SINISTER

Books by Lisa Jackson

Stand-Alones

SEE HOW SHE DIES
FINAL SCREAM
RUNNING SCARED
WHISPERS
TWICE KISSED
UNSPOKEN
DEEP FREEZE
FATAL BURN
MOST LIKELY TO DIE
WICKED GAME
WICKED LIES
SOMETHING WICKED
WITHOUT MERCY
YOU DON'T WANT TO KNOW

Anthony Paterno/ Cahill Family Novels

IF SHE ONLY KNEW
ALMOST DEAD

Rick Bentz/ Reuben Montoya Novels

HOT BLOODED
COLD BLOODED
SHIVER
ABSOLUTE FEAR
LOST SOULS
MALICE
DEVIOUS

Pierce Reed/ Nikki Gillette Novels

THE NIGHT BEFORE
THE MORNING AFTER
TELL ME

Selena Alvarez/ Regan Pescoli Novels

LEFT TO DIE
CHOSEN TO DIE
BORN TO DIE
AFRAID TO DIE
READY TO DIE

Books by Nancy Bush

CANDY APPLE RED
ELECTRIC BLUE
ULTRAVIOLET
WICKED GAME
WICKED LIES
SOMETHING WICKED
UNSEEN
BLIND SPOT
HUSH
NOWHERE TO RUN
NOWHERE TO HIDE
NOWHERE SAFE

Books by Rosalind Noonan

ONE SEPTEMBER MORNING
IN A HEARTBEAT
THE DAUGHTER SHE USED TO BE
ALL SHE EVER WANTED
AND THEN SHE WAS GONE

SINISTER

LISA JACKSON
NANCY BUSH
ROSALIND NOONAN

ZEBRA BOOKS
KENSINGTON PUBLISHING CORP.

ZEBRA BOOKS are published by

Kensington Publishing Corp.
119 West 40th Street
New York, NY 10018

ISBN 978-1-62490-977-1

Printed in the United States of America

PART ONE

by
Lisa Jackson

Chapter One

God, it was cold. As in hovering just *under* freezing. But then, what could you expect in western Wyoming in the dead of winter? Amber's thoughts swirled like the snow coming down in front of her headlights, thousands of tiny flakes dancing in the twin beams that cut through the rugged countryside.

Man, this place was a black hole, but according to her GPS, there was a town in the valley ahead somewhere. Less than five miles, thank God, and hopefully she would find a twenty-four-hour service station to take a break and fill up. Her gas gauge still showed a quarter tank, but you had to be careful out here in the middle of nowhere. Miles of nothing but darkness—that was her impression of Wyoming. Amber hated the feeling of isolation; it made her nervous as hell.

Then again, everything made her nervous these days, not the least of all being Robert's parents. She'd met them once before, of course, during the summer, and they'd traded a few barbs. But this time, a visit of three freakin' days with the whole family in attendance for Thanksgiving, Frankie and Philip Petrocelli had been at each other's throats. From the moment Phil had sliced into the turkey incorrectly until midnight, when Frankie had stumbled on the stairs from "one too many" Manhattans, they'd shown their absolute abhorrence for each other.

And to think she was considering marrying into that bunch of lunatics. "Smarten up," she said, glancing in her rearview mirror. Robert was usually such a sweetie, the exact opposite of his bitter, venomous parents. But this visit had shown her a different side of her fiancé. For most of her stay, he had withdrawn to a near zombielike state in the wake of his parents' vitriol. Really, the only time he'd snapped out of his daze had been when his ex-girlfriend Joy "happened" to drop in. Only *Joy* had been able to pull him out of his dark shell.

Although she had planned to stay till Monday and drive back with Robert, when Robert's parents had started arguing again over something at lunchtime, she'd been glad to zip up her suitcase and tell those crazy Petrocellis adios, *sayonara,* au revoir and good riddance.

"The apple doesn't fall far from the tree," she said aloud as she fumbled with the radio's dial. She found a station but could barely hear Adele's voice over the static, so she switched it off, only making her already bad mood worse.

Maybe she should rethink the whole "till death do us part" thing. Maybe her whole future with Robert wasn't meant to be. The story of her life. In all of her twenty-six years not one man had turned out to be even near "the one." While her high school and college friends were busy planning weddings and putting the final touches on their nurseries, here she was, contemplating breaking up with the only guy who had ever seriously talked about marriage.

"Big deal," she said sourly as she squinted through the windshield. Already Robert was mad at her for cutting out early. She didn't know if she could patch things over, and she didn't know if she really cared to.

The glass was beginning to fog despite the struggling

heater that barely warmed the interior of the car. These mountains were ghastly cold—a no-man's-land.

Reaching across the seat to her purse, she fumbled for her pack of cigarettes and found there was only one left. *Great.* Though she had sworn she would quit, another one of Robert's ideas, she didn't plan to put an end to her nicotine habit until New Year's Day. That gave her the next six weeks to enjoy smoking as much as she wanted. Then at the stroke of midnight, she would quit cold turkey.

As she saw the neon sign for a diner come into view, she lit up and even dared crack the window just a smidgen so that the smoke could get sucked out. Not enough to put her hand outside, not in this cold, but just enough space to keep the smoke from filling up the car.

God, she missed California. Another fifteen hours to go to reach Sacramento, depending on the weather and road conditions and how long she could stand it. She'd come a long way from Billings already, over the Montana state line and clear across the state of Wyoming. She wondered how much longer she'd be in this big-ass state.

As she signaled to turn off the highway, she saw that the diner was also a bar. Big Bart's restaurant also housed the Buffalo Lounge, where one could hear live music every Saturday night, according to the backlit sign posted high overhead.

Finally! The night was starting to hold some promise!

Instead of getting a hot cup of coffee and a hamburger, she decided she'd splurge and order a drink . . . oooh, maybe even an *Irish* coffee. Yeah, that sounded good. With whipped cream and, if she could talk the bartender into it, a drizzle of crème de menthe for the holidays. Mmmmm.

Her stomach rumbled in anticipation as she pulled into the near-empty lot of the roadside establishment. She hit a pothole disguised by a layer of snow and it jarred the car, probably nearly taking out the front axle of her fifteen-year-old Honda in the process.

"Shit!" she muttered under her breath. Fortunately the Civic was tough and had made it through more than its share of abuse in the four years her brother had driven it before selling the little sedan to her.

Grabbing her purse, she slid outside, locked the door, then braved the snow to reach the double glass doors framed by a half-lit string of Christmas lights. Oh, yeah. Right. Merry effin' Christmas!

As she stepped inside, a wall of heat hit her head-on. At last. She hoped to thaw her toes before starting back out again. The hallway led to a landing, and then split. Amber paused to check her reflection in the mirror at the landing. Even though her eyes were a little tired and puffy, her black hair, with its blue tint henna, shone in the dim light. Fabulous. It was worth every penny Andre had charged. Turning away from the well-lit dining area, she headed toward the lounge, where the sound of country-western music bounced against the walls.

She took an empty seat at the end of the bar and ordered her Irish coffee from a tall, thin bartender with a gold tooth that glimmered when he smiled.

"ID?" he asked.

Amber sighed as she rummaged through her purse, annoyed that she kept getting carded when she was so over twenty-one. Locating her driver's license, she thrust it over to the bartender.

"One Irish coffee comin' your way, Amber." He winked at her as he handed it back over, which only aggravated her further.

As she waited for her drink, she noticed there were two other patrons at the bar, and a few couples at the tables sprinkled around a small dance floor located in front of a stage. Apparently, she had missed the Saturday-night crowd. If there had been a band, it was long-gone, the stage empty, aside from a couple of mics shoved toward the back wall.

The drink came with the requested green drizzle and a complimentary if pathetic Irish accent from the gold-toothed barkeep. "Here ye be, missy!"

Amber perused a bar menu, half listening to a Randy Travis ballad that oozed through hidden speakers. As she sipped her drink, the tension in her shoulders and neck muscles eased up, and she decided to give herself a break. To hell with her diet. So what if she needed to drop five pounds? It wasn't as if she was going to try and squeeze into a wedding dress anytime soon. So thinking, she ordered chicken strips and fries then finished her drink.

Nearby, a group that had been drinking beer scraped back their chairs, then took up pool cues at the billiards table near the far wall.

Pool balls began clicking loudly, the two couples laughing, bantering and placing bets as an upbeat country tune she didn't recognize filled the room. Her toes had stopped tingling as her order came and she dipped a greasy fry into a paper cup of ranch dressing. Yep, her blood had begun flowing again. When the bartender asked her if she'd like another drink, she nodded. She was already feeling the effects of the first, but that would change once the food hit.

For the first time she noticed the guy at the corner of the L-shaped bar. A cowboy from the looks of him. Wearing a black Stetson dipped low over his forehead. He was a big guy, tall with broad shoulders. Just her type. She'd always liked tall guys, something she'd never mentioned to Robert, who was only a few inches taller than she was. But this cowboy? Yup. Hmmmm.

He'd been staring at her, not directly, but through the mirror behind the bar. When she met his gaze in the reflective glass, he looked away quickly, but only for an instant.

Then he was back again, his eyes intent. He smiled slightly, lifted his glass and took a big swallow from his beer.

She did, too. It wasn't really flirting, just an unspoken "hi" to a fellow patron of the good old Buffalo Lounge. Along with his Stetson, he was wearing a heavy jacket and jeans, which seemed to be the uniform of all the male patrons around these parts.

Don't do it, Amber. Don't toy with a man you don't know. Think of Robert, and for God's sake, be careful. So he's hot. So what? Be smart. For once in your life, don't do something just for the hell of it, for the adventure. You know it's never worth it.

She exchanged a few more glances as she delved into her second drink. A few minutes later, she caught his eyes on her again. He touched the tip of his hat, then left a few bills on the bar and slid off his stool. With one last look, direct this time, not through the glass, he nodded, as if acknowledging their silent conversation, then headed toward the back of the building, either to hit the bathrooms or take the rear exit.

Dang. A part of her felt ridiculously disappointed as she watched him disappear into a darkened hallway. Maybe she was being stupid. The Irish whiskey had muddled her brain a bit and the best thing she could do was get over it. After all, she was unofficially engaged (no ring, mind you) to Robert, and when he returned to Sacramento she was going to have it out with him. Either there was a sizeable diamond under the tree this year or he was getting a big kick in the backside on New Year's Day. Cigarettes weren't the only thing she'd be giving up for her New Year's resolution. She was swearing off loser men who couldn't commit.

Leaving half of her overcooked chicken strips in the basket with a few fries, she accepted a third drink from the bartender. She nursed it, along with a glass of water, for another half hour. By the time she paid her bill, Amber's head was a little fuzzy. Hmm. Maybe she wasn't in the best shape for driving . . . but she couldn't stay here.

Even though the roads were pretty much empty at this time of night, she knew she couldn't make it to Sacramento. Even Salt Lake City would be a stretch. Elbow on the bar, she rested her head on her fist, sorting her weary thoughts.

Find a motel—that was the only option.

Gathering her purse and zipping her jacket, she decided she'd just drive a little farther down the road and stop at the first motel she came to. She could flop for the night. In the morning, she would set out fresh and make it all the way to Sacramento.

"Sounds like a plan," she said as she walked through the frigid night toward her car. Clouds covered the moon and snow was still falling, drifting against the buildings. Shivering, she made her way to her Honda, then stopped short. Her front end was listing badly. The tire she'd hit on the pothole earlier had totally deflated.

"Crap!" she muttered under her breath, her heart sinking. She didn't have Triple A, and though her father had taught her how to change a tire back when she'd learned to drive, she wasn't sure that her spare was functional or if she had a jack or whatever the hell it was she needed to change the flat.

Now what?

She could go inside, ask for help, or take a cab to . . . *where? Shit.* Whether she liked it or not, she'd have to depend on the kindness of strangers. The bitter wind that roared through the valley cut through her coat and stung her eyes. No one would last out here for long.

"Need help?" a rough voice asked.

She turned to find the guy in the black Stetson walking across the parking lot.

Relief swept across her worried mind. "It's my tire. Flat as a pancake."

"Let me take a look." He walked to the driver's side and crouched down near the front wheel well. "Yep. It's bad. See here?" He pointed to the tire and moved back, so she could see the damage. Though she really didn't need to lean down to see the damage, she did it just to appease him.

Wasn't it funny how some things just worked out? That the tall cowboy from the bar would turn out to be her savior, her Good Samaritan—maybe a friend and a lover if things developed right. You couldn't fight destiny.

"Doesn't look like I can drive—" Her eyes were trained on the wheel when he moved sharply, startling her.

Before she could get away, he yanked her body hard against his.

"Hey!" she said, half-scared, half-intrigued, until he shoved something over her mouth, his hand thickened by a leather glove that muffled her cry.

Panic shot through her. What the hell was going on?

Her mind raced through all the horrible stories she'd heard about rapes and abductions. Oh, no! Not her. She had to stop him. Someone had to stop him . . . someone leaving the bar . . .

She struggled in his arms, kicking against his legs, but he was unflinching. A tall pillar of a man.

"Be a good girl, and you won't get hurt," he whispered into her ear, his voice sizzling with malice.

Oh, Jesus. Talk some sense into him. Stand tough! Wasn't that how you were supposed to deal with a potential rapist?

Her gaze combed the parking lot and the building, willing the door to open and someone to rush to her rescue. *Please . . . open that door!*

She felt him shift, one of his hands lifting, and she used that moment to kick and writhe and try to beat him off. She bit hard on the glove, tasting dust and dirt and old suede.

He didn't so much as flinch.

She threw her weight against him, and his rumbling laugh, deep and throaty, convinced her that her struggles were useless.

Think, Amber. Somehow you have to outwit this son of a bitch!

In the slight pause she saw the knife in his free hand. The long, sharp blade glinting in the weak glow of a security lamp. *Oh, dear God . . .*

This time, when she tried to jerk away, he lifted her off her feet and dragged her, wiggling and twisting, to a dank patch of snow behind the Dumpster. No one from the bar would see them back here. No one!

"Let me go!" Her words were muted by his hand, but in the next second—a dark spiral of hope—she gasped as he flung her down.

Free!

It was her last clear thought before her head hit the frozen ground, sending an explosion crackling through her vision. Pain and fear shot into her system, but through the misery something called to her.

Get up! Escape! Now!

Her head ached and her bones felt heavy as she tried to pull herself onto her feet. Confused, she thought she might get away . . . but when she opened her eyes, he was on top of her, a heavy weight crushing her chest, pressing into her throat.

"I said, be good!"

In the weak light, she could only make out the glint in his eyes. A sickening glimmer of pure evil that chilled her very soul.

"You're hurting me," she croaked out. "Why are you hurting me?"

His voice was a knowing whisper as his lips curled into a cold grin. "Practice makes perfect."

Then he lifted the knife again. And in that last fragile instant, while snowflakes fell around her and the faint hum of music from inside the bar reached her ears, Amber Barstow realized she would never make it home to California.

Standing outside the entrance to the cave, the killer watched snow fall on the valley below. From up here, through the haze of white, it was possible to see the river, a dark snake winding toward the smattering of lights, hundreds of bulbs illuminating the snow-blanketed streets of Prairie Creek, Wyoming.

A night owl screeched, and then there was quiet.

He wiped the blood from the blade of his knife on his worn jeans and thought about what the future would bring. As he cleaned the sharp steel, a ghost of a smile crawled across his lips and the pleasant hiss of anticipation buzzed in his ears.

No one knew.

No one suspected.

The girl had been dead a week and not a soul anywhere around was looking at him.

Wind whistled through the canyon, rattling snow from branches, churning up white clouds, bringing the cold from the north. Good, he thought as he ducked between rocks to the hidden entrance of his cave where a campfire was already burning, black smoke billowing upward near the skinned carcass of a coyote dripping wetly against the rocky floor.

This was a good kill.

A kill accomplished with only his bare hands and his knife. He relived the first thrust of his blade through the coyote's shaggy hide. Listened again to its howl of agony, its snapping teeth going still. That was it. The rush of the kill, the feeling of flesh surrendering, the life struggle that was about to come to an end, the shudder of death.

He'd hunted animals for years, he thought over the hiss of the fire. But they were easy prey. Easily outwitted.

Humans, though? They were the ultimate test, the supreme target.

His thumb stroked the hilt of the knife as he recalled taking the woman. He ran his tongue over his lips at the memory: the suddenly limp body in his arms, blood flowing from her neck, shock in her eyes as she let out her last gurgling breath. Now he felt an erection begin to rise. She'd been so naïve: a bleating little lamb to the slaughter. Killing her had been child's play. Disabling her car and luring her in, waiting for just the right moment for her to lean forward, her balance off, the way she'd fought him and then later, the smooth feel of the knife plunging through and running beneath her skin.

Remembering brought a shudder to his large frame, but she was, of course, just a rehearsal for the main event.

He'd hidden her body well. He'd gutted her atop a tarp, long after throwing her in his car, leaving no trace of blood in the parking lot. No one suspected. No one even seemed to know that she was missing. Poor Amber. That was her name, according to the California driver's license he'd found in her purse.

But now it was time to go to the next level. That's why he was here. That's what he'd come for. The Dillingers . . . their ranch spread out below him . . . their souls black . . . their time near.

He had to be extracareful now. Every kill had to count.

Holding the knife above his head with both hands, he felt the power that came from the killing enter him, uplift him, send him to a higher plane.

Do you feel me? he silently asked them, his prey.

I'm coming for you.

Chapter Two

Sabrina's hands were full as she shouldered open the glass door of the Prairie Creek Animal Clinic. This morning she balanced a cup of coffee she'd grabbed at Molly's Diner, her purse, computer case and the business mail she'd picked up from the P.O. box.

"Oh, good, Dr. Delaney, you brought the mail," Renee called. "Look what I found yesterday!" Waving an envelope from behind her desk, earbud already in place so she could answer the phones wirelessly, the clinic's receptionist was already rearranging the pamphlets and business cards on the counter. Though it was a good ten minutes before the clinic officially opened, Renee's computer monitor with the day's schedule was glowing as Sabrina slipped inside.

Sabrina paused on the mat to stomp the snow from her boots as the scents of antiseptic and disinfectant greeted her. Padded benches lined the walls, and the floor was scratched from thousands of anxious paws that had crossed the threshold, but now this veterinary clinic was half hers. That had been a big personal goal—to work in her own practice and stay in Prairie Creek. Every day she thanked her lucky stars that she could check that big one off her bucket list.

Well . . . almost every day, she thought as she put her

coffee down in exchange for the fat parchment envelope that Renee was waving.

"Looks like a wedding invitation!" Renee said cheerfully.

"That it does." It was an invitation she had thought she'd dodged. Practically everyone else the Dillingers knew had gotten one, and she'd wondered, hoped maybe, that she'd been overlooked. As Sabrina noticed that the postmark was dated six weeks earlier, Renee's smile fell a bit.

"I know. My bad," Renee said before Sabrina could say a word. "I, uh, it . . . I think it got shuffled into the junk mail and recycling somehow and then . . . wow, I don't know, I saw it poking out of an old magazine, so I pulled it out and saw that it was for you. Sorry."

"Okay," Sabrina said. "But—"

"I promise I'll be more careful with the mail. I really don't know how it happened." She blinked behind her glasses as if she might break down into tears.

"It's fine. Truly." And it was. Renee Aaronson was usually reliable, and she had a charming way with the customers. She was able to juggle several phone calls, all the while dealing with a yapping Chihuahua or a freaked-out Siamese or, worse yet, their overly worried owners. Sabrina almost admitted to Renee that she would prefer the invitation should go back in the recycle box, but she didn't want to dump her life story on the young woman.

"Seriously, Dr. Delaney, it won't happen again."

"Good. So," she said, to change the subject, "are we busy today?"

"Swamped." Renee glanced at the computer monitor. "Wow. Yeah. Appointments back-to-back. And that's before the emergencies."

"I'd better get at it then," Sabrina said, already pushing open the short swinging door to the back of the clinic with her hips. Quickly, she made her way down the short aisle to her cubbyhole of an office, where she peeled off her jacket, slipped on a purple lab coat and exchanged her boots for shoes.

A quick check in the mirror behind the door showed her honey-blond hair still in place, swept back into a braid that usually held through most of her hectic day. Frowning, she assessed herself with cold eyes. Her face was still smooth, and her amber eyes softened the sharp line of her high cheekbones and nose. Not quite the same girl who'd fallen in love with Colton Dillinger almost twenty years earlier, but all in all she'd held up pretty well.

"It's all that talking with the animals," she said aloud, recalling how her sister, after observing her treating a lame horse, had dubbed her Dr. Doolittle.

Once behind her desk, she slit open the envelope. She knew what it was of course: an invitation to the nuptials of Pilar Larson and Ira Dillinger, to be held the weekend before Christmas.

She wondered if Colt would be at the wedding too, and what he would think of her if they came face to face. Looking at the engraved script on the invitation, she shook her head. What was wrong with her that she could let a romance nearly two decades old still get to her?

"Perfect," she said, noticing the enclosed RSVP card, the date for responding long past due. She thought about making up an excuse and not attending the event, but since the Dillingers were the best customers of the clinic, that seemed like poor form. Davis Featherstone, the Rocking D's ranch foreman, already knew that she was on duty that week as Antonia was going to be out of town. "So I can't even lie my way out of it."

"Lie about what?" came a voice from the doorway. She turned to see Antonia herself walk in. Her shiny dark hair was swept back in a twist that only a few women could pull off without looking schoolmarmish. Toni was one. "Talking to yourself. Am I interrupting some morning affirmations?"

Sabrina tapped the heavy stock card against her desk. "My invitation came. A little late, but it's here."

She snatched it away for a closer look. "You must have been on the B-list." At thirty-four, an ex–beauty pageant finalist, she was as smart as she was good-looking.

"Just lost in the mail. But now it's a problem because I don't want to offend our biggest client, but there's no way I can go."

"Why not?"

"Colt could be there."

"So, *that's* why every relationship you've had since has been lukewarm. Now I get it!" She shrugged; then, no longer teasing, added, "Look, you've both moved on, right? He has a family and bought a ranch up in Montana."

"Had a family," Sabrina corrected a little too quickly. Colton had lost his wife and daughter in a terrible automobile accident.

"That's right." Toni sucked her breath through her teeth. "That was tough, but it's been a while. "The point is he does have a life, one without you."

"I know."

"And you, you've got this fantastic clinic with an even more fantastic partner."

Sabrina rolled her eyes, but the point was well taken. Her romance with Colton was ages ago. There was lots of water under that particular bridge. She pushed the reply card away on her desk. "You're right."

"Scuttlebutt on the street is that Colton refuses to attend the wedding anyway. Besides, a big bash like this hits Prairie Creek once in a century. You can't sit home just because you don't want to run into an old boyfriend. Do you know that statistically, ninety percent of all childhood sweethearts don't last?"

"You're making that up. And it's easy for you to push me out there. You've already got a husband."

Antonia grabbed a pen from her pocket and leaned over the desk, turning the RSVP card her way. "You would think I was signing you up for the wet T-shirt contest in Jackson Hole." She checked off a box, tucked the card into the small envelope and licked it. "Done. Now you're committed, and you're going to have a blast."

"Not likely." Sabrina reached for the small envelope. "I'll come up with an excuse."

"Nope." Antonia scurried toward the door with the invitation behind her back. "Do it for our clinic. Think of the animals who need you to keep the peace with Ira Dillinger."

"That's not fair." Sabrina folded her arms.

"It's good business," she said with a smile.

"I'm telling you, I'm not going. I'll get the flu."

Antonia held the envelope high. "Oh, Renee? I've got something that needs to go out in the mail today," she called, disappearing down the hall.

Sabrina made a sound of exasperation. Was she overreacting? Colton Dillinger had been out of her life for a lot longer than he'd been in it. He'd moved on long ago, and she sure as hell had tried to, though it had been something of a losing proposition.

"But it doesn't matter anymore," she said aloud. Colton Dillinger was out of her life. Forever. He'd proved that well enough. And she'd moved on. After all, it had been eighteen years. Too long a time to carry a torch or hold a grudge.

She heard the buzzer at the front door and looked up to see one of her patients—a corgi/beagle/God-knew-what-else mix of a dog and as bad-tempered a little beast as they came—being carried in by its owner.

Pasting on a smile, she dropped the invitation from her mind, then headed down the hallway and into an examination room.

"Hey, there," she said to the dog, which promptly pulled

its black lips into a snarl and, with wildly rolling eyes, started barking loud enough to raise the dead.

"Don't do anything I wouldn't do," Colton Dillinger told the cattle as he closed the door of the holding pen. The wind was howling outside, rattling the roof and walls, nearly obliterating his words, and some of the cows were complaining, lowing loudly, their hooves shuffling in the straw. For a moment he thought of the person who had convinced him that it was healthy to talk to your cattle.

Sabrina Delaney.

He smiled. He'd heard Sabrina was a vet these days. Made sense. She knew her way around animals of all kinds.

Colton had been rounding up his livestock these past few days with Cub Jenkins, his foreman, and some of the other hired hands, needing to get the herd under cover before the next blizzard came barreling down from Canada and hit Montana. Cattle weren't given much to panic in the snow, but the wind, sometimes, if it was fierce enough it could send them searching for cover, often right into obstructions that killed them. During one blizzard when Colton was a kid, some stray cattle had bunched together at a fence to get out of the wind and suffocated each other. And everyone had heard tales of the huge number of cattle lost during the blizzard of 1949.

Sure, the storm currently ripping through this part of Montana in a frigid Arctic blast was probably just a little howler compared to the whiteout of '49, but Colton knew what had to be done to secure his stock. Latching the door to the pen, he pulled his scarf up over his nose and stepped into the blast of snow and ice. A few minutes in this stuff and he'd be a dead man. He mounted Mojave, a Kiger gelding that was his main workhorse, able to change gears and get the job done in the blistering wind and snow.

If only some ranch hands could be as reliable. He snorted, his steamy breath warming the center of the frosted scarf.

Inside the stables, he gave Mojave a well-deserved brush-down, then braved the wind one last time. According to the forecast, the weather was about to break. "'Bout time," he muttered under his breath. His livestock were secure, safe and tucked into the barns and sheds of the ranch, but they were starting to get restless, and he couldn't blame them.

The warmth of the house seemed to melt his face as Colt kicked off his boots then hung his jacket on a hook by the door. He strode past the bacon grease congealed in a cast-iron skillet on the stove. It'd keep till morning.

In the den he dropped down at the fireplace and stoked the fire. Another log and some old paper would do it. He reached into the paper bin and his hand closed over the fat parchment envelope.

The invitation.

He slipped out the engraved card and read it one last time. It had arrived weeks ago, a creamy envelope that was the harbinger of bad news.

The honor of your presence is requested . . .

Like hell. Big family wedding, his old man tying the knot.

His sister Ricki had been bugging him about making an appearance, and much as he'd like to see all his sisters, there was no way Colton could be in the same room with the bride, Pilar Larson, a gold digger of the first order.

He tossed the invitation into the fire and rocked back on his heels to watch his father's latest decree curl and burn in the licking flames. He didn't want to see Ira, he didn't want to see the Rocking D, he didn't want to see Pilar, and he wasn't sure he wanted to see Sabrina because even though it had been a long time ago, they hadn't left on the best of terms.

Whatever the hell was happening in Prairie Creek, he wanted no part of it.

* * *

On a clearing near the treed area of the Rocking D known as Copper Woods, Davis Featherstone slid a shovel from the back of his truck and spotted the boss's Dodge Ram in the distance, purring up over the ridge. Wet snow gave way under his boots as he went over to the men who waited astride their horses, all ready to herd the near-grown calves back to shelter. Winter coats shaggy, the mix of black Angus and white-faced Herefords had strayed earlier, but they were complacent now.

Probably hungry and thirsty, Davis thought. Even with all this snow around, cows couldn't figure out how to get a drink. He'd heard of them dying of thirst in the snow.

Not that he'd let that happen to Dillinger steers. Not yet thirty, he may have been young for a ranch foreman, but he was a cattleman. He could have run this ranch blindfolded.

Except for the dead coyote.

The slaughtered animal had thrown them all for a loop. It wasn't just the place of esteem that coyote had in Shoshone stories of creation; it was the way the creature had been mutilated. Sliced and carved.

"Will you dig a hole?" Davis asked the men.

The two men, both Shoshone, exchanged a cautious look. "We'll dig," Mick Ramhorn said. "I don't mind being part of a proper burial. But I won't touch it."

Davis held up the shovel. "Might as well get started. The boss will have to do the grunt work this time."

The men got off their horses and began searching for a good burial spot, a tall task in the deepening snow. Lou started digging while Mick retraced his path through the snow to the truck for a pickaxe.

Turning away from them, Davis looked back once again toward the tree where the coyote lay. In just the past few minutes, snow had collected on the carcass. If you didn't know, you'd think it was just a boulder at the base of the tree.

If you didn't know.

Wind stung his face as the scene washed over him again. He closed his eyes, but it was still there, last night's vision of a thin, lithe spirit dancing in the snow, a dark shadow waving pine branches like feathers as she twirled and circled the dark mound at the foot of the tree.

A snow spirit dancing in the night.

Standing at the trail's end at the edge of the woods, he had thought the snow and cold were messing with his mind. As he watched and waited, however, he realized he recognized the snow sprite: Kit Dillinger.

He had left her to her snow ritual, thinking it was the harmless dance of a woman whose only home was out here in the valley, away from houses and people and the problems they caused. But he had thought wrong. When he'd returned this morning on his way to search for strays, he'd brushed snow from the mound. As he'd removed the branches, alarm had shot through him at the sight.

A dead coyote, half-skinned and mutilated.

"I hope you've got a good reason for calling me out here." Ira Dillinger slammed the door of his truck and stomped over. He was a tall man, and a force to be reckoned with. "Because some of these snowdrifts are taller than a damned elephant." He trudged up to Davis and demanded, "What the hell is that?" as he stared at the mutilated carcass at his ranch foreman's feet.

"A dead coyote."

"What the hell happened to it?" Keeping his distance, Ira crouched down for a better view.

Davis looked away, able to see it all in his mind. Chunks of fur and flesh were gone; blood covered the rest, the coyote's head nearly severed from its spine, legs sliced at the joint, at least one tooth missing. No wild animal had feasted on the dead cur. No jagged bite wounds were evident, but it was hideously carved. Not the killing of any hunter Davis had ever seen.

Ira scowled. "It's like a mad butcher had at it."

Davis nodded. This was no cougar or wolf attack. "Someone stripped him with a knife."

Scanning the horizon, as if he could find the culprit hiding in the stands of snow-covered aspen that rimmed this valley before it gave way to white mountains, Ira frowned. "I don't like it."

Davis nodded. "I thought you'd want to see it. That's why I radioed you." The ranch hands used walkie-talkies since cell phone use in the area was spotty at best.

"You know I got no love of coyotes," Ira admitted. "The only good coyote is a dead one."

That was cattle ranching. Most ranchers shot coyotes to keep them from attacking young calves. That was different. A quick, clean shot was the way of the West, but no one, at least no one he worked with, advocated torture.

"But this is weird. Some sicko playing survivalist?" He spat a stream of tobacco juice onto the snow.

Davis said, "The men are spooked."

"Well, they'll feel better once they clean it up and we'll call it done."

Davis Featherstone shook his head. "None of the men will touch it. That's why I called you."

Ira's face flushed red. "It's a dead coyote. You can leave it until the snow stops, but after that, have someone cover it with dirt and bury it."

"Coyote is a part of Shoshone legend. A real trickster, but responsible for the creation of the Shoshone people. Messing with a coyote, that's what you call bad karma." Davis nodded toward the men on the other side of their horses, where a mound of dirty snow was growing. "They won't go near it. It's like a bad totem to have a hand in the evil."

"Of all the pansy-ass . . ." He took off his Stetson and slapped it against his thigh, bits of snow flying, to reveal a head of thinning gray hair. "Don't act like a damned dead varmint is the work of some higher power."

"It's not God's work we're afraid of. It's the devil." Davis's arms were folded across his chest, solid and intractable.

"And you don't have hands around that aren't Shoshone?"

"Not too many wanted to travel in the blizzard."

"Fine. Get me a tarp and a shovel. Everything's damn near frozen, but I'm not about to leave that corpse out here to attract cougars and wolves." They were the enemies of a cattleman, and he'd be a fool to leave bait sitting out here.

In the meantime the men had carved out an impressive ditch in the nearly frozen-solid ground. By the time Ira dragged the carcass over, the pit was deep enough for a burial. Davis sent the other men on their way and took a shovel to cover the poor creature with dirt.

Ira stared across the fields. "You think one of the Kincaids is behind this?" he asked suspiciously, mentioning the rival family with a ranch down the road a piece. Ira always thought the Kincaids were behind everything bad that happened.

Davis kept his own counsel and didn't say what he was thinking: that the dead coyote was a bad omen, and that he'd seen one of Ira's own flesh and blood literally dancing on the animal's grave. But then, Ira hadn't seen what he had.

"Just keep a cool head about it," Ira said as they finished up. "And keep this to yourself."

"I don't share business with Sam, if that's what you mean." Davis's brother, Sam Featherstone, was the sheriff of Prairie Creek.

"Well, good. And tell the other men to shut up about it if they want to keep their jobs here. We don't need anyone poking around at the Rocking D, looking into my family's business."

"Okay, boss."

Although the slain creature was under the dirt now, covered with dignity, a knot of dread was still lodged in Davis's throat. He shouldn't be afraid of a seventeen-year-old girl who was skinning animals on the ranch. Kit Dillinger, he could handle her.

The real fear was the thing that drove the rage . . . the lust to kill and deface the victims. If Kit was possessed by a bad spirit, he would see to it that she got help. He would take her to rehab personally. Shit, he knew plenty of people there.

And if it wasn't Kit doing these things, and a big part of him hoped that it wasn't, well, God help them all. There was true evil among them.

Run, old man, the killer thought, dropping his binoculars to stare at the disappearing vehicles of Dillinger and the foreman. The other men had led the stray cattle off a few minutes ago, but these two had lingered to bury the kill.

An amusing sight, watching grown men dig in the midst of all the snow. Poor bastards. Little did they know that this was just beginning. If they were going to serve old Ira, then they'd be busy indeed.

Taillights winked as Ira Dillinger hit the brakes before turning and driving over the ridge. The killer smiled to himself and dropped a hand into the pocket of his cargo pants. There he ran his finger over the sharp fang he'd pulled from the coyote's jaw. It rattled against the molar he'd taken from the California girl before hiding her body. Just a little memento, to help relive it.

Jangling with the thrill of it.

He licked suddenly dry lips.

The wind slapped him in the face and he backed away

from the cover of scrub oak and pine, inching his way toward his cave. He'd have to move soon, find a new place to hide out. Especially since he knew his message had been delivered. But he'd expected as much.

He would need to back off, stay out of sight. He couldn't always have this bird's-eye view of their torment, though there were plenty of other ridges around the valley that would give him a good vantage point.

And it was just so damned good to see the old man squirm.

Chapter Three

Colton sprawled in his easy chair in front of the fire—more embers now than flames—and sipped at a glass of scotch. The blizzard was shrieking around the corners of the house as he stared at the glowing red coals, his thoughts drifting. He was reminded of another fire, the one that changed his life, the smoke and crackling flames casting a gray haze over what had once seemed like a bright future. Colt had lost his uncle, he'd lost his girlfriend and he'd pretty much lost track of his own clear path.

There had been terror that night, roaring terror, along with a realization that being born a Dillinger didn't make one infallible. Well, yeah. These days, he knew that first-hand.

Straightening, he saw that he'd forgotten to include the RSVP card in the fire, where his father's initials were entwined with those of Pilar Larson, a woman who could well be his daughter.

Pilar . . .

He'd briefly been enthralled with her once himself, after Sabrina, after leaving his father and the Rocking D twelve years earlier. He'd spent a whole lot of time on the rodeo circuit and he'd met Pilar during those days of drinking and riding. Horses and women. The circuit had been a great place for both.

Pilar had been in the picture for a while. A bender that had lasted a few weeks before he surfaced and shook himself free of both his ghosts and her. Even low as he'd been at the time, he'd still possessed the wisdom to see that a woman like Pilar would suck his soul dry if he let her get too close.

Shortly afterward he'd moved to Montana and bought the ranch. Met Margo at a rodeo in Nebraska, and bit by bit, he'd climbed out of what could have been a very dark hole. They'd had Darcy, and Colton had left the rodeo circuit behind for a family that he'd cherished. But it all had come screeching to a halt with the car accident that had taken them from him.

He'd been thrown into a dark depression, and only recently had he felt the fog lifting and the desire to possibly live life again. He'd been lucky that Cub and the hands had held the ranch together while he'd been dealing with his grief. A little over ten months earlier he'd run into Pilar at his mother's funeral where, coincidentally, she'd connected with Ira, and though he'd tried to avoid her—he didn't want to revisit his rodeo days any more than he wanted to talk about the family he'd lost—Pilar had been intent on cutting him from the herd of mourners and getting him alone.

"Rourke is yours," she'd told him without preamble, referring to her eleven-year-old son whom she'd brought in tow. "It shouldn't be a surprise, Colt. Look at him. He's got that Dillinger red in his hair, and he's stubborn, just like you."

Colton had felt his soul shrink to a nugget. "You're lying," he accused, furious with her. "Rourke is Larson's son."

Pilar gazed at him, almost with pity, as if she found his denial pathetic. "Rourke is not Chad's son," she said, referring to her deceased husband. "He's a Dillinger."

"What's your game, Pilar?" he'd demanded.

"Get a DNA test," she stated flatly. "Then you'll know."

He'd wanted to strangle her. Such a beautiful liar. But then . . . then he looked at Rourke and started to wonder. A kid . . . *a son?* He hadn't believed her, but she wasn't wrong about the boy's red hair. Colton was dark, like his mother, and also like his brother, Tyler, and their youngest sister, Nell. But sister Ricki was a redhead and Delilah, the middle child of Ira's brood, had hair a red-gold color. Ricki and Delilah had taken after Ira and so . . . maybe had Rourke? Was it possible? Surreptitiously, his eyes had followed Rourke all around the funeral events, both during the service and the reception at the house afterward, where everyone met for food and drink and a remembrance of Colton's mother.

Then Pilar had sent him Rourke's DNA, and Colton had seen if it was a match. It was. He was Rourke's father. On that, she hadn't lied. While he was figuring out what to do about that news, Ira, steeped in grief, had turned to Pilar to assuage his loneliness. And Pilar had turned right back! He couldn't believe she would have the brio to date his father! Even knowing what an opportunist she was, he just hadn't seen it coming.

After that, he'd just stayed incommunicado from Ira and Pilar. He wasn't sure what to do about Rourke, but until this damn wedding was over, he was staying in Montana.

The ice in his drink had melted, so Colton poured it out and started over, this time taking the scotch neat. "What a joke," he said to his dog, and as if he understood, Montana thumped his tail. Part German shepherd and Lab with a smattering of mutt, Montana had come with the ranch when Colton had bought it. His name had been Breezy or something equally stupid. Colton had redubbed him the name of his newly adopted state and they'd hung out ever since.

He carried his refreshed drink back to his chair. His old man was going to be stepfather and grandfather to the same kid. That was both mind-boggling and sad. Ira just didn't know what he was getting into. Pilar had agreed to keep the truth about Rourke's paternity a secret as long as Colton coughed up child support. Pretty soon, the woman would be robbing the Dillingers from both ends.

"You know what they say?" he asked, continuing his one-sided conversation with the mutt. "'There's no fool like an old fool.'" Was he referring to his father or himself? He wasn't sure. Though barely sixty-six, Ira wasn't exactly ancient, but he was certainly proving the adage true by marrying Pilar.

The thought curdled the contents of Colton's stomach even as he remembered Pilar's ample curves, wild energy and perfectly arched eyebrows. Her smile was infectious, the twinkle in her eyes hinting at mystery. A beauty by any man's standards, Pilar was complicated and sexy, but, Colton knew, with a heart as small and cold as the money she was so fond of. Why couldn't the old man see that he was being played like an old fiddle?

Hell. What man would open his eyes to that kind of duplicity while his cock and ego were being stroked with equal perfection?

You weren't immune to her, were you?

No. And he had the son to prove it.

And now, damn her, she was marrying his old man.

So in the end, who was the bigger fool?

The specter of the animal carcass stuck in Ira's craw as he drove toward the ranch house. Much as he'd tried to dismiss his foreman's warning of bad totems and karma, an ill feeling needled him, like a burr under the saddle.

Despite the blinding snow, he veered south, cutting over toward the buildings of the original homestead. Set in a white thicket of cottonwood and pine, the burned-out shell of the once-grand old house came into view. He'd been born there, in the upstairs bedroom that was no more. Now there was just an insubstantial frame of blackened timbers on the first floor. One of the two tall chimneys had collapsed in a pile of rubble; the second still stood tall, though the stones were black as ebony.

Ira eased up on the gas and let the Dodge Ram idle as he eyed the ghost of the home he remembered from his childhood. Long before the fire, this place had been abandoned for the newer, more modern ranch house that he still called home.

Cutting the engine, Ira stared out the windshield as snow crystals tapped the glass. He caught a glimpse of his reflection in the rearview mirror. Yep, Father Time had left his mark with the lines etched in his face. Once compared to "a young" Clint Eastwood, he felt like he'd aged a hundred years since Rachel's death. No one had made the Eastwood comparison in a while. His once-red hair was now gray, holding only a hint of its former hue, and when the hell had these crow's-feet near the corners of his eyes become so prominent? He still had the strong Dillinger jaw, a blessing from his ancestors, and his eyes, mounted over a Roman nose, were as intensely green and sharp as ever.

Shoving open the driver's side door, he braced against the snow blast and buttoned his jacket a little tighter before kicking a path through the snow to the back of the building. Snow caked the rusted gate that hung at an angle.

Inside what had once been the backyard, he glanced to one side where his mother had always tried to plant a vegetable garden. Snow coated the twisted remnants of fruit trees, their discolored branches having been devoid of leaves or fruit for nearly a quarter of a century.

Covered with snow, the old homestead was pretty as a picture, but the charred ruins still pained Ira. After all these years, he was still mad as hell at Judd. Furious and disappointed and lonesome. Judd had been the closest thing Ira had had to a friend.

Ira scowled at the remains of the old house, half blaming

it for the loss of his younger brother. Blessed with a helluva lot more balls than brains, Judd had sneaked out here and met Mia Collins, when the fire had broken out. Ira, of course, had known that his brother was head over heels for the woman and, truth be told, she had been breathtaking in those days, in that same sensual manner that Pilar Larson possessed, and he'd felt damn guilty ever since. Ira certainly had no room to talk when it came to being a cheater, but he still felt he shoulda put his foot down where Mia was concerned, talked some sense into Judd, reminded him that he had a wife, a son and a daughter. But he hadn't. He'd tacitly abetted the affair, letting it rage hot and wild, and it had come down in a burst of fire.

He shivered as his mind flashed to the sirens and the flames. The acrid black smoke that burned his throat and obliterated the stars as it billowed into the sky. Judd and Mia had been locked inside. Mia had escaped, helped out by Ira's own son, Colt, which had damn near scared the shit out of Ira, watching his son brave those scorching flames to save her.

Judd hadn't had a savior. He'd died inside that inferno, and Ira only hoped the smoke got to him before the fire did.

No one had ever figured out who started that fire. Arson, the fire chief said, but who had set the blaze?

There'd been talk of a drifter—a firebug—who'd roamed down through most of the Plains States and into Texas. Maybe he'd done it. That would explain the string of fires in Prairie Creek eighteen years ago—blazes that hadn't hurt anyone, aside from the insurance companies that had to cough up dough to mend the fire damage.

But Ira had always thought it was the Kincaids. Sheepherders who owned the neighboring parcel of land, the Kincaids had been at war with the Dillingers for as long as Ira could remember. In the past few years the rivalry had boiled down to a relationship of simmering distrust. Grazing rights, water rights, the issues of cattle guards and whether or not to pave roads—any issue was fodder for dispute with the Kincaids. Most recently the Kincaids had thrown up some cabins near government land at the base of the mountains with a plan to turn the serene landscape into a goddamned retreat, or some such folly. Once the shacks were done, they had demanded that the Dillingers keep their cattle away from the tourists. Ira had tried to look the other way and laugh it off. The Major's health was failing, and an unfair battle wasn't worth winning. Still, the rivalry lived on.

"Son of a bitch," Ira said now as the wind kicked up, momentarily blinding him with a spray of tiny ice crystals. Blinking, he stared up at falling snow and remembered the newel post at the top of the stairs, its varnish worn down to the wood from being rubbed for good luck by generations of Dillinger children. In his mind's eye he saw the faded pattern of the hall runner that separated the north side bedrooms from the south. A boxy, square bathroom had sat at the end of the hall, an add-on when indoor plumbing became a must.

All gone.

Ira should have bulldozed the place years before, but he'd held on out of nostalgia and respect for his brother. Rachel had pushed a little, but when Ira had pushed back, she'd quickly given it up.

Now Pilar wanted the ruins razed, cleared away for a guest house with a built-in pool *inside* the house. Aiming to finance her dream, Ira had been working on a deal to sell oil rights. That woman kept forgetting that she was living on a working cattle ranch now, but there was a trade-off in these things. She made Ira forget that he was pushing seventy, and if he needed to build a pool to keep his wife happy, so be it.

Somewhere in the distance, he heard the cry of a wolf.

Darkness was settling in so he squared his Stetson on his head again, then made his way to his rig. It was time to look ahead, not backward. He had a new life stretching in front of him.

He still had a few years left on this planet and he intended on making the most of them.

Marrying Pilar Larson was the first step.

And, damn it, he wanted his children at the church to witness the event.

Colt was the key. Firstborn, possibly the most obstinate. If he came, the others would capitulate. Ricki was already involved, and the other two girls—Delilah and Nell—would probably show. Despite their stubborn, self-centered antics, they'd learned the meaning of family duty from their mother. Tyler was a wild card, but his wife, Jen, wouldn't miss a Dillinger event for the life of her; she was too damned interested in the value of Tyler's inheritance to stay away for long. Too bad: Ira despised her.

Disgusted with his offspring, Ira fired up the Dodge Ram and did a quick turn. As he glanced in his rearview mirror, a shadow skittered across the house.

A shadow of *what?*

"Jesus," he whispered, his heartbeat racing.

Quickly he turned in the driver's seat to stare through the rear window.

Nothing . . . just snow clinging to the charred bones of the old building.

Flipping on the wipers, he eased onto the gas again. He was losing it tonight. That was it. Seeing the mutilated coyote corpse and then visiting this old homestead where too many Dillinger ghosts resided was messing with his mind.

He sniffed at himself for being a sissy. He'd grown up Wyoming-tough and there was little in life that really scared him, and what he'd "seen" could have been nothing more than one of the floaters in his eyes that sometimes caused tiny shadows or flashes to appear in his range of vision.

Nothing to worry about.

As he drove toward the heart of the ranch, where the "new" house stared from a copse of pine, windows glowing brightly in the gloom, he ignored the little chill that slid down his spine and concentrated instead on how to get Colton to come to the wedding.

Chapter Four

"Brook!" Ricki Dillinger called over her shoulder as she stood at the kitchen sink, arms deep in warm suds. "If you've got anything that needs to be put in the dishwasher, bring it in now!"

As usual, her daughter didn't respond and probably hadn't even heard the request. "Great." Ricki frowned at the photo on the windowsill of a bright-eyed, giggling child of four. "What happened to you?" she said aloud.

That little girl was long gone. At fourteen, Brook rarely scared up a smile and barely spoke to her mother except to criticize or pout.

"Brooklyn? Did you hear me?" Again her request was met with teenaged silence—loaded, negative space punctuated by voices from the television. *"No, Mom, I cleared all my dirty dishes last night,"* Ricki mimicked her daughter as she finished cleaning the coffeepot. Sometimes it was lonesome, living alone with a teenager. Ricki craved adult company, but she was relieved to be away from the hornet's nest buzzing around her ex in New York.

Loneliness beat addiction any day of the week.

Ricki glanced out the window mounted over the sink of this house she'd claimed a year before when she'd returned home to care for her mom. Beyond the sheet of softly falling snow, she spied her father's Dodge Ram pulling into a garage designed to hold six vehicles. Good. He'd be alone. Tonight the bride was out. Pilar had farmed her son off on friends and had headed to Denver for a "girls'" getaway. Tonight was Ricki's last chance to talk some sense into her father.

Tossing her dishrag into a hamper, she then rounded the corner to the living room, where the TV was tuned to some reality show about an outrageous celebrity family. But the overstuffed chair where Brook had been camping out was vacant, aside from her favorite rumpled quilt. Only then, over a hysterical shrieking from the television, did she hear the sound of the shower running. Using the remote she found buried under two magazines and a power bar wrapper, Ricki switched off the television. She tossed the remote onto the coffee table, then walked into the hallway.

"Brook?" She rapped on the bathroom door and yelled, "I'm going up to the main house." Again, no response. "Brook?"

"I heard you!"

"Then answer the first time," Ricki called through the panels, but knew her words were lost in the teen void. She went to the closet and grabbed her coat and scarf.

In my next life I will not uproot my only child and move her across the country. When they had left New York, Ricki had told Brook about her three-month plan to care for her mother in her final weeks. *A good death,* Rachel Dillinger had said in her gutsy way that exuded courage and tore at Ricki's heart. She'd passed away on Valentine's Day, and as they were planning for the funeral, Ricki had realized she had no intention of booking a flight back to New York. "I need to stay on for a while," she had told her sister Delilah after the funeral. "I think it will be good for me, good for

Brook, too." Back in Queens, trouble had been brewing amongst Brook's friends. One girl had gotten expelled for setting fire to a trash can, and she'd almost dragged Brook into the clink with her. Others were making up stories that, though untrue, had gotten other parents riled up. Tension was the order of the day, so, in many ways, Brook had also needed a fresh start.

"If you make it a month living with Dad, you're a better woman than I," Delilah had muttered. Living in Santa Monica, her sister was a thousand miles and several light-years away from Prairie Creek. Her youngest sis, Nell, too, had expressed her feelings on the subject with a laugh and then, "Good luck with that. If you hadn't noticed, he's a pain in the ass at the best of times."

Oh, she'd noticed.

Shortly after the funeral, she and Brook had packed their things and moved over to the old ranch foreman's quarters. It was twice the size of their Queens apartment and rent-free. The small house had a kitchen and bath, and two small bedrooms that gave them both enough privacy, while Ricki was able to have her daughter close enough to keep an eye on. So far, this place had served them well, and there was plenty of work for Ricki to do on the ranch. Her old riding skills had come back to her, and the physical labor, the endless vistas and the big sky had been therapeutic.

But things were changing here at the Rocking D. Pilar would soon be the lady of the house, and already Ricki could feel herself becoming enmeshed in her father's dealings with his bride-to-be. Maybe it was time to find some other line of work away from the ranch. It was one thing to live here, another to be under her father's thumb twenty-four-seven. Next chance she got, she planned to head into town and check with Molly, the owner of Molly's Diner, to see if she needed anyone to wait tables for her.

Tucking her wild red curls under her scarf, she stepped

into the boots she'd left by the front door. Seconds later, she was outside and marching up a winding path to the main house, where lights were blazing in windows that seemed to reach to the sky. New-fallen snow stretched over every surface as far as the eye could see, a blanket of white, covering the pale grass and frozen earth. The wind had kicked up, keening, almost a voice in the night, warning of more storms to come.

She understood Dad's desire to begin a new life. Ricki was looking to build a new life, too. But she wasn't going to hook up with someone half her age to do it.

She knocked on the door out of courtesy, then let herself in, leaving her boots in the tiled foyer. "Hey, Dad, it's me!" she yelled, unwrapping her scarf only to spy the carry-on bag standing at the foot of the stairs.

So he was serious. Earlier in the day he'd mentioned that he might have to head up to Montana to convince Colton to return for the wedding.

No time like the present to have that talk.

"Going somewhere?" she asked as she headed down the wide hallway to the great room situated at the back of the house. A gourmet kitchen occupied one end and opened up to a casual seating area, complete with soaring ceilings, wood beams and a massive rock fireplace that climbed one wall a full two stories.

"To Montana." Her father was seated in his favorite recliner. "In the morning."

"Are you out of your mind? You're actually flying in a blizzard just to make sure that Colton comes to your wedding?"

"It's not a blizzard." He glanced out the window and snorted, as if he could measure the intensity of the storm.

"Yet." She paused, then added, "Y'know, you can't force Colt to come back, Dad." She went to the clock in the nook of the wall, her mother's gold clock. Under a glass globe, the clock had a gold pendulum that rotated underneath—an object of fascination for her as a child. “You’re wasting your time and energy.”

“It’s not a waste. I’ll take the plane over to Cheyenne afterward. Got some business to take care of.”

Her father stared at her hard, his gaze boring into her as it had all of her life. “And Colton is a part of this family. He needs to be here.”

“He’s got a history with Pilar. It’s . . . awkward.” Ricki wouldn’t give up the things her brother had told her in confidence, but she shouldn’t have to. Wasn’t it enough that their father was about to marry one of his son’s ex-lovers?

“Colton is a big boy, and Pilar’s not the only filly he chased. He’ll get over it.”

Not when you expect him to stand in the church facing the son he never knew he had. It was a heartbreak, the way Pilar had manipulated Ricki’s brother, the way she was manipulating Dad right now. Ricki made a stab at the big issue. “Colt and I have been talking about this wedding.”

“Tell me something I don’t already know.”

“We’re worried about you,” she said, walking closer to the recliner where he sat, reading glasses propped on the end of his nose, half-drunk glass of whiskey on the table at his side. The television, a behemoth of seventy-some inches or more, was turned to a satellite station that catered to rodeo and stock car enthusiasts, but, thankfully, the sound was muted as her father was scanning the newspaper.

“Call it off, Dad. Call it off and I will stand behind you one hundred percent. Or at least postpone this wedding. Give yourself some time to grieve for Mom and readjust to life on your own.”

He stared up at her as if she were speaking a foreign language. “I’ve made the adjustment, and I don’t have to live alone. Pilar and her boy moved in two months ago.”

"Pilar's half your age."

"I know how old she is."

"You're old enough to be the grandfather of her son. The great-grandfather even! It's kind of sick."

"American families are no longer the typical two parents, two point five children." Ira glared at her over his glasses. "You of all people should know that."

Ricki frowned and turned back to the clock. "Thanks for reminding me." Yes, she was divorced with a fourteen-year-old daughter and a wayward ex-husband back East, and she wasn't a perfect parent, but she was trying.

"We're not talking about me, Dad. We're talking about you marrying Pilar, a woman young enough to be your daughter who just happened to have had an affair with your son. A woman who's already sent one husband to his grave."

"Damn it, Ricki. You sound like a broken record!" He yanked off his reading glasses. "I'm marrying Pilar because I love her and I don't want to spend the rest of my years alone."

"Mom hasn't been gone a year."

"Ah. So now we're getting to it." He reached down and hit the lever that lowered his footrest. "How long am I supposed to wait?" Climbing to his feet, he squared his body in a stance Ricki knew well from police work. Confrontation.

She hated confrontation, but she had learned to stand her ground. "The last time our family was together, we were burying Mom. To come together again, ten months later, for your wedding . . . it just feels wrong. All I'm asking is for you to give it time."

"What's an acceptable waiting period for you, Ricki?" His voice was rising. "Am I supposed to read Emily Post or consult a high-priced therapist to figure it all out?"

"Dad, calm down."

"I was calm until you sashayed in here and started telling

me what to do. You think I was born yesterday? I know Pilar is younger than me. I know she dated your brother. I know exactly when your mother died, thank you, and I loved her all my adult life. But she's gone, Ricki. And I'm not one to sit around and cry in my whiskey."

"No," she agreed reluctantly.

"You're wasting your time and mine." He threw himself back down in the recliner and grabbed the newspaper, snapping it open. "The wedding's in less than three weeks, and I'll thank you and your siblings to shut up and show up, if you know what's good for you."

"What are you going to do, send us to bed without supper?" She fought back the annoyance flaring in her chest. "I'm over thirty, Dad. Idle threats don't work anymore."

"Don't let the door hit you on the way out," he muttered, eyes glued to his paper.

"Fine." Nothing was more infuriating than her father when he was in a snit. Ricki stalked out, pausing in the hallway to retrieve a stack of mail that had been left for her. "If I can't get you to postpone the wedding, at least leave Colt out of it."

Again, he refused to look up at her. "My plane leaves in the morning."

"Then have a great trip." She tucked her mail under one arm and wished she could make a more dramatic exit, but she had to pause to put on her boots. Still, she gave the door a good slam behind her.

Ira was an ornery cuss . . . and so was Brook, his granddaughter, Ricki thought as she headed down the path to her "home." The place looked charming right now with its windows glowing against the snow. Ricki had tossed out the idea of stringing up some Christmas lights around the door, but Brook had just told her "whatever" as she'd tapped in another text message.

Unlike Ricki, Brook did not want to be here.

"It was only supposed to be temporary . . . a visit," she'd reminded Ricki over and over again. "You lied!" The accusation was usually accompanied by the slamming of a door and furious text messaging to her father, decrying her horrid situation out here in the middle of nowhere.

"Someday, you'll thank me for this," Ricki said as she stomped the snow off her boots on the front porch. Inside she found her daughter lounging on the couch.

Rudolph, the white kitten Brook had adopted two weeks earlier, was curled on the back of the couch, while a quilt was tossed over Brook's legs. She was splitting her attention between the Real Housewives of Somewhere and her cell phone, where she texted with lightning speed.

"Homework done?" Ricki asked.

"Yeah."

"All of it?"

"I said yeah." She sounded bored rather than irritated, as if she'd expected to be interrogated.

"Okay." Ricki was opening a Visa bill when Brook started up.

"I want to go home," she said with a sad little sigh.

"You are home."

"I mean to New York." Her voice, for the first time in a week, held some passion, some hope.

"That's not going to happen right now, honey."

"Mom! You don't get it. I *hate* it here! I hate everybody here. They're all weird."

"No, they're not."

"I told you I bumped into that old Kincaid lady, and she looked like she wanted to kill me!"

"You knocked her purse down when she was coming out of her daughter's dress shop," Ricki said with forced patience. Georgina Kincaid wasn't a forgiving sort on the best of days. She could just imagine how she felt after Brook barreled into her.

"And she had drugs and a gun, Mom," Brook reminded her. "They fell out on the sidewalk."

"And I told you her husband is really ill. Stop arguing, Brook. The Major isn't well and Georgina's taking care of him."

"Aren't we supposed to hate the Kincaids?" Brook lifted her brows.

"Where do you get this? Never mind." As soon as she said the words she wished she hadn't because prolonging an argument with her daughter was exhausting and a waste of time. Besides, she knew who Brook had been listening to. Ira used every opportunity to bad-mouth his neighbors.

"I don't have any friends here," Brook said morosely. "Not real friends, not like Sophie."

"Give it time," Ricki said. "You'll make some friends."

"How much time? We've been here like . . . an eternity already!"

"Maybe Sophie can come for a visit."

"Why would she want to? There's nothing to do here, and . . . and Dad said it would be okay for me to move in with him and Oona. When he said I could come for Christmas, I asked if I could move back and he said he'd like that."

Oh, Jesus. Ari, you bastard! "You talked to him? Tonight?"

"Texted. He was at some gig. Taking a break between sets."

And probably getting high. With Oona.

"He must have forgotten about Grandpa's wedding. You need to stick around for that."

Brook rolled her eyes in a classic save-me expression as the cat hopped onto the windowsill to stare outside. "Why?"

"Because Grandpa wants everyone there."

"Big effin' deal."

"Watch it, Brook." Seeing the set of her daughter's jaw, that Dillinger jaw, Ricki added, "Look, if your dad and I can work something out, after the wedding you can probably visit him." She hated herself for the lie. Ari Vakalian didn't want his daughter living with him. Ari could not handle his daughter, and after a few days, Brook would not be able to cope with her childlike father. Ricki knew it. Ari knew it. And, though she wasn't showing it, Brook probably knew it as well.

Denial. It was a family trait that ran through the Dillinger clan gene pool as much as red hair and obstinacy.

As she walked toward her bedroom, Ricki glanced at a picture of her family, taken years before, when she was just a child. All of her siblings were gathered around their parents on the porch of the "new house." She stood between Colt, the oldest, and Delilah, who was two years younger than she. Tyler stood on the step below while Nell, the youngest, was huddled up against their mother's leg.

Now, Ricki's lips twitched as she saw her youthful self, full of promise and idealism, her hair falling around her shoulders in a tangle of flame-colored curls. Her skin was tanned from the long Wyoming summer, her teeth not yet straightened, a skinned knee poking out of her cut-off jeans. Her brothers and sisters were all staring at the camera, all displaying a strong Dillinger chin and eyes that varied from green to gray.

"Headstrong! That's what you are, every last one of you!" their mother had said often enough. That day on the porch, Rachel Dillinger was smiling broadly. Ira's arm was draped across her slim shoulders and her fingers were entwined with those of three-year-old Nell, whose ringlets were dark brown with hints of red, her legs and arms still chubby.

How happy the family had seemed.

How *united.*

Back in the day.

When they were all young and the world was wide open to them.

Before reality and heartache had set in.

Before Rachel Hargrove Dillinger had contracted uterine cancer and died long before her time. With a pang of heartache Ricki felt that adulthood wasn't what it was cracked up to be.

She glanced back to the living room where Brook was slouched on the couch. Her daughter, like so many members of the Dillinger family, knew her own mind and had the blistering temper that went with it. Though Brook took after Ari with her olive skin, brown eyes and dark hair, the Dillinger genes wouldn't be denied. When the sunlight hit her just right, there was a scarlet glimmer in her hair, and the Dillinger jaw was unmistakable, especially when it was set. Which was most of the time.

Like grandfather, like granddaughter.

Leaving Brook to the housewives and her love affair with her phone, Ricki shut the door of her bedroom, plopped onto the end of the bed and speed-dialed Colt.

When he answered she said, "Thought I'd call and warn you to brace yourself."

"Okay." She heard the hesitation in his voice.

"You're about to have a visitor, Colt. Muhammad appears to be coming to the mountain."

Chapter Five

"The hotel is superb. Just beautiful," Pilar gushed to her fiancé over the phone. He had been in a piss-poor mood when he'd called, but she'd done a good job of cheering him up.

She wiggled her newly lacquered toes propped on the chaise and reached for her lemon drop. "It's actually sort of a spa. All the gals got mani-pedis and hot stone massages." She sipped her drink, her tongue flicking over the sugared rim as Ira responded.

"I'm glad you girls are enjoying yourselves," Ira said. "Just hurry on back, darlin'. You know I miss you."

"Mmm, miss you, too," Pilar said.

"Is it snowing there?" Ira asked.

"Uh-huh." She lifted her chin to take in the white stuff dancing past the golden hotel lights. "I'm surrounded by white." That included the posh white bedding that had been so heavenly for sleeping, and the bed stacked with cushy pillows in all shapes and sizes. "Sitting in the lap of luxury. You know, after the wedding, we really need to come back here. I was thinking maybe we could get a condo here and split our time. There's so much going on, all the time, and

Rourke would have much better educational opportunities here."

Ira's laugh cackled over the line. "There's plenty of education to be had here, the good old-fashioned kind."

She hated the way he did that, laughing off her ideas. He forced her to do an end-run around him to get the things that she wanted . . . the things she needed. She ended the call with fake kisses and tossed the phone on the bed.

She collapsed against the puffy white comforter, her head and arms landing on a stack of cushy white pillows. She dreaded going back to Ira and that big-ass house in the sticks. Everything about this place just oozed luxury. She squeezed a fat, square pillow to her chest and wiggled her toes. If only there was a hotel this nice in Wyoming. But no. She was stuck out on the prairie, with cows serenading her instead of handsome bartenders.

Rolling over, she tapped her phone to search for "luxury bedding" and eventually saw photos of posh comforters and pillows. King size, right into her shopping basket. Buy now. Yes, yes, yes.

How easy was that?

It was about time to redo their bedroom and get rid of those old floral sheets that Ira's first wife had picked out. Not her style. If she couldn't live in a luxury spa, well, she would make her home into one.

Wiggling into the soft bedding, she imagined herself at home in this wonderful fluff. Yup, this was just the thing she needed to keep her sanity back in Wyoming. Atop sweet-scented bedding, anything was possible. She could close her eyes and pretend. In the dark, a man was a man; the parts were the same, and they worked the same way. In a bed like this, she would be able to close her eyes and ride her husband like a wild woman and almost believe that she was making love to Brad Pitt.

Almost.

It wasn't as if she didn't care for Ira, she did. Maybe she even loved him, and it wasn't his age that bothered her a bit. No. It was the fact that he was insistent that they live in that tiny little town in the middle of nowhere. Prairie Creek was in his blood, but it just wasn't in hers. Yet. Probably never, but she'd try to make the marriage work because she desperately wanted to be Mrs. Ira Dillinger.

Somehow, in her transformation, she would rid Ira's house of Rachel Dillinger's ghost, even if she had to have Mrs. Mac and those little maids scrub it away, inch by inch.

In town, Sabrina stayed late at the clinic to take on a feline emergency.

"I'm sorry to call you at this hour, but I was just so worried about Buster!" Sally Jamison's round face was twisted into a knot of concern. With a grunt, she hauled her cat carrier onto the reception counter of the clinic. Though Sabrina's expertise was large animals, three days a week she covered after-hours emergencies and gave Antonia a break. Tonight, it seemed, was her lucky night.

"Come on out of there, baby." Deftly, Sally unzipped the carrier from which guttural, low growls and an occasional hiss erupted. She reached inside and the cat screamed his discontent. "Be good, baby."

Slowly she pulled out the huge gray tabby. Buster, a.k.a. "Baby," wasn't happy. His gold eyes were nearly black, the pupils dilated. His ears had flattened to his head and he showed his needle-sharp teeth in hisses aimed at Sabrina as if she were the devil incarnate. He tried to scramble off the counter, but Sally held him firmly. "You're okay," she said, trying to stroke Buster. In response, he cringed and took a swipe at her with one meaty paw.

"What's going on with him?" Sabrina asked.

"He just won't eat, no matter what I give him."

Sabrina fought a reaction. It was obvious the cat hadn't missed a meal in years.

"He threw up yesterday—not just a hairball—and . . . well, I'm just worried about him. When I checked on him at lunchtime, he was listless and hardly moved and . . ." She lowered her voice. "He's been missing the litter box. On purpose. He either just lies in the box on top of the kitty litter and won't come out or he . . ." Her nostrils flared as she tried to come up with delicate words. "He's been doing his business on one of the rugs in the bathroom. It's . . . well, it's just not like him. He's always been a very neat and tidy kitty. Never has accidents. Or, um, never did, did you, baby?" She made little kissy noises at him, then added, "And he howls sometimes, too."

"When he's urinating?"

"I . . . I don't know."

Buster glowered, moans of fury emanating from deep in the cat's gut.

Just then Sally's cell phone rang shrilly, startling the cat. Fortunately, one hand remained clamped on him as she fished in her purse for her cell phone. Apparently she was used to his antics. "It's the shop. I have to take this. Sorry. We're so busy at work, I've been running around like a chicken with my head cut off. Christmas, you know. All the parties and the big wedding."

Sabrina gestured for her to go ahead as she checked Buster's record.

"Hello? Yes, I can hear you! Uh-huh . . . Oh, Cal, don't tell me that. If we can't get that specific rose, then she'll have to pick out something else and you know how Pilar can be. I'm just saying . . . did you call her? Still in Denver. Well, how is she going to approve flower samples from there? For the love of . . . Okay, I'll call her." She let out a long-suffering sigh. "I know. Love you, too." As she hung up, she rolled her large eyes toward the heavens. "Cal has the devil of a time with the shop when I'm not around."

"Let's take Buster into an examination room," Sabrina suggested, leading the way.

Sally carried the unhappy cat into the small room and placed him on the table. Immediately, he tried to escape.

"You poor thing," Sabrina said, trying to console cat and owner. "Nobody likes to be sick." Buster growled through the exam, but allowed Sabrina to look him over, even weigh him and take his temperature without delivering a bite or a swipe of claws.

"Looks like an infection, but let's see. I'm going to have to do some tests, including a urinalysis to make sure there's no blockage."

"I'll have to leave him?"

"Yes."

Sally frowned as she eyed her pet. "Well, if that's what it takes. But can I pick him up tomorrow?"

"Probably. We'll call you."

Sally helped transfer Buster into his carrier again and while the cat growled his displeasure, she bundled up in her coat and gloves. "I guess I should have noticed something was wrong earlier, but I've been working round the clock on the Dillinger wedding." She lowered her voice as she zipped her down coat. "Pilar changes her mind more often than most people change their underwear. It's been hard on everyone in my shop, but Emma is really getting hit hard."

Emma Kincaid was a local dress designer—a talented seamstress who could stand up to any top-notch salon in Cheyenne or Denver. "Emma told you about the dresses?" Sabrina asked.

Sally was nodding. "Just when Emma was about finished with the first one, Pilar saw something different in some magazine, something she thought would be more flattering. And the same was true of the second dress. As if this were her first rodeo. Hah!"

Sabrina had heard the same story over coffee at Molly's Diner.

"And you know Emma's just about the best seamstress this side of the Mississippi."

"Emma is terrific," Sabrina agreed.

"As to the flowers," Sally went on. "Oh, my Lord! She can't make up her mind. First it was the peonies, had to be peonies, then, once we found some, she decided to go with lilies, until someone told her people would be reminded of a funeral and with poor Rachel, you know, barely cold in her grave, Pilar decided against lilies. Now, she's settled on roses and baby's breath, right where she should have been from day one. Oh, but she still wants some birds of paradise, has a thing for them, despite the cost. Dear Lord! Pray she doesn't change her mind again." Sally crossed her gloved fingers to make her point. "It's driving us, all of us at the shop, crazy. Especially Mia, her being kind of related to the Dillingers, you know. Her daughter being Judd's and all."

Oh, Sabrina knew. Only too well. Mia's daughter, Kit, was seventeen, and she spent most of her time traveling the Dillinger lands, communing with the animals and the land, by all accounts. No one and nothing could keep her in school. Mia, who wasn't Sabrina's favorite person by a long shot—she was too needy and grasping and intent on burrowing into the Dillinger clan by hook or by crook; she still used the injury she'd sustained in the fire eighteen years earlier as a lever to extort guilt and money—had all but despaired of Kit and given up trying to get her to conform. Kit was a wild child and had no use for convention, whether it was the law or not. She was a Dillinger by blood and simply roamed their lands as she pleased, living in her own world. She steered clear of her mother, and Sabrina wondered if maybe Kit was as loath to be around Mia as she was.

"Everyone at the shop tiptoes around Pilar right now. Especially Mia. She really wants the wedding to go well."

Does she? Sabrina wondered. Mia wasn't eager to share the spotlight with anyone and especially someone as exacting and beautiful as Pilar.

"I think Mia's hoping Colton will show." Sally adjusted her stocking cap on her head. "I wouldn't put it past her to make a play for him. She finds a way to remind everyone that he saved her from the fire, and, well, he's a Dillinger, and we all know how she feels about them."

"I heard Colton wasn't coming home."

Sally cocked her head to one side. "I heard that too, but my money's on Ira getting his way."

Sabrina really didn't want to think about Colton.

Sally gave her a hard look. "You were involved with Colton once, too, weren't you?"

"Too long ago to count," Sabrina said, deflecting the conversation, as she reached for the cat carrier. "I went to school with his sister Ricki."

"I know, my son graduated with you two. You remember Jeff?" There was a gleam of pride in her eyes at the mention of her only son. "Ricki's back in Prairie Creek, too. I guess all that big-city cop business just didn't take."

Sabrina was tempted to point out that Ricki had come back because her mother was dying, but there was no point in correcting someone like Sally Jamison.

"Well, anyway, I'm sure Jeff told me you dated Colton when you were a senior."

"High school romance, Sally."

"Sometimes they're the most tricky to get over."

Sabrina managed a smile she didn't feel as she led the way to the reception area. "Thanks for bringing Buster in. We'll give you a call as soon as we know anything."

"You're a godsend," Sally said as, finally, she headed out the door.

By the time Sabrina locked the door behind Sally, her heart and head were swimming with pain. Why did she let Sally rile her about something that had ended when she was a kid?

"You know," she told Buster, "your Sally and gossip are like salt and pepper; you never find one without the other."

The cat hissed in response.

"The worst part is that now I'm stuck going to the wedding and maybe facing Colt again."

Buster arched his back and glared at her.

Sabrina ignored him, her mind on Colton whether she wanted to think of him or not. She'd shared a few words with him earlier this year at his mother's funeral—just enough to know that her heart still stupidly raced a little when he was near. It was ridiculous after all this time. Colton had married, had a child, and suffered an unbelievably tragic loss, and yet Sabrina's thoughts kept traveling back to her own time with him, remembering how much she'd loved him, how hurt she'd been when he left her high and dry.

"It isn't about you," she told herself sternly, but she already knew she wouldn't listen.

She'd always felt this way about Colton Dillinger. She'd been seventeen and flattered by his attentions. A couple of years older, he'd been a rodeo rider with a little college under his belt, rough-and-tumble, a cowboy in the making. All muscle and sinew, with a square jaw and a sexy smile that matched the irreverent spark in his eyes, Colton Dillinger had been trouble, a man to avoid. And she hadn't. Sabrina had found him dangerously fascinating and been hooked from the moment his lazy smile had stretched across the stubble of his beard and his eyes had found hers. That fall, when she should have gone away to school, she'd changed her mind and taken classes at the nearby community college. Because of Colton Dillinger. Because she'd thought she'd marry him and have a passel of Dillinger babies. Because she'd been willing to set aside her own dreams to be with him.

Oh, how foolish she'd been. Yeah, their love had flamed hot that fall, but after the fire at the Dillinger ranch, things had begun to fall apart. She'd wanted to get serious; he'd been aloof. The blaze that had killed Judd and nearly crippled Mia had also destroyed any of Sabrina's girlhood fantasies where Colton was concerned and had changed the course of so many lives.

"We were kids." She let her thoughts fall away for a moment of intense focus as she drew blood from the cat's neck. "There." She managed to withdraw the needle and her hand before he could snap a paw at her.

In many ways the blaze at the Dillinger ranch eighteen years earlier still smoldered, its embers still hot enough to burn, its smoke black enough to always obscure the truth. Colton had left Prairie Creek soon afterward with hardly a word to Sabrina. She'd longed for him to come back for too many years to count.

Now, ironically, she hoped he stayed away.

From inside Mojave's stall, Colton heard the door to the stable creak open, felt the cold rush of wind stream into the stables and heard a familiar tread on the old floorboards. He didn't even have to look away from the hoof he was trimming to know that his father had arrived. *Great.*

"About time you showed up," he said, keeping his voice neutral.

Mojave, whose testy disposition was renowned, snorted impatiently while Montana was rousted from sniffing at a hole in the floorboards. The dog growled, lifted his head and barked sharply.

"I've been expecting you." Colt dropped the gelding's foreleg and straightened to find Ira closing the door behind him. How many times had he been in a similar situation, alone with his father in a building that smelled of dust, urine and horses?

"Ricki called, did she?"

"Yeah."

"Figures. You kids are thick as thieves."

"Not kids anymore." Colt was thirty-nine, Ricki not far behind. How old did you have to be for your parents to leave you alone? He traced the dorsal stripe of the gelding, patted him on his rump, and earned another disgruntled snort from Mojave. Colt slipped through the stall door and faced his old man.

"Always will be kids to me. That's the trouble with you all. I can't trust a one of you."

The feeling was mutual. "You're not talking me into coming to that farce of a wedding of yours, if that's why you came."

His father glanced over at the stall where Mojave was staring back at him. A couple of boxes over, Scarlet, a roan mare, nickered softly. As the old man scanned the row of stalls with a practiced eye, Colton rubbed the anxious mare's neck.

"Nice herd ya got here," Ira commented.

"They'll do." Colton opened the barn door.

"The bay. Your primary stud?"

"Rocky would like to think so. He's the old man around here. Trouble is, he always acts half his age around the mares. His ego is a lot bigger than his . . ." His father's eyes narrowed a bit as if he'd been waiting for a jab. Colton added, "But you didn't fly up here to see the stock, did you?"

"Nope."

Colt braced himself for the battle that was about to go down. "Let's head inside and you can try to convince me to go down to Wyoming. I'll make you coffee and tell you no. And you can fly home, feeling good that at least you tried."

Ira made a sound of disgust.

Whistling to the dog, Colton left the lights on but secured the door. Ahead of them, Montana bounded along the path of broken and flattened snow leading to the house. Half a step behind, his old man followed through the bone-deep cold to the house, probably little more than a cabin by his father's standards.

"You work this place alone?" Ira asked.

"Cub Jenkins is my foreman. I let him hire the crews when we need 'em."

"Trustworthy?"

"No, Dad. I hire the biggest crook in the county. What kind of question is that?"

Irritated, Colt stomped up the two steps to the porch and opened the door. He'd owned this place for more than a decade, and his father had never bothered to visit. Even during the dark days after the accident, Ira had flown up for the funerals and stayed in a motel, not out of a sense of privacy for Colt but as a clear message that Ira's world revolved around Ira's ranch and he had no use for anything beyond Dillinger land.

As soon as Colton opened the door to the mudroom, Montana bolted inside and checked his empty food bowl parked in the kitchen. "You were fed," Colton reminded the dog as he shed his coat and hat and hung them on a peg near the back door. "Want coffee?"

Ira shrugged out of his jacket and hung it and his Stetson on an empty peg. "Got anything stronger?"

In a cabinet over the refrigerator, Colt located a half-empty bottle of Jack. He handed it over with a glass he snagged from the dish rack. "Don't tell me it's 'five o'clock somewhere,'" he warned. "I know that already."

"Time, just another man's restraints, another man's measure. Means nothing." As if to add emphasis to his theory, the old clock near the stairs counted off the half hour. Ira poured himself a stiff shot and held up the bottle for Colt to do the same.

Colt shook his head. "If time means nothing, why the rush to get married? You're not dying, are you?"

"Hope not."

"Then why not slow down a little? What happened? You've got Viagra with an expiration date or something?"

"Funny." Ira tossed back a swallow and walked through a dining alcove to the living area, where he warmed the back of his legs near the fireplace.

"Mom hasn't been gone a year."

"And she wouldn't want me to waste time."

"She also wouldn't want you to do something stupid."

"Rachel's dead, son, and that's that. I want to spend the rest of my years enjoying life."

"And Pilar is gonna bring you joy?" Colt decided he did need a drink. He found another glass and poured himself a healthy shot.

There was a smug twinkle in Ira's eyes. "She already does."

Colton rubbed his eyes, as if he could wipe away the image of an old fool in bed with a sexy woman. "If things go south, it's not so easy to undo a marriage vow. It'll cost you."

"I'm not a man who looks at the road behind him." Ira pointed his glass at his son. "I keep my sights on what's ahead. I thought I taught you to do the same. You can't let regret eat away at you."

Colton raked back his hair, staring at the fire. Regret was a bitter taste on the back of his tongue. It clouded his days and clung to his nights. Any man approaching forty was liable to have a tool belt full of regrets, but Colt's was heavy enough to stop him in his tracks some days. Regret over lost love. Regret that he hadn't been there to save his wife and daughter. Regret that he'd let an itch below the belt take him on a bender with Pilar all those years ago, producing a kid who was now a victim of his two irresponsible parents.

"Some things take time," Colton said, eyes on the fire.

"Well, some things can't wait for you to throw your damned pity party. Take a stand, son. Get your ass down to Prairie Creek and be a father. Show Rourke what it's like to be a Dillinger."

Rourke . . . a Dillinger.

Colt met his father's measured stare. "Pilar told you."

"Of course she told me. We're getting married. I know you're the boy's father. You think she'd keep that from me?"

"It wouldn't be the first time," Colton pointed out coldly. "She let Chad die thinking the kid was his."

"Again . . . you're kicking up dust in the past. We gotta look at the future. You're the boy's father. What are you gonna do about it?"

Tossing back the whiskey, Colt felt the burn of his future. "Does he know?" Ira nodded and Colt ground out, "Goddammit."

"Show up for the wedding. Smooth things over with Pilar, get to know your son."

My son . . .

Unbidden, the image of his baby girl, Darcy, came to him—her soft, toothless smile, the light in her green eyes as she looked up at him, helpless and trusting . . .

Colt felt sorely tempted to throw his glass in the fire, but he crossed to the counter and placed it down carefully, his nerves strung taut with rage. "I'm not gonna let you manipulate me."

Ira shook his head and strode to the back door, reaching

for his coat. "Don't take this out on me. That boy needs to know his father and I'd like to see you at my wedding."

Colton shoved the bottle of Jack into the cupboard and let the door bang shut.

"You know, son, there was a time when you couldn't do enough for me."

"Pilar'll have you in the grave before the year is out."

"At least I'll die happy," Ira came back. "Which is more than I can say for you, living like a hermit up here. When was the last time a woman even stepped foot in this place?"

Colt had no answer. His head hurt and there was a sour taste in his throat. His father knew that Colt was Rourke's father and he still wanted to marry Pilar.

Ira paused, one hand on the doorknob. "Come on, son, let me buy you breakfast." Casting a glance at the unwashed fry pan on the stove, he added, "Or lunch. Whatever you want. Your choice."

"Nothing appears to be my choice."

"The boy's your son," Ira repeated stubbornly. "That's all I'm sayin'."

"Pilar already asked me for child support."

"That a problem?" Ira asked with a lift of his brow.

"Happy to support Rourke. Just thought it was kind of ironic that you'll be supporting Pilar."

"Let it go, Colton."

Colton managed to keep himself from making another smart comeback. He had no use for Pilar, but Rourke was a different matter. Ira was right in that regard: he had a son, no matter how many ways he tried to deny it. That had been proven by a simple paternity test.

As if sensing him weakening, Ira wrapped one arm around Colton's broad shoulders and urged, "Oh hell, make the trip to Wyoming. Do it for your old man."

Colton stepped free of his father's grasp but not the emotional net he'd cast. Ira had woven that too well. No,

Colt wouldn't go for the wedding, but he would go for Rourke.

"Okay," he said.

"Okay?"

"Okay, I'll go. For Rourke. And get that shit-eatin' grin off your face," Colton growled, "or I might change my mind."

Wisely, for the first time in creation, Ira did as he was told.

Chapter Six

First the storm had dumped ten inches of snow over the region and then the wind had raced through, blowing the powdery white stuff into drifts against buildings, fence posts, farm machinery and you name it. Sheriff Sam Featherstone's boots crunched through the snow's crust a week afterward, as he walked up to the abandoned car and slid the thin metal strip of the Slim Jim between the window and rubber seal. The vehicle had been left at Big Bart's Buffalo Lounge since before the storm swept through and it was now half-buried in snow. Sam worked the Slim Jim and suddenly the lock popped open.

"Looks like you've done this before," Bart O'Day said, his breath a cloud of white.

"Once or twice." Sam unlocked the rest of the Honda Civic, which sat listing toward its flat tire. He opened the glove box on the passenger side. "Says it's registered to an Amber Barstow, Sacramento." The name and address matched the information that had come up when he ran the license plate back at the precinct.

"That's good, right?"

"Not good or bad, just consistent."

Bart, the owner of the bar and grill on the outskirts of

Prairie Creek, had called the sheriff's department about the car and Sam was checking it out. The wind had died down, leaving a vista of white snow and blue sky from the wide-open stretch of land that hooked off the interstate. It was so clear today that the purple and black shale fingers of the mountains seemed to rise up from the field beyond Bart's parking lot. On days like this, you just had to take a breath and appreciate the fact that you were in God's country.

"You say the car's been here a week?" Sam asked again.

"More or less." Bart shifted from left foot to right, his belly zipped so tight into a red jacket that it seemed a small pin might pop it. "I figured it was just a flat that happened during the bad snow. You know how people walk away from a vehicle and come back with friends when the storm clears. But no one's claimed it."

"There's no stolen vehicle report for this Honda." Sam jotted down the girl's name on a piece of paper. "And this Amber Barstow didn't leave a message with any of your staff that she'd be back to pick it up?"

"Not a word."

Sam handed Bart the slip of paper. "If we're lucky, she bought something at your place and used a credit card. Can you check your receipts for the day that you noticed the car left here, maybe a day or two before, see if you find her name?"

"That might take a while, Sam."

"It'd help us pinpoint the time when the car was abandoned."

"I'll get Shelly on it." Bart started toward the building, then turned back. "What you gonna do with the car, Sam?"

"Probably get Bud to tow it into town. Unless you want to add it to that rust heap out at your place?"

Bart waved him off. "My wife says one more old junker and she's divorcing me for sure. But I'd like it out of here. With holiday travel, the lot fills up sometimes."

"I'll take care of it."

An abandoned vehicle was generally not cause for alarm, but something about this one tickled the hairs on the back of Sam's neck. He gloved up and checked out the car, leaving things where he found them.

It appeared that Amber Barstow was on a road trip. There were two spent coffee cups in the holder, an empty pack of cigarettes on the passenger seat, and—most telling—a suitcase full of clothes and toiletries in the trunk. No purse, but the blister pack of birth control pills in the travel case showed that the last pill had been taken on a Friday.

Today was Thursday. That would place the girl here Friday or Saturday, depending on what time of day she took her pill. The makeup case had been so full, Sam had found it hard to stuff everything back in. All the tan-colored lotions and creams. Plastic packs of eye shadow and blush. Lipsticks and a bunch of pencils in red and brown for God knew what. As he replaced the pill pack and tucked the shiny silver cosmetic bag away, he felt like a voyeur. Even after eleven years of police work, it felt wrong going through a strange woman's possessions. A violation of privacy, and Sam valued privacy. Still, gathering evidence and putting it all together—assembling the puzzle—that was what kept his head in the job.

So. No purse or cell phone, but a fat suitcase of women's clothes and a good stock of makeup. Most women wouldn't go too far without their belongings, say if a friend had picked her up here. Clearly Amber Barstow intended to reclaim her car. So where the hell was she?

Sam checked up on Amber, and by the time he was walking into the restaurant, he had learned that Amber Barstow had not been reported missing, and he had the photo from her driver's license on his iPad, ready to show around.

The lunch rush was winding down in the restaurant, so

Bart's wife, Shelly, who worked as the primary waitress, was able to take a minute and look at Amber's photo.

She stuck her pen behind her ear and frowned. "Face doesn't ring a bell, but I do like your iPad. It's so slender." She held the device up so that Bart could see it from his spot at a table in the back, where he was going through rubber-banded stacks of receipts. "See this, honey? Mm-hmm. This is what I want for Christmas!" Shelly handed it back to Sam. "I've been hinting around, but he'll probably just get me some earrings or perfume again."

"You don't recall this woman?"

"Mmm . . . no . . . ask Carol or Jane."

Sam was about to check with the other waitresses when Bart let out a hoot. "I got it. Amber Barstow," he hollered, holding a receipt high in the air and motioning Sam to the bar. Sam let out a slow breath and walked over to Bart, not liking that he'd shouted out the woman's name.

"She was here Saturday, right?" Bart asked. Sam was scanning the receipt as they moved down the dim corridor. "Maybe she came to hear the band. You know, we have live music on Saturday nights."

"It says her server was Grady," Sam said.

"Well, just your luck. Grady's working now."

Bart clapped Sam on the back as they stepped up to the bar to talk with the wiry man with the gold tooth and pale eyes. Grady Chisum was not Sam's favorite citizen. The man had been at the center of dozens of barroom brawls before he decided to clean it up and malinger on the other side of the bar.

It took Grady no time to recall the woman. "Amber," he said, almost with an "aha" attached to it.

"You know her," Sam said.

"Nah. She just came in that one night. She in trouble?"

"That's her Honda Civic outside, the one with the flat tire," Sam said.

"I just want her to get the car out of my lot," Bart said, holding the receipt up to Grady's face, which he turned away from.

"Irish coffee with a green drizzle on top," he said as he hung the glass he'd been drying in the overhead rack. "Yeah, that's her. Dark hair. She was kind of quiet, kept to herself most of the time. She checked out a guy at the bar, but I don't think they hooked up or anything."

"She was alone?" Sam asked.

"Yup. And so was the other guy. Didn't recognize either of 'em. He had a dark jacket and a black Stetson. I can't remember what she was wearing, but she was shivering when she came in. It took her a while to unzip the jacket and relax."

"Did they leave together?"

Grady squinted. "Don't think so, but I'm paid to pour, not to babysit."

Sam went back outside to talk with Bud Thomas the tow truck driver. Since the car's owner wasn't a missing person yet, he wasn't going to voucher all the possessions in the car, but he didn't want the vehicle going all the way over to county impound. "Just take it back to town," Sam told the driver. "Leave it in the lot behind the precinct."

"Will do," Bud said, his breath steaming the cold air.

By the time he rolled into the lot back at the precinct, the muscles in the back of Sam's neck sang with tension. He cut the engine to his county-issued Jeep and rotated his neck far enough to hear his vertebrae crack. The neck ache was chronic. Like the Jeep, it came with the job. Lately, the department was on overload. They were down two deputies, one from retirement, the other a pregnancy, and he was having some difficulty getting anyone qualified to take the jobs.

The holiday season was always stressful and seemed to bring out the worst in some people. Domestic violence reports were on the rise, along with the usual traffic accidents, power outages, drunk drivers, poachers and fights. But he had a niggling fear about the abandoned vehicle. He sincerely hoped Amber Barstow was all right.

Locking the Jeep remotely, he walked through the back entrance of the low-slung cinder block building housing the sheriff's department. The smell of floor wax and burnt coffee greeted him, and he hadn't stepped five feet into the common lunch area when Naomi Simmons, a secretary for the department, chased him down.

"The furnace is on the fritz again," she said, perpetual scowl in place. "All the front offices are freezing." She was bundled in her down jacket and scarf and dabbed at her red nose with her tissue.

"Call maintenance and—"

"I did. You know what Mel told me? 'I'll get to it.' You know what that means. *When* will he get to it? That's what I'd like to know. Hopefully sometime before the New Year!" She was really getting worked up now, and Sam figured the influx of adrenaline might be just what she needed to get her blood flowing again.

Gary Rodriguez, one of the deputies, was seated at a round table, immersed in the newspaper, but he looked up at Naomi, then looked down again quickly, as if he wanted to make sure he stayed out of the line of fire.

"You want me to talk to Mel?" Sam asked.

"Like that'll do any good, but yes."

"Get him, or someone from maintenance, on the line for me," he agreed. The last thing he needed was to handle this detail himself, but he couldn't have the staff freezing, either. He needed a little patience here, a trait the Shoshone were known for, though Sam often felt he'd been shortchanged in that department.

Naomi stormed to the coffee counter, tried to fill a cup from the carafe marked HOT WATER and found it empty. "Fan. Tas. Tic." Jaw set, she filled her cup at the sink and slid it into the microwave. As her mug twirled to the right temperature, she scoured the basket of tea bags and grumbled about there not being any peppermint.

Sam grabbed a cup of black coffee and wound his way through the rabbit warren of hallways to his office, the largest in the building, but by no means plush.

He'd barely sat down when his phone rang and Naomi connected him to the lackluster Mel Gervais who promised to "get right on it."

"Sheriff?" he heard as he was hanging up.

He glanced up.

Katrina Starr, Prairie Creek's youngest detective, stood in the doorway to his office. Petite, barely five-foot-three, she was an intense woman, who was far too serious for her twenty-eight years. "That detective from Sacramento called back while you were gone."

"Any word on Amber Barstow?"

"He got a call from her parents this morning, and they filed a missing person's report." Katrina frowned. "Amber Barstow is officially missing."

Colton zipped his duffel bag closed and told himself he was making a big mistake. Despite all his vows to the contrary, he'd decided to return to Wyoming, not for the wedding, but to try and connect with the son he'd never officially met. He couldn't imagine how Rourke would respond to a face-to-face with the absentee father who'd sired him. Probably not well. In fact, if Colton had been told that he wasn't

Ira's son, but the progeny of a love 'em and leave 'em cowboy, he probably would have spit on the pretender.

The old man had taken off yesterday on the private plane he'd hired, but Colton had decided against flying with him. The quarters would be too damned tight, and he'd needed to square things up before he headed south. He left Jenkins in charge of the stock and there were plenty of ranch hands available to help out. Jenkins had also agreed to put out food and water for Montana, who now followed his every step. That dog did not like the sight of a duffel bag.

"You'll be okay," he said, kneeling down to scratch the shepherd behind his ears. "I won't be gone long." Montana whined and looked up at him with accusations in his dark eyes. The dog *knew* Colton was lying. Whining, wagging his tail, he begged to be let in on the adventure.

"Now don't look so pathetic," Colton said, then caved. "Okay, you're right. This might take a while."

Sensing that his mission was accomplished, the dog took off, claws clicking frantically as he raced to the front door.

Colton shouldered his bag and followed after the excited mutt. "Yeah, I know," he said as he reached for his jacket. "I'm a sap."

Montana barked expectantly as Colton shrugged into his coat, reminded himself to call Cub to let him know that Montana was taking the trip with him, slapped off the lights and walked outside into a rush of bone-chilling cold.

He had a long drive ahead of him, but the distance wasn't the difficult part. Nope. Even with the weather he could probably make it in a little over eight hours. It was what was on the other end that was the problem.

When he'd fled to Montana, he'd been escaping all the pain and blame and family bullshit of Prairie Creek. That place had closed around him like a noose, choking the living breath out of him.

And now? With Margo and Darcy gone, he could see that

his time in Montana was coming to an end, too. He had to get out of Margo's kitchen. He'd given up trying to sleep in the bed they'd shared. And Darcy's room? Although Ricki had packed a lot of stuff up for him when she'd visited the previous spring, he'd stayed away from the bedrooms at the back of the house. He was on his way out, that was a given, and had been ever since he'd lost them.

His next move? That was still up in the air.

He was damn sure it wasn't Prairie Creek.

Whistling to the dog, he opened the driver's-side door of his Explorer. Montana leapt inside and took his spot on the passenger seat as Colton stowed his bag in the back.

Half a minute later, he was behind the wheel and heading back to the place he'd sworn he'd left forever.

Chapter Seven

It was after two, and with the lunch rush over, Sabrina hoped to grab a quick burger and a quiet ten minutes to herself in a booth at Molly's.

As she sat down, Cordelia, one of Molly's waitresses, asked, "Do you want fries with your burger?"

"No fries. Salad or fruit, if you can do it."

"Milk shake?"

"Just black coffee."

"Trying to cut down on the carbs?" Cordelia motioned to the patrons behind her. "That's all I been hearing for the past two weeks. Folks are trying to trim down to squeeze into the formal wear in their closets. Seems like most of the town has been invited to the big wedding."

"Really." Sabrina hadn't even thought about what to wear yet. She had bigger issues and forced the question that had been preying on her ever since she'd concluded she'd have to attend. "Have you heard about whether Colt Dillinger is coming for it?" Cordelia was always a good source of information.

"Jury's still out, and I call it a fifty-fifty chance. I think Ira's up in Montana now, trying to rope him into it. But the big surprise was when those invitations went out to all the

Kincaids. Pete Murray said he thought his eyes had gone buggy when he was sorting the mail down at the post office. He almost called Pilar to make sure it wasn't a mistake, but figured he'd mind his own business."

"I bet that was a shocker," Sabrina agreed. Pete was a reliable postman, but nosy as the day was long.

Cordelia hitched a thumb to the rear of the restaurant where Georgina Kincaid and her husband, the Major, sat finishing their lunch. "I know they're going. Hunter and Emma, too. Of course, Emma's not surprised, considering she's making Pilar's gown. Or should I say gowns in the plural. Did you hear that Pilar has her working on three?"

"That's the buzz." Sabrina put the cloth napkin on her lap and glanced at her empty coffee cup.

Cordelia said, "Lemme bring that to ya."

As she disappeared into the kitchen, Georgina and the Major rose from their table. The Major, once a big bear of a man, now moved slowly, stooped over and stepping carefully as if he were walking down the galley of a rocking ship. Georgina went to the register to pay the bill, but the Major kept motoring toward the door, slow and steady.

Sabrina was sorry to see him failing. The Major had always been kind to her. His daughter Mariah—now there was the polar opposite of her daddy. That girl could have been the prototype for one of the characters in *Mean Girls* when she was younger, and she hadn't improved much with age.

The Major paused at Sabrina's booth and lifted a hand toward the windows overlooking Main Street. "How's that for snow?" he said.

"Quite a bit," she agreed.

"Should go tobogganing," he observed.

"I'm hoping to do some snowshoeing this weekend if we don't get dumped on again."

He nodded. "Good."

Word had it that the Major was suffering from some form of cancer and that he was dying by inches. Sabrina couldn't be sure if he really knew who she was, but really, did it matter?

By contrast, his wife passed by with a scowl and a prim nod. That was Georgina's best greeting since Sabrina had helped her ranch hands vaccinate scores of lambs the previous spring. Georgina Kincaid was quite a piece of work, but in her face you could still see some of the acclaimed beauty from her youth.

She was able to stave off the chill of Georgina's stare when Cordelia brought her a cup of piping hot coffee. Checking her cell, she saw an afternoon and evening loaded with appointments, including a visit to the Dillinger ranch to check on the stock. And Sally still hadn't returned her call about Buster. Another busy day, but TGIF. At least, she only had a half day of work tomorrow and Sunday . . . maybe she really would get out the snowshoes and take a walk in the snow. This time of year, she was stuck in the clinic for far too many hours.

The diner was emptying out, giving her the quiet she craved. Doc Farley, who rarely worked on Fridays, waved as he left with his wife, Nora. Two men took their coats and cowboy hats from hooks by the door. Sabrina didn't recognize them, but one nodded a greeting and the other touched the brim of his hat. That's how folks were around here, friendly, making a point to say hello. It was one of the aspects of small-town life that had kept her here in Prairie Creek when her mom had fled to a larger city.

She was cradling the hot mug when the door jangled and in bustled Sally Jamison. She waited on the slate landing, scanning the restaurant with her hands on her hips.

"Sally?" Sabrina called, lifting a hand. She really didn't

want the queen of gab to join her, but they did have business to transact.

Sally bustled over. “I’m not ignoring your call, I’ve just got so many plates in the air, and if Pilar doesn’t make a decision on her flowers soon, they’re all going to come crashing down.”

“No worries. Do you want to join me?”

“No can do,” Sally declined, but she slid onto the banquette opposite Sabrina anyway. “I’m meeting Pilar here to get the house measurements and go over some final choices. *Final* being the operative word.”

“I was calling about Buster. You got my message that he has a urinary tract infection? You’ll need to continue his medication. You can pick him up when you have a free minute, any time before six.”

“You must think I’m a terrible mommy, not getting back to you sooner.”

“I know you’re busy.”

“Crazy is more like it. I just got an order for twenty more wreaths for the Boy Scouts. Twenty! Mia and I are going to be up all night bending wires.” She looked up at the wall clock. “I’ll head over to pick Buster up, just as soon as I finish here with Pilar.”

“Renee has your instructions and paperwork all ready for you.”

“Thank you for taking such good care of my baby.”

“You’re very welcome.”

Sabrina expected Sally to get up and find Pilar, but she settled in and hunkered closer. “So”—she folded her hands on the table—“did you hear that the cops found an abandoned car out at Big Bart’s, some little Honda, I think, and the car’s owner, a young woman, has been missing since the Saturday after Thanksgiving.”

“Uh-oh.” Sabrina sipped her coffee, thinking that it was

a long time to be missing, especially in this weather. "Have they released any details?"

"Only that she lives in California."

"I wonder what she was doing out this way."

Sally shrugged.

Sabrina hoped that the florist was exaggerating the details of the young woman's disappearance. "I'm going to start locking my doors." The front door opened. Sabrina caught a glimpse of Pilar stomping snow off her boots and her heart sank.

Sally lifted her head, spied Pilar just as the door shut. "Pilar?" she called, waving. "Over here!"

No, not over here, Sabrina wanted to say. The place was dead and there were plenty of other tables. But all at once Cordelia appeared with her burger, and Pilar was right beside her with a big hello and a little wiggle of the hand, telling Sabrina to scoot over.

"I haven't seen you out at the ranch in a while," she told Sabrina as she sat down beside her.

"I guess you just miss me. I'm there at least once a week. Out in the barn. Sometimes the stables."

"That explains it. This time of year, I don't go out there much." The smile on her lips fell away as Pilar turned to Sally. "I got your message and my heart is broken. Tell me you've found some birds of paradise?"

"I have, but it's not that simple." Sally looked up as Cordelia approached the table again. "I'll have a tuna salad on toast, please."

Pilar ordered a fruit salad and a lemon water. "I'm just back from Denver, so I'm having a little culture shock again. Everything here is . . . different."

Some of us like Prairie Creek just fine, Sabrina thought. She bit into her burger and kept her thoughts to herself, not that she had a chance to get a word in with Sally and Pilar who had started blathering over flower and measurement crises.

"What do you mean?" Sally said to Pilar. "I thought you were bringing me the measurements today. We can't start the garland without them."

"No. You said you were coming out to the place while I was in Denver, to get them yourself," Pilar insisted. "I'm sure I told you that I don't even know what to measure and, really, I don't have the time for this."

"And I said I was too busy. I offered to send Mia, but you said Ira didn't want her poking around the house."

Pilar rolled her eyes and sighed. "How am I supposed to manage all this on my own? I should never have let Ira talk me out of hiring a wedding planner."

"Maybe you should talk to Ricki," Sally suggested. "She's been a big-city girl for a while and she's there at the ranch. She could have some great ideas and—"

"Oh, Ricki," Pilar said in disgust. "She's too busy helping her father run the ranch. Besides, she was a cop. Not exactly a high-fashion profession. I swear, there's going to be a wedding catastrophe if I don't get someone to help me pull this thing together."

Sabrina kept her gaze on her salad, just in case Pilar got any ideas about hooking her in. But apparently playing doctor to the livestock also failed to rate high enough to deal with wedding decisions, in Pilar's mind.

"I'm sure one of Ira's other daughters will give you a hand once they get here," Sally said. "In the meantime, I need to get going on the garland for your house . . . the church, too."

Pilar squeezed her eyes shut for a second, then, when she opened them, seemed to be in control again. "Fine. Just send Mia over. Tell her to come tomorrow afternoon. I'll deal with Ira. We're doing a dress rehearsal in the church at four. She can come to the house and measure there first, then I'll make sure she gets into the Pioneer Church while we're there. Reverend Landon is a little sensitive about people breezing in and out of his church while a service is going on."

"Tomorrow afternoon then." Sally tried to pour oil on troubled waters and forced a smile as she smoothed her napkin on her lap. Fortunately, at that moment Cordelia arrived with their food. "Trust me, Mia will take care of everything."

"Right." Unimpressed, Pilar examined a cube of pineapple on the tines of her fork, then popped it in her mouth.

"Any chance she'll run into Colton while she's out at the ranch?" Sally asked. Sabrina tried not to react as Sally went on. "You know how she is about the Dillingers."

"Oh, yes," Pilar said tightly. "Doesn't everyone?"

Sally nodded. "You know, Mia never lets any of us forget that it was Colton who saved her from the fire."

"She's got to be ten years older than he is," Pilar pointed out as she raised an eyebrow.

Sabrina thought, *Careful, Pilar. Do you know what people in town are saying about you?*

Sally pursed her lips in a mixture of sympathy and bewilderment. "It's just that he's all she's been talking about lately."

Pilar shook her head. "I don't think Colt's coming. Ira flew up to Montana to try and persuade him, but Colt won't budge. Poor Ira. His son is breaking his heart, but then that's nothing new for Colton Dillinger, is it?"

Sabrina dropped a crust from the bun onto her plate as the conversation finally moved on. For once, Pilar Larson had spoken the truth, and it killed her to no end that she still had feelings for Colt.

The years seemed to evaporate as Colton sped down the state road that cut through the canyon and followed the winding path of the creek from which the town had taken its name. Guarded on either side by hills that rose to craggy mountains, Prairie Creek Valley widened to the south, closer to the Rocking D, which was located ten miles out of town and included thousands of acres of ranch land. He slowed as the gateway that marked the entrance to the Rocking D Ranch came into view. Something in his chest sparked—the desire for home, though it wasn't his home anymore, hadn't been for years.

His tires sang over the cattle guard, and then acres of white surrounded him, sparkling in the gold of the setting sun. Dillinger land stretched out all the way to the snow-capped shale mountains. His teeth locked as he passed the spur of road leading to the old homestead house. Did the place still smell of death and heartache?

A handful of small trucks were parked in the drive of the main house, and workmen's ladders were still leaning up against the house. White lights lined the windows and doors of the first floor, giving the house a golden glow against the snow.

Christmas lights. So Mom's tradition was being carried on.

The minute Colt cut the engine, Montana lifted his head from the backseat where he'd been sleeping and started barking. "Let's check it out, buddy," he said, climbing out of the cab. The dog jumped out and began turning circles in the snow while Colton stared up at the cedar and glass building that looked more like a modern cathedral than a ranch house. He didn't recognize anyone working on the Christmas lights, but then it had been years since he'd spent any amount of time here.

Montana sniffed the fence posts, then trailed Colton as he climbed the porch steps, rang the doorbell and wondered about the best way to get past Pilar to his son.

His son.

His throat felt thick at the thought of having a kid in this world. Well, maybe something good had come out of his time with Pilar. He'd been so young and brash back then. He'd liked ranching, but working under his father's rule had crushed his spirit. He'd missed Sabrina, but he'd known that he wasn't what she needed. Not then. Not when he only thought about roping and riding and how to escape Prairie Creek and the aftermath of the fire that had taken his uncle.

Pilar . . . she'd been a distraction. And in those days, he'd been looking for one. Luckily he'd found Margo and then they had Darcy . . .

His chest constricted and he hitched his duffel farther up his shoulder and stepped inside the house. Montana followed him in, claws tapping on the wood. The dog paused and smelled the molding, and Colton found himself taking a deep breath, too, as he headed down the long hall to the back of the house.

God, it still smelled like home.

Must have been Mrs. Mac's cooking, or maybe the cleaning stuff she used. There was something reassuring about the odors of wood smoke and lemon, and—all rolled together, the smells and the wide-plank floor and the sun hitting the clock in the nook—it all reminded him of his mother. This had been her home, the land and family that she loved, and her spirit lingered here. The feeling was strong. Right now, Colton could almost believe she was in the kitchen trying out a new cobbler recipe or upstairs going over the books. If he didn't know better, he'd think Mom was haunting the place, giving Pilar a bit of a poke.

He dropped his duffel onto the floor.

"Who's there?" Janice MacDonald emerged from the kitchen, wiping her hands on a dish towel. "Colton . . ." She beamed with pleasure. "I was wondering if we'd see the Montana cowboy for the wedding," she teased, patting his shoulder. "But you're too skinny. What do they feed you up there?"

"Beer and Jack Daniel's," he answered, smiling.

"Well, that's no good for you. Your father is away in Cheyenne, but let me go get Pilar."

"That's okay. If you can just show me where you want me . . . ?"

"I'd better get her," Mrs. Mac said as she headed up the stairs. "She'll want to see you and she's the boss now."

Good God.

He didn't believe for a second that Pilar was in love with Ira, but it seemed she'd do anything, including messing with Rourke's well-being, to please the old man. Colton suspected that the exotic beauty wanted a direct hand on the Dillinger wealth. Well, she could have it. He didn't give a rat's ass about his father's empire.

Except where his kid was concerned.

And that was going to be the tough part.

He rubbed the back of his neck in frustration. Things were already sticky and they were only going to get worse. A helluva lot worse.

"Colton?" Pilar's voice greeted him before she appeared.

Montana's ears perked up and he gave a low growl.

"Stay," Colt ordered under his breath, and the dog sat on the entry floor, just as his father's bride swept through the archway leading to the back of the house.

She was as beautiful as he remembered. Thick, jet-black hair wound into a knot at the base of her skull, full lips and dark eyes that still sparkled with a sexy mischief. Dressed to the nines in a sweater and tight jeans, Pilar was still a knockout. He could still appreciate her attributes, though what he mostly felt upon seeing her again was wariness.

"So you decided to come after all," she said, beaming up at him. "I'm thrilled. It's so good to see you." Were those tears she was blinking back manufactured? "It'll mean so much to your father."

"I came to meet Rourke."

"I know." She sniffed and ran a finger under each of her eyes to stem the tears. "He's upstairs in his room. I'll get him."

"Hold on a minute." Colton put a hand on the banister, blocking her little hop up the stairs. "Before you drag him down here, how's he doing? I mean, with all this."

"All this? Oh, the marriage and you being his father and all."

"Yeah, 'and all.'"

She lifted a shoulder. "You know how resilient kids are. He'll get used to it."

Colton didn't detect much compassion in her response. "I thought you agreed to keep it quiet. Then Ira tells me he knows, and so does the boy."

"Your father is the only one I told . . . besides Rourke, of course. But I had to tell Ira. There can't be secrets between a husband and wife."

"Did you learn that from lying to Chad all those years?"

"Whoa. Low blow, Colt. Below the belt, and I don't want any crude jokes about that, okay. Come on, everyone has a few secrets. Even you. You can't tell me there isn't someone special in your life that you shared our secret with."

She had him there. "The only person I told is my sister Ricki, and she knows how to keep a secret."

"Well." Pilar put her hands on her slender hips. "That explains why she's so cold to me . . . and so nice to Rourke. He likes her, you know."

"I don't blame him. Ricki's good people."

"Hard to believe, coming from one Dillinger to another," she said dryly as she turned back to the stairs. On the first landing, she paused and looked down at him, and for the first time he saw real concern in her eyes. "Please remember

Rourke's my son. I love him with all my heart. A mother's love, you know. Unconditional."

He was surprised at this emotional outburst, but as if understanding that she was baring her soul a little too much, she squared her shoulders and glanced into the foyer. "One thing." She wiggled a finger toward the door where Montana sat on the mat. "We don't allow dogs in the house."

"Since when?" He couldn't remember a day when his father's favorite hunting hound hadn't been curled near his chair by the fire.

"New rule. I'm allergic. We have barns and stables and all kinds of outbuildings." Her edict pronounced, she hurried up the remaining stairs, her heels clicking on the hardwood before she crossed the catwalk and disappeared into a hallway.

"Don't move a muscle," Colton told the dog. He could hear muffled conversation from upstairs and then the sound of her returning footsteps.

"Come on," she whispered to the boy who was following her down the stairs.

In that second, Colton's life changed forever. Aside from his reddish hair, the kid was the spitting image of Colton as a youth. He even moved awkwardly as Colt once had, all legs and arms. How Pilar had passed him off as Chad Larson's son was a mystery. Watching the kid trudge down the stairs as if he were walking toward the hangman's noose, Colton felt an odd glitch in his throat.

"Rourke," Pilar said. "This is Colton Dillinger. He's Ira's son—the one I told you about. Do you remember what I said about him?"

"Chad was my father," the boy retorted intensely.

"I know you always thought that, but it's not true," Pilar said brusquely. "Chad raised you as if you were his own, but Colton is your real father."

"You're a liar!" Rourke accused, turning to face his mother.

Colt shifted his weight. This wasn't going well, but then he'd never thought it would.

Pilar said firmly, "I never told you the truth before because I didn't think you were old enough to understand that—"

"But I'm old enough now?" he charged, defiance flashing in his eyes, the same kind of rebellion that Colton had felt. "Now that you're sleeping with the old man, I'm old enough to know that you screwed his son, too?"

Whoa!

Pilar gasped, and for the briefest of seconds Colt wondered if she might slap her son. To ward it off, Colton caught her wrist. Fury burned in Pilar's dark eyes as she spun to face Colt.

"The boy's got a point," he said.

"I don't need you standing up for me!" Rourke's face was flushed. "Let go of my mother."

Colton slowly released her and Pilar smoothed her sweater, lifting her chin in defiance. "This is starting off well. Now, let's go into the family room and try again, so we can all get to know each other."

"Fuck that!" Rourke pushed past his mother and headed for the stairs. "I can't believe you're doing this to me!"

"Rourke, come back here right now!" she demanded.

With his head down, the boy bounded up the steps and disappeared around the top landing without looking back.

"Rourke!" Pilar hollered.

Watching him flee, Colton felt a mixture of relief, guilt and compassion. And part of him wished that he could escape up the stairs as well.

"I'm going to drag him down here by his ears, if I have to," Pilar declared, starting up the stairs.

"Unconditional love?" Colt threw back at her, and when

he saw a shaft of pain in her eyes, said a little more softly, "Let him go."

She started up the first few steps. "But he just swore and disrespected me and you, and he *never* uses foul language—"

"Give him a little time to get used to things."

"I'm getting married in a week!"

"It's not a deadline for Rourke, though. You and Dad are in the all-fired rush to get married. Give the kid a break. And, if he doesn't want to see me this trip, I'll come back some other time."

Pilar paused on the landing and crossed her arms over her breasts. With an angry glance cast to the second floor she said, "Look, Colt, I'm not going to let my son swear like one of Ira's cowhands."

"*Our* son," Colton reminded her as somewhere upstairs a door slammed so hard the timbers of the house shook and Montana gave out a startled little woof.

"I did not raise that boy to be defiant!"

"He's eleven. You hit him with some pretty big news. And there's plenty more attitude just around the corner."

"Not from my son."

"Yeah, you're right. Doesn't run in the Dillinger family. Or with you, for that matter. I'll bet you gave your mother fits as a teenager." She glared at him as he added, "Sometimes, you just have to back off a little, Pilar," then picked up his duffel bag and whistled for Montana to come.

"Where are you going?" she demanded.

"Looking for a place to stay."

"But you can stay here. I'll have Janice get one of the guest suites ready."

"Nope." Colton shouldered his bag and headed toward the door, his boots finding their way across the familiar planks of the floor. "Wherever I bunk, the dog goes, too."

Chapter Eight

Seven o'clock on a Friday night, and Sam had to hustle to stop into the downtown shops before they closed. This time of year, Main Street wasn't exactly bustling after dark, even though his department was working overtime due to being short staffed, two more deputies down with the flu. That's why he, after his regular shift, was braving the cold in the streets of the town, helping pass out flyers, despite the work piling up on his desk and computer. He caught Hub Booman at the cleaner's and Aura Calo at the bookstore just as they were closing. The barbershop, pizza place and realtor's office had come next. He'd been lucky to be able to hand off the flyer to Cal in the flower shop; Sally would have held him captive in conversation for half an hour.

By the time he headed toward Molly's he had covered most of the merchants and he was bone weary. Tomorrow morning, with hopefully a full crew, he'd get one of his deputies to hit the daytime businesses, like the bank and the feed-and-seed shop.

A blast of warm air carried the scent of fresh baked rolls and roasted meat as he opened the door. It smelled good. Classic rock was playing on the jukebox, and the dinner crowd was tucking into plates of fried chicken, roast beef and gravy, or the Friday spaghetti feed.

Sam went straight to the bulletin board by the door and tacked up one of the flyers. MISSING—AMBER BARSTOW. The e-mailed photo from the young woman's parents had printed up nice and clear, her dark hair shining, her smile carefree and giddy.

If only that photo could speak. Tell him where she was. Already she'd been missing more than a week, and Sam didn't like the idea that she'd been last seen here in Prairie Creek. It was his responsibility to find her, and he didn't think he'd sleep a wink until that happened.

But he needed to eat, and he wouldn't mind spreading the alarm about Amber in person. In Prairie Creek, that meant putting the word out at Molly's Diner.

The stools at the end of the counter were taken by the crew from Slim's barbershop, with Slim himself at the end chewing on a breadstick. Paul Nesbitt, the town mayor, was there with his wife, Chrissy, sitting alongside Ricki Dillinger.

And that was the only empty seat, right next to Ricki. Sam hesitated as he unzipped his jacket and considered grabbing dinner at the saloon instead. He didn't have anything against Ricki. Hell, growing up best friends with her brother Colton, he'd ridden and corralled cattle alongside that girl. There'd been years of campfires and competitions, shooting matches and horse races. Ricki had been like a sister to him, and he'd missed her when she flew out East to be a city girl.

But now, Ricki was back, and Sam wasn't feeling so brotherly anymore. It pissed him off. Feelings. Shifting tides of emotion that were about as easy to stop as a cold front coming down from Canada.

"Sheriff?" The mayor twisted around on his stool. "Pull up a stool and grab some grub."

"Sounds good." Sam shook off his jacket and hung it on

a hook, trying to grow a thick skin in the process. "I've been passing these around town." He held up the stack of flyers, then passed a few out to the patrons at the counter. "We've got a missing person, last seen at Big Bart's."

"Sorry to hear that." Paul held the flyer away to accommodate his farsightedness. "I heard there was some commotion out by Big Bart's today. A search party?"

Sam nodded. He'd spent most of the day organizing the search, but even with men and women from all the nearby law enforcement agencies, the county was a huge parcel of land to scour, and snowdrifts and freezing temperatures didn't help.

Leaning close to her husband, Chrissy sighed. "Pretty girl. These things always scare me."

"She got any friends in the area?" asked Henry, who'd been cutting Sam's hair since he was five.

"That's what I'm trying to find out. I'm hoping someone might come forward once we get the word out. Her car was abandoned with a flat tire, and it would be great if a friend picked her up." Safe and sound. That's what Sam had told his own daughter when she used to wake up from a nightmare. *Don't worry, you're safe and sound.* He wished he could say the same for Amber Barstow.

"When was the last time we had a missing person here?" someone asked.

"Never happened while I was sheriff." Sam took the empty stool beside Ricki, who was studying the flyer, staring at the photo in the same way he had.

"That's a question for the town archives," Paul said. Running an insurance agency with Chrissy, Paul was a big fan of facts and statistics.

"There was a guy in the sixties," Slim offered. "Vietnam vet. Turned out he went off in the woods and shot himself."

Sam saw that Ricki was halfway through a roast beef platter. "How's the beef tonight?" he asked.

"Melt in your mouth."

"I'll take one of those, Cordelia. And water." He turned to Ricki, who was usually not part of the Friday night crowd at Molly's. "What are you up to?"

"Treating myself to dinner. Just dropped my daughter off at the high school for the basketball game."

"That's good. Glad she's making friends."

"Well, actually I had to force her to go, mean mother that I am." Ricki pushed the flyer back on the counter and picked up her fork. "What are you working, four to twelve?"

"I started at six-hundred hours with the search party out by Big Bart's. I'm down one deputy with another on maternity leave, a few more are out with the flu, but this isn't something I can put off till after Christmas."

"Does the state have a missing persons unit?"

"Naw. Highway patrol is more focused on the highway. Right now I'm coordinating the multistate search, but if we don't find her the FBI is probably going to get involved."

"Coordinating a multistate search and passing out flyers yourself?"

"As I said, right now, we're short staffed."

Ricki glanced again at the flyer. "She lives in California?"

He nodded. "She was visiting her boyfriend's parents for Thanksgiving, just outside Billings. Apparently things didn't go so well, so she drove back on her own. Headed out of there Saturday morning." Generally Sam didn't go over the details of a case with folks in town, but Ricki was different. A former NYPD cop, she knew law enforcement, and she was into it, but then she was Ricki.

As they ate, they discussed possible scenarios for Amber Barstow. Sam wasn't buying the theory that she'd hooked up with a friend—or the cowboy in the black hat—and left her car abandoned for nearly a week. "She left a suitcase in the trunk of her car, stuffed with clothes and makeup. And birth control pills. Would you go off for a week without your birth control pills?"

Ricki put her Diet Coke back on the counter. "Nope. And most women don't part with their makeup bag." She raked reddish curls from her forehead, a gesture he'd seen a thousand times but never tired of. "This is bad, Sam."

He nodded and told her about his phone interviews with Amber's parents, her fiancé, and Bill Russell, the Sacramento cop who had interviewed Amber's employer and searched the missing woman's apartment for clues. "I've got a Skype interview set up with Amber Barstow's boyfriend." He checked his watch. "In about an hour."

"Wow." Her green eyes were hopeful. "You've pulled together a lot of information in twenty-four hours."

The praise felt good, but he only said, "It's not enough. Not until we find her."

Sabrina's afternoon had been chock-full. She'd handled a collie with a broken leg and an injured hawk found by a farmer's boy, two phone consultations with vets in neighboring towns and a sheaf of paperwork. It was after seven when she was able to hang up her lab coat for the day. Of course she wasn't finished working; there were always calls to the surrounding ranches, and tonight she was scheduled to visit the Dillinger ranch.

Traffic moved slowly through the small town. Friday night brought people in for dinner or a movie, and pedestrians bundled in thick jackets or coats hurried along the sidewalks. Breath fogging as they talked, people passed lampposts and bony trees strung with sparkling white lights lining Main Street.

Caught behind a flatbed as it lumbered through the two stoplights in the heart of the town, Sabrina told herself the delay didn't matter. She was late already, but she'd called ahead and explained that she'd been hung up at the clinic. Davis Featherstone, foreman at the Dillinger ranch, had said he'd wait for her. So her workday had stretched from eight hours to ten, or maybe more.

Silver garlands had been strung over Main Street with decorative bells and stars in the center, and she smiled up at one as she passed under it. There was nothing like Prairie Creek at Christmastime.

Sabrina had thought about leaving this part of Wyoming. She had for a while, during college and veterinary school, but she'd come back when her father had his first heart attack. He'd survived it, then had another that had taken his life. Her mother had wandered around in a fog for six months before she'd packed up the house and moved down to Cheyenne to live with her sister. Now, even though she was the only Delaney left around these parts, Sabrina had stayed in this little town of hundred-year-old buildings, most with western facades. Maybe she was just a nostalgic ninny, but Prairie Creek seemed to be indelibly etched in her heart. The fact that she and Antonia were able to partner up and buy out Doc Storey, the man who had been the town veterinarian for as long as Sabrina could remember, had made staying all the more appealing.

Now, she drove past the winking neon lights of Big Bart's Buffalo Lounge, a local watering hole located just outside town, and thought about the Dillingers. She'd worked for them for a lot of years and had a decent relationship with Ira, and she didn't want to mess that up. It was just as well Colton wasn't coming to the wedding. Or was he? Even though Pilar had confirmed that detail, Sabrina wasn't convinced. She understood that Ira Dillinger wanted all of his kids at his wedding and Ira usually got his way.

She downshifted as she approached the Rocking D spread and drove across the cattle guard at the main gate.

Another hundred yards down the lane, she passed the spur that led to the charred remains of the old homestead house.

Suddenly cold inside, she shuddered through the memory of that night, about what she and Colton had been doing while fire roared just down the road. That had been the night she and Colton had first made love, but it had turned out to be the beginning of the end for their relationship.

"Oh, God, stop it," she said aloud, angry at herself. She wasn't going to buy a one-way ticket down memory lane. At least not tonight. To clear her mind, she adjusted the heat in her old rig as the windows were beginning to fog over again.

As she rounded the final bend, the Dillinger ranch house appeared in the darkness. Situated on a rise, festooned in Christmas lights, the interior lamps glowing warmly behind walls of glass that rose to a tall, peaked roof, Ira Dillinger's home was as grand and modern as the old homestead house had been rustic and time-worn. Sabrina had always thought that the architect who had been commissioned to draw up the plans for the new place had attempted to mimic the mountain peaks surrounding this part of the valley.

A ladder was propped against the side of the house and others were lined up by the driveway. No doubt getting ready for the impending nuptials. An older Explorer was parked near the garage.

Sabrina's heart nearly stopped as she pressed the brakes. Was that a *Montana* license plate?

It was.

"Crap!"

Instantly her heart rate went into overdrive. So much for all those rumors that Colton Dillinger wasn't returning.

Ricki wasn't one to sit around and mull things over. When an idea came to her, she acted on it, as evidenced by her defection to New York City and her wayward marriage to Ari. But tonight . . . tonight it seemed like she was getting a nudge from fate or kismet or one of those phenomena that shines on your face until you finally wake up and say, "Yeah, I get it."

Earlier, Sam Featherstone had sat down beside her at Molly's. He'd mentioned that the department was understaffed. They'd even discussed the girl who had gone missing. If that wasn't invitation enough to visit the sheriff and ask about a job, she didn't know what was.

She'd picked up three girls from the game, dropped them at the yogurt shop with twenty bucks, and driven the four blocks to the sheriff's office. On a roll now, she pulled open the door of the sheriff's office and was greeted by a blast of heat. "Wow. It's warm in here."

"Thank the Lord, because earlier today we had no heat at all, and that is not acceptable." Naomi Simmons folded a page to mark her spot in the fat paperback she was reading. "It's hard enough working the late shift, but in a chilly office . . . ?" She hugged her sweater, handcrafted with a smiling Rudolph, and pretended to shiver. Rudolph's nose, a red jingle bell sewn into place, actually gave a muffled jangle. "I just don't have the tolerance for that anymore."

A transmission barked over the police band radio. "Excuse me," Naomi said, turning away to answer.

Ricki smiled. The smell of burnt coffee, the radio dispatch, the Christmas decorations strung haphazardly from the ceiling, the battered desk chairs and the path on the floor worn from the steady tread of boots past the front desk . . . God, she missed this. Hard to admit, but true.

As Naomi handled the dispatch, she eased the zipper of her jacket down and paced past the big clock on the wall, which was next to a photo of Sam and his staff and a handful of plaques from civic organizations. There was a swear jar on Naomi's desk, a tin that probably contained sweets, and a photo of her with her husband and kids—two boys, who seemed to be college age. In the photo, Naomi wore a print dress with cabbage patch roses that made her look like a grandma. She was one of those people who had always seemed old for her age—even back in junior high.

"So, Ricki," Naomi said, finished with the call, "you got police business, or did you just come in to check the temperature?"

"I need to talk to Sam."

"Well, you're in luck. He's back in his office, fretting." Naomi pointed a finger down the hall.

Ricki headed in that direction, thinking that the boss would rip you a new one if you walked into his office in NYPD, but here . . . here folks didn't stand much on formality.

She knocked on the office door marked SHERIFF and poked her head in.

Sam looked up from his computer screen. "Hey, Ricki. Come on in."

"You still Skyping?" When he shook his head, she pushed the door and came right up to his desk. "I've been thinking about it, Sam, and the only solution for both of us is that you have to hire me. Make me a deputy. I need a job and you said yourself you're understaffed."

His brows shot up and he rolled his desk chair back a couple of inches as if to get a better look at her around the computer. "Did I miss something . . . like a job application?"

"I'll fill one out, and you can check my record, but it's good, you know that. I did twelve years with the NYPD, three years in mounted and four in the detective bureau, but I'm not going back. I'm here to stay. And as I said, since I need a job and you need a deputy, it's a win-win situation all around."

Sam leaned back in his chair and frowned. "It's never a good idea to mix business and friendship."

"Mix-schmix. I'm all business, Sam."

"Mix-schmix?"

"NYPD's got one of the best departments in the country—in the world, maybe—and I'm as good as it gets. Not to blow my own horn, but I'm *it,* Sam. I'm the best you'll find for a hundred miles around here. Maybe the best in the whole state of Wyoming."

"Just the state, not everywhere west of the Mississippi?"

"Well, I didn't want to brag."

"Too much." His gaze found hers and for the first time since seeing him again, she saw a spark of humor in his eyes. "Best in the state," he repeated. "Can't beat those credentials."

"No, you can't," she said, deciding to ignore his gently teasing tone.

"There's still the issue of friendship. I've known you since you were a kid, and I used to feel like we were family."

"I know. You and Colt were like brothers. But it's not nepotism, Sam. We're not related and that's something. And . . . you know, it's way too hot in here." She pulled off her jacket and plunked it onto the chair. "Anyway, it's hard to go a mile in this town and find someone you're not related to."

"That's one of the things I like about Prairie Creek," he said, as if to divert the conversation from the hiring question.

"Me, too. Lots of family." And hers was getting bigger with her father taking on Pilar and Rourke. Rourke she could deal with, but Pilar . . . She just wished Dad would wait.

"Stick Windham was on me to hire him a few months back, but I just don't hire friends."

"Then you're making a mistake. Besides, he's your bud. Our friendship is different."

"We got some history between us," Sam said.

A shiver whispered over her skin. "But you have some kind of history with every staffer in that photo out front. You were born and raised here and so was I." She tipped her face to the ceiling and let out a frustrated breath. "Come on. You know I'm a hard worker. I'll run your investigation or assist stranded motorists who forget to chain up. I'll even make coffee and fix your crooked garland if that's what it takes. Hire me now, Sam."

He squinted at her. "Why so desperate? What's the rush?"

"I miss police work," she admitted. "I need the money. Got a daughter to raise. And I need an excuse to get away from Dad . . . and Pilar . . ." She couldn't stop herself from grimacing.

Sam snorted, then he laughed. "You don't hold back."

"So I'm hired?"

He raised his hands. "Give me some time to think about it. A day or two."

Undeterred, she pointed to one of the Amber Barstow flyers on his desk. "You don't have a minute to think right now, Sam. Not with that girl missing. Come on, you were even handing out flyers yourself. That's how understaffed you are." She turned and sat down in one of the visitor's chairs, then took a different tack. "How'd it go with Amber's boyfriend? If you don't mind my asking."

"Unfortunately the interview just confirmed my thinking." He moved the mouse on his desk and clicked a few times. "Here. I've got this paused on the most revealing part. Two minutes of this, and you'll get the gist."

Robert Petrocelli's body language showed a young man beaten down and weary. His horn-rimmed, oversized glasses could not mask the dark circles under his eyes, and his shoulders were hunched forward.

"She wanted a ring, you know?" Robert admitted. "She wanted to get engaged and I was, like, 'Why now?' But I might have done it. For Christmas, you know." He cleared his throat. "I can still do it. When she comes back. I can give it to her for Christmas . . . on Christmas Eve. I heard you sent out some search parties today. Can I help? What if I fly out there and help you look for her?"

He sounded hopeful, but Ricki heard the desperation, the undercurrent of fear that he might never see his girlfriend again. "He seems like the real deal. Did anyone else see her drive off alone?"

"Robert's parents, and a neighbor." Sam paused the screen again.

Ricki considered. "That looks real, how distraught he is. I don't believe he hurt his girlfriend."

"Right now Robert Petrocelli isn't considered a suspect."

"Have you gotten a look at Amber's phone records? Bank statements?"

"Katrina got ahold of her bank and cell phone records today. Nothing unusual. The last call on her cell was to her parents, Saturday afternoon. She was upset that she'd missed Thanksgiving with them and was on her way home. Withdrew two hundred bucks back in Sacramento before her trip, then a few credit card purchases, mostly for gas and food. The last one was Big Bart's Buffalo Lounge."

"So money is probably not the motivation." Ricki plucked a flyer from his desk, and as she studied Amber's brown eyes and shiny black hair, a dark feeling came over her. It wasn't looking good for Amber Barstow. "Random abductions are rare, statistically speaking, but so far no red flags among her family or friends. We can check out the people she worked with, but it's looking like a random strike. Someone local, maybe?" She nodded at the computer. "You have any sexual predators in your database that might fill the bill?"

Sam cocked his head to one side. "I know what you're doing, Ricki, and you're a pro, all right. But while I appreciate your feedback on the case, I can't go any further. Not tonight."

She tossed the flyer on his desk, stood up and stretched like a cat. "Am I taking advantage of you? Compromising your high standards?" She had meant it as a barb against his stubbornness, but somehow it sounded like a tease.

His mouth, that sexy, wide Sam mouth, was set now. Way too grim for a man that handsome. It occurred to Ricki that she would have to stop thinking this way once they were officially working together. She would have to work on that.

"Right now, I'm saying no. Besides, it's late. Don't you have to pick up your daughter from the game?"

"Been there, done that. I just dumped Brook and her friends at the yogurt shop. But I guess I should go pick them up before they eat the shop out of crushed Snickers." She snatched up her coat and turned to the door, then paused. "If it was random, we need to look at the last place she was seen." She turned back to him. "Big Bart's?"

"We've been there. She left alone, apparently without her car, but the bartender saw her checking out some cowboy at the bar. Nobody he recognized. Black Stetson. Grady said he was a big guy, but that description matches half the men in town."

"Hmm. Yeah. Anyone else see Mr. Black Stetson?" Ricki asked.

Sam shrugged. "I haven't had a chance to track down other patrons who were there that night."

"Maybe one of them will know something."

"Maybe, but don't even think about talking to Grady on your own. Right now, you need to skedaddle and I need to get back to work."

"Okay." She backed out the door. "Not to state the obvious, but you *have* been working these past few minutes, talking with me." He rolled his eyes, and she saw that it was time to retreat. "Just saying."

On the way out she wished Naomi a good night, then stepped into the cold air and restrained the urge to do a happy dance in the parking lot.

She could read the situation. Sam would cave. He would hire her, and pay her to do the work she loved. And getting to work with someone she'd always had a thing for? A bonus.

She smiled to herself. She just needed to get him to say yes.

Chapter Nine

A dark figure stood by the trough with a black mask of a face and an axe lifted against the inky night sky. Light from the round moon, laced by thin clouds, glinted on the blade of the axe.

Folding his arms against the eerie cold that swept around the Dillinger barn, Davis Featherstone watched as she swung the axe down with a fury.

"Yaaahh!" Her cry ended on the crack of impact.

Davis stepped away from the building, his boots crunching on the snowpack as he approached her. She was using the axe blade to fish ice chunks out of the horse trough when she noticed him.

Kit Dillinger pushed the ski mask up so that it bunched over her forehead. "Their drinking water was frozen, and I know a cold horse doesn't need to be drinking ice water this time of year."

"Nothing makes an animal sick quicker than dehydration." He stepped back, out of the way of flying ice. "Next time, you might want to use one of the plastic rakes to fish the ice out. That much water, it can make the axe blade rust."

Kit yanked the dripping axe from the water and frowned, as if she'd been caught stealing it. "Want me to go get a rake?"

He shrugged. "Next time."

Davis hated pointing things like this out to her, because he knew the girl was hard on herself. Maybe it was because she chose to live as a hermit most of the time, setting up camp wherever the spirit moved her on Dillinger land. For three years she had been scavenging on this land, ever since she'd dropped out of school. Her mother, Mia, pretended that Kit lived with her in that small house in town, but everyone knew the truth. Kit was a child of the valley.

Last week with the latest blizzard bearing down, he rode out to find her and offered up an old shed a few miles out. "It's barely more than a shack, built as a hunting shelter, I think, but you're going to need to stay inside," he'd told her.

"I can't stay inside," Kit said matter-of-factly. "But I'll use it for sleeping."

"I don't want to ride out here one day and find you frozen to death. You're underage and there are laws about these things."

"So?"

"Look, Kit, since you refuse to live with your mother, or anyone, and you won't even stay here with the animals, at least use the shed."

She almost smiled. "Nah."

Sometimes, watching her, Davis found it hard to believe she wasn't some Indian revivalist or some new age granola looking for attention. But Kit's eccentricities were genuine. He suspected that she went for days without seeing another human, and she seemed to like it that way. On a bad day, Davis craved a bit of isolation himself, so he understood. But most of the time, he worried about Kit out in the valley, a young woman, barely more than a girl, fending for herself completely on her own. It was an ancient way of life, living in communion with the land, hunting small prey and gathering roots and herbs, but still, he worried about her.

As he watched, Kit moved down to break the ice on the

other trough. With another wild cry, she smashed the axe through the surface and then bailed the chunks of ice out. When he didn't immediately leave, she dropped the axe, looked at him hard, then swept the ski mask from her head and shook it out.

Her hair was pulled into a long, coppery braid with wisps around her face. Thin but strong, fast but graceful, Kit was a beautiful girl. Whenever he looked at her he saw Dillinger there—she was Judd's daughter, no denying that—but she'd also inherited a wild and free spirit that was at odds with convention.

"That cold front passed, but we've got plenty more winter on the way," he said.

"I like the snow. It brings quiet."

He nodded, wishing he could ask her about the ritual he'd seen her performing in the distance. Somehow, though, it didn't seem wise to face the issue head-on. When you trapped a wild animal, it had no choice but to lash out at you. He would wait and think on it.

"Good work today," he told her, nodding toward the stables. "The horses are always happy when you're here."

She lifted her elfin face to the moon. "They don't want much from me. Just a good brushing and clean hooves."

"You can go now. It's getting late."

"There are still a few horses who need to have their hooves picked. I can't leave without tending to them."

"You should be gone already." Hearing the sound of an arriving truck, he added, "I got Sabrina coming out to check on those pregnant mares."

"Babylon?" Kit asked. "She's restless. I was just cleaning her hooves. She could barely hold still for me."

Babylon was the mare Davis had been most worried about. "I worry that she might hurt herself, banging up against the stall."

Kit grunted. "Sabrina's good."

Not as good as you, Davis thought, knowing Kit's sixth sense where animals were concerned was a gift from the spirits who moved her.

As they headed toward the door, Kit yanked up the black skirt she wore over her blue jeans to wipe off the axe blade before handing it back to him.

"Good?" she asked, turning away.

"Good," he said, watching her leave, wishing he could call her back, knowing it was fruitless.

Inside the stables, he heard a female voice talking, soft and low. Following the sound, he found Sabrina Delaney in Babylon's stall, rubbing the mare's sleek brown neck.

"Hey, Davis." Sabrina didn't even look away from the horse. "I already checked out Queenie. She's in good shape."

Davis nodded. "This one's more of a worry."

"When I came over, she was pawing the floor of her stall," Sabrina agreed. She let herself out of the stall, then turned back to face the tall, rangy mare. "What is it, girl? Feeling nervous?"

"She's high-strung," Davis said. "Always has been."

"Some of us women are just born that way, right, girl?" Sabrina said as the mare stretched her long neck over the stall gate and nudged Sabrina with her nose. "Yeah, I know, it's tough."

"So far, she hasn't been a problem," Davis said. "Kit knows how to calm her down."

"Was it Kit who cleaned her hooves? Because whoever groomed Miss Babylon did a great job." As if she understood, the bay snorted, her dark ears twitching at the conversation. When Davis nodded, Sabrina added, "That girl is something else with animals."

"She said you were good, too."

"Really." Sabrina arched a brow. "High praise, indeed."

Davis nodded.

"You look worried," she said.

"I am worried," he admitted.

"Kit lives off the grid by choice. We all know Mia. Her relationship with her daughter isn't a good one. They couldn't be more dissimilar." When Davis didn't respond, she said, "Let's keep an eye on Babylon, but I don't see any reason to worry or medicate her. She's healthy. Bright eyes and a gleaming coat. Make sure she gets enough exercise and try to keep her calm. Avoid any undue stress." She picked up her veterinary kit.

Davis looked behind him. He wanted to be sure Kit wasn't within earshot, but the girl was long gone. "Have you handled any weird cases lately?" he asked her intently.

Sabrina met his gaze and said slowly, "I treated a wild hawk today, which isn't my usual."

"Ritualistic animal killings. Mutilations."

"What? No. Why? What's happened?"

"Ira asked me not to talk about it."

"Now you really have to tell me."

"We found a mutilated coyote carcass on Dillinger property."

"Mutilated how?"

"Skinned. Sliced. By a human, not an animal."

"Did you call the authorities?" she asked, making a disgusted face. Davis understood. Of all the creatures on the planet, humans were by far the most cruel.

"No law against killing coyotes."

"I know, but . . . Look, can I see the carcass?"

"We buried it out in the valley."

"Can you unbury it? The ground's frozen, so it should be intact." She put down her veterinary kit to zip her jacket. "You've got my interest piqued. As least show me where it is. I'll come back in the morning."

Suddenly, Davis wanted to end the conversation. He had hoped Sabrina would have an explanation, a way around the facts that were staring him in the face, the evidence that all pointed to the one person he wanted to believe was free of blame. "In the morning," he agreed. If that would get her off the trail right now, he would take a ride out with her.

"You've got me spooked, Davis," she admitted.

He shook his head. She wasn't the only one.

Sabrina stared into Davis Featherstone's granite face. For a man so young, he possessed a gravitas she generally only saw in people who'd lived a long time. "So call me in the morning and we'll figure out a time," Sabrina told him as she grabbed her kit and headed toward the door.

"Tomorrow," Davis said.

Just as she turned away from the foreman, the door to the stables opened and along with a rush of cold air a man appeared.

Colton damn Dillinger. Big as life.

A shepherd followed him inside as the pale barn light washed over a face she'd recognize anywhere, despite time, distance and years. His jaw was a bit tighter, his features more angular, all reminders of a boyhood long vanished. He seemed to have filled out, still long and lean, even rangy, ever the cowboy.

Her heartbeat ran light and fast, which was ridiculous. *It's over, Sabrina. Long over. Remember that. For God's sake, remember that.*

"Sabrina?"

Dear God, even his voice was familiar.

Colton's gaze caught hers. "I thought I saw you drive in."

"You don't miss a trick."

"Ouch." His lips twisted a bit. "I probably deserved that."

"And more." The words just came out, repressed for what seemed like forever.

He dared step a little closer and he seemed taller than she remembered, and, of course, even more broad-shouldered. "Okay, let's start over." When she looked up sharply, he held up both hands. "Sorry, bad choice of words. I meant the conversation."

"O-kay," she allowed, but was looking for a way to end this. Conversation with him was pretty much pointless. They had been lovers long ago, it didn't work out, and now they were making awkward small talk.

He made a stab at it again. "So, you're the vet for the Rocking D. I guess some things have changed in eighteen years."

Some things, but not everything. The thought was irritating. The same attraction that had brought them together so long ago still sparked between them. Stupidly. Yes, dammit, after eighteen years, the chemistry was still there. And she hated it. Time to end this. Now.

"I was just leaving." She nodded toward the door, hoping for a quick escape.

"Is there a problem with the herd?" Colt asked.

"She was just checking over one of the broodmares," Davis interjected, and Sabrina realized she'd forgotten the foreman was standing nearby. That's what seeing Colton did to her.

Obviously, Davis saw his quick exit. "See you in the morning," he told Sabrina, then headed toward the rear of the stables.

"I heard you took over Doc Storey's practice," Colton said, drawing her attention back to him again. She smelled the scents of leather and soap and horses on him, the combination reminding her of a hot night of making love to him. Oh, God. "Good for you," he was saying. "It's what you always wanted."

What I wanted was you, she thought and hated herself for it. *He left you, Sabrina. Don't ever forget.* She didn't bother with a fake smile and just said, "I've been practicing for a few years now." Tightening her grip on the handle of her bag, she ignored the fact that he was still too damned handsome for his own good. Two days' growth of beard and long hair poking out from beneath his hat only added to that rugged cowboy charm.

"For what it's worth, I'm glad Dad hired you to take care of the stock." He tipped back his hat, and the sincerity in his eyes struck a chord deep inside her. *It's because you're tired and run-down and vulnerable. This isn't a true feeling; no attraction lasts eighteen years.*

She looked away from him. A headache pounded in her tired brain, and the last thing she needed right now, the very last thing, was dealing with Colton Dillinger. Of course, she'd thought she was long over him, had convinced herself that if she ever saw him again, she wouldn't feel a thing.

It was mortifying to know she was wrong.

What she felt at the sight of him was a ludicrous blend of anger, humiliation and desire. Was she curious about him? Hell, yes. But she wasn't going to go there. She'd grown up in the past eighteen years, and though she suspected passion could still run hot between them, plenty of things had changed. She had a life here . . . and he had one in Montana. End of story.

"Are you okay?" he asked.

"Fine, really, but I have to go," she said and turned away before he could recognize the lie in her eyes. Marching through the snow to her truck, she tried to think rationally, to push aside any of those old unresolved feelings for him that still lingered. Not old, she told herself, more like ancient. He wasn't a part of her life now and never would be. She made her living from treating livestock in the area, and Ira Dillinger's ranch represented the lion's share of cattle and horses in the valley. She needed the Dillinger business and couldn't risk blowing it with anyone in the family, even Colton.

She absolutely couldn't have him know how she felt.

Yanking open the door to her truck, she swung behind the wheel and threw her bag onto the passenger seat.

"Wait!" Colton was jogging through the snow, his dog bounding behind him. He caught up with her, his boots sliding a bit in the snow, just as she slammed the door shut. The alarm that reminded her she hadn't buckled up began to *ding,* so she yanked the seat belt strap over her shoulder and clicked it in, then fired up the engine so she could roll the window down.

"Are you sure you're okay? You look a little pale."

She stared at the dashboard to avoid his penetrating eyes. "I'm just tired, and it's been a long week." *And I was just hit with the terrible realization that I've thrown away eighteen years of my life pining for you.*

For a second he hesitated, as if he didn't know what to say. "It's . . . it's good to see you again."

"We don't have to pretend that we're friends, Colton," she said.

"What?" He was as surprised by her tone as she was.

"I'm sorry. You caught me at a bad time."

"I'd like to think we are friends." He seemed sincere.

Perfect!

"Good. Yeah. That's great. We're friends."

"What the hell, Sabrina?"

She was acting nuts and she couldn't help herself. Shaking her head, she threw the truck into reverse. Before she could leave, he clamped a gloved hand over the open window ledge. "I've got to go," she said, staring pointedly at his fingers.

Why in God's name could she remember every touch, every moment with him?

Because for a long while after he left, you reviewed it night after night, alone in your bed, wishing for him, wanting him . . .

"I was a shit back then," he said, picking up on her feelings as if she'd voiced them.

"You were."

"I'm trying to say I'm sorry if I—"

"If you what?"

"I don't know. Hurt you."

She gritted her teeth. She felt tears burn her eyelids, but she held them back and blamed them on how tired she was. "And I was really . . . young. So, okay. Good. We've apologized. We're all kumbaya now, okay. Look, who cares, anyway? It was so damn long ago." She tried to laugh it off, but her throat was too tight.

"Sabrina . . ."

"Stop! I know you've been to hell and back, Colton. I heard about your family and I'm sorry about that, for you. I really am. But . . . this is . . . oh, hell, I don't know what this is. Listen, Colton, I've really got to go."

His jaw tightened and he glanced away, but his gloved hand was planted firmly on the window. "Could we talk, sometime?"

"Sure. Fine. Whatever. I, um, I guess I'll see you at the wedding. Everybody thought you wouldn't show, but, well, everybody was wrong: Here you are."

"Ahh . . ." He nodded as if he finally understood. "You didn't think you'd have to see me."

She had no answer to that as a gust of wind blew through the cab.

"How about we grab a cup of coffee sometime?" he persisted. "It'll give us a chance to talk. Catch up on the last eighteen years or so."

She took a deep breath, trying to think clearly. Impossible, with Colt's face in the open window, just inches away from her. "I don't think so."

"Sabrina, come on."

She fought with herself. “I don’t mean to be . . . petty or hold grudges, but maybe it’s my nature.”

“Yeah, right.” His smile, as boyish and irreverent as she remembered, slid across his jaw. “I’ll call you. I’m sure someone here has your number.”

“I didn’t say ‘yes.’”

“Just a matter of time, darlin’.”

God, he was irritating. “I wouldn’t hold my breath, if I were you.”

“It’s a date, then.”

She let out a disgusted breath. “We’ll see.”

“That we will.” His cocky grin mocking her, he slapped his palm on the window ledge and stepped back.

Sabrina hit the gas and, wheels spinning in the snow, fishtailed out of the drive and drove into the blessed darkness.

The killer stood beneath the low-hanging branches of a pine and stared through a veil of falling snow to the tall windows of the Dillinger house. Without any shades the glass soared to a peak, allowing the lights within to blaze brightly into the night. Ira Dillinger, that old prick, saw no reason for privacy, no need to shut out the rest of the world. Of course not. Imagining himself as king of this part of Wyoming, Ira Dillinger feared nothing. He considered himself and his family impervious.

Guess again, old man.

All of Dillinger’s false pride was about to come to a crashing, brutal end. Which would be perfect.

From his hiding spot, he smiled at the thought of the havoc he would wreak. Soon. He salivated at the thought and touched the handle of his hunting knife buried deep inside his pocket. Life as he knew it was going to change for the old man. Ira Dillinger and anyone close to him was going to learn about fear.

Quietly, he slunk through the shadows, staying close to the thicket of trees that flanked the machine shed. From beneath the roof's overhang, he found a new vantage point, where another window was visible.

Anxiously, he waited.

He listened to the sound of an owl hooting in the distance, barely audible over the pounding of his own heart.

His eyes were trained on the window. Through the glass that soared nearly thirty feet to the roof's peak, he had a view of the wide plank staircase leading to the second floor. The grand main staircase. He told himself he wouldn't have to wait long and, as expected, within ten minutes, he spied Pilar Larson mounting the steps to the upper story.

His guts tightened as he surveyed her.

Silken black hair shimmered blue in the light from the chandelier. Her dress was clingy, showing off a slender, toned body with firm breasts and rounded hips. Her calf muscles flexed with each step. His heart raced a little faster as he watched her stride across a catwalk to disappear from his line of vision.

Though it was risky and he couldn't afford to get caught, he took a chance. Moving silently around the outbuildings at the back of the house, he kept to the shadows and hoped the light snowfall would cover his tracks as he made his way until he was in position to view the master bathroom window.

Again, he waited.

Again, he was rewarded.

Within three minutes, lights came on and Pilar stepped into view. As if she knew he was watching, she bent low. Probably turning on the water of the large soaking tub located beneath the window. And then, as the tub filled, she started removing her dress. Slowly she bunched the fabric and hiked the dress over her head, an unwitting striptease. Next she unhooked the bit of black lace that was her bra and dropped it as well. Her breasts fell free, dark nipples exposed. He felt his throat tighten, his pulse jump. She rotated her head as she shook out her hair, black tresses tumbling past tan lines on her taut skin.

Mesmerized, he stared, his damned cock actually twitching in the cold as she bent over, breasts dangling. Rising again, she pulled her hair into a ponytail mounted high on the back of her head. Quickly she shimmied out of her panties, dimmed the lights and stepped into the tub. Squinting, he watched the windows begin to steam.

His guts twisted as she disappeared and he imagined what it would be like to slide into the tub with her, mount that hot, tight body. The water, almost uncomfortably warm, might be oiled or perfumed. Her body would be slick and oh, so sweet. Her mouth would round with surprise and pleasure as he drove himself deep inside her. Hot. Wanting. Willing.

He was really hard now.

If he closed his eyes . . .

NO! Stop it!

He took a step backward and blinked, his fantasy withering along with his cock. Sucking in a deep, angry breath, he felt the ice in the air freeze his lungs.

His head cleared in a rush.

He couldn't be distracted.

Not by Pilar Larson or anyone else.

He wet his suddenly dry lips with his tongue and turned away, his fingers clutching the knife in a death grip, his imagination running wild. He thought of what he would do to that bitch if he ever got her alone. Thought of the seductive feel of the first cut, the knife's blade probing beneath a layer of smooth skin. Despite the bitter rush of wind from the north, a cold smile twisted his lips as he slipped away.

Soon, he thought, reminding himself that there was work to be done first.

Practice makes perfect.

But then . . .

Again his imagination took flight and he saw her naked, lying beneath him, gasping for breath, soaked in sweat, not realizing that the orgasm he'd educed from her would be her last, until she saw the glimmer of the metal blade descending . . .

Chapter Ten

"I love you. I've always loved you, Sabrina, you know that. I'm so damned sorry . . ." Colton's voice was earnest, his gray eyes filled with sincerity as he leaned across the bed and moved over her, skin on skin. Far away, a coyote howled, its cry jarring, as if the animal were in pain. Before she could ask about it, Colton kissed her. Hard. Sabrina's skin tingled and when his lips found hers, she sighed into his mouth and felt the warmth of his naked flesh against hers.

"I love you, too," she said, feeling his hardness against her abdomen and the fire burning hot, deep inside her as the coyote's whines faded. Making love to him was so easy, so natural. "I've never stopped . . ."

Bleep! Bleep! Bleep!

Annoyingly the alarm clock broke into Sabrina's dream. The sweet sensation of Colton's body against hers faded as she slapped at the clock and pulled herself to a sitting position. She closed her eyes for a second, wanting to fall back into the warmth of that sexual fantasy, but it was gone. Damn.

Throwing off the covers, she snapped on the light. Her cat, a sixteen-year-old Siamese that she'd adopted when the owner had been forced to move into a retirement home, stretched lazily on the covers. "Come on, Claudia, it's time to get up and at 'em."

And time to let go of silly schoolgirl dreams. Spending just a few moments with Colton yesterday had already started messing with her psyche. She'd come home to her townhouse and for the first time in years, she'd felt lonely. Empty. There was a hole in her life Claudia couldn't fill.

The cat followed her from the kitchen, where she started coffee brewing, and into the bathroom, where she took a quick shower. Stepping from beneath the spray, she wrapped a towel around her torso, tried to comb out the wild tangle of her hair, then stared at her reflection in the mirror, calling herself names for hanging on to what had mostly been a high school crush all these years.

And it wasn't like she hadn't had other relationships. She'd dated a number of different men. She'd even kind of thought she might marry Brent Bywater, but somehow that had just slipped away. Her fault probably, she realized now. All because of Colton Dillinger.

Growling beneath her breath, she tossed off the towel and threw on her clothes, then headed into the kitchen. Her morning routine didn't vary much, though, she had to admit, her dream was the best she'd had in a long while. Even if Colton Dillinger had filled the part of her lover.

"It's been too long," she admitted to Claudia as she flipped on the TV, then scrounged in the refrigerator for cat food and yogurt. While Claudia turned her nose up at her tuna delight, Sabrina folded the yogurt into a small bowl of granola and frozen blueberries.

Her mind was already on the day ahead and she was waiting for the weather report when the story of the missing woman came on. Her head snapped to the television when she heard that there was concern of foul play and the sheriff's department was asking anyone who had seen or heard from Amber Barstow to contact the department.

"What happened to you?" Sabrina mused. During the summer, Prairie Creek had its fair share of tourists longing for a taste of the Old West, but this time of year few people visited. And now, in the heart of the holiday season, a woman was missing. Sabrina stared at the photo of Amber Barstow on the screen. She didn't look familiar. Sabrina sincerely hoped she would turn up alive and well.

In minutes, she'd finished her morning routine and gathered her things. She wanted to get into the clinic early. "And quit thinking about Colton," she told herself as she hurried down the stairs leading to her basement garage.

So he was back in town for a while. So what? So he wanted to talk. Big deal. Life went on, despite any predawn fantasies she may have had.

Colton awoke in the bunkhouse feeling both rested and restless. His thoughts were on Sabrina. He hadn't realized she'd never forgiven him, until he was in the moment. It bothered him to think how much his thoughtless actions had hurt her when he'd left her and Prairie Creek behind. He'd learned to anesthetize his feelings when he'd lost his family; it was the only way he'd been able to cope. But Sabrina's feelings were still raw, at least where he was concerned.

Well, Ira had given him her number, so he would call her soon.

At least she was willing to talk to him, sort of. With his son, that wasn't the case. After the confrontation with Pilar and Rourke, Colton had decided to crash in the building erected for the hired hands. Since it was winter and the summer workers had moved on, and the two full-time hands had homes in town, he had the bunkhouse to himself. He was tending the fire, trying to take the chill off the drafty bunkhouse cabin, when someone knocked on the door.

He opened it to find his sister Ricki holding up a thermos. "Room service."

He grinned and she gave him a bear hug, clapping him on the back.

"I was getting worried when I couldn't find you last night," he told her. "Thought that maybe you'd packed up and hightailed it back to New York after all."

"You were worried? How did you think I felt when I figured that I might be the only one of Dad's kids here for the big wedding," she charged, then laughed. "Okay, deep down, I knew you'd cave." Ricki poured two cups of coffee from the thermos. "And I figured you'd end up here, rather than at the main house."

"So now you're clairvoyant?" He accepted the steaming cup and stood at the window where he looked across a small portion of the Rocking D's snow-flocked acres.

"Close enough."

"Look into your crystal ball and tell me if I ever get close to Rourke."

"Ahh, yes. That's a tough one. Especially if you're going to try and do it without everyone knowing your business and all the dirt about you and Pilar. Word gets around fast."

"So much for your powers of divination."

"So you saw him? I take it he didn't exactly welcome you with open arms?" She capped the thermos and took a spot next to him at the window.

"He made a point of telling me I wasn't his father and that he already had one."

"And?"

"I figured that would happen, but he had a meltdown, swore and stormed up the stairs. Really pissed Pilar off." He took a sip of the hot coffee, which hit his empty stomach hard.

"She needs to give the kid some time."

"Yep." He glanced over his rim. "Maybe I shouldn't have

come here so soon, especially with all this wedding crap. Rourke's mother is getting married—not a very reassuring time for him."

"Well, if you're looking for advice, I'm fresh out. Got a teenager of my own who has her own set of daddy issues."

Colton scratched the stubble on his chin. He and Ricki had always been close, even when she'd lived back East. Though they didn't talk on the phone or e-mail or text weekly or even monthly, there was a tight bond between them, a connection that spanned distance and time. It was as easy to talk to her now as it had been when they were two gangly devil-may-care kids who had raced bareback on their horses across the dried-up pond in the heat of late summer.

She told him about her frustrations with Brook, who wasn't adapting to life in Wyoming and was trying to find any way possible to return to New York.

"I can't really blame her. When we came out here, the plan was for me to take care of Mom. But after Mom passed, I realized I didn't miss the craziness of the city as much as I thought I would. And this is a great place to call home. Wide-open spaces, slower pace, fresh air . . ."

"And a break from the ex?"

"Exactly. Ari will always be Brook's father. I just hope she didn't inherit his addictive behavior."

Colton had heard about Ari's problems, more than once. "I think you made a good choice." He finished his coffee and she poured him another quick, last shot. "This place would be perfect if it wasn't for Dad's iron fist."

"You might find it hard to believe, but Dillinger drama puts the fun back in dysfunction, compared to Ari and his chaos." She sighed into her coffee cup. "He's got a serious addiction, Colt, and I'm afraid it's going to kill him."

"Drugs will do that."

She nodded. "It was compromising my position with the police department, and his behavior was doing a number on Brook. I don't think she knows about the drugs, and I haven't been able to destroy her image of her father, not yet."

"You know I won't say anything." He took another slug of coffee.

"Good. And speaking of sensitive matters, I take it you saw Sabrina last night?"

"You know about that?"

"Give me a break. Everyone on the ranch knows about it. Come on. Spill."

Sure, he'd spent most of last night thinking about Sabrina, but that was about as far as it went. And she'd made it pretty clear how she'd felt—that he was a bastard of the lowest order—so he wasn't ready to talk. He noticed his sister looking at him expectantly as she sipped, and he wished Ricki would leave well enough alone. Some things you just didn't want to discuss with your sister. "I said I'd call her sometime, but there's a chance I'll catch her again this morning. She's coming back to see Davis over some coyote trouble."

"Good luck with that. You know what they say about a woman scorned."

"Don't remind me."

Laughing, she patted his shoulder and gratefully changed the subject. "Bet you're starved. If you and Montana want to head over to our place, I'll make you breakfast."

"You're on, sister."

"Thirty minutes. Gives me time to drag Brook out of bed. Nothing fancy. Bacon, eggs, toast and jam. Maybe some apple butter, if you're lucky."

She left, and Colton headed into the washroom. He showered, shaved, fed the dog from a new bag he'd picked up along the route from Montana, then headed to the foreman's house. Ricki was as good as her word and kept his plate full until he pushed himself away from her small table and lifted a hand in protest when she tried to scoop a second serving of bacon onto his plate. "Enough, woman!"

About that time, Brook stumbled down from the upper loft, a white kitten on her trail. Fortunately Montana was preoccupied, warming himself near the heat register, and didn't care when the kitten, a white lump of fluff, hopped onto the ledge of the bench surrounding a built-in banquette.

"Get down, Rudolph," Ricki said, making a shooing motion while Brook plopped into a big chair in front of the television. With hair falling out of a ponytail on the top of her head, Brook wore pajama bottoms, a T-shirt and a surly attitude.

"Too early for TV," her mother admonished as the teenager, wrapped in a thick blanket, picked up the remote and was about to click it on. "Say hello to your uncle and have some breakfast."

Swiping back hair from her eyes, Brook looked up at Colt. "Hi," she said without enthusiasm.

"Brook," her mother admonished. "You can do better."

So Brook said to Colt, "Ya wanna watch some TV?"

"Your mother made a great breakfast," he said.

Brook lifted a shoulder. "I don't eat in the morning."

Ricki drawled, "Then you're going to have a hungry day, because I told Pilar you'd keep an eye on Rourke this afternoon while they do a dress rehearsal at the church."

"I'm on vacation!" Brook complained as she made her way to the couch in the living room and scrounged in the cushions for the remote.

"Yeah, well, too bad."

An argument ensued, Brook refusing to eat, Ricki not allowing "some stupid reality show" to be turned on. Ricki finished with, "Besides, we have tons to do."

"What?" Brook asked suspiciously. "I'm *not* babysitting. Not for Rourke. He doesn't even like me."

"He doesn't even know you, but this will give you a chance to get acquainted. You're on."

"Oh my God, this is *so* unfair!" Brook scrambled off

the couch, adjusted the blanket around her shoulders and marched away.

Ricki let out a long sigh as she raked her hair from her eyes. “Maybe you shouldn’t ask me for advice about parenting. Seems I’m not that great at it.”

“Who is?” Colt got up and reached for his hat and jacket from a curved coatrack near the door.

“But I can give you some advice about women.”

He slid one arm into his jacket. “I don’t suppose it would help to tell you I don’t need any.”

“You and Sabrina had a good thing going once. You were way too young to make any promises for the future then, and you’ve been through some really hard things since, but I always thought you and Sabrina were made for each other.”

“So now you’re a matchmaker? Really? It’s not your style,” he said, exasperated.

“Oh, come on. You know what I mean. You always kind of thought of Sabrina as ‘the one that got away,’ even if you were the one who pushed her aside.”

“You need a job.” Colt sent her a look that he hoped would end this conversation. “You spend too much time making up romantic fantasies.”

“I do need a job, but you’re a rotten liar. You know you still care for her, no matter how hard you argue against it. As for that crap about romantic fantasies, you know I’ve always been a straight shooter.”

He couldn’t argue the point. In fact, Ricki had always been a feet-on-the-ground, cut-to-the-chase kind of woman. He’d never understood her getting all wrapped up in a dreamer like Ari Vakalian.

“So, like it or not, here’s my advice on the topic. You might just have a second chance here with Sabrina. If I were you, I wouldn’t blow it.”

“She doesn’t want it, even if I did.”

“Oh, bullshit. Sometimes things happen for a reason.”

"I don't believe that and neither do you."

She bulldozed on. "Maybe you're back in Prairie Creek to hook up with Sabrina again."

"I'm back in Prairie Creek to get to know my son. And you can tell Brook I'm willing to lighten her load. I'll be with Rourke." He squared his hat on his head. "Even if it kills him."

As usual, the morning at the animal clinic brought a procession of sick animals and worried owners, but Sabrina's schedule had an opening around ten that worked for Davis Featherstone. This time, the drive to the Dillinger ranch filled her with conflicted feelings. Colt was back and he wanted to talk. Did she want that, too? Did she? Did she want—hope—to start over?

"Don't get ahead of yourself," she muttered, but there was no denying that she felt a bit of expectation now that hadn't been there before. "Idiot," she muttered, sending herself a meaningful glance in the rearview mirror. What was the old saying? Hurt me once, shame on you, hurt me twice, shame on me. She'd best remember it.

Davis had given her instructions to drive through the north gate and along a gravel access road. It sounded simple, but now that it was snowing again, white mist suspended over the road and billowing around cliff sides, it could be tricky. In these parts, one wrong turn of the wheel might have you bottoming out over boulders, plowing into drifts or flying off the edge of a hidden cliff. Still, she found a fresh set of tire tracks—the foreman's truck, she hoped—and followed them down into the canyon. He'd texted that she wouldn't be able to miss the spot as it was wide-open and he'd be there.

He hadn't lied. As she followed the tire tracks into the valley, she spied his old truck and two men standing near a shallow grave. Two. Had he brought Ira along? She squinted through the dancing lace of falling snow.

No such luck.

"Colton," she said aloud as her pulse accelerated. She had to fight down the swell of heat rising inside her. Oh, Lord . . . What was wrong with her? She was way too old for this.

Throwing her truck into park, she noticed Colt eyeing her every move as she slid to the ground and walked over. In the light of day, he was striking against the pristine white of the prairie. The dark cowboy of her fantasies. For a split second she remembered her dream and how it had felt to have his long, sinewy body stretched over hers. Naked. Flesh to flesh.

She needed to shove that image out of her mind for good.

But when he looked toward the approaching truck and smiled at her, a piece of her cold heart melted. Which was just plain dangerous.

When Davis had explained to him about the dead coyote, Colton had jumped into the situation, mostly because he knew Sabrina had taken an interest in it. Normally, a dead coyote was considered a blessing—one less predator for the baby calves—but after he and Davis arrived at the burial site, and after Davis put him to work exhuming the poor critter so that the foreman could avoid any "bad karma," Colt saw the problem.

This animal had been skinned by a sicko. No doubt about it. Not someone looking for fur and meat or simple extermination. This was the work of a butcher trying to send a message.

To whom?

Now that Sabrina's truck had stopped, he had to tamp down the urge to run and greet her. Instead, he watched the way she maneuvered through the snow, walking fast, her cheeks flushed, a purpose to her stride. Her gaze, when it landed on him, was strong and steady. *A woman from a girl,* he thought. Maybe Ricki was right. Looking at her, he remembered those feelings from so long ago, and it did sort of feel like she was the one who got away.

Snowflakes accumulated on her baseball cap as she bent over the animal, frowning. “Strange behavior,” she muttered, shaking her head as she examined the way the carcass had been butchered. Glancing up, she let her gaze meet Colton’s for the briefest of seconds before she eyed the surrounding hills once more. “Isn’t this the middle of the Rocking D?”

“About,” Davis said, and it was true. Acres of Dillinger ranch land stretched in every direction from this valley. Access wasn’t easy; a person had to make his way through a series of gates to get to this particular spot.

Sabrina asked, “Did you call your brother about it?”

“Sam has his hands full with that missing woman,” Davis said. “It’s not a crime, killing a coyote, and Mr. Dillinger asked me not to say anything.”

“I know. But this is disturbing,” she said. “Whoever did this is sick.”

“Don’t worry about Ira,” Colt put in, but his attention was on Sabrina. The tip of her nose was red from the wind, snowflakes catching on the strands of hair escaping her cap.

“It’s too cold to linger out here, and I’ve got a tarp in the truck.” Sabrina straightened and headed for her pickup. “I’d like to take the carcass back to the clinic, keep it on ice, take a closer look when I have time.”

“Okay,” Davis said, but a line had formed between his brows.

“I’ll help you,” Colton said, and followed Sabrina to her pickup. They grabbed the tarp, and then Davis and Colton wrapped up the coyote’s remains and hauled them to the bed of her truck. He, Davis and Sabrina discussed what the mutilated carcass could mean. Was it a warning to the

Dillingers? But who? And why? A strike from the Kincaids? That was far-fetched. Though their feud was long-standing, who would mutilate a coyote. Again, why? Or just some psycho with no message at all? Just getting his twisted rocks off.

Colton wasn't sure what to believe, but he'd be willing to bet that Davis knew more than he was letting on. Something was eating away at the foreman, and though it might take some time to get to the truth, Colt was determined to get to the bottom of it.

"If this is a threat from one of the Kincaids," Colton said, "it's outside of their usual tactics, unless something's changed that I don't know about."

Sabrina shook her head. "Well, we know it's not Emma Kincaid. She takes in strays. Dogs, cats, even brought in a wild fox with a broken leg that she found on the side of the road last year. I don't see her as someone taking a knife to a coyote. Certainly not like this."

Davis said, "But the others. Alex and Blair. Wild kids."

Blair Kincaid had his mother's icy blue eyes and demeanor, but Alexandra took after the Major with reddish-brown hair and a sunnier disposition. "I haven't seen either of them in years since they moved away," Colton said. "They haven't been invited to the wedding, have they?" When neither Sabrina nor Davis answered what was really a rhetorical question, he said, "I'll have to ask Ira."

"Alex was just a kid. She was never really a problem," Sabrina said. "But then there's Mariah."

Colton distinctly remembered Mariah Kincaid. Dark-haired and dark-tempered. A natural bully if there ever was one. "What about Hunter?" he asked.

"Works for the fire department," Sabrina said.

There was irony there, as once upon a time some people in the town had felt that the Major's oldest child had set fire to the old homestead. There was talk of seeing him at the site just before the place went up, though Colton had never believed he could be capable of arson, let alone murder.

Colton felt the bitter cold of December settle in his bones. “Hopefully this is the end of it.”

“And not the beginning,” Davis agreed, heading to the cab of his truck.

Colt closed the tailgate of her truck, then followed around to the front. Sabrina tugged open the door and nearly went down in a slippery patch of snow glazed with ice.

“Whoa there.” Colt reached for her, catching her around the waist. His hands gripped her hips, and for a moment there was the tactile memory of the flare of her hip bones, the curve of her waist. In his arms she seemed frail and strong, delicate and yet all woman.

He held her to him, enveloping her with his arms, lingering a moment.

Her eyelids flickered in surprise. They stared at each other and then she gently pulled herself free. “I . . . I’ll call you when I . . . when I get a chance to examine the carcass,” she said breathlessly.

“Okay.”

He didn’t move as she climbed into her truck and fired it up. He stood there in the middle of the snow-capped expanse and watched as her pickup bounced down the rutted, white lane near the fence line. A snow cloud almost took it, but she hit the brakes and her red taillights glowed through the white storm, then she took a turn at the north gate and the vehicle disappeared.

A part of him wanted to chase her down.

And do what? Remind her that you were too young for a wife and she was barely legal? That seeing your uncle’s burned body had changed your devil-may care outlook on life? That you just wanted out of Prairie Creek?

Davis was already behind the wheel of his truck, its engine idling loudly, exhaust visible in the cold air. Colton climbed into the passenger side and the foreman put the old Ford into gear. Cranking on the wheel, Davis followed the fresh tracks of Sabrina's rig as Colton wondered how the hell he could get close to her again.

She was the first glimmer of light he'd seen in so many long, dark winters. But they had a past . . . a past he had fucked up.

How do you change the mind of a stubborn woman like Sabrina? An impossible challenge. Against all odds, against all reason.

But then maybe Ricki was right that "things happen for a reason," a saying he'd found trite and patronizing, something people would say when there was no explaining a tragedy, but this time . . . Maybe it was good he'd come back to meet his son. Maybe it was time to put the memory of all he'd lost aside and concentrate instead on what he could possibly win.

From his perch near the cave's entrance, the killer trained his binoculars on the threesome who had collected on the valley floor. Despite a curtain of falling snow, he recognized them. The ranch foreman, one of the town vets, and Colton Dillinger, the old man's eldest.

So the prodigal son had returned. Reason to celebrate. Add one more Dillinger to the guest list . . . at the Pioneer Cemetery.

Not only was the oldest son back in the picture, he was out in a snowstorm digging up the coyote carcass. Another dutiful Dillinger.

"Good job, Colton." He'd been afraid the dead coyote would be buried deep and forgotten, like so many other Dillinger secrets.

But not this time. Not only did they dig up the corpse, but the vet was taking it with her in her pickup.

They were bothered.

Good. He wanted to set them on edge.

This was a good development, he thought smugly. The message had not only been sent; it had been received.

And now, it was time to ramp things up.

A rush of anticipation sizzled through his blood as he considered his next act, one that would make the death of a coyote pale in comparison.

His next move would strike at the heart of the happy couple's upcoming ceremony. He had defiled their land. Now it was time to defile their church.

Fantasizing about the surprise in their eyes, the stunned expression on their faces when they came upon the horror, got his juices flowing. He licked his lips and rattled the teeth in his pocket for good luck.

This one, too, would be a test, but then, weren't they all? His mother's words echoed through his brain. *Practice makes perfect.*

Chapter Eleven

"I know it's disturbing," Sabrina admitted to her partner. Any skinned creature was a gruesome sight, and this one was distressing.

"I just don't know why you brought that damned thing *here,*" Antonia said as Sabrina bent over the dead coyote on the metal table. During a break between patients, Antonia had walked into the little-used unit behind the clinic to check on Sabrina's "lapse in judgment," as she called it.

"I want to know what happened. The coyote figures prominently in Shoshone legend. Some of the men were really bothered by this, and I thought it might help to get it off the ranch. Besides, this is a concern. I wanted to examine the carcass, and I'm glad I did. Look at this." She had used a clamp to wedge the coyote's mouth open to examine the area. "He's missing a tooth, but it's not from an accident."

Folding her arms in front of her, Toni leaned closer. "It's an extraction, complete with incision." She shook her head. "Who does oral surgery on a coyote?"

"The same psycho who skins him."

Antonia turned on the hot water in the small sink. She lathered up and scrubbed her hands, but looked into the mirror mounted over the sink, her reflected gaze meeting Sabrina's.

Sabrina opened the door of the refrigerated unit and slid the carcass onto a shelf. "I know it's weird. That's why it bothers me."

"This is Wyoming." Antonia dried her hands on a paper towel. "Dead animals come with the territory, but yeah, this is out of the realm of normal for around here."

"Agreed."

"Do what you want. I know you will, anyway. As long as he's quarantined out here and doesn't affect the patients, I don't really care."

"I'm going to call the Dillingers, just to let them know about this missing tooth. At least they should know what kind of a kook they're dealing with."

Antonia smiled and cocked her head. "A good excuse to talk to Colton. Right?"

"No. He's an old flame, long extinguished. You know that. Geez, Toni, you're as bad as the rest of the gossips around this town."

Toni shook her head. "I'm just saying that ever since you've known about the wedding and the fact that Colton might be returning, you've been different. Now that he's here . . ." She shrugged.

"Save me." Sabrina went to the sink, happy to turn away so that her friend couldn't see her expression.

"I just wonder why you won't admit it, not even to yourself."

A good question, Sabrina thought. Was she that transparent? If so, why the hell was she kidding herself?

Mia Collins blew a kiss toward the old homestead house as she passed the turnoff that went by the charred remains of what could have been. Then she made the sign of the cross over her chest. She wasn't even Catholic, but whenever she thought of Judd Dillinger and how horribly he'd died and how she'd miraculously escaped the same hellish fate, she sketched a quick cross and whispered a prayer. She'd been Judd's lover and she'd dreamed of being his wife. No matter that he'd had Lila and their two children. Mia had always just assumed Judd would divorce Lila, let her raise the kids, then someday, somewhere, they would walk down the aisle together. She'd even envisioned herself as playing a dutiful stepmom, if called upon.

I remember, Judd. I always remember.

It had been eighteen years, but Mia still keenly felt his loss. Certainly more than Lila ever had. Judd's wife had tucked Garth and Tara under her arms and torn out of town like she'd just been waiting to leave. In a blink she'd married that rich Alaskan oil man. Mia had been holding her breath wondering if Lila had been sent an invitation to the wedding, but Pilar hadn't mentioned whether Lila was coming or not. There was a chance she wouldn't show. Lila had blamed Ira for being complicit in Judd and Mia's affair, so it seemed highly unlikely she would show her face around Prairie Creek again, and she'd married just as fast as she could, or so Mia had heard.

"No one else remembers you, Judd, but I'll never forget," Mia said as she kept her eyes on the snowy lane. She had been working at the seed shop when they'd met. She'd been freaking out because she was turning thirty, and he'd been so kind and well-dressed and flattering. He'd told her she didn't look a day over twenty-one, and he called her Sunshine. That was his name for her.

She sighed and touched the crystal dangling from her rearview mirror. Judd had given it to her, saying she'd brought the sparkle back into his life. She'd known he was married, but she still had felt sorry for him. He'd said his wife wouldn't let him touch her anymore, with the young kids and all, and a man had needs.

She'd discovered those needs for the first time in the storeroom of the seed and feed when Judd had followed her back on the sly. The secrecy, the excitement of knowing that Deke Everly could come in any time, all that pressure had added up to make the sex really good. "Explosive," Judd had called it, and she'd slapped him on the shoulder, pretending to be a prude, though she'd really gotten off, too.

After that, they met in a lot of different locations. A motel on the interstate a few towns over. Picnic areas at the state park. And some nights he thought it was okay for them to hook up at Big Bart's. "I need some Sunshine today," Judd would tell her when he came into the seed store. And she would tell him that all seeds needed sunshine to grow. Ha.

The night of that deadly blaze, she and Judd had been so into each other, creating their own heat, that they'd been sort of oblivious to their surroundings. Judd had built a cozy fire in the main hearth, warming up the place, creating a love nest that naturally had smelled of charred wood and smoke. So when more smoke began to fill the room, it had taken them a while to notice.

And then there was a blank spot in her memory. She knew a lot of people didn't believe her, but the next thing she remembered was Colton Dillinger carrying her away from the fire. His strong, young arms saving her. He'd been her hero . . . still was. Colt was the only Dillinger who didn't seem to blame her for Judd's death. As if. She'd been devastated by that terrible night, too. She'd lost her lover, and her health had been compromised forever.

Really, sometimes those Dillingers acted like *she* had started the fire, when she was actually a victim of it. Ira had been a first-class son of a bitch when he learned about Mia's pregnancy. Mia had been forced to sue Judd's estate for support, but she'd gotten a paltry sum out of them. Her lawyer had advised her to take what was offered, and ever since she'd felt cheated. Of course that little nest egg was long gone, but the real point of contention now was respect. Her daughter, Kit, was a Dillinger, but she'd been reduced to scavenging the badlands when she should have been raised in a nice house like this.

Trimmed in snow and white lights, the house was pretty as a Christmas card. Mia parked, killed the engine and fingered her keys with a sigh. Part of this could have been hers. She could have been a Dillinger living . . . well, like Pilar. Instead, what did she have besides this pretty little crystal? Nothing! Life was not fair.

Wanting to keep her hands free, Mia left her cane in the backseat and carefully made her way along a path that had been shoveled free of snow. Though she still limped slightly, she walked as tall as was possible and barely had her finger on the doorbell, when it was thrust open.

"Oh!" Pilar was on the other side. "I forgot you were coming today. Good. Finally! Ira is in the great room, so don't bother him."

Mia pursed her lips to keep from snapping at the little bitch. Bother? As if she were selling magazines door-to-door. "I'll be quiet as a mouse," Mia said, trying to keep the spite out of her voice.

"Perfect." Pilar stood back, giving her room to pass. "I've had such a day. The church rehearsal is still on. Ira is bowing out, but you can still get into the church. And I've got a million and one things to do." She actually did seem a little harried.

Good. That's what you get, Mia thought, not giving a fig who was coming to the church. She just wanted to get the measurements for Sally and be on her way, far from all the painful memories.

"You can start on the staircase here," Pilar said, gesturing toward the wide wood staircase that was the focal point of the entry room. "We're doing a garland all the way up."

"I've got the design from Sally." Conscious of Pilar's eyes on her, Mia unspooled her tape to check the height of the newel post.

"But I don't think we're doing any decorations on the back staircase—the one off the kitchen."

"Nope. Nothing there." If Pilar was so busy, why was she standing there watching her? Mia started the slow climb up the stairs, pulling herself along from the railing. Stairs were a problem for her.

Pilar sighed audibly behind her.

Mia gritted her teeth, knowing she was keeping "the bride" waiting. "Why don't you go take care of those million and one things, and I'll come find you if I have any questions," she suggested. "And I promise, I won't bother Ira."

"Well, if you're sure," Pilar said, then added, "I'll come back and check on you in ten minutes."

Control freak, Mia thought. Was it any wonder that Pilar was stressed about the wedding, when she wouldn't leave the people she'd hired, like Mia, alone to do their jobs? With Pilar out of sight, Mia paused to take off her coat and smoothed down her cashmere sweater, pleased at how the V-neck exposed just the right amount of cleavage. She had donned her Sunday best for this appointment, and she didn't appreciate Pilar treating her like a cleaning lady.

Measuring the stairs was difficult, with Mia's unsteadiness, but in a few minutes she was done with the banister and moving on to the other areas. Working her way into the great room, she found Ira sitting in his chair and reading a magazine with the flat screen tuned to some show about Wall Street and investments.

"Hello, Ira." She held up the tape and smiled. "I'm here to get the right dimensions for your wedding decorations."

He looked her up and down, his eyes lingering. Was he checking her out? He was, the son of a gun. That was not what she'd expect from a man his age; well, in truth he wasn't all that old, only in his sixties, but he *was* a man about to be married. "Do I need to move?" he asked.

"No. You're fine where you are. I'll work around you."

"Good." He picked up his magazine but didn't look away.

Aware that his eyes were still on her breasts, she went over to start working on the windows in the connecting room, separated by a wide arch but visible from Ira's chair. That way, he could check out her butt. Men seemed to like full curves in the rear.

She moved on to the dining room, smiling to herself. Dillinger men . . . She'd always had a thing for them. Pilar appeared a minute later, walking right past Mia as if she were invisible.

"So we've had a wonderful change of plans with Colt here," Pilar said, perching on the arm of her husband's big recliner. "I'm heading to the dress rehearsal, and Rourke is going to spend some bonding time with his dad. They're going to watch some college football at Ricki's."

Colton was here?

And what was that about Rourke's dad? Chad Larson had died years ago . . .

"I'd like to watch a little football," Ira said. "Maybe I'll join them."

"Hold on. This is a chance for Colt to finally get to know his son. I don't think you need to be there."

"What the hell? It's not like I'm not involved. I'm going to be Rourke's stepfather. I'm already his grandfather." He shook his head as if he, too, couldn't believe the weird familial ties. Mia didn't blame him.

"Well," Pilar said, "Just don't get in the way." Pilar pressed a kiss onto Ira's forehead. "Okay?"

"I know how to handle my family," he said gruffly.

Mia jotted down the measurement as the news washed

over her. Colton was Rourke's father? She nearly fell over and had to grasp the windowsill to keep herself on her feet. Wow . . . *wow* . . . This was some hot gossip. When she heard the news, Sally was going to be annoyed that she herself didn't come to measure.

"They could have bonded years ago if you'd let out the truth," Ira was saying.

"Don't you go second-guessing me," Pilar said, half scolding as she draped an arm over his shoulders. "I was protecting my son, and I think I did a damned good job. You men don't understand the mommy instinct, so don't even try."

The tape measure slid back into the case with a *thwack* and Mia cringed, hoping they hadn't heard it. If they had, she figured that would end the discussion, but no, they either had forgotten, or didn't care, that she was in the other room.

"You should come with us to the church," Pilar said. "I could use a little help. It's your wedding, too, you know."

"I'm not stepping foot into that church until it's absolutely necessary," Ira groused. "Why we have to use the Kincaid church and not the one in town, I'll never know."

"The Pioneer Church is perfect, and the Kincaids deeded it over to the historical society years ago. Trust me. It'll be so much more quaint and intimate, for lack of a better word, than stodgy old Saint Ursula's."

Ira growled, but Mia heard Pilar stop him with a loud kiss.

Mia found herself hating them both. She couldn't wait to tell Sally or someone about Colton being the father of Pilar's kid. How unbelievable was that? Really kind of incestuous if you stopped and thought about Pilar sleeping with son and now father. Mia's attentions might lean toward Dillinger men, but that didn't mean she didn't like to have some dirt on them.

Half an hour later Mia had finished up and nearly ran

into Pilar, who was hurrying out, her arms full of makeup and toiletries. The nervous bride-to-be barely said a quick "I'll see you at the church," before dashing out the door while juggling her bags. The second she was gone, the big house seemed quiet. Almost peaceful with only the muted sound of the television. Mia gathered her things and was walking to her car when she recognized the wraithlike figure sitting atop the pillar and post fence near the parking area. "Kit!" she declared, a hand covering her chest. As always, when she saw her daughter Mia felt a bit of pride, a lot of love and a ton of guilt.

"I thought that was your car," Kit said.

In her down jacket, jeans, saggy skirt and beanie, Kit was a bundle of disappointment. Mia worried about her. Day and night. Kit should be in school instead of doing God knew what around the Dillinger ranch on a December day colder than a witch's tit.

"You want to come home with me, Kit? I've got a stop to make, but then I'll take you back to the house." Mia squeezed her daughter's arm and was surprised at the rock-hard contours of her biceps.

Kit disengaged herself from Mia's grip with a sharp tug of her arm. "I'm feeding the horses today. None of the hands want to come in on a Saturday."

Mia nodded, unable to stop her mouth from curling into a pout.

Kit stiffened. "Don't cry."

Although Mia shook her head, she couldn't deny the tears stinging her eyes. This was all so unfair: Pilar soaking up all the Dillinger money while Mia and Kit had to rough it.

"I'll come home later," Kit said reluctantly.

It was more than Mia could have hoped for from her strange and distant daughter. This had been their lot for years, half-estranged, Kit almost defiant and Mia not wanting to cross the line and get the police involved. Since Kit would soon turn eighteen, it seemed a moot point.

She dashed away her tears and swallowed hard. "I've got to run over to the church, but when I get home, I'll put on a pot of black bean chili."

Kit simply nodded.

"I'll leave the pot on the stove." Mia wanted to pull her into her arms and hug her tight, but she knew from experience that the more she tried to rein in her free-spirited daughter, the more likely she would lose Kit forever. So Mia forced a smile, then headed back to her car. Life was full of disappointments, but you had to move on. Hadn't Judd taught her that so long ago? A person just had to keep moving. At least Kit was coming home for the night.

"This isn't gonna work," Rourke said as he and Colton walked down the hillside to Ricki's place.

"What isn't?"

"I already told you, I have a dad."

"Okay." The sky was a vault of white and the air had that brittle winter feel, as if it were sprinkled with minute shards of ice, tiny pieces that burned your lungs when you took a deep breath.

Colton glanced over the rise in the direction of the valley where they'd dug up the coyote this morning. He thought of Sabrina and was almost embarrassed at how badly he wanted to set things straight. Annoyed at himself, he kicked at the curtain of snow over the trail. Damned if women weren't the most difficult creatures to deal with.

"So don't do this," Rourke said.

"Well, I am your father, whether you like it or not. And I want to get to know you."

"Nobody asked me what I want."

"That's true."

"How long is it gonna be before I can go home?"

"Awhile."

The boy looked him up and down, a hard scrutiny. Grudgingly, he picked up his pace, snowflakes sticking to his hair and shoulders. "I'm just saying, this is lame."

Colton had decided neither he nor Rourke was ready for a heavy one-on-one session, so he'd enlisted Ricki's help. The plan was to make homemade pizzas, catch a football game on television and maybe, if the mood was right, play some cards. Colton figured he'd take it slow with the boy and let things develop on their own.

Following Rourke up the shoveled walk to Ricki's, Colton wondered how he'd stepped into all this relationship muck all at once. He was suddenly faced with putting things right with both Sabrina and the son he never knew. Since Margo and Darcy's deaths, he'd stayed away from relationships, but he couldn't back off with Rourke. Their tie was for life. Whether the kid liked it or not. And he wasn't going to give up on Sabrina, either, now that he'd found her again. Funny how she'd gotten under his skin with just a glance. Maybe she'd always been there and he just hadn't noticed.

Ricki met them at the door in an apron. She shuttled them both inside, where the scent of rising bread dough mingled with the sharp tang of tomato sauce and a faint smell of wood smoke from the fire blazing in the stove greeted them.

"Aren't you domestic?" he observed as Rourke kicked off his boots and flopped onto the couch.

"Where's Brook?" the boy asked as his gaze skated around the small living area.

Ricki hooked her thumb toward the back of the house. "In her room. Why don't you tell her to come join us? Otherwise she might have to suffer the indignity of having sausage on her cheese pizza."

"I heard that!" Brook appeared from the back of the house, cell phone in hand. "I *hate* sausage. I'm a vegetarian."

"Since when?" Colton asked.

Ricki answered dryly, "Last week."

"Meat is not good for you, Mom." Brook clicked through several channels. "Sophie's been doing the no-meat thing for two months and she feels great."

"Sophie is Brook's best friend. She lives in New York," Ricki explained. Then, seeing that her daughter had settled on another reality show about a B-list celebrity's life, she called, "Hey. We're watching college football today."

"Ugh!" Brook dropped the remote onto the coffee table. "Why?"

Ricki said, "Uncle Colton's a fan."

Brook pulled a face and her gaze shifted to her uncle and she asked again, "Why?"

Colton said, "Because I love seeing two teams trying to beat the crap out of each other."

Brook gazed at him as if he were a Neanderthal, but Rourke slid an appreciative glance in his direction. "I like the Cowboys," he said. "But Colorado State's going to be tough to beat."

"You want to hold your head up here, you gotta go with Wyoming," Colton said, settling onto a corner of the sofa as he changed the channel. "Here we go. Looks like Wyoming already scored a field goal."

Rourke didn't comment. Out of the corner of Colton's eye he saw the boy put his feet up on the coffee table, just like he had.

"Call me when the pizza is ready." Brooklyn started down the hall, shouting back, "The *vegetarian* pizza."

Ricki handed a can of root beer to both Colton and Rourke and they popped them open at the same time. Rourke groaned when the Cowboy receiver missed a pass.

They watched companionably for a few minutes, then a commercial came on. "So . . . do you hate my mother?" Rourke asked.

Colton felt his jaw drop as he wondered where Rourke had heard that. "'Course not. Your mom takes good care of you and wants what's best for you. So do I."

Rourke shrugged. "I heard you used to be in the rodeo. What did you do?"

"Mostly roped calves." He turned the soda can in his hand. "Do you ride?"

"I'd like to, but Mom says it's too dangerous."

"Around here, horses are a way of life. I can hook you up, get you going if you want. Nothing too rough. I can talk to your mom."

"She won't like it." A smile threatened Rourke's lips.

"Yeah, well." He shrugged.

"So, can you show me some roping tricks?"

"I might remember how."

Rourke said scornfully, "You can't have forgot how."

"Why? I'm pretty old."

"Not that old," he said wisely.

Colt looked over at Ricki, who was beaming at the kitchen counter. It was just like a woman to turn to Jell-O inside over a guy moment. *Progress,* Colton thought. He and Rourke both turned back to the TV. He had no illusions that he could completely break down the wall between them today, but maybe he'd get there eventually.

Chapter Twelve

Sabrina and Antonia walked to Molly's Diner from the clinic. They closed the veterinarian office at four on Saturdays but left an emergency number listed on the door.

"Who would do that to a coyote?" Antonia asked for about the fifteenth time as they bent their heads against the wind.

"I don't know," Sabrina answered, just as she had every time. She adjusted her scarf as they entered the restaurant. An icy draft followed them in, fierce enough to rattle the diner windows.

"So, Colton was there with you," Antonia said as they slid into a booth opposite each other.

"That's right." Sabrina reached for a menu left on the table.

Antonia lifted her shoulders and smiled. "So . . . ?"

"There's nothing between Colton and me."

"Yeah, I know. Nothing."

"I'm telling the truth." Sabrina snapped open the menu though she knew it by heart.

"But there could be, right? I mean, do you have his digits?"

"No."

"Does he have yours?"

Sabrina lowered the menu and eyed her partner. "I'm sure he's learned my cell number by now."

A smile bloomed across Antonia's lips. "What are you going to do when he calls?"

"Talk to him, probably."

"Probably?"

Sabrina shook her head. She wasn't ready to go there . . . at least not yet. But a little part of her was actually warming to the idea of seeing Colton again and she couldn't help feel a bit of anticipation at the thought. There was a part of her, a very silly part, she thought, that had never stopped loving him, which, of course, was ridiculous.

The door opened, and Mia Collins came over in a flurry of snow and cold air. "Good afternoon, ladies." She took off her wool cap and shook it, sending wet flakes flying toward the table.

Antonia scooted out of the way of the snow and Mia took that as an invitation to join them, which sent Antonia's brows sky high. Mia wasn't a friend to either of them and both Sabrina and her partner weren't big fans of hers. The woman clung to the past and hung on to the Dillingers any way she could. Sabrina had once told Antonia, "If I end up bitter and deluded like that, promise that you'll shoot me." It was only half a joke.

Antonia pasted on a smile. "Hi, Mia. What's up?"

"I just came from Pilar's dress rehearsal at the Pioneer Church," Mia said as she hung her coat and hat on the hook at the edge of the booth, "and I gotta say, I wish Molly served something stronger than coffee." She slid in next to Antonia with a sigh.

"That bad?" Sabrina asked, eyes on Antonia.

"I was there to measure for flowers, but of course Pilar put me to work taking pictures so she could see herself from a hundred different angles. I swear, when you look up *vanity* in the dictionary, there must be a photo of Pilar Larson."

"Harsh," Sabrina said.

Mia shrugged. "I call 'em as I see 'em."

"Sounds like Pilar," Antonia said with a shrug. "How was the dress?"

"Beautiful, but I think she's going to make Emma change it again." Mia lowered her voice. "But that's not the big news. I overheard earlier that Pilar's son, Rourke, was supposed to be at the rehearsal but didn't come, and do you know why?" When both women shook their heads, Mia leaned forward and delivered the news. "It's because he was spending time with his *father,* Colton Dillinger. Turns out Chad wasn't the boy's father at all. Pilar had an affair with Colt."

Sabrina's heart did a painful little dive.

"I don't believe it," Antonia said scornfully.

"It's true. Pilar and Ira were talking about it. Ira said he was the kid's stepfather and grandfather."

"He could've meant anything by that," Antonia said. "This sounds like another one of the stories that circulate about Pilar."

Sabrina could barely breathe. This had to be a lie, right? Gossip generated by bored minds.

"It's going to be all over town. Pilar got knocked up and pawned the kid off as Chad's." Mia sat back and folded her arms, her eyes glittering like a cat who'd just pounced on a mouse. "Can you believe that? Those Dillinger men sure are a fertile breed." Mia wagged her head back and forth, grabbing one of the laminated menus. "What are y'all having?"

"Excuse me a minute," Sabrina said. She felt hot and couldn't see straight. It was nothing to her. This wasn't her story. But Colton . . . with *Pilar?* She ducked down the hall by the restrooms.

Her cell phone rang at that moment and she looked down

at the screen. She didn't know the number, but she thought the area code was Montana.

Her throat was tight. She didn't want to talk to him. She felt too raw, too let down. Even though her emotions were all out of line, she couldn't help it.

The cell phone rang her default tone once again and she screwed up her courage and answered, "Hello?"

"Hey, Sabrina." Colton's warm tones came through the phone. She could tell he was happy. Could hear it in his voice. What would he hear in hers?

"Hi," she said shortly.

"You want to get that coffee tomorrow?" he asked.

"I don't know. I've . . . got a lot to do."

"On Sunday? Okay, then, how about dinner together tomorrow night?" he pressed.

"I don't know." That at least was the truth.

"Is something wrong?"

"No, I just . . ." She drew a breath and told herself there was no time like the present. If she wanted an honest relationship with Colton—no, wait—if she wanted *any* kind of relationship with him, including just friendship, they needed to be straight with each other. Starting now. "I just heard that Rourke is your son."

For a long moment, there was only the sound of the wind in the background and she sensed that he was standing outside. "Where'd you hear that?"

"Is it true?"

He made a strangled sound, then ground out, "Yes, but it wasn't supposed to be out there yet."

Her heart dropped again. "Oh. When would it be out there?"

"Listen, I can't really get into all this right now. I'm at Ricki's and—"

"Don't worry. You don't need to explain. It's your life, Colt, and I'm just—a friend. Let's talk later. Good-bye."

Her hand was shaking as she slid her cell phone from her ear and ended the call. Damn it all. She really needed to get her head together where Colton Dillinger was concerned, but she feared it wasn't going to happen.

The killer stared into the lantern in the center of the cabin and watched the dancing flame. It was time.

And it was time to get out of here. He stood and surveyed the dilapidated shack. It had probably been used for a hunting cabin back in the day, but now it stood empty, the thin walls shaking when the wind raced through this section of the valley.

With no electricity or running water, the place had all but been forgotten, but it had provided him the shelter he'd needed. Located close to the Dillinger spread and tucked into the woods, he had been able to come and go without being noticed. There were many other hideaway spots for him to lie low; he had a particular cave he liked.

But now things were about to change, so it was time to move on.

Besides, the old hunger gnawing inside him, his constant companion these days, was raw. Angry. The beast needed to be fed.

Ignoring the cold that blew through cracks in the walls, he reached into his backpack and pulled out a near-empty bottle of Jim Beam, who had, of late, been his only friend.

Well, except for the girl.

"Here's to you," he said, lifting the bottle and looking into the darkened corner of the room where she sat, propped against the wall. She was permanently seated, frozen that way. Her eyes were hollow, her skin a transparent, bluish tone, and the drizzle of blood on the corner of her mouth had dried and frozen in place.

He took a long swallow and grabbed one end of the tarp, shaking it open. He couldn't keep her hidden here forever. And though she hadn't started to decompose yet, not with these frigid temperatures, he was tired of looking at her. The thrill was gone.

"Sorry, baby, but I'm going to have to let you go," he said as he finished his drink. Capping the bottle, he tucked it into his pack again. Opening the tarp was easy. Dragging her onto it was more of a challenge, but he was strong. Smiling to himself, he secured the tarp with baling twine from a spool he'd stolen right from under the old man's nose. *Take that, you prick!*

Hoisting her half-frozen and oh-so-dead body onto his shoulder in a fireman's carry, he hauled her outside into wind so cold it iced his eyeballs. He closed his eyes and felt his way to the pickup, thinking of the corpse's destination.

The perfect way to ruin a wedding. A sacred place, defiled.

"This is good-bye, darlin'," he said as he tossed her into the truck bed next to the gas can. Her body landed with a hard *thunk* and the old can rattled. "It's been fun, but it's over." He double-checked to see that the tailgate was secure. He wouldn't want her sliding out before he was ready.

A gust of wind screamed through the canyon, and he climbed inside. He slammed the door against the wind, fired up the engine and tossed his gloves on the other seat. Anticipation thrummed through his body, and he couldn't resist digging into his pocket and touching the teeth. His trophies, sharp and smooth. The sound of them clicking against each other brought him a pang of satisfaction.

Only two so far, but by this time tomorrow he'd have at least one more to add to his collection.

Yep, he thought, shifting the truck into drive, it was time to hit the Dillingers where it hurt.

* * *

Sabrina twisted off the knobs of the shower and wrapped a towel around her body. The hot water had eased the kink in her neck, but not her mind. Nothing could wash away the ache of disappointment. Colton had forgotten to fill her in on a big chapter in his life.

He had a son.

She kept trying not to think about it. No point in probing it under a microscope, because it was what it was. But it stung, and no amount of sweet-smelling shower gel or hot water could wash that kink away.

She unwrapped the towel and let her dry hair spill over her shoulder. Still naturally blond and thick. She was considering putting it up in a twist when she saw one dark paw slip beneath the door.

Claudia, ever curious, was sending her a message. "Okay, okay, I get it." Sabrina opened the door and the cat poked her dark head inside. "Hey, there," Sabrina said as Claudia stepped into the small room and hopped onto the closed lid of the toilet.

The doorbell chimed and Sabrina gritted her teeth. Thinking they would go away or leave a package if it was a deliveryman, she rewrapped her hair in a towel, and put on her bathrobe. She was determined to ignore them, but then the bell became persistent.

She'd wanted a night to hole up in her sweats, drink a little wine and throw herself a pity party—uninterrupted—but the incessant bell was not going to allow that.

Hurrying down the stairs in bare feet, she peered through the peephole.

Colton Dillinger leaned insolently against the post supporting the roof of her small porch. So, he was here. She should have known he wouldn't wait to try and explain.

"Okay . . ." she warned herself, her heart beating a little

faster as she turned the latch. "You are the worst kind of fool," she muttered as she opened the door.

He straightened, all six foot two inches of him. Snow feathered the air behind him, a dotted halo of white surrounding the man she had spent most of her life alternately dreaming about and trying to forget.

"What're you doing here?" she asked.

"From our phone conversation, I kinda thought maybe we should have a face-to-face." The timbre of his voice caused a little spark of adrenaline to shoot through her body.

"Hey, it's not my business. I shouldn't have said anything to you. I was out of line. I, um, hope things work out for you and your son, I really do." Oh, Lord . . . she could feel tears gathering behind her eyes. "So, um, I'm going to say good night."

She swung the door closed, but it met with a barrier.

Colt's boot.

"C'mon, Sabrina," he said.

I don't want you here. But she released her grip on the door. "You're really going to do this, aren't you."

"Uh-huh."

"Great." She turned back to the living room.

He stepped inside and closed the door behind him. He followed her in, his boots ringing on the floor, and echoing in her heart. What the hell was he doing here? Why was she even letting him inside?

Because you want him here. You know it and he does, too. All those defenses you built up over the years, Sabrina, they're thin as paper and falling down. You love him. You've always loved him, and that's the problem. Oh, God . . . She folded her arms over her chest protectively, hoping he didn't notice the fact that she was trembling.

He tossed his jacket and hat onto the arm of her overstuffed couch. "Look, I'm sorry you found out about Rourke before I could explain."

"It's all right."

His sharp gaze met hers and charged her with the lie. "It's clearly not."

"It's not my place—"

"You keep saying that, but you're looking at me as if I've hurt you, or let you down, or both. Which I get, because I took off after the fire. But this"—he spread his hand—"I didn't know about Rourke. I fell in with Pilar in the wildest of my rodeo days. It wasn't long, and I know what you're going to say—it was long enough."

"I wasn't going to say that."

"After Pilar I pulled my life together. I met Margo and I guess I put the demons to rest. And then Darcy came along and we were happy, but then . . ." He lifted a hand and let it drop. "You know the rest."

"I'm sorry you lost them," Sabrina said, her resolve turning to water.

He nodded. "It's been five years. I'm okay. I don't want this"—he moved his hands to include her and him—"to be some kind of . . . grief counseling." He hesitated, glancing up at the ceiling. "Oh, hell. I know this is sudden, and trust me, I didn't expect it, but the truth is I just want a chance to start over, or pick up where we left off, or just plain spend time together."

He was killing her with this. Making her feel her fears were insignificant, and maybe they were. She gestured for him to sit down, and when she sat on the couch, he dropped down beside her. For a moment she remembered making out on her parents' sofa, and then later, making love. To this very man.

"Before I reached the age of twenty I was crazy in love with you," he admitted. "But I knew I was too young to take on a wife, and you were barely legal. Then there was the fire, and everything got screwed up in my head. A shitload of guilt. I was on a downward spiral, and I didn't want to take you with me. I loved you, Sabrina, but I knew you deserved better."

"I loved you, too," she whispered, a lump forming in her throat.

"I'm sorry for being young and stupid."

"No . . ." She lifted her hands, warding him off. "It was what it was." The fact that she'd never gotten him out of her system wasn't his issue.

"Who told you about Rourke?"

"Mia Collins. She overheard Pilar talking about it."

"Mia. Huh. No one was supposed to know yet except Ira."

"Ira knows?" she said, surprised.

"It was the leverage that got me to come to the wedding." He sat back on the couch and let his head drop back. "But I'm glad I'm here. I was hanging out with Rourke today for the first time, watching football at Ricki's. Trying to get to know him a little better."

"How'd that go?"

"Okay, I think. He wants me to know that Chad Larson's his father, no matter what anybody says, but he liked that I was on the rodeo circuit. I told him I'd try to get him on a horse, though Pilar thinks it's too dangerous."

Sabrina almost laughed. "Way to get in good with the kid's mom."

"Yeah." He grinned. "She'll probably have me tarred and feathered."

He turned to her, and though she didn't face him, she was acutely aware of the heat that came off his body beside her. What would it take to turn, to slip into his arms and lose herself in his warmth?

Don't think about it, she told herself.

"I can't turn back time. I don't even want to. But I'm here now, and when I think about the future, it's hard to imagine it without you," he said.

Oh, how she wanted to turn to him and burrow into his

warmth, to trust him again. Was it possible, or just a pipe dream?

To give herself some room, she stood up and went to the window. "What exactly do you expect of me?" she asked, turning back to him now that there was a safe distance between them.

"A chance." He cocked his head. "I'll make it worth your while."

"Dating," she said. "Spending time together."

"Whatever you want to call it. You and me together. That's what I want."

And what about when you go back to Montana?

"What about you? What do you want?"

Yes. What? She closed her eyes for a second and bit back the response that leapt to her mind. *I want you, Colt. I've always wanted you.*

"I can't think with you draped on my couch," she said honestly. "A few days ago—no, wait—even today, I was telling myself and the whole world that I was over you, that there was nothing between us."

"A lie."

"Probably. Yes. But . . . this is all too fast . . . I need some time, so I think you'd better go."

"If that's what you want."

She couldn't respond because, damn it, she really didn't know what she wanted.

He grabbed his hat from where he'd tossed it and got to his feet. "Okay, I'm out of here. But I'll be back." He actually cast her that roguish smile of his. "I'll wear you down, Sabrina. You know I can be a persistent bastard."

"I do know that."

His boots clicked on the vestibule floor and then he was gone, as quickly as he'd come. Through the door, down the steps and across her lawn, where his boots made impressions in the blanket of fresh snow.

She picked up the cat and stroked Claudia's soft fur as Colton climbed into his truck and drove off. She stood at the door for a minute or two, watching his taillights disappear in the night, and scolded herself for feeling like she'd just made a terrible mistake.

Colton switched on his windshield wipers and turned off the radio. With snow falling and a few drinks under his belt, he knew he had to keep his focus on the road.

When he'd left Sabrina's house, his head reeling, he'd stopped at a local watering hole for a couple of beers and a hard mental shake. It was good to see some of the old guys at the bar, but it didn't make him feel any better.

It felt like he'd blown it. He'd thought that he could convince Sabrina to give him another chance, but now he wasn't so sure.

He drove out of town still chiding himself. Just seeing her again had awakened long-slumbering feelings in him, but she didn't seem to feel quite the same.

He considered turning around, driving back to her house and pleading his case all over again.

"Don't be stupid," he told himself, glancing in the rearview mirror.

He switched on the radio only to hear the plaintive notes of George Michael singing "Last Christmas." Before he heard the sad lyrics about "once bitten, twice shy," he snapped it off. This isn't helping, he thought as he barreled down the state road toward the Rocking D.

Half a mile farther he noticed a glow on the horizon, an eerie yellowish shadow. All but obscured by the snow, it seemed to move and shift like a ball of light.

What the hell?

Fire?

A large ball of it on the hill beyond the fence line.

"Jesus! No!"

With a sick feeling he realized the old Pioneer Church, the site of his father's wedding, was going up in flames!

"Son of a bitch." In his mind's eye and only for a split second, he saw the fire eighteen years ago, the raging flames, excruciating heat and charred beams of the old homestead.

He hit the brakes and reached for his phone, intent on calling 9-1-1, but his cell wasn't in the cup holder. It wasn't on the dash, or in the empty seat next to him and it definitely wasn't in any of his pockets. He figured it must've slipped out of his jacket pocket at Sabrina's place.

"Damn it to hell," he muttered, hitting the accelerator, his tires spinning. The Explorer shuddered, sending snow spraying to the side of the road as it jumped forward.

He switched on the emergency flashers and repeatedly hit the horn, hoping to wake up anyone who might be nearby, though the few surrounding houses were, for the most part, empty, the result of his father buying out the ranchers at the bottom of the market.

No doors flew open.

No porch lights snapped on.

No one raced across his porch to help.

"Damn!"

He reached the lane that led to the church and turned the wheel. His heart raced, his blood pounding in his ears. In horror he stared at the approaching inferno as thoughts of the fire that had shaped his youth clamored to the front of his brain. This time, he hoped to God there was no one inside.

Chapter Thirteen

Slumped on the sofa, Sabrina snapped off the news where warnings about another storm bearing down on this part of the state, and a plea for anyone who had seen the missing California woman to come forward, topped the hour. Depressing news. Even the tips on roasting a Christmas goose had made her feel bad, since she had no plans for the holiday.

Mom was going to be in Cheyenne with her sister, Mavis. Though Sabrina had invited them both to come to dinner in Prairie Creek, she and Mavis had decided to stay home for the holidays. Sabrina had secretly fantasized about spending Christmas with Colton, but now that seemed remote. Probably impossible. Of her own making, sure, but she felt the need to be cautious. She'd carried a torch for him half her life. She needed to be smart. Decide if this was what she really wanted and whether she could believe Colton felt the same.

Word would be out by next week's wedding that Rourke was his son. After that, Sabrina would see Pilar and Rourke in town. She might run into him when she went out to the Rocking D. It was going to be hard, any way around it; Prairie

Creek was just too small not to have Colton's affair with Pilar be a hot topic.

But was she being too self-protective? Ira knew Rourke was Colt's and he was dead set on marrying Pilar anyway. Maybe she should just throw caution to the wind and go for it.

She loved Colt; that much she now knew. Well, maybe she always had, deep down. Denial always made life so much easier, until it made it harder. The truth was Colton Dillinger was the only man she'd ever really loved and she had never gotten over him, no matter how much she'd tried to deny it.

Here's your chance, Sabrina. Admit that you love him. Be honest. That's what you want from him, isn't it? What have you got to lose?

Turning off the lights, she wondered what it would be like if Colton were still here, if she had taken him by the hand, led him upstairs . . . They were adults; what would making love to him hurt?

She was about to head upstairs when she heard a buzzing coming from the couch. Digging through the cushions, she discovered Colton's cell phone. A text message from Rourke glowed on the screen. With the lock on, she could only read the first part of it:

> when r u talking to mom about riding? I want to go with you ok?

Sabrina stared at the words and knew how important it would be to have Rourke reach out to him.

"Change of plans," she said to the cat. Though it was after eleven, she tossed on her jeans and sweater, then found her jacket, socks, boots and gloves. With the cell phone tucked in her pocket and her heartbeat accelerating, she set out to track Colton down.

* * *

With the Ford's headlights flashing, his horn blaring, Colton drove over the final rise and stood on the brakes in front of the conflagration that had been the small, historic church.

Flames, spitting and hungry, shot skyward through the roof while black smoke billowed in the snow flurries. As he watched, a window splintered, spewing hot glass, the roar of the rolling flames thunderous. He flung open the door to his SUV and, despite the freezing temperature, the heat hit him in a wave. Snow was melting around the burning building, while flakes continued to fall.

No vehicles were parked in the lot, but there was one set of tracks in the otherwise pristine snow. His heart thudded, adrenaline spurred by fear racing through him. Dear God, was anyone inside? If so, how could they survive?

He couldn't wait for firefighters.

More intense, stark images of the fire eighteen years earlier swept over him as he ran forward. Mia, her hair aflame, screaming and rolling off the porch. The smell of burning flesh. His uncle's grotesquely charred body.

The steps to the main doors were still intact, and as he blinked against the smoke he realized the fire was on the far wall of the building, rising above the altar like a ghostly monster. The steeple tower was still, for the moment, standing. He would start with the church bell.

Quickly, he backtracked to his SUV, stopping to hit the PANIC button on his remote. The blaring horn began pulsing into the night. *Ehh! Ehh! Ehh! Ehh! Ehh!* He grabbed gloves and a towel from his trunk and quickly soaked them in the melting snow. Holding the wet rag over his nose, he slogged through the smoke and watery snow to the broad front porch.

The front doors hung open, the entrance a great yawning maw of darkness from which smoke boiled. Squinting, holding his breath, he peered inside, shined his flashlight over the interior. The altar was engulfed, the curtains behind the pulpit a mass of flames, the pews at the front of the church already burning.

He knew the building. He had explored it as a kid. Past a coat closet, he found the door to the bell tower and inside, the ropes that were still attached to the ancient bell overhead. Throwing his weight on the chain, he yanked hard and was rewarded when the bell began to peal.

Bong! Bong! Bong! The bell tolled through the night, echoing in the tall tower and drowning out any other sound but the car alarm and the pounding of his own frantic heart. The noise was deafening, but it didn't smother the questions blaring in his mind. What had happened here? Why was the church ablaze in the middle of a snowstorm?

Coughing, he threw his weight into the ropes. As the bell pealed loudly, he considered the hazards and extent of this fire. Even if the church burned to the ground, there were no other buildings nearby. Granted, the church was a piece of Prairie Creek history, but buildings could be replaced.

People couldn't.

When two more windows blew and the crash of exploding glass punctuated the ringing bell, he knew it was time to get the hell out.

His hands were blistered from the ropes, his body soaked in sweat as he finally let go and backed out of the tower closet. Shooting a glance toward the burning altar, he winced against the heat as flames enveloped the first three rows of pews . . . and then he saw her.

Sitting in the third row, a woman faced the altar.

"Oh, Christ." How could she stand the heat?

He didn't have time to think. Holding the towel over his face, he raced down the aisle toward the wall of heat. Overhead, the old beams creaked. His eyes burned and smoke forced him to stay as low as he could and keep moving forward, passing row after row of pews whose varnish was already blistering.

"Lady!" he screamed. "You have to get out of here!" But she would know that. She *had* to. If she was aware. But she wasn't. She had to be passed out from the fumes. Or worse. Gritting his teeth, he forced himself forward. Heat scorched the air around him, sparks flew and the smoke seared his lungs as he finally reached the pew and grabbed the woman by the shoulders.

"Come on!" he barked through the mask of the towel.

She didn't move.

He lifted her onto one shoulder and that was when he knew. She was already gone. Dead.

Creeaaak! Old timbers splintered overhead and another window shattered. The building shuddered and Colt knew within minutes the whole roof would collapse.

Without thinking, Colton threw her over his shoulder and raced to the front doors of the church, the wall of heat pressing against him, closing around him, melting the air so that he had to close his eyes and navigate by memory.

His knee banged into a pew, but he kept moving forward. A deep crackle overhead told him the old roof was giving out. Off to the side, a chandelier dropped down and smashed onto the pews. Flaming debris followed. The hair on his arms singed.

Two more steps!

He threw himself out of the building, carrying the woman, leaping down the stairs, his boots sliding on the wet snow. Somewhere over the honking of the Explorer's horn and the *whoosh* of the conflagration behind him, he heard the scream of sirens.

Thank God!

Relief soaked through him along with cold, fresh air.

He hauled the dead woman far from the flames to the

other side of his truck and laid her gently on the ground to see her face.

Blood drizzled from her lips. Her dark hair was shiny, as if she had just brushed it, but her skin . . . His stomach lurched at the sight of her skin. The skin had been stripped from her arms and torso—almost peeled off in a horrendous way that reminded him of that dead coyote.

Despite the mutilation, he recognized her. The missing Amber Barstow. Her picture had been on all of the newscasts in recent days, as well as highlighted on the front page of the local paper.

Through the blur of smoke and falling snow he saw the flashing lights of emergency vehicles as they rolled into the pristine white parking lot.

Amen.

He sank down into the snow of the parking lot and stared at the dead girl. *What happened to you?* he wondered. A coughing spasm overcame him. He turned away to spit in the snow, then looked back at her. *What the hell happened to you?*

The glow on the horizon was unmistakable: fire.

Sabrina slowed as she tried to figure out the location of the orange flames burning through the haze of falling snow. The old Pioneer Church?

She didn't think twice, but cranked on the wheel of her truck as she reached the turnoff. From the flashing lights, she could see that the fire department was there, but she was a licensed EMT. Maybe she could help. Heart in her throat, the wheels of her truck slipping a little, she hit the accelerator and bumped up the lane to the rise.

Emergency vehicles were already on the scene, strewn haphazardly across the snow-covered parking lot. Firemen pumped water high into the air, creating dazzling fountains that fell onto the church, fighting the flames, sizzling against white-hot timbers. Smoke billowed out of the open front doors and through gaps in the roof.

At this time of night, chances were no one had been inside.

As she turned her truck to park away from the emergency vehicles, her headlights hit a familiar truck. Colton's truck.

Oh, God.

She threw the truck into park and bolted out. "Colton!" She wove around the pump truck and lunged toward the double doors.

"Stand back!" a fireman ordered. A man she recognized as Hunter Kincaid stepped in front of her, blocking her way.

Sabrina pounded the arm of his heavy coat. "Colton Dillinger!" she screamed. She must have sounded like a lunatic but she didn't care. "I'm looking for Colton Dillinger. His truck is here and—"

Another fireman said, "We're clear. No one else in the building."

"*Else?*" she repeated. "No one *else?*" Was she too late? Had Colton been caught in this horrid inferno?

Oh, God, she couldn't lose him now. All the cold fear she'd felt eighteen years ago came back in a rush. "No!" she cried, tears filling her eyes.

"Stand back," Kincaid said, all business. "Now!"

"Sabrina . . . Is that you?"

She turned and found Sam Featherstone standing near his department-issued Jeep.

"What the hell are you doing here?" he asked as she made her way toward him.

"Looking for Colt! I know he's here. His rig's right there!" She jabbed a finger toward his SUV. "And, and . . ."

Then she saw him. Covered in soot, black from head to toe, but standing upright, tall and rangy as ever, he emerged from behind his SUV.

"Colt!"

He tossed his blackened gloves into the snow, then looked up at her.

"Oh, God." Her knees threatened to give way, and she willed herself not to sink to the ground in sheer relief. Instinctively she ran to him and threw herself into his waiting arms. "I thought you were dead," she cried, clinging to him, not caring who saw.

For an answer he kissed her, hard. She could feel the pounding of his heart. "You're not getting rid of me that easily," he said on a shaking breath, keeping her tight against him.

Sabrina bit back a sob. He was alive! *Alive!* "What were you doing in there? For the love of God, what happened?"

"Nothin' good," he whispered into her hair. "Nothin' good until now."

She couldn't let him go again, couldn't deny what had become so crystal clear to her in the past few hours. "I want to start over. I do. I do, Colton. I don't know what was holding me back."

"Good. Good." He held her like he'd never let go, but then he finally lifted his head and guided her farther from the noise of the trucks and the shouts of men and the hiss of the dying fire. "I want a new beginning, too. With you."

"I've been too careful. I won't be anymore."

"They've got it now. Let's get out of here," he said.

The distraction was working.

From his own truck, the killer had witnessed the lights and sirens of emergency vehicles tearing up the narrow streets of Prairie Creek, on their way to the biggest fire to hit this part of Wyoming since the Dillinger ranch blaze nearly two decades earlier.

No one would suspect the fire was only a diversion meant

to direct attention outside of town. As soon as he was satisfied all the rescue vehicles and police were on their way to the church, he drove to the far side of town, parked his truck in the deserted lot of a school and strode, head down, along the sidewalks where others had trod.

The night was quiet, traffic on the main street through town hushed by falling snow. Even the few sounds that escaped from a late-night bar or the dog barking from an apartment were muffled by the snow.

Her house was small, unkempt, a cabin where the neighbors were far enough away that, unless something went very wrong, he could do what he had to do and get out unseen. His hand slid into his pocket to finger his trophies once again. Soon hers would be among the teeth now massaging his fingers.

Then he located the house key, the one he'd stolen from her purse as she'd set it down when he'd asked her advice on a bouquet for his girlfriend. As she'd looked into the case of cut flowers, he'd lifted her set of keys deftly. With that weird limp, he knew she could never make it back to the front counter in time to catch him in the act.

Now, he slid on his gloves and took her key ring from his pocket as he stole around to the back of the house. He knew she had no animals and that her untamed daughter was camping out in one of the Dillinger cabins.

Everything was coming together perfectly, he thought, as he slipped the key into the back door and felt the lock spring open.

Waiting for her sleeping pill to kick in, Mia tossed and turned in the worn groove of the double bed she'd slept in most of her life. The room was dark except for the glow that filtered in through her window shade. With the ground outside covered in white, the light from the street lamps was magnified and darkness was never complete.

The house still smelled of chili, and the pot still sat on the stove, ready for Kit to reheat when she got home.

If she got home. She'd promised, but then Kit couldn't be counted on unless you were a horse, or a cow, or a god-damned dog.

Mia was sick of waiting for her, sick of living alone. It galled her to no end to think that her daughter, a Dillinger, mind you, had turned into a strange animal whisperer that other people looked at as if she weren't right in the head.

"What do you do out there?" Mia had asked her daughter countless times, but Kit just looked away and shrugged. "Talk to me," Mia had demanded, but her words never penetrated Kit's veil of secrecy. It was downright embarrassing.

Mia knew that the Dillinger foreman, Davis Featherstone, encouraged her, tossing food here and there in return for work in the stables. Mia had told Featherstone in no uncertain terms to leave Kit alone, but the man had looked at her as if she were speaking a foreign language. That was typical of the help Mia got from the Dillingers—none.

The first wave of slumber teased at her brain. She let her breath out slowly and stared at shadows playing on the ceiling, shadows reflected from tree branches outside her window. Finally, she might be able to sleep.

Turning over, the bed springs creaking a bit, she thought she heard something. A soft *click.*

The back door?

Had Kit come home after all?

She listened hard. Nothing. Huh. Oh, well. Had she really expected her daughter to follow through? Her eyelids were getting heavier and she almost had Pilar's sneering face out of her mind.

Thump.

The soft sound of a door closing. The kitchen door.

So Kit was sneaking in again, trying not to wake her mother. Didn't she know better? Mia was happy to have her home. "Honey?" Mia called toward her opened bedroom door to the darkened hallway.

Nothing.

Just the *tick* of the clock at her bedside, her mother's favorite, and the quiet hum of the furnace.

"Kit?" she called again and then listened.

Silence. Nothing but the beating of her own heart.

And yet Mia sensed she wasn't alone.

The hairs on the back of her arms lifted a bit.

"Honey, this isn't funny!"

She rolled over to turn on the bedside lamp just as the door to her bedroom opened further. In the half light she saw the silhouette of a man, a big man, dark against the white woodwork.

"Who the hell are you?" she demanded.

Her blood ran cold.

Frantically, her fingers scrabbled across the scarred nightstand, reaching for the lamp, for the clock, for anything.

He leaped across the room. She screamed bloody murder, but he was on her in an instant. A gloved hand muffled her cries as his body pressed her hard against the mattress.

Fear screamed through her body. Her fingers curled over the clock and she tried to strike him with it, but he used his free hand to rip it from her fingers and toss it aside.

"Don't!" She tried to plead with him. "Don't hurt me!" But her words were muffled by the fat glove. She wriggled and writhed, trying to get him off her, but he was too strong. Her broken body was unable to dislodge him.

She felt her bladder release as he yanked something from his pocket and held it up.

A knife. Its long blade gleamed dark silver in the light from the window.

She screamed again, but it was a feeble noise behind his big hand. A shiver rippled through her body and she struggled harder, intent on shaking him off. She twisted and bucked and tried to pummel him with her fists, but even as she fought, she realized her efforts were futile.

He was stronger, and he had a weapon.

A very sharp weapon.

God help me, Mia thought as he leaned closer.

His breath was hot against her ear as he whispered, "Practice makes perfect."

And then the knife descended.

Back at the bunkhouse, Colton kicked open the door and carried Sabrina in, all the while his lips pressed to hers in the kiss begun when he'd insisted on carrying her through the deepening snow.

He burned to have her, with all the heat and fury of the fire he'd dodged earlier in the night. His kisses were hungry, greedy, but she answered with a fervor that said she shared his desperation.

He ended the kiss and moved his mouth along her jaw, his lips teasing the silken texture of her skin. "Sabrina . . ." he said unsteadily.

She tried to answer but instead just brought his mouth to hers again, kissing him back with all the pent-up passion she'd kept locked away all these years.

He buried his fingers in her hair, awed by her openness. This was no seventeen-year-old virgin anymore. She was a woman—mature and smart and sexy as hell.

Her hands slid down to tug on the lapels of his flannel shirt. Two snaps popped open, and she cocked an eyebrow. He yanked up her sweater to run his hands over her warm flesh. Everything about her excited him. The crevices of her back and shoulder blades. The slope of her belly. The sweet mounds of her breasts. He pulled her bra down to suckle, feeling like an amateur, a teenage kid desperate to score, but he couldn't hold back.

He had to have her. Now.

Feeling her nipple harden under his lips, he moaned and lifted his head. "You sure?"

Stars burned in her eyes, but she said, "Maybe we should stop and think this over."

"What?" he expelled in disbelief, then he felt her silent laughter.

"Woman," he muttered, tearing at the remaining snaps of his flannel shirt. Then, "Talking's overrated."

She pulled off her sweater, flung it aside, then hopped up from the cot to unfasten her jeans. "You got that right," she said with a smile as she peeled off the denim. Then she grabbed his hand and led him to the shower. They plunged beneath the hot spray, locked together, their hands exploring all the forgotten places, their mouths forging new pathways, until Colton pulled her onto his hard shaft and Sabrina's arms and legs encircled him and they rhythmically made love until they were both gasping and half falling against the tiles, laughing, and then gripped by desire. Sabrina cried out as they both climaxed at the same moment, and shuddering, Colton held her as tightly as he could, his heart full.

"The one that got away," he said, to which Sabrina looked up at him with love and questions in her eyes.

"Later," he told her and then kissed her hard again.

PART TWO

by
Rosalind Noonan

Chapter Fourteen

Ricki Dillinger squinted down at the dead woman, her gaze following the line of skin that had been stripped from around her neck, exposing muscle and cartilage down over her shoulder and chest. Behind her, the conflagration of the church lit up the sky and sent waves of heat her way.

“I told you it was gruesome,” said Wiley Cook, the EMT who was young enough to be her son, but had heard of her reputation with the cops in New York. She’d convinced him to unzip the body bag for her by bamboozling him into thinking she was working for the sheriff now. No lies, just wishful thinking.

“Poor thing,” Ricki said, focusing her cell phone to snap a photo. “Just passing through Prairie Creek and someone did that to her.”

“Some crazy person,” Wiley said. “Like the mad butcher in that movie.”

“You’re right on that,” Ricki agreed, capturing another image just to be sure. It wasn’t a fresh corpse. Signs of decay were evident, though Ricki suspected that the freezing temperatures had delayed decomposition. Rigor was pretty far along, and the body was frozen in a sitting position.

“She must have been sitting for a while,” Ricki observed.

"That's how your brother found her—sitting in one of the pews. He didn't know she was dead, and the fire was spreading fast."

"Right." This was liable to set Colt back a few years. "But she couldn't have been in the church long," Ricki said. "They had a dress rehearsal there this afternoon."

Wiley shrugged. "I don't know about that. I'm guessing whoever set this fire left her there."

Ricki muttered, "He probably killed her, too."

So the woman's killer was out here, close by. She thought of her own daughter, sleeping alone in the cabin, and picked up her phone, putting a call in to Janice MacDonald, the Dillinger housekeeper who lived in the small quarters at the back of the main house. "Sorry to wake you," she said when Janice answered, then quickly explained about the fire and the killer on the loose. "He's probably long gone, but would you mind going over to the foreman's house to stay with Brook until I get back? Bring one of Dad's guns with you."

"I have my own," Mrs. Mac told her, a subtle reminder that Ricki was not in New York City anymore.

As she ended the call, Wiley asked, "Should I close her up?"

Ricki took one more look at the corpse. "I think I'm done. Thanks for taking the trouble."

Wiley's easy smile faded as he glanced over her shoulder, and before Ricki could turn around she heard Sam Featherstone's gruff voice ask, "What's going on over here?"

Wide-eyed, Wiley scrambled to zip up the body bag, as Ricki faced Sam. She held her phone up. "Got some images for us to look at. Sometimes when you send the body on to the medical examiner, it takes a while to get a report back, and you forget how things looked."

"I know," he said curtly.

"Where will she go? Cheyenne or Jackson?" Ricki asked, unfazed by his tone.

"Jackson." Sam's dark eyes held a flicker of annoyance. "But you're not on this case, Ricki."

"I'm aware."

A loud crack and subsequent shudder of roof timbers interrupted her. Collectively their heads whipped up to see the roof begin to cave.

"Get back!" someone yelled.

Sam grabbed her arm in a proprietary way that made her do a quick double take, but he was just doing his job. They moved back another twenty feet, behind the vehicles.

A voice crackled on the radio and Sam held up a pointed finger for Ricki to wait while he adjusted the volume on the device clipped to the collar of his jacket. "Kit's heading your way," Naomi's voice came through.

"She's coming all the way out here?" Sam frowned. "Did you tell her there's a fire here?"

"I did, but I swear there's something wrong with that girl."

Most of Prairie Creek would agree on that, Ricki thought.

"Thanks for the heads-up." Sam signed off on the radio and stared at the roaring fire.

"It's burning fast," Ricki said. "Do you know if they found any signs of accelerant?"

"Haven't talked with the fire chief yet. I've been focused on Amber Barstow."

Ricki nodded toward her father, who stood off to the side, talking with firefighters. "Dad said this is only the third big fire in eighteen years. The old homestead, the bakery fire and now this."

Sam's eyes were distant. "The bakery fire was an explosion. Bad gas line. This?" He shook his head. "No reason for a church to be engulfed in flames in the middle of the night."

"Probably arson." Ricki sighed. "With the homicide, you got a killer who appears to be a real psycho."

Sam rubbed his knuckles against the side of his jaw. "I'd appreciate you keeping that under wraps for the time being."

"You're going to have to warn the public about him. Might as well do it now."

"I don't want to sound the alarm until we know what we're dealing with. Did you see the way the victim is carved up? It could be a cult, some weird ritual. In which case, we'd be scaring the public without reason."

"Whenever someone turns up dead, I'd say that's a good reason."

"See, that's where law enforcement in a small town differs," he said. "It's more complicated than it looks."

Ricki wanted to tell him that Einstein said that you should keep things simple, but she kept her mouth shut, distracted by headlights meandering up the hill, the car veering off the snowy roadway, then bouncing back on.

Sam noticed, too.

"Drunk driver?" she asked, squinting into the darkness.

"It's a wagon. A Subaru." Sam frowned. "Looks like Mia's car."

"It's Kit driving." Did the girl even have a license? Ricki wondered. Probably not.

They both watched in a mixture of curiosity and horror as the car turned into the parking lot so erratically that it spun around and slid into a snowdrift. When it appeared to have made a soft landing, Ricki and Sam hurried over.

"Kit?" Sam peered in through the driver's-side window. "You okay in there?"

The door flew open and she emerged, eyes round as quarters, skin pale as the moon. She rushed to Sam, grabbed his arm and tugged frantically. "Come." Her voice was taut, springing from a dark place. "My mother. Come, help."

She pulled him toward the car, as if she could push him inside.

"Calm down, Kit. Did you say your mother needs help?"

She just stared at him through wide, wounded eyes.

"Tell me," Sam urged.

But she couldn't bring forth any more words.

"Where is Mia?" He looked around.

"Her house . . . in town . . ." Kit forced out, then doubled over. Panicked or sick? Ricki couldn't tell.

"We'll go there," Ricki said, putting a gentle hand on Kit's shoulder. She knew the girl didn't like to be touched, but she had to get through to her. "Over this way. The sheriff will give you a ride in his Jeep." The girl's body trembled as Ricki guided her around the hoses and trucks. Sam jogged over to Gary Rodriguez, one of his deputies, to let him know he was leaving the scene.

Ricki opened the back door of the Jeep. "There you go."

Kit climbed awkwardly inside, fumbling, as if she'd lost control of her limbs. She stared straight ahead, helpless and vacant, and Ricki's heart lurched with fear. Something was really wrong. Then she noticed the dark stain on Kit's jacket and hands. Blood.

When Sam returned to find Ricki in the passenger seat, he said, "This is no time for a ride-along."

"Deputize me, Sam. You need help and I've got the experience and know-how. So stop fighting it. Whatever happened in town, Kit's in shock." She lowered her voice. "And she's got blood on her hands."

He shot a look in the backseat, then turned back and started the engine. "Fine," he clipped out. "You're officially an employee of Prairie Creek."

"Thank you, Sam." She switched on the lights of the roof rack, and held on for a bumpy ride.

Hiring Ricki went against Sam's better judgment, but having her beside him, listening as she gently talked to Kit, he began to revise his opinion. She did know how to talk to people, though Kit wasn't giving them much. The girl never did, but this was something else.

The neighborhood was dark and quiet as they pulled up outside Mia's cabin. The whispering snow that covered everything in white helped muffle the sound. He killed the engine and turned to Kit, but the back door was already open, the girl flying out into the snow. Ricki and Sam wasted no time following.

"Kit," he shouted. "Don't go in there. There could be . . ."

But she was loping ahead, an elk in the snow.

The front door was open a crack, a small mound of snow piled up on the floor, before Kit pushed it open and stomped inside. "Mia?" she said, hurrying down the dark hallway.

"Kit, hold on there," Ricki called, following her.

Sam flicked the light on and drew his gun. There were footprints on the hallway linoleum. Bloody prints. "Shit."

Ricki turned back and noticed. "Aw . . . fuck me."

Words that Sam rarely heard from a woman these days. It would take some getting used to Ricki, who danced around the prints in a late attempt to preserve a crime scene, but kept moving down the hall.

Sam did a quick check of the living room and kitchen as he passed. No one, but then he didn't expect there to be since the dark footprints on the floor were already dry, turning brown. From the bedroom came the noxious smell of a slaughter yard and the sound of whimpering, like the cry of a wounded dog. Stepping gingerly, Sam followed Ricki to the doorway, where they both paused, able to make out Kit's shadowed silhouette leaning over the bed.

Sam flicked on the light to illuminate a world of horror. A crimson pool on the floor. Shattered glass and detritus scattered through the ransacked room. Stepping around the pool of blood where Kit stood silent as a grave, he saw her. Mia lay on the bed, naked from head to toe, her neck severed in a deep gash. Her face seemed untouched except for a line of blood trailing from her mouth. But her body . . . the massacre was organized and repulsive. The skin of her shoulders and arms carved off in almost an ornamental way. Same with her stomach and thighs. She'd been skinned . . . butchered like an animal.

Kit just stared down at her mother, so Ricki stepped forward and put a hand on the girl's shoulder, her boot stopping just short of the puddle of blood. "I promise you, we're going to find whoever did this to her."

Kit seemed to see something inside her own head, some tableau that darkened her eyes and turned her features blade hard, but then she turned to Ricki and nodded.

It was pushing three A.M. when Ricki pulled Sam's Jeep into a spot in front of the foreman's house and killed the engine. She had a headful of gruesome images and a silent girl in the passenger seat, but somehow the edginess of it all was as familiar as a comfortable old pair of slippers. Police work really was a chronic sickness.

"Okay, we're here," she told Kit, who moved like a sleepwalker as they shuffled through the light powder that had fallen during the night. Ricki gave a courtesy knock so as not to startle Mrs. Mac, then stuck her key in the door.

The older woman was sitting up on the couch, fuzzy blanket on her lap and a revolver sitting on the coffee table. "I'm glad it's you." She pushed the blanket aside and smoothed back her hair. "I'm not too happy to hear there's a killer roaming around this area."

"You and me both."

Mrs. Mac's dark eyes were stern as Ricki motioned Kit inside.

"Kit's staying with us tonight."

Mrs. Mac nodded and took in Kit's bloodstained appearance as she lifted her parka from the hook by the door.

When Kit hung back, Ricki prodded her. "It's cold. Come in. Stay for a while. You can leave when you want to." That got the girl to cross the threshold.

As Kit stood in the hallway, Ricki paused to peek in on Brook, sleeping peacefully in a lump under her zebra print quilt. Her hair fell over the pillow, and her pale face looked blissfully serene. Sleep was one of the few times Ricki saw her daughter at peace these days. She closed the door and thanked Mrs. Mac, who was hovering by the front door.

Ricki slung her own jacket on the hook. "You want me to call Dad to walk you back up to the house?"

"No need." She slid her gun into her coat pocket. "My good friends Smith and Wesson will take care of me."

Ricki turned to Kit. "Bathroom's down the hall. There's a pull-out couch in the living room." Kit didn't move for a moment, then finally walked stiffly into the bathroom and shut the door.

Mrs. Mac whispered, "What's going on?"

Ricki exhaled. "Janice, Mia's dead."

Mrs. Mac's hand flew to her chest. "Mia's gone?"

"Looks like the same person who killed Amber Barstow killed Mia." At least, that was Ricki and Sam's guess based on the body carving. When Sam asked her to get Kit out of there, the techs from the state lab had just started collecting evidence. It would be days, maybe even a week before they got a complete report back.

"Oh, my Lord."

"I know." Ricki knew that the full impact of it hadn't hit her yet; she was too tired and wound up and sick to wrap her mind around it.

Mrs. Mac nodded toward the bathroom. "Does she know?"

"I'm afraid she found her."

"Good Lord in heaven. Who would do such a thing?" She shuddered.

"I don't know, but I plan to find out," Ricki said. "Thanks for coming over."

"Anytime. You get some sleep now."

"I will." Ricki was throwing the bolt on the door when Kit emerged from the bathroom, decidedly cleaner but still skittish as a new colt.

She zipped her jacket to her chin, shivering despite the warmth of the cabin. "I need to go." She moved toward the door, but Ricki stepped in her path, effectively blocking the way.

"You're in shock, honey, and there's real danger out there."

"No." Kit was stoic.

"Sam told me to keep watch on you, and he's right. So just unzip that coat and I'll show you where you can sleep."

Kit backed against the wall, hugging herself and hunching over. Emotional implosion, Ricki thought, moving closer to her.

"Just get some sleep here, where you're safe, and after you're rested, we'll go from there." She purposely kept her distance, knowing Kit would bolt if she felt cornered.

She suspected the girl suffered from some variation of autism, but it wasn't a concern to folks around here who put more emphasis on hard work than on education. Kit was a hard worker.

She was relieved when Kit moved to the pull-out and yanked open the bed as if she'd been doing it all her life. Ricki got her some bedding and then went to her own room. Tired herself, she quickly took a shower and crashed onto her own bed.

Hours later, in the utter silence of the middle of the night, she got up to check on both Brook and Kit. Brook was sound asleep in her bed, but when she got to the living room, she saw the pull-out bed had barely been disturbed and Kit was gone.

The sun was rising behind the gray shale mountains as Davis Featherstone opened the stable door at the Rocking D and released the horses to the field. From the looks of it, Kit had done a good job with them the previous night. Their hooves had been picked out, and they were dry and content. Kit was good with animals; that was why he'd been so thrown by the dead coyote, and before that, last summer's skinned lamb. Despite her inclination to live on the plains, Kit had never seemed to favor hunting . . . at least, not until lately.

The bluish light of morning on the snow-covered plains had a sinister tint. Two dead, both women. After he'd caught the scent of smoke and ash on his way in this morning, he'd stopped into the lodge and gotten word from Mrs. Mac. There was a killer out there. Looked as if the same guy had killed that woman passing through town and now Mia Collins, too.

Kit's mother.

His blood had run cold when Mrs. Mac had told him. "Where's Kit?" he'd asked.

"Safe and sound with Ricki. But you should know there's a killer out there, and he seems to be a firebug, too. Burned down the Pioneer Church. Pilar's going to have a cow when she finds out. Not about the dead women, mind you, but the wedding."

Davis knew that wedding was a thorn in Ira's side. If he were the old man, he'd elope and call it a day.

Now Davis gave a shout to move the horses along, but they knew the routine. Even in the snow, he turned them out each morning. The open space and sunshine served them better than a day in the dry, shadowed stables. He patted

Pepper's neck and gave the appaloosa some loving. When he turned back, he saw the Jeep with the roof-rack of lights approaching. His brother Sam.

Although his brother was the sheriff, Davis wasn't a fan of the law. The law didn't feed hungry families or care for children when their parents beat them down. Sometimes he thought Sam had forgotten where they came from when he'd married that rich girl. For a while, that big house and baby girl had lifted him up, separated him from their past. Even though Sam's wife had hightailed it back to Denver, taking the daughter along, some of the entitlement had stuck. And the law and order halo remained.

Sam wore a black bomber jacket with his shiny gold star pinned to the chest. Did he remember the day a man in the same uniform had come to take their mother away?

Sam's face was wan, tired. "You hear about last night?"

"Two murders and a fire." Davis tramped through the snow, toward the gate. "You had a busy night. How's Kit handling it?"

"In shock, I think. She's staying at the ranch until we find this guy."

"You sure? She doesn't like confinement."

"Ricki took her home," Sam said, and Davis let it go.

"What makes you think it's a guy?"

"Just playing the percentages. Besides, the killer has this way of carving up the victims."

"Carving them up." Davis spoke slowly. He didn't want to hear this. "Like . . . how?"

"He's got knife skills. He sliced off the skin of their arms and legs and left the muscle and bone, like a hunter saving a skin."

A hunter . . . or a huntress.

Davis swallowed hard, but he couldn't clear the salty taste on his tongue. He couldn't dismiss the image of Kit swaying around that coyote near Copper Woods, dancing in the snow, bowing to it and lifting her arms to the sky in some ancient ritual.

He turned away to latch the gate. Yesterday, he had worried that she'd gone over the edge, killing the coyote and skinning it, cutting out a tooth as Sabrina had mentioned. But now . . . two women were dead, carved up in the same way. He slammed the steel gate. This wasn't Kit. It wasn't. Couldn't be. That wasn't how she was made. But the facts were there. As their grandmother used to say, you can bury the truth, but it will always be waiting there, under the dirt.

And Kit didn't get along with Mia at all.

"Word's traveling fast." Sam took his hat off. "By this afternoon, half the town's going to be loaded for bear, and we don't even have a suspect in sight."

Head down, Davis kicked a snowdrift off the path, not wanting his brother to see the emotions warring inside him. How he wanted to protect her. How he wished he could dance with her. And yet, there was the vein of fear, the possibility that her skillful hands had carved off those layers of skin. "Why did you come here?"

"The first victim was found in the Pioneer Church, just down the road. I was wondering if you've taken on any new hands lately. Anyone passing through?"

"Someone you can pin the blame on?"

"Easy, brother."

"Ira Dillinger doesn't take kindly to people who are passing through. The work here goes to local guys." And Kit. Kit got first priority.

"Got some names for me?"

"Don't push it."

"Then take a minute. Get the bug out of your ass and tell me who's been working here in the past month. Unless you want me to subpoena the Rocking D's records. Ira will be thrilled."

"I don't hire killers," he snapped.

"He's out here, Davis, and I'm casting a net to find him. This is how it works."

This was always how it worked, with Davis resisting and Sam doubling the pressure. "Fine." Davis gave him names: Lou McCoy and Mick Ramhorn were on the payroll. Stub Everly and Catfish Griffin worked by the hour.

But he conveniently left Kit out. No one would suspect her, anyway.

No one but him.

Chapter Fifteen

The next morning, Ricki woke up with an ache in her shoulder and a feeling of dread. Kit hadn't returned and she really didn't know what to do about it. She stood in the kitchen with a cup of coffee and rolled her tender shoulder as her mind slid to a gruesome image of a raw shoulder stripped of skin, its musculature and bone on display like a med school cadaver.

Mia.

Amber Barstow had been cut in the same way.

Last night, on the verge of sleep, Ricki had worried that the killer might have done his handiwork before cutting his victims' throats. What if he had drugged them or bound them in place so that they felt every cut . . . every raw nerve flaring with pain?

She didn't want to believe any human being on this planet could be so cruel, so heinous. At least the medical examiner would have some information on the cause of death and the timing of the wounds.

But where was Kit? The girl had been on her own so long, she probably didn't even think about others, and now with Mia gone, her last tether to people may have been severed. Ricki's gut was churning with worry.

Just as she was about to call Sam, her cell phone blooped. Snatching it up, she saw the message was from Davis: Kit is here at stables.

Ricki nearly collapsed with relief. Good. She recalled that one of the mares was close to foaling and it made sense that Kit would be there rather than here.

Ruffling the curls on her forehead, she yawned. Another few hours of sleep would be nice, but she knew it would be impossible with the investigation just starting. Part of her couldn't wait to tell Brooklyn that she had a job now, but the other part could only imagine the barbs that would come from her daughter once she learned there was a killer at large. *I thought we moved here for a better quality of life, not a hack-job from some psycho. Thanks, Mom.* Yeah, Ricki could wait for that conversation.

And apparently, Brooklyn could wait, too. When Ricki poked her head in, her daughter was curled up in bed and breathing slowly. It was just after eight, and Brook rarely made it out of bed before noon on Sundays.

She called Davis's cell and he answered on the first ring. "Yeah, she's here. Won't leave Babylon's side. I told her to go, but she won't."

"You heard what happened to Mia."

"Yeah." He was sober.

"Davis, I hate to do this to you, but can you make sure she sticks around? She might be . . . vulnerable." She didn't want to come out and say that the killer might have her in his sights, too, but Davis seemed to get the message.

While she was on the phone with Davis, Sam rang in, and she signed off and took his call. "Morning, Sheriff."

"Did you get some sleep?"

It seemed like such an intimate question, and she had to brace herself to answer in a level voice. "A few hours."

"Good, because you've got a full day ahead. I'd like you

to coordinate a search of the Rocking D, since you know the lay of the land. I mean, if you're still on board."

"Absolutely."

"Got some volunteers here and loaners from nearby jurisdictions. I'm sending one group out with Gary to search the Kincaid ranch, especially near the church. I'll send a group out your way to help, but I don't know the best way to cover the land there."

"In this snow, we're better on horseback. I can have Davis supply us with horses. If you got a few who don't ride, I can have them cover the access roads, as long as they have a four-by-four," she suggested.

"Sounds like a plan."

They discussed a few other details, and to her surprise, Sam brought up Brooklyn. "Speaking more as a parent than a sheriff . . . I don't know what you've got planned, but I don't like the idea of your daughter out there alone while you're gone all day. After all, we had a strike right near you. Can she spend the day with a friend or something?"

"Good idea." Here she was, ready to lam out of here, leaving her daughter alone in a fairly isolated cabin. "I'll take her up to the main lodge. Pilar will be around with Rourke, and Mrs. Mac will be there all day." Maybe Brook could help Pilar rearrange the wedding plans.

After they ended the call, she went into triage mode. She called Davis again, about the horses this time, woke up Brook and jumped in the shower. Half an hour later, she left a sullen but quiet Brook sitting on a stool at the kitchen counter, watching as Mrs. Mac beat together butter and eggs.

"Cookies." The older woman pointed to the drawer by the ovens. "And you can help me decorate them. There's an apron right there."

"Isn't that great, honey?" Ricki plunked the apron over

her daughter's head and patted her shoulder. "I'll be back as soon as I can."

Brooklyn rolled her eyes but didn't dare complain in front of Mrs. Mac. Good. This might force Brook to spend some time with her family, get to know them at least a little.

Out in the corral, Sabrina was walking one of the quarter horses around. A boy was standing by. "T-Rex is a very gentle horse," Sabrina was saying. "He's got a great temperament."

"When do I get to ride?" the boy asked. On closer inspection, Ricki realized it was Rourke.

"As soon as Colton gets the okay from your mom."

"She'll never say yes," he muttered gloomily.

"Your dad's pretty persuasive," Sabrina assured him.

Inside the stables, Colton was helping Davis and one of the hands saddle up horses. Davis put a blanket over a quarter horse and nodded at Ricki. "How many horses will you need for your search party?"

"I'm thinking six altogether. I'll ride Rio. The other volunteers will go out in a truck."

"Hardly a search party." Colt lifted a saddle onto the horse. "We're going to join in. Sabrina and Davis and me. You need us, and I don't mind beating the bushes for this monster. If he's here on Dillinger land, I say let's track him down."

"After you talk to Pilar about Rourke riding?" Ricki suggested.

"How'd you know about that?" Colton asked.

"Sabrina." She inclined her head to where Sabrina was having Rourke lead the horse.

"He's eager to get to it, but today's not the day," Colton said.

"And Pilar's going to go with that?"

"He's a Dillinger. He's going to ride," Colt said in a tone that allowed no argument.

Kit emerged from a stable leading a white and gold Arabian. "I'm going, too." She looked Ricki in the eye.

"That's not such a good idea." Ricki shifted from one foot to the other. "Protocol doesn't allow family members to be working on a case they have ties with."

"It's just a search party." Colton straightened and tipped back his hat. "Not a jury."

"Colt is right," Davis said. "The lay of the land changes all the time, and nobody knows those plains better than Kit."

Ricki held her tongue with an effort. In New York, a young woman would not be allowed to help search for her mother's killer. But then, she wasn't in New York anymore, was she? "All right then. What can I do to help you get these horses ready?"

Half an hour later, Rourke was back at the house, and two search parties of six set out. Ricki and Davis led one, and Catfish Griffin, a ranch hand, acted as guide for the police volunteers. They would use the ranch walkie-talkies for communication.

Ricki now realized that Sabrina was here not as the ranch vet but as Colton's girlfriend—a recent development that her brother seemed pretty happy about. As they headed out, both parties following the farm road that had been cleared of deep snow a day ago, Colt's dog followed along behind them, stopping now and again to mark the edge of the road and frolic in the powder.

Sabrina pointed out, "Montana is coming with us."

Colton twisted to look back at the trotting dog. "Yeah, he does that sometimes."

"The dog doesn't know the ranch," Ricki pointed out, "and the snowdrifts are deep."

"Yeah." Colt shrugged. "We're going to have to keep an eye on him, because I can make him follow, but I don't have a command to make him go back."

"Sounds like that dog has you pretty well trained," Davis

said dryly, and despite the somber tone of the morning, everyone chuckled.

Even Kit smiled.

The snow had stopped sometime during the night, and though everything was blanketed in white, most of the trails were still apparent. Ricki looked out over the white sweeping hills and plains and wondered if he was out there, lingering. She didn't think so, but you never knew. You just never knew.

The charred ruins of the old Pioneer Church reeked of smoke. Every few minutes wind stirred up dry snowflakes mixed with ash from last night's fire and sent the icy cinders around behind the short standing wall to pummel Hunter Kincaid in the face.

"Are you done yet?" Casey Rawlings, a volunteer firefighter, called from the parking lot, where he was keeping a lookout.

"Almost." Hunter removed a spray bottle from his satchel and adjusted the nozzle to produce a steady stream. He turned on the video feature of his phone, then pointed the spray bottle at the seal at the top of the church's propane tank and squeezed.

Thick dishwasher soap squirted out with a *splat.* He kept spraying, surrounding the valve and saturating the seal with the soapy mixture he'd brought from home. Hunter knew the fire inspector who'd been here earlier in the day had fancy chemicals and test kits, but for this test, dishwasher liquid was just as effective. If propane was leaking out anywhere around the seal, the gas would make the solution bubble up.

The bigger the gas bubble, the greater the leak. Another thing he'd learned in the two years he'd spent training in Jackson's fire and rescue. Two years wasted, as far as Lieutenant Whit Crowley and his hooligans were concerned.

They considered the local fire department to be their private men's club, a place for beer and poker funded by the county. Anyone who got in the way of tradition was not welcome, to the tune of threats and maliciousness that bordered on criminal behavior. They felt Hunter was a traitor in their midst. He'd heard the jibes—comments about him being a reformed firebug, based on the mistaken belief that he'd had anything to do with the Dillinger fire—but he ignored all of them.

"Almost done?" Casey called. "I'd hate for Lieutenant Crowley to find out we brought a truck all the way out here."

"Fuck him," Hunter said under his breath, then shouted back: "There's no leak." Not even a small bubble.

Imagine that. Crowley and his men had been wrong again. In their investigation this morning, they'd cited the propane tank as having a leak. That meant a fine for the church, as well as the expense of repairs. Refitting the tank or replacing it completely. And to get the work done, a person usually called the only plumbing and heating specialist in town—none other than Whit Crowley.

It was a nice little give-and-take.

He turned off the video, packed up his stuff and tramped round the side of the building over well-trodden snow.

Casey paced beside the truck with all the energy of a nervous nineteen-year-old. "What do you mean, there's no leak? Do you think Crowley and the guys fixed it?"

"Not unless the church forked over a grand this morning. It's just like the other propane tanks at every fire we've worked in the last year or so. Crowley claims a propane leak, writes up a violation, then gets paid the big bucks to fix it."

Casey punched gloved fists together. "That's gotta be against the law."

"No one's been the wiser, that is till you helped clean up at the Olsen fire." He put his bags into the back of the truck and clapped Casey on the back. "You prepared to be a whistleblower?"

"Are we going to lose our jobs?"

Hunter wasn't so sure. He didn't think the fire chief, Jack Raintree, was in on the scam, but he may have been turning a blind eye to it. At the very least, a lot of folks in Prairie Creek were on friendly terms with Whit Crowley. "Don't worry about it just yet," Hunter said. "We can't come out with any of the evidence until we have more of a case. I should have started collecting evidence on those home fires when they happened, but who knew?"

"A thief among us," Casey said dramatically. "I can't wait to lock him up and throw away the key."

"That would be satisfying." Crowley behind bars, where Hunter himself had almost landed, more than once.

The two men got into the truck, and Hunter started it up.

Casey said, "This time, they're saying it's arson."

"'Fraid so. I found multiple points of origin, and gasoline markings and residue. Whoever set that fire was hoping for some major damage. That makes it different from the other house fires we've had. This firebug went whole hog."

"So it wasn't Crowley's men?"

"I don't think so, since it doesn't fit their pattern. We'll see. But you can bet Crowley will be approaching the church about replacing their propane tank for them."

"Do you think the lieutenant knows we're on to him?" Casey asked.

All these questions . . . he hoped Casey would use some discretion. "Nah. He can't see past the dollars he's shoving into his wallet."

"I don't want to get kicked out."

"They can't fire you. You're a volunteer."

"They can shit-can me, and I really like this job. At least, the fire part."

"Yeah." There was something irresistible about fire. The way it captured the eye, the way it circled objects and swelled, roared or disappeared in a cloud of ash. Hunter knew that attraction. Half the guys on the rescue team probably felt that lure, but it didn't make them any worse at their job. Hunter used to argue with his old man that it made him a better firefighter.

And it did. To capture and kill the beast, you had to understand it.

Sam hadn't planned to drive out this way today; he trusted Dillinger and Rodriguez to handle the searches. But when Gary called with word of the old hunting shack on Kincaid land that looked like it had been recently occupied, Sam figured it would be worth his while to head out.

The old cabin was brittle with cold and neglect. Two old camping chairs and an ancient Coleman stove were the only furnishings left behind. At first glance, it appeared to be a bum lead.

Unless you knew what you were looking for.

One of the camping chairs was stained, probably with body fluid, if the smell was any indication. The odor of rotting flesh was something Sam knew he would never forget.

Deputy Gary Rodriguez stood over a brown stain on the floor marked with a card labeled #11. "Do you think this is blood, Sheriff?"

Sam nodded and rubbed his chin, bristly since he hadn't shaved for twenty-four hours. "And the blue fibers from a tarp . . . not to mention the empty bags. Those are good finds. It figures he'd want a tarp to move the body."

Rodriguez folded his arms. "Yeah, but leaving the bags behind? It seems a little obvious. Not too bright."

"Some criminals are not the sharpest pencils in the box,"

Sam said. "And some of them enjoy leaving a trail. It's like a tease." The empty tarp wrappers had already been collected as evidence; Sam had grinned when he recognized the price label from the Handy Hardware store, right on Main Street in town. Soon as he could, he'd check with Phil Turner about the tarps.

For now, Gary would wait here for the techs from Jackson. "Appreciate you sitting on this crime scene," Sam told Gary. "We'll know more once the guys from the lab comb through it."

Gary nodded. "You headed back to town?"

"Nah." Sam zipped his jacket and opened the flimsy plywood door. "I gotta stop over at the Kincaids. Last I heard, Georgina Kincaid's holding the other search party back at gunpoint."

Rodriguez looked incredulous. "Seriously?"

"That's what I'm hearing."

Ten minutes later, he passed under the gate marking the Kincaids' Double K Ranch and proceeded until he came up on the dark Suburban parked and waiting within sight of the ranch compound. He rolled down the window of his Jeep and faced Larry Park from the sheriff's office in Lander. Two of his deputies were among the searchers in the back of the vehicle.

"Where's she aiming?" Sam asked.

"Into the air . . . so far," Larry answered.

The tinted rear window of the Suburban rolled down, and Katrina Starr leaned out. "It's Georgina doing the shooting, Sheriff. I tried calling on the home phone, like you said, but no one answered."

Sam said curtly, "I'll go talk with her."

"I hope you got bulletproof glass in that vehicle," Larry called as Sam pulled away.

"I hope she recognizes that it's me," Sam muttered as he

bumped along the drive, slowly approaching the two-story, dark brown ranch house that had been considered beautiful in its day. Now the brown trim was blistered and the stenciled double doors seemed dated. He rolled to a stop, put the Jeep in park and waited.

Within a minute, the front door flew open. A woman stepped out, lifted a rifle to the sky and fired.

The report rattled Sam's Jeep as it echoed through the canyon.

Sam quickly opened the door and stepped into a foot of snow. "Hold on there!"

"Get off my land!" Georgina turned and swung the gun toward him.

He ducked behind his Jeep, not taking any chances. "Dammit, Georgina. Hold your fire, or I'll have to run you in!"

"Sam?" she called. "That you?"

"It is. Put that gun down so we can talk."

"Fine."

He peered around the hood of the vehicle and watched as she lowered the butt of the rifle to the ground and propped it up in the doorway.

"I want those trespassers off my land!"

Now that she wasn't armed, he closed the distance between them. "Those trespassers are law enforcement, Georgina," he said tightly. "A search party. We've had two homicides in Prairie Creek. We have reason to believe the killer has been hiding out on or near Kincaid land."

"We're not harboring a criminal here, Sheriff. So take your people and go."

"This is a killer we're talking about, and we've already found evidence that he's been holing up in that hunting shed. The one on Horseshoe Ridge."

"What?" For the first time her demeanor changed and she looked toward the hills with concern.

"We need to search the area. This is one bad dude. Not someone you want hiding out on your property."

"I got my rifle here, and the Major's still a crack shot when he feels inspired."

Sam put his hands on his hips and stared at the woman, half-annoyed, half-amused, though he would never show it. An aging beauty in her sixties, Georgina Kincaid had always been known for her eccentricities—Wyoming tough but well pampered. Even so, she'd never been this foolish.

"Did Hunter tell you about the fire at the church?"

"He did. Burnt to the ground, he said. It's a shame, what with the big Dillinger wedding supposed to go off next weekend." Her eyes glimmered. She didn't look all that dismayed. The feud might be simmering on low, but it ran deep. "Still, doesn't feel right, letting intruders roam on Kincaid land."

Sam wanted to point out that they'd built half a dozen rental cabins to bring "intruders" in for an "authentic ranch experience." In the past few years, the Kincaids had delved into a number of offshoot businesses—all half-baked efforts to make a profit off their failing sheep ranch.

"As sheriff, I can't turn my back on this one, Georgina. I'll get a court order to search your land if I have to, only I don't think you want the town to go to that expense, and in the time it takes, this guy might burn down those cabins you built for your retreat."

She let out a sigh. "Well, that would be just awful, though they might be damaged already. The Major has been too sick to drive out there anymore, and frankly I haven't had the time."

"If you like, I'll check on the cabins when I'm out that way. Give you a report. And that search party out there?

Think of them as family. Except you don't have to feed them dinner."

She sent him a dark look, but said, "Just get them off our land before the sun sets, or this gun won't be for show."

He knew her bark was worse than her bite. Hell, the old bird wasn't even able to ride out and check on the back acres anymore. He walked toward his Jeep, then turned back. "Give the Major my best, and from now on, point your rifle at wild elk not deputies."

"I'll do what I can, Sheriff," Georgina said in a tone that made Sam doubt she was seriously listening to him.

Chapter Sixteen

At the moment, Delilah Dillinger wished she were anywhere but here in this stuffy Santa Monica studio, shooting a commercial on a beautiful afternoon.

"Too much orange. Get me some different lighting gels," demanded the director.

"Light Amber? Spring Yellow? Oklahoma Yellow?" Delilah Dillinger handed the gels over to the photographer and receded into the background, not wanting to distract anyone from the mission of setting up lights and cameras for the shoot. Today they were filming a commercial for Fun! Fun!—an energy drink sold on the Japanese market—and since the director was Franco Denazi, a gorgeous metrosexual Delilah had once dated, she knew the day was not going to be fun-fun at all.

The gels were changed and everyone held their breath as Franco considered the effect. "No, no, it's all wrong." He raked his hair back and paced into the shot, where a giant toy plane sat in front of a backdrop of clouds. "Am I the only one who gets it? Can't you see what I'm looking for here?"

Apparently not, Delilah thought, sinking farther back into the shadows. As Franco continued his tirade, she lapsed into speculation over what had attracted her to him. Desperation, maybe? She'd had her ups and downs during her years in Hollywood, first trying to make it as an actress, but circumstances had shut that down just as she'd felt she'd been about to score a decent role. She'd made an income in production ever since—behind the camera instead of in front of it—and though she didn't mind the work, it hadn't really been part of her plan. And nowhere in all of these years had she found a soul mate, a lover or even a close male friend.

Yes, there were many things she loved about Southern California, but the men were not among them. She missed real men, the kind with calluses on their palms and muscles born of moving hay bales and riding a horse for ten hours a day instead of pumping iron at the local mirrored fitness center during a lunch break. There was something to be said for a cowboy who could pick you up and hold you as if you were light as a feather. A real man who wouldn't be caught dead wearing pink or sporting jewelry. A real man responded with hunger to a woman's touch.

Trying to tune out Franco's artistic tirade, she turned to the kitchenette of the studio and eyed the bagels and croissants reserved for the talent. There was a bowl of Jolly Rancher candies for everyone, but she sensed that the noise of unwrapping would put Franco over the edge right now. She was famished, but she would have to delay gratification, the story of her life these days.

Her boss, Martha, motioned to her, and Delilah snapped to. "The talent needs coffee," Martha said, motioning to the actors waiting behind a partition at the back of the studio.

Delilah nodded. Once upon a time she'd been the talent, and though she used to feel twinges of envy watching the actors run through their lines, now she wasn't sure she felt much of anything except a sense of time slipping by. Or, maybe that was her biological clock ticking . . . loudly.

She headed out to pick up the drinks. Her duties usually didn't include coffee runs, but they were short-handed and she'd been demoted on this commercial, thanks to Franco's power play. Whatever. She had started out in this business doing the scut work, and her ego could survive a few coffee runs. Now, she took orders from the Japanese talent whose sparse English somehow included the term "caramel macchiato," and headed out.

The exterior staircase of the Santa Monica building plunged her into sunshine, and she smiled to see that the marine layer had lifted so that she could see the ocean, a glimmering patch of blue in the distance. It was warm, even for Southern California. Like summer in December.

As she made her way down the stairs she took her cell off silent mode and saw half a dozen text messages from her siblings. Nell, Ricki and Colt had been bombarding her, with Ricki demanding that she come be the new wedding planner and Colt saying he'd buckled under so she should, too. Nell had chimed in, too, expounding on what fun it would be to have a sibling reunion. Only her younger brother, Tyler, and his wife, Jen, had left her alone.

Wedding planner. She supposed she could do it. She certainly possessed organizational skills. But she wasn't all that keen on helping out Pilar, who was a piece of work and always had been. And then there were the murders in Prairie Creek, and what appeared to be an arsonist who'd set fire to the Pioneer Church. Crazy.

In the coffee shop, Delilah placed her order, then set up a text to all of them, saying: If we're having a reunion, let's find a place without Pilar. Without a killer on the loose. Without snow. Sunny and 78 in SoCal!

Colt responded: It's always about you, Del.

She smiled and texted back: You got that right.

And then the phone rang. Ricki.

"Did you make your reservation yet?" her sister asked as soon as Delilah answered.

"Fat chance. I'm not a wedding planner. I got a job here, y'know, and I'm in the middle of a shoot."

"Those would be dangerous words if you were in my line of work. Which is part of my news. I'm now a deputy with the sheriff's office."

"Really. So you're definitely staying?"

"Looks like it. But here's the deal: you may not be a wedding planner, but you could do it in your sleep. You're made that way."

"Thanks for the vote of confidence, I think."

"There is no hope for this wedding without you. Pilar's floundering for a new venue, and she's convinced the whole thing needs to be postponed."

"And this is bad, why?"

"Dad doesn't want to wait. He wants Pilar, period. We're not going to stop him, so what the hell. I gotta go now, but we need you, girl. You're the best party planner I know. You can help Pilar pull this off."

"Pilar was a classmate, not a friend. And to help her marry my father? The ick factor is pretty high." The barista called out that her drinks were ready, and she popped on her headset and put the phone in her pocket.

"Dad wants her for his wife and you know how he is," Ricki added.

Oh, she knew. All the Dillingers seemed to have that bulldog trait, herself included.

"Look, I gotta get back to work," Ricki said again. "Call me later. I'll even meet you at the airport."

"Don't plan on it. I'm totally tied in here." She paused at the bottom of the stairs to shift the drink carrier in her arms. "We'll talk later."

"When you show up in Prairie Creek."

"Maybe," was all Delilah allowed.

Inside the studio, they had just finished a take and Franco

was sending the talent off-set while the fake airplane was sprayed to reduce the glare of the lights on its high-gloss patina. Delilah distributed the drinks and sipped the skinny latte she'd bought for herself. If she had half a brain, she would have picked up a yogurt or an energy bar, but she'd been too engrossed in conversation with her sister.

The Dillinger guilt was almost as bad as the Dillinger denial, and now her mind was stuck on Prairie Creek. She didn't think much of Pilar, but the fact that the Pioneer Church had burned to the ground was frightening. And with everything else that was going on, it was as if Alice had slipped through the looking glass again. Murders in Prairie Creek while she was safe here in Los Angeles?

Sipping her coffee, she *pinged* a fake poinsettia dangling from a garland someone had strung over the kitchenette area of the studio. Dust went flying. At home, the lodge would be lit up like a box of gems. She could see the lights, glowing on the pristine snow. Maybe they'd even hook up the horses and go out for a sleigh ride, in honor of Mom.

They finished another take, and Franco called for a ten-minute break. She smelled his approach before she saw him, his cologne a mixture of orange, cinnamon and jasmine. Not terrible, but not the way a real man should smell.

"I hear we have a dinner date," he said.

"We do?"

"Oh, Delilah, I meant to tell you." Martha squeezed her arm. "Franco needs you to accompany him to the Commercial Critics' Awards tonight. I told him you would drive."

"We'll leave from here, as soon as we wrap," Franco said. "Let's swing by my place first, so I can change."

A few dates did not make Delilah his piece of property. She stared at the sickly garland and fought back a surge of injustice. But it wasn't Franco's fault. He was who he was and she'd always known that. If it was anyone's fault, it was her own.

"There's been a change of plans," she heard herself say, as surprised as anyone that she'd spoken aloud. Disillusionment had been with her a long time. Too long, she realized.

"What?" Franco's voice revealed his annoyance.

Across the room, heads turned as the production crew listened. No one defied the director on a shoot. At least, no one who wanted to continue working in the biz. "I've got to get to the airport. My family back in Wyoming . . . there's been a sudden death."

Now the room went silent. *Details!* Their faces begged. *Give us details!*

She handed Franco her half-sipped latte, patted his shoulder and walked out of there, following one of the basic rules of the entertainment industry. Always leave them wanting more.

Ricki sat down at the wide pine table—the dinner table of her youth—and plotted her escape. After hours of searching in the snow, a family dinner by the roaring fire seemed just the thing. But Pilar was cranky, and Ricki had a million and one things to go over with Sam—things she couldn't really cover over the phone. Mrs. Mac had put out a nice spread with lamb chops and baked potatoes, but Ricki's mind was elsewhere. She kept thinking about the caves they had discovered; Kit Dillinger and her refusal to come to dinner as Babylon was in the final stages of her pregnancy and would probably foal tonight or tomorrow; and lastly, their doer, who may or may not have set fire to the Pioneer Church. The case was building, and though Sam said he could wait until after dinner, Ricki was impatient.

From his spot at the table Rourke was pouting but seemed

to have moved to Colt's side, which she could tell amused her brother but pissed off Pilar no end. Good.

"I have an announcement to make." Pilar put her crystal goblet down with all the pomp and circumstance of a queen. "The wedding is off."

"That's not what we decided a few hours ago," Ira growled, his patience thin.

"Our church has burned to the ground!" Pilar pressed a napkin to her mouth as her eyes flooded with tears. "The wedding's coming right up and there's nowhere to have it."

Ira slugged back some wine and grumbled, "We'll figure it out. There are a hell of a lot worse problems around here than this, Pilar."

Go, Dad. Ricki could see that her father was on edge, but the reaction around the dinner table was barely a ripple. Rourke shot his mom killing looks, Colton chewed steadily, Brook tore apart a roll and Sabrina was cutting her meat. No one wanted to get in on the fight.

Ira raked a hand through his silver hair. "I thought we agreed that we would have the wedding here. We got the biggest house in all of Prairie Creek."

"For the reception, Ira. That's what we planned. But I couldn't possibly stage the ceremony here, too. Where would we seat people? There's no aisle for my train."

Cutting into her meat, Ricki wondered why her father was attracted to a woman with the same emotional maturity as her fourteen-year-old daughter.

"How about the front staircase?" Sabrina suggested. "I always thought that would make a pretty entrance for a bride."

Pilar waved her off. "My gown was perfect in the church, but I can't wear it on that staircase. It'll snag at every turn."

"Screw the staircase . . ." Ira said. "You don't need an aisle to make a wedding legal. We're having it here."

"But we don't have the staff to switch over from rows of

seating to tables and chairs, and . . ." Pilar pressed trembling lips together as she reached for her ever-present glass of champagne, an affectation that began the same time as the wedding plans and looked to be developing into a habit. "I can't do this on my own. I knew I should have hired that wedding consultant from Jackson."

"Well, hire her now," Ira said.

"I can't. She's booked eight months out."

"Then hire someone else."

"Don't you see? There is no one."

Ricki's patience was tapped out, especially when she thought about Kit, waiting for new life in the stables after she'd just lost her mother. Meanwhile, here was Pilar boohooing about her disrupted wedding plans. In the next few days, when the medical examiner released Mia's body, there would be a funeral to plan. Now *that* was something to cry over.

Ricki let Pilar whimper and whine until she could stand no more. "Here's an idea. Delilah's coming tomorrow," she said. "She's done event planning before." Delilah had called and let her know she was on her way, though she wouldn't be thrilled that Ricki had nominated her to the whole family.

Colton scowled at her as he chewed.

Nope, Ricki thought. Not thrilled at all.

"Aunt Delilah's coming?" Brooklyn's eyes brightened. "Can she stay with us, Mom?"

"We'll see," Ricki said, turning around to Pilar, who was sitting back now, changing tack. "Delilah's got the know-how to pull this wedding off in six days, and do a good job of it, too. Besides, everyone else is on their way. Nell's flying in and Tyler and Jen are bringing the kids. If you're going to get married, you'd best do it while family is here."

Pilar sipped her champagne, considering. Well, at least the whimpering had stopped.

Ira turned to his bride. "I'll call Delilah after dinner, get her thinking about it. That way she can hit the ground running."

"She's always had an eye for design," Pilar said grudgingly.

"Yup." Ricki wiped her mouth and put her napkin on the table. "If you'll excuse me, I need to get into town and meet with Sam." She picked up her plate and pointed to Brooklyn. "Stay here at the main lodge until I get back, okay? I won't be long."

Snow whispered over his shoulders as he held the binoculars to his face and warmed to the scene beyond the wide windows of the mansion. A family gathering, all the Dillingers basking in the warm yellow light of the big dining room. Such a handsome family Ira Dillinger had there, but no one was crying for Mia Collins? How quickly they forgot the dearly departed.

Although dangerously close to the lodge, he was well hidden in darkness while they moved like actors on a stage, on display for him to dissect with his eyes.

One at a time, one at a time, he reminded himself. He didn't want to get greedy and ruin the plan. And while the flock might be hard to control, it was so easy to bring a single lamb to the slaughter.

Reaching into the pocket of his pants, he fingered the sharp edges of the teeth. His charms. Mia's tooth had been harder to extract; surprisingly deep roots for such a shallow person. But he had it now, a fat molar to round out his collection.

He studied the women behind the window and wondered who would be the next. As his hand moved down, he felt the erection jutted up near the clicking teeth. Smiling, he seared his sharp eyes through to the women in the display case.

Pilar Larson, Ira's prize, with round breasts and the black

hair of a vixen. He would do evil things to her, and she would lap up every abuse like a thirsty cat. Ricki, the tough one, strong and fierce as her flaming red hair, moved into the kitchen. He would have her moving under him like a sleek gazelle. Sabrina, the sunshiny vet. It would be easy to trap her in the shadowy barn one night, press her into the corner until she squealed like a pig.

And then there were the young ones. Kit, the missing one, the wild child who would submit to his glimmering blade. And Brook, a kitten-girl, a rosebud ready to be plucked. Would young blood be sweeter?

He would find out. He would have his taste.

Fat flakes danced in the air as Ricki pulled into the parking lot at the office. She hoped this new snow wouldn't be a problem for her sisters, both flying in tomorrow.

"Hey, there, Ricki." In his white suspenders and red Henley shirt, Chet Norcross looked like Father Christmas himself.

"Merry Christmas," Ricki said, remembering Chet as Mr. Norcross, her high school civics teacher. "You're looking festive."

The dispatcher adjusted the mouthpiece of the cordless device sprouting from his thick, snow-white hair and beard. "My wife and I are big fans of Christmas, and I like to play up the Santa angle." His chair swiveled toward her and she saw that he had gained weight over the years. Yup, that belly was like a bowlful of jelly. "Welcome to our little family. I heard you hit the ground running, already supervised a search party out on the prairie."

"I did. I was hoping to bring Sam . . . the sheriff, up to speed on it. Is he around?"

"Back in his office. I think he's been working the case nonstop since the fire last night. Maybe you can talk some sense into him, get him to sleep. We got a room with some bunks in the back if he really can't tear himself away."

Ricki knew how a homicide could drive a person day and night, fill your thoughts and haunt your dreams. "I don't think I have any sway with him, but we'll see." The precinct was quiet, with lights off in the break room and interrogation room. She headed down the hall and knocked on Sam's half-open door. "Sheriff?"

His head was down, resting on folded arms. Knowing Sam, he had to be near exhaustion to pass out at his desk. She stood there for a moment, longing to smooth down his dark hair and massage his shoulders. The instinct was more maternal than sexual, but the sexual part definitely was there, too.

"Just resting my eyes," he said without moving.

"You might want to consider resting your eyes back in the bunk room . . . or even at home, where you can get decent sleep. Fuel the brain. Keep the pistons firing."

He lifted his head, his eyes half-closed. "Too much going on." Straightening, he sat tall, looking professional once again in his navy fleece. "So Kit showed you some caves, where he seemed to be hiding out. Tell me about it."

"That's pretty scary—you snapping out of sleep to the facts of the case." She took a seat in the chair facing his desk. "Do you always do that?"

"I don't always have two homicides to solve. So tell me about the caves."

"Colt and I knew the general location, of course. Davis, too. But Kit knew exactly how to find the paths, even with the snow. She told us she's used the caves for shelter at times, but not recently. Said she's been staying in a little shed in the woods since the snow started. That maintenance shed down by the creek." Ricki immediately felt anxious. Kit had spurned Ricki's attempts to help her, but she couldn't help worrying about her. "One of the caves had signs that it had been used recently," she went on. "A fire ring. Bloodstains, which might be animal. And a deer carcass, partly skinned with its throat slashed."

Sam rubbed his chin, dark with stubble. She'd bet that he really hadn't gone home all day. "Maybe a hunter used the cave?"

"And left his prize deer there? I don't know any hunter in this area that would leave behind enough meat to feed his family for a year. And when I mentioned how it was carved up that way, partially skinned, Sabrina and Colton said something about a coyote that had been skinned and abandoned on the Rocking D. Did you hear about that?"

"No, but ranchers kill coyotes and mountain lions all the time."

"But this was different. Skinned like the other corpses. Sabrina took it in to her lab for a closer look and she said someone had even cut out a tooth."

Sam squinted at her. "A tooth?"

When she nodded, he turned to his monitor and started clicking the mouse. "Then we have a pattern here," he said grimly. "The preliminary report from the ME showed that crude tooth extractions were performed on Barstow and Collins. In Mia's case, it was a molar and the killer had to dig deep."

Adrenaline tingled in her veins—a mixture of "aha" and horror—as she jumped up and leaned over his desk to view the report. "He's taking a tooth, one from each of his victims."

"That assumes that Barstow and Collins were killed by the same person who skinned the coyote and deer," he said.

"Well?"

He ran his knuckles over his chin and nodded. "Seems likely."

"I started to suspect this when I saw that Barstow and Collins were carved up in the same way. But now, with these animals and the missing teeth, I feel him breathing down our necks. He's out there, Sam. We've got a serial killer in Prairie Creek. A twisted one, with some wicked knife skills."

"Those teeth . . ."

"They're trophies. Trinkets. Maybe he keeps them in jars. Maybe he's stringing them into a necklace."

Sam let out a heavy breath. "Lot of folks in these parts know how to skin and quarter an animal. It's a matter of survival. But this guy's an expert."

"Not just experienced. Trained. When I saw Mia Collins all carved up, it made me think of my biology class at Wyoming State. You know, in the lab when they slice off a cat's skin and pin it back. Those perfect cuts so you can see the muscles and bone . . ."

"Maybe a surgeon, or taxidermist," he suggested.

"Or a butcher. A meat cutter knows anatomy . . . and talk about knife skills."

"Maybe he's just passing through. Serial killers wander."

"Maybe," Ricki agreed. Neither one of them said anything for a moment. Looking at him, Ricki felt a surge of energy. Tossing out ideas with Sam got her mind spinning, her investigative juices flowing. They were on the same wavelength.

He pulled out a notepad. "Let's get a list of possibles. Persons of interest. Surgeons, doctors, butchers . . ."

"Does Clyde Denowski still do taxidermy?" she asked.

"He's the only one that I know of within a hundred miles."

"And how about Dodge Miller? He used to have that expensive butcher shop off Main Street."

"Had to close. With the bad economy, people couldn't afford expensive cuts of meat at his prices. Most people buy their meat at that wholesale store in Lander."

"So what happened to Dodge?"

"He's working at the wholesale store now, always complains about it when I see him. Hates the drive out to Lander."

"Maybe we should talk to him," Ricki said.

Sam was nodding. "First thing tomorrow." He stretched and yawned. "I'd do it now, but most people don't take kindly to having the sheriff drop in this late at night. That's okay. I've got to go over these reports more closely."

"Let me know when the information comes back from forensics," Ricki said.

"Will do. It could be that the place was used by some hunters, but from the smell, I don't think so. I wouldn't be surprised if our killer moves from place to place, staying ahead of anyone who might be out there. Those acres are fairly deserted, but you've always got stray cattle and ranch hands, as well as the odd wanderer like Kit Dillinger."

She thought hard for a moment, knowing she needed to talk to him about her failure to keep Kit contained. "One of these days Kit's going to have to come back to earth long enough to plan her mother's funeral. As far as protecting her, it's not easy. She wants to be near the animals and she's hanging out at the stables. I can't get her to come back."

"Kit could be the killer's next target. She'll be able to roam free again someday, but not right now."

"Well, good luck with that. Maybe she'll believe that if she hears it from you. Or from Davis. She respects him. And he seems really worried about her. There's something weird there . . . can't put my finger on it. Can you ask your brother about it?"

"Apparently my brother can't be trusted."

"Say what?"

"I drove out to the Rocking D just after dawn to talk with him. I wanted the names of his recent ranch hands. Routine part of the investigation. He was in a foul mood, but now that I hear about the coyote, I know he's holding something back. He didn't say a word about it."

Ricki thought back to Davis's discomfort in the caves. "You need to talk to him again."

"I have half a mind to arrest him for obstructing justice."

"Spoken as a bossy big brother. I know because I have one." Her cell phone buzzed in her jacket pocket. "But there comes a point when age is no longer the great dictator." She glanced at her phone. "It's Brook. Sorry." She took the call. "Hey, honey. I'm right in the middle of something."

"When are you coming home?" Brook's voice was shaky.

Ricki was on her feet. "What's wrong?"

"Pilar sent me home. She said I'd be fine if I locked the door. So now I'm here alone with Rudolph and . . . I thought I heard something out by the woodpile."

"Good God." When Sam looked up, she said tersely, "Pilar booted Brook out and she's alone at the foreman's house." She covered her phone. "She thinks she hears someone outside."

Sam leapt up and grabbed his jacket. "Let's go."

Ricki followed him out the door, phone pressed to her ear. "Did you lock the door behind you?" And had she locked the kitchen window? She always opened it when she cooked bacon and she was pretty sure Kit had escaped through it.

"Of course I did. Why did Pilar do that to me?"

"I'll have a talk with her. Do you want to go back to the lodge? I'll have Grandpa come get you."

"No." Her voice cracked. "I'm too scared to go out in the dark, and I'm not opening the door to anyone."

"Okay." Ricki climbed into Sam's Jeep, a knot in her throat. She told herself her daughter would probably be fine, that it was merely Brook's vivid imagination, but her galloping heart wasn't listening.

What was the noise that Brook had heard? The sound of *him* trying to get into the house?

"I'm on my way," she said tautly. "Stay on the phone. Just keep talking to me."

Chapter Seventeen

With lights flashing, Sam sped down the state road, ignoring the snow that shimmered in the headlights. As he listened to Ricki's end of the conversation, he considered the choice words he would have for Pilar Larson, sending Brook out alone after dark when there was a killer at large. Foolish. Irresponsible. Reprehensible.

He had no patience for people who didn't take care of their own family. Maybe he wasn't winning any awards as father of the year, doing the long-distance parenting thing, but he made sure his daughter, Ava, got what she needed. Hearing the strain in Ricki's voice, he hoped to God Brook was safe. She was priority one.

And once he was out at the ranch, he'd have some face time with his brother. Davis had been holding back, and Sam wanted to know why. Sam wouldn't stop till he cut through to the truth.

"Stay calm," Ricki told her daughter. "Try to watch TV. One of those housewife shows."

Sam could hear the strain in Ricki's voice; she was right to worry. The image of bare bone and muscle and skin curling at the edges flashed in his mind, and he tamped it down, focusing on the road.

"You want to be able to hear if there are any more sounds? That's actually a good idea. Where are you hiding? The closet. I hear Rudolph there. Yes, I've heard those stories of animals that have saved people's lives. Okay, honey. You just stay put. We'll be there in a flash."

Ricki was still talking with Brook when they came to the turnoff for the Rocking D. He slowed the vehicle as they headed toward the main gates. He could tell Ricki was anxious, but she put up a good front for her daughter.

The foreman's cabin in sight, he turned to Ricki and mouthed: "You have a gun?"

She pressed the phone to her jacket and reached for the small five-shot clipped to her belt. "My off-duty pistol. It'll scare Brook's socks off if she sees it."

"Then don't let her see it." He drew his gun. "I'll clear the interior with you, then check outside. She said she heard something by the woodpile, right?"

"Yes. The wood's stacked under the living room window, on the west side."

That pile needed to be moved—too combustible to sit against the house—but they could work on that later.

"We're here, honey. I'm just unlocking the door, and Sam and I are going to search the place when we get inside."

The door open, they moved in one at a time, pressed against walls, clearing the place, room by room. Standard defensive tactics, and Ricki played them well, like a seasoned dance partner who signaled right or left or blinked when it was time to swing around. At times like this, Sam felt like he'd had Ricki beside him all his life.

"Brook?" Ricki called into the small bedroom. When the girl answered, Sam headed outside to check around the house. He shined his flashlight on the woodpile, which seemed to be intact. Could have been an animal burrowing in. Another reason you didn't want a stack of wood leaning against your house.

Inside, he found Ricki hugging her daughter. "I'm so proud of you," she said. "It was really smart to hide in the closet."

"Don't leave me here alone again, Mom."

Ricki's mouth tightened. "You were supposed to stay at the big lodge. Pilar is such a—piece of work." She had to bite back what she really wanted to say.

Brook pulled her zebra print blanket tighter over her shoulders. "Where's Kit?"

"At the stables," Ricki said, hoping it was true.

"I'm going to head over there now," Sam said, tucking his flashlight under his arm. "I think you and your mom should be sleeping up at the big lodge. Don't they have some spare rooms up there?"

"Only about half a dozen," Ricki said. "You're right. It's not safe for Brook to be sleeping here alone while I'm out and about doing police work." Again, she hugged her still-shivering daughter. "Why don't you grab some stuff and put your boots on."

Brook looked up at Sam. "Can I bring Rudolph?"

Ricki opened her mouth to say yes, then stopped herself. She didn't want to weaken her position when she took on Pilar. "We'll leave him for now, but he'll be fine. I promise."

Brook seemed about to argue, but apparently her fear was too great and she simply nodded jerkily.

"You're safer up there," Sam told her. "We don't want to take any chances."

There was a meow, and Brook bent down and scooped the white kitten into her arms. "Will you miss me?"

As Brook took the kitten off to gather her things, Ricki clapped a hand on Sam's shoulder to steady herself. "Nothing is so scary as thinking your kid is in jeopardy."

Sam rubbed her back—a move meant to comfort, though the contact charged him up in a way that didn't seem quite right for a man on duty. "She's going to be fine."

He dropped his hand away when Brook returned. He would have to learn to keep it to himself. As he and Ricki shifted Brook's pillow and clothes up to the lodge on the hill, Brook was surprisingly polite and cooperative for a kid her age. Pilar was in bed when they arrived, but Ricki gave Ira a piece of her mind, and Sam followed it up with a stern warning to keep the doors locked and look after his granddaughter.

"I'll lock the doors and turn on the alarm," Ira agreed. "But I've got a cabinet full of guns, and I always keep a revolver upstairs beside the bed, just in case."

Sam frowned. "Mind you don't shoot a family member with that." Domestic disputes comprised the majority of the shootings in Prairie Creek. "And be careful. You've got a child in the house. Have you familiarized Rourke with guns? Does he know how to shoot?"

"Hell, no. Pilar's mollycoddled him," Ira grumbled, "but I'll get him going." Then he glared balefully at Ricki. "I talked to Delilah. She's no wedding planner."

"I know," Ricki said, exasperated, "but she's a planner, at least."

He waved her off with a dismissive hand and Sam was amused to see Ricki roll her eyes after his back was turned.

After Brook headed upstairs, Sam thought he'd be saying good night, but Ricki told him she was coming along to the stables. "I won't sleep until I know Kit is okay."

Sam couldn't help thinking it would be nice to have her along.

When they entered the stables they saw the horses had been fed and settled in their stalls for the night, but there was no sign of either Kit or Davis. Ricki looked in on the pregnant mare; she was resting comfortably for the moment, it appeared. Sam tried to reach Davis on his cell. "No luck," he told Ricki.

"Well, we've got two horses missing, and one of them is

Luna, his mount, so he may be out there, out of range of cell service. I'm hoping Kit is with him."

"Does he usually work this late at night?" Sam asked.

"Sometimes. As long as everything gets taken care of, nobody really cares what hours he works."

They decided to ride out and follow the tracks leading away from the stables. Ricki showed him the tack room, and he lifted two saddles onto horses she brought over. Working together, they had the two horses ready to ride in a few minutes.

The wind had died down, and snowflakes lingered in the air like a white mist. He could get used to this, having Ricki by his side. He sat high on his mount as she pointed to the tracks in the fresh snow.

"Two sets of tracks, heading down toward Copper Woods. I hope that's our mark," Ricki said.

"You have to wonder why Kit would go out in this storm. Where the hell is she going?"

"Nobody knows what she does out on the prairie, or exactly where she stays. She just wanders, and as long as she doesn't hurt the stock, Dad doesn't mind."

"Where was she the night of the church fire?" Sam mused aloud. "When her mother was killed?"

Ricki stared at the fields of white as their horses plodded down the trail. "You think Kit might be the killer?" Her skeptical tone indicated that she thought he was way off base.

"We need to consider everybody. That's all I'm sayin'. Everyone knows she and Mia never got along. And she's been in the vicinity of both murders."

Snow collected on the Stetson she'd grabbed from the barn, and there was something about the contrast of Ricki's soft, feminine face under a carved, manly hat that appealed to him.

"I don't suppose you tracked too many people in New York on horseback," he observed.

"Try none. They use the mounted police mostly for crowd control and parades."

He nodded, suddenly sober. "It's a dark day in Prairie Creek when a kid like Brook isn't safe at home alone." He didn't want to think about the things that had happened on his watch. They needed to end the killing, stop the predator. "We've got to get this guy."

"Damn straight."

Their words fell off and the only sound was the tapping of icy snowflakes on their hats. A companionable silence, Sam thought as he stole a look over at her. Yeah, he could definitely get used to this.

Concealed by a snow-covered pine, Davis watched her dance in the snow and felt a growing alarm. Was Kit a killer? Had animal instinct taken over, defying the laws of man? To leave tonight while Babylon drew closer to birth meant she had something to do that was pretty damn important.

Kit was so far afield . . . so out there.

Davis Featherstone knew how it felt to live on the outside. Cast out from the safety of a family. Outside the circle of the law.

When he was seventeen, right around Kit's age, he'd pushed all the limits. Beer and girls and weed. He'd gambled away the few bits he could scrape together. He'd been at the center of plenty of barroom brawls, drunk out of his mind. Wasted and hungry. Surly with the teachers who wanted respect for their useless knowledge. At his best, he was a decent ranch hand. At his worst, he was a common criminal.

One night, feeling his oats, he'd stolen a shiny new truck and made a run for Vegas. He hadn't gotten too far when the cops found him. The cops had tossed him into jail for grand theft auto. But the vehicle's owner had demanded that the charges be dropped. He claimed that the truck had been a loan to the kid.

Ira Dillinger was the owner of that truck. He'd saved Davis from doing big-time in a state prison. He'd also given him steady work as a ranch hand and a place to stay in the bunkhouse, away from the violence at home. The boss had saved Davis's life, but no one had been able to reach Kit in the same way.

She was one of a kind. A snowflake.

Davis looked back in the shadowed forest, checking Luna, who waited quietly where he'd tied her to a tree. Part of him felt like a cad for spying on Kit; the other part wanted to sweep her up on his horse and gallop back to safety.

But so far, he'd taken the easy out, just hanging back in the trees. He watched her sway in the falling snow, dancing around the same tree where the coyote had been abandoned. What was it about this spot near Copper Woods? And what was in that white mound, now dusted with snow? *Another coyote?*

Something in her hands sparkled like an icicle when she held them up in the snow. What was it? She moved toward the white mound, then plunged her hands in.

Was she trying to bury the shiny object?

He had seen enough . . . maybe too much. He came forward, emerging from the cover of trees.

"Kit."

Lost in another world, she leaned forward, her hands submerged in snow.

"Kit." He moved closer, calling her until she jerked up and snapped her head toward him.

"Davis?" Her eyes were full of sorrow, her cheeks tracked with tears. The sight of her tweaked a chord of emotion deep inside him, plucking at feelings he'd thought had died with his unhappy childhood. "What are you doing here?"

"Kit, what is this?" When she didn't answer, he said, "I

saw you here earlier this week with that coyote. I didn't want to say anything when we came across that deer in the cave today, carved up the same way, but I saw you doing this ritual with the coyote carcass. Right here, with the coyote against this same tree. Dancing the same dance."

She pulled her hands from the snow mound, rolled back on her haunches and wiped her gloves. "This is a sky tree. The coyote was dead so I brought him here to let his spirit rise to the sky."

"The coyote wasn't the first time I saw you with a skinned animal." He hated pinning her down—it was torture for a free spirit like her—but it had to be done. "Last summer . . . remember when I ran into your camp down by the meadows? There was a skinned lamb hanging from a tree."

She stared at him. "I ate it. Roasted it over the fire. I was hungry."

"You should have come to me. Mrs. Mac will feed you any time, you know that. You can't just kill a lamb."

Kit rose to her full height, faced him. "I didn't. Mountain lions were attacking him. They did the damage. I scared them off, but it was too late for the lamb." She rubbed her gloved hands together, as if kindling a fire. "That wasn't a good day."

Davis tipped his hat back, not sure what to think anymore. He didn't think Kit was lying to him—there wasn't an ounce of dishonesty in this girl—but it was impossible to get a solid answer out of her.

Her eyebrows rose over her smudged face. "I'll pay Ira Dillinger back. I have some money buried over by—"

"It's not the money," he interrupted. "It was probably a Kincaid lamb, anyway. But, Kit, what is all this?" He looked toward the white mound. "Another carcass?"

"No . . . it's stuff that belonged to my mom." She reached into the snow and removed a glass prism, and then lifted a white trash bag from the snow, shaking out a thick pelt of brown fur. "My father gave it to her," she said.

"Ahh . . . Why are you burying them here?"

"These are what she valued. They need to be buried here, so her spirit can rise to the sky." She then reached into her boot and pulled out a hunting knife, sleek and sharp. A two-inch blade, better for precision cutting. "I don't hurt animals. I try to help them."

"What about people?" he had to ask.

"I don't hurt them either."

She was right. She was as she'd always been. He'd let himself think terrible thoughts because he'd been too scared for her. "I know. But people make judgments. They jump to conclusions."

"They're going to think I killed my own mother because I'm good with a knife?" she said incredulously.

"It's possible."

"They'll be wrong."

"We'll have to make them see that."

Ricki and Sam stood watching from the woods as snow whispered through the branches overhead.

"Oh my God," she breathed. "Is that a knife?"

"Wait," Sam said, putting a hand on her arm.

At that moment Kit looked over at them. "Who's there?" she demanded.

As Ricki and Sam stepped out, Davis scowled at them. "Are you kidding me? Even out here, I can't be left alone."

"We were looking for Kit," Sam said, facing his brother squarely. "What's your problem?"

"Leave Kit alone," Davis snarled.

"What is this stuff?" Ricki asked, pulling up the prism and fur.

"Put them back," Kit said tautly, and Ricki, meeting the girl's gaze, set the items back on the snow.

"Is somebody gonna tell me about this?" Sam asked.

Davis looked to Kit, then back to his brother. "It's too cold out here for the whole story. We'll go back to the stables. Check on Babylon."

"Then come to my place," Ricki said. "It's warmer."

After a moment, both Kit and Davis nodded curtly.

Forty-five minutes later, after a stop at the stables to see Babylon, the four of them convened at the foreman's house. Ricki tried to keep quiet while Sam did the talking. His voice was low and nonjudgmental and sexy as hell, though it seemed to annoy Davis. She sensed a bit of bad blood between the two of them, though they remained civil.

Davis and Ricki shared the sofa while Kit insisted on sitting on the floor. Leaning against the fat sofa arm, Ricki warmed even more to Kit as Davis told the story of how he had worried that Kit's firsthand knowledge of the area and her knife skills would make her a suspect in the killings. "I didn't know the coyote had been all carved up when she found it," Davis said, raking back his dark hair. "She just took it to the sky tree, trying to do the right thing for its spirit."

Sam's voice was level, reserving judgment. "To carve up a human body like something in an anatomy textbook, that takes skill."

"I cut the throat of a mountain lion caught in a trap once," Kit said. "He was howling in pain. I had to do it."

It was a roundabout way of professing her innocence, but Ricki believed her completely. As Sam continued the questioning, Ricki tuned out the voices and focused on her, the animal whisperer who understood creatures so well but had no one to understand her. Her hair and eyes were so distinctively Dillinger, and yet she lived a world apart, self-exiled.

Did she ever get lonely? There was definitely grit under those round eyes and long fingers, but there was also a good heart. Ricki believed her.

"So . . ." Sam summed things up. "You were burying the crystal and fur coat as a sort of memorial to Mia."

She nodded, then got to her feet, dusting off the seat of her pants.

"Where are you going?" Ricki asked.

"The stables."

"You need to stay with someone," Sam said sternly, "for your own protection."

"Stay here," Ricki offered. "Brook's up at the main house. You can have her bed."

"I'll be at the stables with Babylon," Kit said firmly.

"I'll go with her," Davis said. "She won't be alone."

Sam looked at his brother, then at Kit, then back at his brother. Whatever he was thinking he kept to himself as he turned to Ricki. "Then I'll walk you up to the lodge."

As Kit and Davis headed out the door, Ricki turned to Sam. Although exhaustion shaded his face, there was something distinctively sexy about the smoky shadows over his dark eyes. "I'm a deputy. I've got two loaded guns and a belly full of vitriol for any intruder who wakes me up before sunrise. And you're the one who didn't sleep last night. Why don't you stay here? It'll save you driving back into town through all that snow. And you can protect me, like the big, bad-ass sheriff that you are."

He rubbed the back of his neck. "I would laugh, but I'm just too tired."

"Then stay. Here." She took his arm and guided him to the back of the house. "Let me show you to your room, sir."

He snorted, then opened his eyes wide when he saw her bedroom with a painting of the prairie on the wall and the double bed with its pale blue comforter. "Your bed? No, Ricki. I'll stay, but give me the second bedroom."

“Here’s the thing about that,” she said, escorting him into her room. “I don’t really know how to explain to my teenaged daughter that a thirty-something man slept in her bed. It seems like something that would be good for years of therapy.”

“Ahhh . . . didn’t think about that.”

“Just promise me you’ll take your boots off first,” Ricki said briskly. “I can’t stomach the idea of boots in my bed.”

Sam sat on the edge of the bed and leaned down to untie his boots. “I should have taken them off at the door. That’s what happens when a man lives alone. You revert back to the old bunkhouse manners.”

The sight of Sam sitting on her bed, stripping down to his stocking feet was just too homey and familiar; it sent a thrill through Ricki’s nether regions. Damn, the man looked good. It was one of those pinch-me-I’m-dreaming moments, and she sorely wanted to tackle him down to a prone position and tangle in the covers with him.

But that probably wasn’t a good idea. No, she needed to choose option B, Brook’s bed.

“Okay, then.” Her palms were sweating, and she wiped them on her jeans, trying to appear casual. As if she put a gorgeous man to bed in her room every night. “There are towels and soap and stuff in the bathroom, and help yourself to anything you want in the fridge.”

“Thanks.” He stood up, tall and solid and only inches away from her. “But I think I’ll just go to bed.”

She could feel the heat of his body through her sweater. “Good night.”

That was her exit line, but she couldn’t move her feet. And why was he standing so close? Was that a signal? An invitation? Because the answer had to be no, though every nerve ending in her body was shrieking yes.

“Good night.” He leaned down and kissed her cheek, his lips like a brand.

That did it. She tipped her face up to him and pressed her lips to his, testing. She couldn't help herself.

He hesitated for a heartbreaking moment, then they were kissing, deep, thorough kisses that sent hormones surging, her body pressed to his.

Want pulsed inside her, a steady, hot burn fueled by the erection she felt straining against his jeans. There was an electric thrill at the knowledge that he wanted her, too. She held her body against his, her tender softness embracing his hardness. He was all muscle and bone, but she fit against him like a glove. She was malleable and soft, and as she melted against him, she savored the way that the spaces between them could be so easily filled.

Physically, they would work well together.

It was the emotional, social bond that would bite them both in the ass.

He slid a hand up under her sweater, cupped a breast and they both groaned in pleasure. This was not high school. This was not two amateurs fumbling around in the dark. But that didn't diminish the tingling pleasure of it all, the sweet sip of the giant cup that neither of them were ready to imbibe in.

Not just yet.

But with her eyes closed and his hand caressing her breast and her hands running over the planes of his muscular body, she could allow herself to forget all the things that kept them apart.

Just for one sweet minute.

Chapter Eighteen

Despite the obvious limitations of the top bunk, Ricki slept well knowing Sam was in the next room. In the morning, she rolled over and caught the savory smell of brewing coffee. Heaven on earth.

She stared at the ceiling and pressed a finger to her lips, as if she could trace the remnants of the kisses. Sam was a good kisser, but that had been no surprise. Sam and Colt were the same age, and so she'd had a close-up view of the many loves of Sam Featherstone as he and her brother skated through high school. She'd always figured that a guy who could land so many pretty girls had to have some secret skills in the dark.

And last night—finally!—she'd been the recipient of his legendary sumptuous lips, warm hands and hard body. Just a short make-out session that left them both wanting more, but still, it had been the fulfillment of a childhood crush—a crush that was quickly blossoming into a full-blown attraction. She was going to have to tone things down now. She and Sam couldn't get involved. She had a daughter to raise, as did he, and he was dead set against mixing business and pleasure. But there was nothing to say she couldn't enjoy having him here, making a pot of coffee in her kitchen.

As she slid out of the bunk and reached for her robe, she heard voices.

"Can you teach me how to shoot?" came the sprightly voice. Brook? What was she doing here? When was she ever out of bed before nine A.M.? Ricki was going to kill Pilar if she'd kicked her daughter out again.

"I could show you a few things." Sam sounded friendly, comfortable. "But you need to ask your mom. She's a good shot. When we were kids, she usually managed to outscore me and your Uncle Colt in target practice."

"Good morning." Ricki found Sam at the kitchen table with her laptop, while Brook leaned against the counter holding a tall glass of orange juice.

"Morning. Hope you don't mind, I jumped on your computer to access my e-mail."

"Go for it," Ricki said, thinking how natural Sam looked sitting at her kitchen table. She stepped close to Brook to get a mug from the cabinet. "Is this my daughter I see, up and about before noon?" Brook looked so sweet, with her hair pulled back and wisps curling at the edge of her face. Ricki was tempted to kiss her, but wasn't sure if that would be welcome.

"Pilar got everyone out of bed. There's an army of ladies attacking the lodge, wiping down walls and vacuuming. I couldn't wait to get out."

"Did she at least have Grandpa walk you down here?" Ricki asked, pouring coffee.

"Mom! You can see this house from their kitchen windows. And Pilar said she's sending Rourke down later. She wants me to watch him while she goes into town to take care of some wedding stuff."

Ricki shook her head. "I won't be here, and you can't be alone here, not with everything that's going on. You can do it up at the lodge."

"She said she'd pay me! And I told you, the cleaning ladies are there. Don't ruin this for me."

"How about out in the barn? Grandpa could give you a riding lesson."

"Grandpa has meetings all day. He told me you need to do an airport run to pick up Aunt Delilah."

"I can't." Ricki sighed. A little support from the family would have been nice. "I need to work."

"I wish I could go along to pick up Aunt Delilah, but I have to watch Rourke," Brook said, but she didn't sound all that upset. Whether Brook admitted it or not, she liked Pilar's son.

"Maybe Colt can do it." Ricki grabbed her cell phone and ducked into the bedroom. "Let me call him." Quickly she lined Colton up for the airport run. He promised to call Ira and straighten it all out, with a word of warning that it still wasn't safe to send his grandson outside on his own. Then she hit the bathroom for a quick shower.

When she emerged twenty minutes later, showered and dressed, Brook was finishing off a plate of cheesy eggs and Sam was studying the laptop screen, a sober expression on his face.

"We saved some bacon and eggs for you," he said. "Plate's in the oven."

"Thanks."

"The eggs are good, Mom. You need to try Sam's recipe," Brook said.

He shrugged. "Onion powder."

"Mmm. Smells good." Using a towel, she retrieved the warm plate and set it on the table beside Sam. "What's the latest?"

"Initial reports are back from the ME and the state crime lab," he said. "You might want to finish eating first."

"Gross." Brook scooted her chair back, brought her dish to the sink and headed off.

"She's a good kid," Sam said when Brook was out of range.

Ricki swallowed a mouthful of creamy eggs. "This move

has been hard for her, but like it or not, we had to get out of there. Her father is dabbling in the drug scene, and Brook was beginning to hang with some kids in crisis."

"Aren't all kids in crisis?"

"If you expect that, you'll never be disappointed." She popped the last strip of bacon into her mouth and took her plate to the sink. "Okay, I'm ready for the hard stuff. Did the crime lab find any links between the cave and Amber Barstow?"

"They did." He turned the screen to her. "I've had some time to sift through it, and I think this is a good time to frame our investigation." He'd highlighted a few lines.

"So, it was Amber Barstow's blood in the cave. He must've kept her there for a while."

"The bloodstains in the shed were hers, too. And it looks like those empty bags held blue tarps. The same blue fibers were found in the shed and on Barstow's body."

"So we know where he was holed up—on Dillinger and Kincaid land. And from there, he went into town, to Mia's place." A tingle ran down her spine at the thought of him being there, so near. "It's like he's been breathing down our necks."

"He was close." The kitchen light shone on Sam's glossy dark hair. "I wonder why."

"The Rocking D is a good half hour from Big Bart's. Certainly not geographically desirable." Ricki took a sip of coffee. "Do you think he's got a vendetta? Anti-rancher?"

Sam shook his head. "Look at the two women he killed. If we're looking at one killer, why Amber Barstow, a stranger? And then Mia? We don't have any prints at all to link the cave or shed to Mia Collins's house."

"Footprints?"

"We got clear ones from the shed and Collins's house. My instincts say it's the same guy, but right now we need to keep it open." He changed the screen. "The ME's report on the two corpses shows plenty of similarities between the killings. In both cases the cause of death was blood loss from a severed neck."

Ricki stared at the report. What a horrifying way to go, looking into the eyes of your killer.

"The two animals and the two victims all had a single tooth cut out. And the medical examiner said the mutilation of the skin was distinctive in both cases. See here?" Sam highlighted a line in the report. "They say Mia's injuries are consistent with Amber Barstow's."

"Another link between the two killings."

"Like I said, I think it's the same guy, but it's not definitive." He clicked to another screen. "Here's a list of the patrons at Big Bart's the night that Amber Barstow was seen there. This isn't everyone, of course. Just customers who paid by credit card or personal check."

Ricki scanned the list. "Two of the Kincaids were there. Mariah and Blair."

"But the time stamp for them appears to be earlier than when Amber was there. Katrina's checking the whole list, but let's pull out the ones that fall into the right window."

"Good idea," she said.

"Looks like Doc Farley was there. Cashed out late. What sticks out is that he knew we were looking for witnesses from that night, but he didn't come forward."

"That's not like Doc." Stuart Farley had taken care of the Dillinger family since before Ricki was born. "Too drunk to remember?"

"The bartender doesn't think so. But he does remember that Doc was there with a woman. Not his wife."

Ricki felt a stab of compassion for Nora Farley. "So . . . how do you want to handle it?"

"We're going to be talking to him anyway, seeing as how the mutilations of our two victims seem to be the work of a professional. I plan to see him this morning. I'll be discreet."

That was one great thing about Sam; he knew how to keep things quiet. Ricki considered other angles that needed to be pursued. "I want to have a chat with Sabrina and Antonia over at the veterinary clinic since we got our information secondhand about the coyote's extracted tooth. We need their statements to go on the record."

"Good," Sam said.

"Has anyone talked to the last people in the church the day of the fire?" Ricki asked. "Pilar and Emma Kincaid?"

"My staff was turned inside-out yesterday, split up in search parties," Sam told her.

"How about I take care of it first thing?"

"Okay. See what you can find out and I'll see you at the town hall at noon."

"Town hall?" She pushed back the curls on her forehead.

"Today is the mayor's Christmas party, and everyone in our office attends."

"Is that the party with the tree-decorating competition? And Santa comes to give toys to the kids?"

"That's the one. You think Brook would like a toy?"

"Fat chance, but Rourke might, if it's the right one." She took a sip of coffee and said, "See there? We may have just found the perfect activity for him today."

An hour or so later, Sam thanked Maddie, Doc Farley's receptionist, who had set him up in an exam room so that he and Doc could talk privately. If he'd gleaned anything from working in Prairie Creek for nine years, he'd learned how easy it was to fire up a rumor and how difficult it was to squash it.

He took a seat on the chair instead of the exam table. A minute later, there was a knock on the door and Doc Farley entered, cordial and friendly. "What can I do for you,

Sam?" The doctor's hair was thick as ever, but graying over a distinct brow ridge, which gave him an air of dignity.

"I just wanted to get in to talk to you without raising eyebrows all over town."

Doc closed Sam's file and laid it on the exam table. "What's this about?"

"Your Saturday night out at Big Bart's, Thanksgiving weekend. As the bartender recollects, Nora wasn't with you."

Farley's eyebrows rose. "What's that supposed to mean, Sheriff?"

"I'm not trying to butt into your business, Doc, but your credit card receipt shows you were at the bar pretty late that night. All I want to know is if you saw anything out of the ordinary. Out in the parking lot . . . or even in the lounge."

Doc pinched the bridge of his nose in concentration. "This is about the girl that was killed, Amber Barstow."

"That's right."

"Sorry, I really wasn't paying much attention."

Sam nodded slowly. "Pretty hefty bill for a man alone, having a few drinks. Did you drive yourself home that night? After all those drinks?"

"No. Jesus, Sam. Why don't you just say what you're thinking?"

"I think you were there with a woman friend."

He shook his head. "Nora thinks I was away on a hunting trip that weekend. She doesn't know."

Oh, she probably does, Sam thought. He'd seen too much to think otherwise. "It sure would help if I could talk with your friend, Doc."

"I'm not naming names. If word gets around, people will be hurt. I can't let that happen." He looked down at one of his hands, flexing it slightly. "Not to mention that it would damage my reputation."

"I understand your concern, but it'll be easier if you tell me her name now. I've got two dead women, and a killer on the loose. A killer who was likely at Big Bart's that night." Sam locked his gaze on the doctor's drawn face. "You were there that night and you haven't come forward. You see my problem?"

"I have an alibi."

"This woman you won't name."

He met Sam's gaze. "That's right."

"I want to clear you, Doc. I really do. But I need your help. I'd like to do it outside the public eye, save your reputation, but I need to talk with your friend. A corroborating witness."

The doctor stared blindly at the wall, deciding what to do.

"I need the name of your friend to prove your alibi." When he was met with more silence, Sam said firmly, "By the end of the day, Doc," then Sam headed out, leaving the doctor grappling with his inner demons.

Getting to work and finding a safe place for her daughter and nephew had proven to be a challenge for Ricki that morning. Pilar was looking to dump her precious kid for the long haul.

"I have a meeting in town this morning, and then I have to get back here to meet with Delilah and get her on board. After that, I have to drive to Jackson for a spa treatment," Pilar had told Ricki. "I won't be back until late tomorrow, and I'm counting on you and Brooklyn to help me out with Rourke."

Ricki wanted to point out that Pilar was leaving town five days before her wedding, making Delilah and the rest of them pick up the pieces, but honestly, she was happy to have her gone. The woman sucked all the air from a room.

After Pilar spun out of the snowy driveway, Ricki had followed with the kids. Brook seemed happy to be earning money for corralling her cousin, and Ricki decided that they could hang out at the sheriff's office and make Christmas decorations for the competition at the town hall party. She wanted to maintain a tone of calm fun, minimizing the fear of the underlying threat that a heinous killer was roaming Prairie Creek.

After checking in with Naomi at the front desk, they started off at Sally Jamison's flower shop, where Brook and Rourke picked out a dozen Styrofoam balls along with ribbons, pins and glitter glue to make ornaments.

Sally's hands were shaking as she finished the transaction, and though the woman chattered on like a mockingbird, Ricki could tell she was a nervous wreck. "What about Mia? Have you found the person responsible?" Sally asked, but Ricki shook her head when she started in and inclined her head toward the kids.

Sally looked over and said, "You'd better walk them back to the precinct. Just to be safe."

"It's just two blocks down Main Street," Ricki pointed out. She handed Brook the bag of supplies, touching her shoulder. "There are people everywhere."

Tears flooded Sally's eyes as she watched the door close behind the kids. "Oh, Ricki, are you sure? It's so dangerous out there. Such a terrible time for Prairie Creek. How can Pilar go through with the wedding with this hanging over us like a dark cloud?"

"I don't know." Ricki grabbed two tissues from the box on the counter and handed them over.

Pressing the tissues to her face, Sally quavered. "Mia didn't really have anyone, y'know. Kit's never been around, and Mia never got over your uncle Judd. Not really. Oh, she had a thing for all the Dillinger men, and she used to date Dodge Miller, but she was alone mostly. Life can be terrible, can't it?"

"Mia dated Dodge Miller?" When Sally nodded, Ricki pressed, "Recently?"

"I think so."

Dodge Miller was the town butcher. Or, at least he had been until his business had dried up. If Dodge didn't get back to Sam soon, they would have to go find him. "I didn't think he spent much time in town anymore."

"He doesn't. He was too bitter about losing the butcher shop. Blamed everyone in Prairie Creek for his own failure, especially the folks with money. I understand he went to your father, asked him to invest to keep the shop going, but Ira said no. Well, that just set Dodge off like a crazy bull. After that, no one could stand to be around him. No one except Mia."

Sally's eyes filled with more tears and Ricki asked gently, "Is there anyone you can think of who had something against Mia?"

"Well . . . Ira. Mia sued for child support from Judd's estate, but she just wanted to be part of your family, y'know."

Ricki nodded. Kit was a Dillinger, and it was no secret Mia had wanted to be considered one as well.

The conversation turned to burial plans for Mia—of which there were none. Her body had not been released from the coroner yet, but as soon as it was . . . well, Ricki had to wonder what would happen. Kit was doing her own unique send-off, and it would be difficult to plan a funeral around the wedding and Christmas.

"Check with Kit," Ricki told Sally. "Maybe there'll be a memorial service sometime in January."

"Kit?" Sally repeated in disbelief.

Ricki knew how she felt. Kit didn't travel the conventional road.

Sally's eyes welled up once again as she promised to do the flowers at cost.

"So sweet of you," Ricki said, zipping up the navy patrol jacket Naomi had assigned her from the supply closet at the sheriff's office. It was a man's medium, way too big for

Ricki, but there was room for a sweater underneath and it made her feel petite under the sloshing hunk of fabric.

Next she stopped in at Emma Kincaid's dress shop, where she walked in on a discussion so heated that the three women didn't seem to notice the bell jingling at the door or the blast of cold air.

"I asked you if you wanted the train to snap off, and you insisted that you didn't." Facing Pilar with her hands on her hips, Emma Kincaid stood her ground, blue eyes sparking with controlled heat. "Honestly, I'm not interested in design number four for your wedding dress just because you don't have a church aisle to walk down."

Pilar was gripping a glass of champagne with taut fingers. "Emma, please. I'm already destroyed over losing the church. I'm paying you a small fortune here. What is the big deal about coming up with another design?"

"Because you want a dress in four days, and I'll wager you won't be happy with it, either. Wear one of the three I've already finished. Or go to a department store when you're in Jackson and buy off the rack."

"Enough," Georgina Kincaid snapped, lifting her stony gaze from Pilar's champagne glass to glare at the bride-to-be. A tape measure dangling around her neck, she looked more like the seamstress than her daughter, who wore high-heeled boots and a tiny leather skirt that was about as practical on the plains of Wyoming as cowboy boots in New York City.

Ricki was surprised Georgina was even helping out, especially with Pilar, as the Kincaid matriarch was as anti-Dillinger as Ira was anti-Kincaid. But then, a number of the Kincaids were on the guest list, so maybe there was a new thawing in the cold war between the two families.

"No one can design a brand-new dress in four days, not with Christmas coming and folks up in Jackson waiting on gowns from Emma," Georgina snarled at Pilar.

There's the Georgina we all know and love, Ricki thought dryly.

Georgina shot a glance Ricki's way. "What do you want?"

"Mom," Emma said, long-suffering. "Can I help you, Ricki?"

"What about the dress?" Pilar asked woefully.

Emma turned back to her. "I'll cut the train for you," she said briskly. "That's the best I can do, though that chiffon is a bitch to hem."

"Could you add some beading on the back? Just give it some detail?" Pilar tried.

Emma was firm. "Just the hem. Take it or leave it."

Pilar handed over the gown wrapped in pink plastic, her face set. "Fine. I need it delivered back at the lodge no later than Friday." She turned to Ricki. "Hi and bye. I've got to get with my bridal consultant."

"Drive careful," Ricki said, watching as the dark-haired beauty pulled on a white fur hat and strode out the door. *And don't worry about Rourke. He'll be safe with me.*

"She doesn't deserve Ira Dillinger," Georgina muttered harshly, which made Ricki give her a double take. Realizing Ira's daughter was in the room, she added, "I'm no fan of your father's, but Pilar is vermin."

"Mom," Emma warned again, then, "So, what can I help you with, Ricki?" She tossed the pink bag of gown onto a settee and approached the front of the shop, her heels clicking on the marble floor.

"I'm working for the sheriff's office now." Ricki looked down at her shield. "Just wondering if I could ask you a few questions about the Pioneer Church? We're still trying to sort out the time frame of the fire. You too, Georgina."

"Dying to blame it on the Kincaids, are you?" the older woman sneered.

"I thought you and Dad were getting along better," Ricki said. When Georgina didn't respond, she went on, "We think you were the last people in the building before the fire started and just want to know what the sequence of events was."

Emma hung the pink bag on a hook, and gestured for Ricki to sit. "I hope I can help you. Anything to put that psycho behind bars. I'm afraid in my own house at night."

We're all afraid, Ricki thought.

Reluctantly, Georgina sat on the edge of a chair and eyed Ricki as if she were some dangerous reptile.

So much for the improving relations between the Dillingers and the Kincaids.

From the dress shop Ricki headed over to the animal clinic, where the young receptionist jumped up from her desk to unlock the door.

"Sorry about that. With this slasher on the loose, we're not taking any chances," Renee said, giving voice to the fear that ran through Prairie Creek like a foul river. What had happened to her childhood home, where a kid could go off on a horse in the morning without a care in the world?

Ricki met with Antonia and Sabrina, who showed her the mutilated coyote kept in cold storage. After viewing the carcass, Ricki agreed with Sam: one killer. Neither Antonia nor Sabrina was able to offer up any real information apart from what she already knew. She made notes on their overall impressions to add to her report.

It was still snowing when she left the clinic a half hour later and headed back to the precinct. It was a good six-block trek, but the walkway in front of the shops had been cleared, and the air smelled of snow and pine, probably from the fresh-cut evergreens lined up outside Handy Hardware.

Halfway down the street, she spotted the sheriff's department Jeep a few seconds before she heard Sam calling to her from the door of the hardware store.

"Hey. How's it going?" he asked.

Her heart lifted. This was her boss; she shouldn't be so ridiculously happy to see him for the second time this morning. "Just heading back to the station house to write up my reports."

"You can give me a preview in the Jeep. I could use your help with an errand for the party."

"Sure." Once inside the Jeep she told him what she had learned from Sally about Mia dating Dodge Miller.

"That's news to me. I'm going to head out his way tonight and track him down," Sam said.

Ricki then told him about her interview with Georgina and Emma—no surprises there—and her conversations with the two veterinarians who had showed her the coyote carcass. "I've never seen this town so scared, Sam. Shop owners are keeping their doors locked, and when I passed by the barber shop, Slim came out to remind me to be careful."

"Glad people are taking this seriously, but I hate it. It's like the whole town is being held hostage."

"How'd your morning go?"

"Doc's being evasive," he said. "He was definitely with a 'friend' the night Barstow was last seen, but he won't give up a name yet." As he spoke, he backed his Jeep into the alley behind Menlo's Market, parking at the loading dock.

"What are we doing?" she asked.

"Just picking up some giveaways for the party."

As they climbed out of the truck, the large door rolled open, revealing two men with a handful of shopping carts.

"Sam!" Donald Menlo called, his round cheeks tinged with red. "It's about time. I got them all ready for you." He gestured to the shopping carts full of turkeys. "Two dozen."

"Good enough. I'll give you a call if we run out." Sam extracted a credit card from his wallet and handed it to Donald.

"We have plenty more if you need 'em. I'll be right back with your receipt."

"This is a lot of turkeys, Sam." Ricki grunted as she hoisted a twenty-pounder out of the cart. "You selling them at the party?"

"We give them away to people in need. Started it a few years back, and it's been a big hit."

"I bet. Sounds like a good idea."

The teenaged clerk lifted a fat frozen turkey as if it were light as a football. Swiftly he moved it to the back of the Jeep.

"You coming to the party, Brian?" Sam asked the kid.

"I have to work. But my mom will be there. She never misses it."

Ricki grabbed another turkey and felt the skin of her hand stick to the plastic wrap. "These are so frozen."

Brian took the turkey from her. "That's how they stay fresh."

"Well, I knew that," Ricki said. "They're just like blocks of ice. I think my fingers are frostbitten already."

"I got gloves in the Jeep," Sam offered.

"We got this," Brian said as he carried two turkeys to the Jeep. "See? Almost done."

Cargo loaded, Sam thanked the young man, who wheeled the carts away.

"I can't believe I was bested by a teenage boy," Ricki said, blowing into her aching hands.

"Every kid wants to be tougher than a cop. Especially a female cop," Sam said.

Ricki grunted an assent.

"Come here." He unzipped his jacket, took her hands and pressed them inside his coat where it was warm. The ache was excruciating for a moment as her hands began to thaw, the numbness fading. But the close proximity to Sam was the true dichotomy of ecstatic and torturous, bitter and sweet. Palms against the wall of his chest, she could feel his heartbeat.

Caught by the intensity in his dark eyes, she murmured, "What are you doing to me, Sam?"

"No more than you're doing to me."

Donald Menlo returned, interrupting their moment, and Ricki quickly extracted her hands and got into the Jeep. There wasn't much conversation after that because it didn't seem necessary. She and Sam were riding the same wave, swimming toward impossible possibilities, forgetting the very real threat of drowning.

Sam left his truck parked illegally, right in front of town hall. The perk of being sheriff. "What if someone steals a turkey?" she asked.

He shrugged. "Then I guess they need it more than I do."

The Christmas party was the quaint, sweet celebration Ricki remembered from her childhood. She watched as Rourke helped little kids who were waiting in line for a pony ride. That boy was a quick learner. At one point Sam steered him away to show him some rodeo photos of Colton among the "Prairie Creek Wall of Fame" in the lobby. Rourke stared hard at his father's pictures as if he were imprinting the images on his brain.

Moving from one table to another, sampling wassail and cider, Ricki looked around for Brook. This was the sort of thing she wished she could deliver to her daughter, all wrapped up in a Christmas bow: the sights and sounds of Christmas. The foundation of a community with backbone and heart. The carefree laughter and conversation that filled the air, along with the song of wandering carolers.

She spotted Brooklyn over at the cupcake stand with her friend, Sara. From here, she couldn't read her reaction, and she knew it wouldn't be cool to rush over there in a burst of enthusiasm. No, Brook would have to accept Prairie Creek on her own terms, in her own good time. She hoped that would happen before she jumped on a bus back to her dad in New York.

Outside, the trees decorated for the competition brought a smile to Ricki's face. One was covered in real candy canes, white lights and red ribbons. Blue lights and sliced-up Pepsi cans adorned another. A third was decked in colored lights and miniature elf figurines. The trees surrounded a hut decorated like a gingerbread house, where Chet Norcross sat in a Santa suit—the role he'd been training to play since retirement from the school district. Kids were happy to pose for a photo with Santa or listen to his recitation of *The Night Before Christmas*.

As the party began to wind down, Sam directed guests out to his Jeep. "If you need a Christmas turkey, be sure to grab one from the Jeep out front."

"Thank you, Sam." A short woman with dark hair shook his hand. "Merry Christmas."

"Merry Christmas," Sam told her. "But thank Menlo's Market. They provided the turkeys."

It was a lie, but Ricki would give him that one. 'Twas the season of love and generosity, and she knew Sam didn't want anyone to suspect he was the one playing Santa.

Chapter Nineteen

As her plane landed beside the majestic Teton Mountains and taxied up to the rectangular terminal framed by rustic-looking timbers, Delilah Dillinger did a quick inner assessment of her feelings. It felt good to be back for Christmas, yes, but she was still ambivalent about returning home to Prairie Creek. Still, it was great to be greeted by her oldest brother, who updated her on recent news.

"Did they find that killer?" Delilah asked.

Colton's brow was set beneath the brim of his Stetson. "Not yet."

"I've got to be nuts, coming back now, while Prairie Creek has its own roving serial killer."

"You can take that up with Deputy Ricki," Colt said.

"Deputy Ricki," she repeated with a smile as they climbed into Ira's Jeep, which Colton had brought to the airport rather than his truck to stow Delilah's luggage. "Didn't know you'd just have one bag," he observed, then added that the Jeep would be available for Delilah's use during her stay, as Ira preferred his Dodge Ram truck.

"There's something else you need to know," Colton said. "Better for you to hear it from me first."

"Uh-oh." Delilah didn't like the sound of that. "What?"

As they drove into Prairie Creek, Colton explained that Rourke was his kid. Hard to believe, but his half-drunk relationship with Pilar all those years ago had produced a son. “I just found out about it recently,” Colt admitted.

“Good. God.” Delilah stared at her brother’s profile, the hard line of his jaw. Her own biological clock had been making noise for a while inside her head, but to hear that Colton and Pilar had a son together made its insistent *tick, tick, tick* sound like a roaring freight train bearing down on her. “That adds a new level of ick to this relationship Dad’s gotten himself into,” Delilah said.

“Yeah, well . . .”

Delilah’s misgivings multiplied when they arrived at the lodge and Pilar grabbed her arm as if they were long-lost friends rather than classmates who ran in opposite circles. She could do little more than drop the handle of her rolling bag and let Pilar propel her toward the living room.

“Thank God you’re here,” Pilar said on a huge sigh. “I only have an hour or so before I have to take off, and I’ve got a million questions for you. Let me show you the mantel first. The flowers aren’t here yet, but you can get a sense of it from the Christmas lights. I think this should be the backdrop for the actual wedding ceremony, but I’m afraid it’s lacking the charm I was hoping for.”

“I’ll be out in the stables,” Colt said, faint amusement in his eyes. The traitor. “Want me to take your bag upstairs first?”

“Uh, sure,” Delilah said as Pilar waved him off.

“Just leave it,” she ordered. “We’ve got a big crew coming in and I don’t know who is staying where. Now, Delilah . . .” Pilar turned away from Colton and immediately switched the topic back to the nuptial arrangements. “I’m thinking we should line the stairs with a hundred tiny votive candles . . .”

As Delilah unbuttoned her coat, she forced herself not

to stare at the doughy look of Pilar's lips, the tightness around her eyes. Plastic surgery. Delilah knew all the signs from living in Southern California. Not that she minded, but what in God's name was her father thinking?

Though wedding planning wasn't on her résumé, Delilah let Pilar go through her wish list. Half of Pilar's ideas just weren't going to work, but Delilah could see solutions to the big issues. And although Delilah really didn't want this wedding to come off, from her conversations with her father, it was clear that he did. Ricki had been right on that.

So, fine. She would keep this wedding moving forward. She could do that for her dad.

Within half an hour, she had convinced Pilar to put on one of the rejected wedding bridal gowns to do a run-through procession down the front staircase. Delilah wanted to see how the staircase worked, and she thought the rehearsal would help put Pilar at ease. While Pilar was upstairs changing, Delilah paced across the vestibule, measuring its width. She was sketching out a schematic on her notepad when the front door opened and in came her niece, Brook, along with a younger boy.

"Aunt Delilah! Thank God!" Brooklyn hugged Delilah tight and pressed her head against her aunt's chest. "Everyone else here is clueless."

"I missed you, too," Delilah said, though she was surprised by her niece's wholehearted reaction. From everything she'd heard, Brooklyn had been withdrawn since she'd moved here, and though Delilah had always gotten along with Brook, they didn't see each other that often.

Over Brook's shoulder she saw Ricki clamber through the front door behind them, stomping the snow from her boots. "I told you guys, either take your boots off or go around back," Ricki said, then smiled up at her sister. "You made it."

Delilah hugged her sister, then was introduced to Rourke. So . . . this was Colt's boy, she thought, trying not to stare.

Delilah wondered why things in her family had to be so complicated. She watched as Rourke went off to the stables to help Colt with the horses.

"Uncle Colt is Rourke's father," Brook said. "Isn't that weird?"

"Brook," Ricki intoned. "Don't talk about your cousin that way."

"It was a surprise, for sure," Delilah agreed.

"I think it's weird. This whole family is weird. Is that your luggage?" Brook stepped away to examine the shiny silver luggage. "It's so retro! What room are you in?"

"I don't know, but I hear it's going to get tight here with Nell on her way and Tyler's family driving up. Everyone's going to be here."

"I have to stay here, too. Maybe we can share a room?" Brook suggested.

Delilah shot a look at Ricki, who asked, "Would that be okay?"

"It'd be great," Delilah said.

"I'll take your bag," Brook said, grabbing the handle. "There are two single beds in the room I'm staying in."

"Sounds good. Thanks, Brook."

Delilah and Ricki watched as Brooklyn lugged the shiny suitcase up the stairs.

"Nice kid you got there," Delilah said casually. "What the hell have you been complaining about?"

"That's the good Brooklyn. You don't want to meet her alter ego."

"She's a teenager. No worse than we were, I'm sure."

"Don't remind me. So how was your flight?"

"Fine, but I was bushwhacked by Pilar as soon as I got here."

Ricki looked toward the top of the stairs. "I'll be glad when this wedding is over."

Delilah handed her the tab of her tape measure. "Hold this against the bottom step, will ya?"

They were interrupted by the ringing doorbell. Delilah was joking with Ricki when she peered through the side-lights and nearly choked as she recognized the woman standing there.

"What's Georgina Kincaid doing here?" she whispered under her breath at Ricki.

"She's here to see me," Ira called from down the hall. He squinted ahead, focusing on his middle daughter as his boots tapped the runner. "Delilah? Good to see you, girl. We'll get together later and catch up." He patted her shoulder as he passed her on the way to the door. "Right now I've got a meeting. Looks like we're getting into the oil business."

"What?" Ricki's head snapped around. "You said you would never drill on our land."

"Not our land. Kincaid land." Ira flashed his daughters a cocky grin, then opened the door and greeted Georgina, just as Brook bounded back down the stairs.

For a moment Brook and Georgina glared at each other, then Ira gestured for Georgina to come into his office, saying that Mrs. Mac had set out coffee and cookies. The older woman tore her cold gaze from Brook, gave a curt nod to both Delilah and Ricki and followed after Ira.

Brook looked at her mother with a "See?" expression, but before Delilah could ask what the hell was going on, a gray-haired man in his forties in a string tie and leather jacket came up the porch and through the open front door.

"Len Mercer, Century Petroleum," he introduced himself, offering a hand to both Ricki and Delilah. Brook had edged away, and now turned and headed back upstairs. Delilah felt much the same way. She didn't want to be involved with any plan Ira had to wangle Kincaid land into an oil deal.

Ira came out to usher Mercer inside, then said, "There's one more coming from Century Petroleum. Send him in when he arrives." Both men ducked inside the den and Ira shut the door firmly behind them.

Ricki scowled as she held the tape measure. "Since when does Dad serve snacks for a meeting?"

"Since when does Dad conduct friendly business with the Kincaids?" Delilah asked. "Brook is right, you know. Our family has issues. As evidenced by you and me working our asses off to make this wedding happen when we know it's a match made in hell."

A third man hurried up the outside steps as Ricki was about to shut the door. He was younger, a tall, good-looking man in a shearling coat with amazing blue eyes. Delilah let her tape measure snap back into its casing as he stepped inside and introduced himself to Ricki, who was standing closest to the door.

"Hi. I'm Tom Unger, from Century Petroleum."

"And I'm Ricki Dillinger, Ira's daughter," Ricki said. "And this is my sister Delilah."

"Hi," Delilah and Tom said to each other at the same time. He extended his arm and shook both of their hands. His grip was sure and strong, a man who could use his muscle when he needed to. Delilah smiled but didn't let her hand linger too long within his. Handsome men, in her experience, were lacking in other areas. Most of them, anyway.

"Delilah?" Tom said. "I always liked that song, but I guess you hear that all the time."

"Mostly I hear, 'hey, there, Delilah,' and people think they're hilarious."

"Delilah just got in from Los Angeles," Ricki said. "We're having a wedding here soon."

"I heard. It's big news around Prairie Creek."

"So, you're doing oil business with Ira," Delilah said.

"Hope to." He pointed a thumb toward Ira's den. "I'd better go."

After the den door closed behind him, Ricki waggled her brows suggestively. "He's cute."

"A lot of them are," Delilah said noncommittally. The last thing she needed was for her sister to start playing matchmaker.

"Cynical."

"Yep. That's what happens in Hollywood. We become cynical, ironic and arch."

"Maybe you just needed to come back to Prairie Creek and find a real man."

Delilah didn't answer as her mind jumped to Hunter Kincaid and the summer of the homestead fire. She saw herself as she'd been that night, waiting for him at the tire swing, the one that had been hung from the lone pine tree with the hollow where they'd left notes for each other. Well, she'd left notes and he'd picked them up, mostly. Love notes . . . from a girl sick with love.

Dropping to her knees to measure the stair width, she vowed to scrub Hunter Kincaid from her mind completely. She'd managed for eighteen years; a few days or a week in Prairie Creek wouldn't change that. If her luck held, she might get through the whole visit without even seeing him. Ira had invited the Kincaids to the wedding because of the proposed oil deal. She now understood that part of the puzzle. But knowing Hunter, she doubted there was any way he would actually attend a Dillinger wedding. Thank God for that.

This whole debacle would be over soon enough. *Then what, Delilah?* she asked herself honestly. *Where are you going to go next? Back to Santa Monica?*

The prospect was fast losing any appeal.

Hard to believe, but as Colton looked around the dinner table, he actually felt happy to be back at the Rocking D.

With Pilar off in Jackson and Delilah and Nell here, it was beginning to feel like old times, the days when they were a family under Rachel Dillinger's steady hand, the days when they worked and played and ate together and gave each other a good ribbing from sunup to sundown. His sisters were here, his brother was on his way, Sabrina was seated on his right, his son—who was actually beginning to like him—was on his left, and his childhood friend Sam Featherstone sat across the table, holding the potted pork chops for Ricki to serve herself. Kit had been invited but was bound and determined to stay at the stables. Davis was with her. Looking down the table, he could see the old man had a little glimmer in his eyes as he held court at the far end.

Damn, but the Waltons had nothing on the Dillinger clan tonight.

"So, can we go riding tomorrow?" Rourke asked eagerly as he broke a roll in half.

"That's the plan," Colt said. He'd broken the news to Pilar that he intended to teach Rourke to ride. She'd objected as a matter of course, then had thrown up her hands and said, "Go ahead. You're going to do what you want anyway."

"And shooting?" Brook asked, showing more interest than in anything they'd seen to date.

Pilar hadn't voiced any objections to Rourke handling a gun, so Colt and Sam had taken Brook and Rourke out to an empty field just before supper. In the purple twilight, they showed the kids how to handle a pistol. Like riding, shooting was a rite of passage for anyone growing up out here, and with the killer still at large, there was no time like the present to prepare the kids to defend themselves.

Colt was going to have to talk to Pilar about the gun issue soon, but for now, he was just content to be with the family. Looking past the edge of the windows, he noticed fat flakes floating through the haze of the Christmas lights.

"Are we getting another blizzard?" Ricki wondered aloud.

"Nah," Colton said. "The winds have died down and the mercury is hovering right around freezing. We'll see snow, but the stock can handle it."

"The snow is probably holding up Tyler and Jen," Ira said. "I thought we'd see them by dinnertime tonight, but they'll get through. The last of the clan, all under one roof." Ira's eyes glinted as he lifted his wineglass. "My progeny."

What an arrogant son of a bitch, taking credit for his offspring. Colton chewed his meat, determined not to let his old man spoil a good dinner. As he swallowed, he felt a steady pressure on his right thigh; under the table, Sabrina's hand slid over his muscles and gave a squeeze, as if staking her territory. He turned to her and caught the fire in her eyes, the flame that quickly ignited at his touch. He could scarcely drag his gaze away. He'd plundered those lips a dozen times in the past few days, but she always left him wanting more. He wondered if he could entice her into slipping out to the barn between dinner and dessert.

"We've got to make the most of this white Christmas," Nell said. "Keep up family traditions. I'm thinking about that old sleigh parked in the storage shed."

Nell had always been the one who stuck with tradition the most.

Scooping up a spoonful of applesauce, Ricki said, "A sleigh ride in the snow? Brook's never done that."

"You sound like a freakin' Christmas carol," Brook muttered.

"But it's so much fun," Nell said. "I think it was our mom's favorite Christmas tradition. Whenever we had snow, she insisted on it."

"I can hook two of the horses up to the sleigh tomorrow," Colton said.

"Didn't Mom have jingle bells?" Ricki asked as everyone but Nell groaned aloud.

"God help us," Delilah said.

"Oh, come on, Del," Colt said. "You don't have to pretend to be cool. You're not in SoCal anymore."

"I bet I can find them," Nell said determinedly.

Everyone finished eating, but they remained at the table, talking and joking. Colton sipped from a mug of coffee, listening to the noise of his big, crazy family and his smaller one—Sabrina on his right and Rourke on his left. Maybe he understood some of the old man's Dillinger pride. Family pride.

There was a pounding noise from the kitchen, and suddenly they came traipsing in—Jen, Tyler and the two kids.

"You missed dinner, but you made it for dessert," Ira said, clapping his younger son on the back. Tyler was a younger version of Colton, with the same dark hair shot with red, the same lean cowboy physique.

"I'm heating up some pork chops," Mrs. Mac assured the kids, five-year-old Haley and eleven-year-old Justin.

"Let me help you unload," Colton said, rising from the table.

And suddenly everyone was up, eager to help—or maybe it was just the lure of the snow. They all donned coats and boots and headed out to the circle of light in the driveway by the large garage. The unloading was done in a minute, but people lingered, talking and laughing. The older kids worked the snow, rolling a large sphere for the base of a snowman. Haley and Nell flopped down on their backs and waved their arms to make snow angels.

Rourke and Justin were talking, working on something together, and Colt felt a flash of pride at the resilience of his son. He strode over for a word and noticed an arsenal of snowballs, stacked in a pyramid.

He stopped short, grinning. Industrious kids.

He leaned down to scoop some snow. As he was rolling it into a ball, the boys noticed him.

"That's a nice-looking stash of ammo," he drawled.

"Stay back," Justin said, "if you know what's good for you."

"Quick word of advice," Colt said as he packed the snowball in his hands. "Aim for the body."

The boys grinned, then ducked as he wound up and whipped the snowball at Rourke. They responded by pelting him with missiles.

"Save yourselves!" he shouted, running past his brothers and sisters to dive behind Tyler's SUV. He grabbed Sabrina and swept her off her feet, taking her along.

There were gasps and howls and laughter as everyone scattered, then re-emerged with snow bombs flying. Colt grinned. Life could be pretty damn good when things came together.

Perfect.

There they were. The Dillingers. One big, happy family. Joy in the air.

How satisfying it would be to drop one of them in the snow with a bullet, quick and clean. But no . . . a knife was the way . . .

He fondled the teeth in his pocket as he watched them play in the golden light of the illuminated lodge. He'd wanted to take another tonight, but he had to be patient. A slight delay. A small sacrifice worth the ultimate reward.

More than a tooth to fondle in his pocket.

A real, live trophy.

A live Dillinger to play with for a while.

The lights of the dashboard cast a glow on Ricki's face as she sat beside Sam in the Jeep. After last night, after that kiss that had turned into a heated make-out session, it had become challenging to be in close spaces like this with her.

That was why Sam had tried to talk her out of coming along for the drive out to Dodge Miller's place, a trailer on reservation land. He valued her as a deputy, but he had to utilize every ounce of restraint in his body to keep the physical heat down.

He wanted her, and he hated himself for it. What kind of boss lusted after his employee?

"I asked my father about Dodge Miller and the loan," Ricki said. "Ira tried to dismiss it as a simple conversation. Then he told me that Dodge brought Mia into it. Dodge claimed that Mia would benefit from the butcher shop's prosperity. Said how he would take care of her, would take her off Dad's hands. That really pissed Dad off. Yes, Mia always hung around, but Dad felt sorry for her, I guess."

"So your father refused the loan."

Ricki nodded. "And Dodge's shop went belly-up because apparently he couldn't get one of the local banks to bail him out."

Sam caught a hint of her sweet scent as she shifted her legs. "Maybe the business wasn't so profitable after all. I don't really know Dodge Miller's finances, but I can tell you, his living quarters are pretty ramshackle. This end of the reservation is a sorry place. You can't see much in the dark, but these houses are modest. Some of them are old hunting shacks without insulation or plumbing."

He was driving slowly now, looking for the turnoff to the access road—just a black hole in the trees. His Jeep bumped along for about a quarter of a mile before the headlights swept over a small, snow-covered trailer.

"I'm going to leave the headlights on," Sam said. "Otherwise, it's pitch-black out here."

"You sure that's not going to piss Dodge off?"

"Chances are, he'll be pissed off no matter what we do."

They stepped out into the cold, still night, noise muffled by the steadily falling snow. Sam knew that Ricki was behind him. She had his back, and that felt good. Being able to have complete trust in your partner was what it was all about.

It took a few knocks to get a response, but finally the door opened a crack and Dodge appeared, cap covering his eyes and flashlight grazing his beard.

The beam of the light blinded Sam for a moment, before he turned down his Stetson and let his eyes adjust.

"Sheriff? What the hell's going on?" Dodge demanded.

"Didn't mean to alarm you, Dodge, but I've been calling you all day. When I couldn't reach you, I decided to take a ride out, talk to you in person."

"I got no desire or reason to talk to you or your deputy," Dodge said as the stink of booze filled the air. "You're wasting your time and gas, coming out here."

"Dodge . . . hold on." Sam already had the tip of his steel-toed boot in the door to keep it from slamming in his face. "I need to talk to you about Mia. You heard she was killed?"

"You got a warrant for my arrest?"

"No."

"Then get the hell out!"

Dodge shoved on the door, but it bounced off Sam's boot, bringing a string of curses from the trailer's occupant, who clasped his hand over the door and leaned into it, his face hidden from view.

"I don't have a warrant, but I could get one." Sam paused as Dodge made a futile effort to inch the door closed. "Why don't you make it easy on you and me and let us in? Talk with us a few minutes. You might know something that could help us find Mia's killer. He's out there, Dodge. And he's not done."

The door opened again, but now the flashlight was gone, a soft light glowing behind Dodge. "You don't know jack shit," he said, his eyes still in shadow. "You just come out here and try to pin it on me."

"I'm not trying to pin it on anyone, just asking some questions. That's all."

"I see."

"Could you tell us your whereabouts on Satur—"

Dodge cut in. "I work my ass off for shit over there in Lander. Ten-hour shifts, most of them in the fridge. I got days when my fingers ache down to the bone from the chill. I lost everything and now I got arthritis, too, and I'm just a piece of meat, owned by someone else. A shit job in a shit world. No one in this town gets that."

Ricki spoke up from behind Sam. "We're just trying to figure out what happened to Mia."

"Who said that?" Dodge's head snapped as if he'd been stung, and he wheeled around and shot the beam of his light on Ricki's face. "You got a woman . . . a Dillinger? Is that fucking Ricki Dillinger playing cop?"

A protective instinct rose in Sam. "That's my deputy," he said firmly.

"Fuck that." Dodge lifted his chin so that his beady eyes could latch on to Ricki, and Sam shifted into Dodge's path, uncomfortable with her being in harm's way. "It's men like her papa who ran me out of business. Buying up all the land and jacking up the price of rent! Greedy fuckers. A dozen Ira Dillingers. That was all it took."

"That may be so, but Ricki is a law-enforcement officer. She's got nothing to do with your business going down." Sam drew himself up, trying to see into the trailer, but a glimpse of stacked pots and bottles was the best he could do. This was a bust; Dodge was too drunk to be reliable, and there was no way they were getting inside.

"They're all alike. Rich bastards." Dodge slapped a hand to his face, his words slowed by the alcohol in his blood. "Money grubbers, counting their coins. Not a single good bone in their bodies."

"I want to know about Mia," Sam said, trying to change

the subject. "About the man who killed her. We haven't apprehended him, Dodge. Don't you want to step up and help us catch him before it happens again? Tell me what you know. Tell me now, or I'll be back in the morning with a warrant."

Sam knew he would probably be back regardless, but it was worth a shot.

"Mia didn't care about me. She only cared about *them*. Well, they're coming down. Get ready for a fall, pretty Ricki. Get ready, because you're all coming down. Down!"

Dodge swayed behind the door and teetered. There was a flurry of motion, a *thump*, and Dodge was on the floor of the trailer. Sam pushed the door in against the man's stocking feet. "He's out," he told Ricki.

Sam bent over the man, saw that he was breathing. "You're the one who's down, my friend." He surveyed the dimly lit trailer, though it was hard to decipher objects in the clutter lit only by a dim light over the kitchen sink.

"What do you think, Sam? A search? Call for an ambulance, or let him sleep it off?"

"Jes' leave me alone," Dodge mumbled from the floor.

"We'll let him sleep it off." Sam stepped back and reached for the door behind him. "Let's check back tomorrow."

"I hate to let it go till then."

"I know."

They waited a few moments until Dodge's heavy breathing turned into a loud snore, then they left the trailer. Climbing back into the Jeep, Ricki let out a sigh. "I know he's hit some hard times, and I'm not saying that he hurt Mia, but that man is one angry son of a bitch."

"Amen."

Chapter Twenty

"I managed to talk our bride out of lining the staircase with little votive candles, seeing as how the gown Emma designed for her is made out of chiffon," Delilah said to Nell the following day as she examined one of the bows she'd tied to the railing, trimming it with a fat pair of clippers. "It could go up in a puff of smoke with the slightest spark."

"When's Pilar getting back?" Nell asked.

"This evening, I think."

"Guess what I found."

Delilah looked up at her sister and saw her eyes were dancing. "I'm afraid to ask."

"The jingle bells. They were in the attic."

"Lucky us," Delilah teased her younger sister as Nell bounded up the stairs to ostensibly find the bells.

Delilah was just finishing up her handiwork when her father came stamping through the front door along with Georgina Kincaid and the oilmen. Ira immediately threw an arm out to encompass his domain, showing off a little as he pointed out the handmade wood finishes on the stairs, the cathedral ceilings, the wide plank hardwood floors and the breathtaking views of Dillinger land, as far as the eye could see. She'd heard it all before, but Delilah thought it was a little obnoxious to be spouting off in front of Georgina—especially if Dad wanted to acquire some Kincaid land. For a successful businessman, Ira could be obtuse at times.

"Really fine place you've got here," Len Mercer said as Ira led the group toward his office.

Realizing he was planning to sequester himself inside for God knew how long, Delilah called, "Dad?" She needed to remind him of the upcoming sleigh ride.

"What?" Ira frowned, letting her know by his tone that he didn't appreciate the interruption while he was conducting business.

"A word, please."

Tom Unger paused, facing Delilah. He seemed amused by the interplay between Ira and her.

"This won't take long," Ira said. "A few hours at the most."

It was already afternoon. "That might be too long," she said.

Delilah could hear Nell's approach as the jingle bells rang merrily on the upstairs landing.

"Dad!" Nell cried, seeing he was about to enter his office.

Exasperated, Ira shooed the others into his office then glared at his daughters.

"We're going on a sleigh ride. How long is this meeting?" Nell asked.

"If I miss it, I miss it," he declared, annoyed.

"Go." Delilah made a shooing motion with one hand. "Nobody's twisting your arm."

He shook his head, hesitated for a moment, then returned to his office, leaving a crestfallen Nell and a totally ticked-off Delilah.

"You're coming, aren't you?" Nell asked her.

"Wouldn't miss it."

As Nell left, Delilah threw a baleful glare at the closed door. Her father was a hard and irascible man. While he pretended to have a strong sense of family pride, it was more show than substance. When he'd called her on the phone the night before she left Hollywood, she'd asked him if he'd sent wedding invitations to the rest of their family—Lila and her husband and children, Delilah's cousins Tara and Garth, in Alaska; Ira's own cousin, Royal Daugherty and his family from Bad Luck, Texas; her mother's sister, Cecile, whom Delilah hadn't seen since she was a child. Ira had snorted and told her no, acting as if she were crazy to even suggest such a thing. For all Ira's delight in his own nuclear family, he had no use for anyone outside it except select residents of Prairie Creek.

"Narcissism," she muttered aloud. The men in her life were lousy with it.

She wanted a baby, but the idea of finding a male to help with that endeavor was fast losing what little appeal it had once had.

Well, there were ways to have babies without getting into a relationship with a man. She had some money saved up. She could take some time off and have a baby and start her own nuclear family, without the autocratic and narcissistic tendencies of a male.

She could do it. But somehow, the idea of being a single parent didn't sit right with her. She had always harbored a notion that she would hook up with a certain lean, long-legged cowboy with blue eyes that could see straight into her heart. A Kincaid; forbidden fruit.

Delilah sighed. Why did she always dream impossible dreams?

Ricki combed over the lab report on her home computer one more time. A new bit of evidence that had come in early this morning: the coroner had managed to identify a second blood type on Mia Collins's body, and that blood had been a match with Amber Barstow.

"We believe the killer used the same knife to carve up both victims, and the knife wasn't completely cleaned," Sam had told her when he'd called to wake her up this morning.

"So it's definitely the same killer," Ricki had said. "Why? What's the motive?"

"Victim selection appears to be random. The only major link is that both murders took place in Prairie Creek."

Sam was right, of course, but Ricki felt there had to be something they were missing. She'd rushed through breakfast and lunch so that she could get back to the computer. Unfortunately Brook had tagged along down from the lodge, and now wouldn't come out of her room. She seemed determined to stay planted in an attempt to avoid the family sleigh ride.

Well, Ricki wasn't going for that. They were going on a sleigh ride, and then Brook would have to go back to the main lodge while Ricki headed out to interview Doc Farley's "secret friend," Allison Waller. Sam had finally gotten her name from Doc, and they'd both thought the woman might be more forthcoming if she was interviewed by a female.

Closing the file, Ricki rose from the computer. "Brook? We need to get going. Bundle up. Layers always work, and you definitely need a hat."

The bedroom door opened and Brook stood scowling in the threshold. "I told you, I'm not going."

"Honey, it's time for the family sleigh ride."

"So? Sophie is gonna call me any minute on Skype. I told her I'd be here."

"Send her a text and reschedule."

"She's going to her aunt's for Christmas. This is our last chance."

"Oh, Brook." Disappointment seeped into the room, separating mother and daughter. "Why do you do this?"

"I had this set up like forever!"

Ricki turned away, drawing in a breath. "Fine." It wasn't fine, but then she had to remind herself that her daughter could be doing far worse things, the kind of things they'd left behind in New York. "Lock the door behind me, and do not leave this house. It's going to be dark soon. I shouldn't even leave you alone here."

"I know how to use a gun now," Brook said airily. "Sam said I'm pretty good. Maybe you should leave your gun with me."

"Yeah, that's just what I'm going to do." Ricki had grown up in a culture with guns, but she wasn't yet ready to pass that on to her daughter. "Stay put. I'll be back as soon as it's over." Ricki left the house, wondering why she bothered.

As soon as her mother was gone, Brooklyn opened the kitchen cabinet. She shoved two Pop-Tarts into the toaster, then went to the laptop and clicked on the Skype icon. Sophie was bursting with all the energy and coolness of New York.

"Aw . . . it can't be all bad," Sophie said.

"The only good thing is that my aunt Delilah is here from California. She makes TV commercials, and she's really nice."

"Really? Do you think she could get you in a commercial?"

Brook sighed. "She used to be an actress . . . I don't know . . . maybe. I wish we had gone to live with her, instead of here with cows."

"So what are you doing for Christmas?"

"Nothing," Brook answered. Nothing she wanted to do, anyway.

Beyond Sophie's smiling face on the laptop, Brooklyn could see the snow-covered landscape outside the window. The big lodge was covered in beautiful lights, and there were two ginormous trees. They'd gone to that Christmas party in town, and although Brook didn't really know anyone other than Sara, it had been kind of fun seeing the town hall set up like a winter wonderland. That little gingerbread house with Santa inside. All the lights and the trees. The miniature train set run by an old man who was so proud of it. Rourke had helped out with the pony rides and had also delivered cups of hot cider to the volunteers.

". . . and I went to see the tree at Rockefeller Center yesterday," Sophie was saying. "We were going to go ice skating, but—"

The screen went black as the connection cut out.

"Oh, shi—" This was just her rotten luck.

The furnace bucked a few times, then the room went dark but for the flicker of flames in the fireplace. Brooklyn shuffled to the windows to open the drapes. Watery light faded in, along with a cool draft.

Mom was wrong about moving back here. This place was creepy. She shivered and took her cell out of her pocket. Well, at least her cell phone still worked, although the battery was low. Where the hell was her charger? Well, it wasn't going to work with the power out. Quickly, she sent a text to Sophie: computer down! this place sucks.

A moment later, her phone buzzed. Sophie!

"Oh my God, can you believe the power went out?" Brook paced away from the window, unable to shake the creepy feeling.

"Thank God for cell phones," Sophie said.

"Really." As Brook talked, she went into her room, grabbed the blanket from her bed and collapsed into the closet where she'd nested the other night when she'd heard that scary noise.

"Did I tell you about the murders?"

"Murders?" Sophie laughed. "Now you're just making stuff up."

"No. No. No, I'm not," Brook assured her. She told Sophie about the woman who was just passing through town, and then how Mia Collins, sort of a distant relative, was killed in the same way.

"Ohmigosh! That's way more dangerous than New York!"

"I know, but my mom is all like, this is a great place to live. And people are just rude here. And strange. Not like New York strange. Like hick strange."

"Well, this relative of yours that got killed . . . seriously? I mean, Brook . . . that's really scary!" Sophie said.

"That's what I've been saying! I didn't know Mia all that well. Kit's her daughter, and she's like a cousin, sort of, and Mom's worried about both of us. Oh. And Mom's a deputy now."

"A deputy?"

"I'm telling you, my mom will never leave! I can't wait till college when I can get the hell out of . . ." Brook's voice trailed off as a strange odor reached her nose. What was that? It smelled kind of . . . like nail polish remover. She sniffed again. No. Now it smelled like smoke. There had been a few logs in the fireplace, but she usually couldn't smell that back in her bedroom.

Letting Sophie talk, she got out of the closet and took a deep breath. Definitely something burning.

"I'll call you right back." She shoved her phone in her pocket and recalled the Pop-Tart she'd left in the toaster. Her pulse raced a little faster as she thought of how mad her mom would be if . . .

She opened the bedroom door to a room of haze. Immediately, her eyes burned, and she choked on a breath. Dark smoke masked everything . . . except the flames rolling over the walls at the front of the house!

"Oh, my God!" Casting a quick look at the kitchen sink, she considered throwing water on the flames, but this was no toaster fire.

Get out. Get out! GET OUT!

She edged forward, snatched up a dishcloth and covered her mouth, her eyes, searching wildly for escapes.

The kitchen door was a wall of flame. And the front? She couldn't even make out the door in the roaring fury of fire!

Whimpering in fear, she backed into her bedroom and slammed the door behind her. The window! She yanked on it and accidentally dropped her phone behind the side of the bunk bed.

Oh, no. Oh, no. For some stupid reason the window wouldn't open.

"Damn it. Damn it!"

She was trapped in a burning house!

Seated between Delilah and Nell, Ricki wasn't allowed to sulk about her daughter during the sleigh ride. It would have been impossible, with Tyler's wife, Jen, acting as the Christmas carol police, calling out new songs and making sure that everyone was singing. Well, almost everyone. Delilah seemed lost in her own world and Colton said he didn't want to scare the horses, and Rourke followed Colt's every move. That, at least, was heartwarming to see how he was accepting his father. Brook could take a lesson from him.

Maybe Ricki's glum feeling was about more than Brook's defection. Maybe it was about Mom. Rachel Dillinger had always said there was nothing like a country sleigh ride to clear the head. She'd been right. And with Ricki's head clear, she realized that she still missed her mother. In some ways, she always would.

As Colt shifted the reins to guide the sleigh team back to the barn, Ricki noticed a dark cloud on the horizon. Not so much a cloud . . .

"Stop the music a second. Someone's got a fire going on our property." Ricki pointed through the purpling skies. "Do you guys see that smoke over toward the east?" The song trailed off as everyone turned to take a look.

"Think it's Davis, doing a controlled burn?" Nell asked anxiously.

"Not this time of year. Not this late in the day." A stab of worry pinned Ricki as she squinted at the black puff on the horizon.

"What is it?" Jen asked.

"It's back toward the lodge." Colton slapped the reins and hollered to the horses, and the sleigh shot ahead down the snow-covered path.

A stand of trees and a gentle rise blocked that part of the landscape from view, but the second that the sleigh broke past the barrier, Ricki's worst fears were confirmed.

The foreman's house was on fire!

The front porch was in flames!

And her daughter was inside.

"Hold on tight!" Colt shouted back.

"Go! Go, go!" Ricki shouted, though it wasn't necessary. Colt had already urged the horses into a run. The sleigh bounced and rocked as its runners strained against the brittle, frozen land.

Beside her, Delilah was already on her cell, asking for the fire and rescue squad.

Nell shook Ricki's arm. "Brooklyn?"

It was hard to hear over the horses' hooves, the rocking sleigh and the pounding of her pulse. Ricki swallowed back the knot in her throat. "She's inside."

Everyone braced themselves as the sled flew over the final rise and slammed back on the path. Ricki's teeth jolted in her head, but she didn't care. She didn't care about anything but the baby girl she had loved for fourteen years.

With the foreman's house in full view now, the fire's fury was undeniable. Black smoke rolled off the roof timbers and mixed with falling snow. The blaze engulfed the entire front of the house, orange and yellow flames licking the beams, outlining the A-frame shape.

Ricki's fingers dug into the seat as the sled drew closer.

Don't panic.

She knew hysteria wouldn't help the situation, but she wanted to bound out of the moving sleigh and dash through the roiling flames.

When they reached the final slope, Colton halted the horses and Ricki scrambled out while the sleigh was still moving. She landed in a drift that covered her boots, but she tore through the snow to get to her daughter.

The wood of the front porch glowed red—pulsing, hot coals. There was no getting through that way, so she raced around to the side of the cabin, hoping to find Brook waiting outside the kitchen door.

But the side door was ablaze, too. A separate fire, suspiciously confined to the exit. There was no way in . . . no way out.

"Oh, my God!" She tore at her hair, veering into the searing heat. "Brook! Brooklyn! Where are you?" Her throat burned. Her eyes teared from smoke.

In the periphery of her focus, her family moved around her, shouting and scrambling and calling for Brook.

If the doors were impassible, Ricki would have to find another way in. She was backing around the house in search of a way in when a crashing sound split the air.

Glass exploded from the window of the rear bedroom—Brook's bedroom.

"Brook?" Pressing into a gust of thick smoke, Ricki could make out a flurry of movement in the window. Something fell over the sill—Brook's zebra blanket. A moment later, there was a denim-clad leg on the windowsill.

"Brook!"

The teen jumped, sailed out the window and dropped into the snow.

Ricki rushed forward. She picked up her daughter from the ground and folded her arms around her, noting the smell of smoke on her, the ash on her face, the coating of soot that made her hair brittle as Ricki stroked it.

"Brook. Oh, my God, Brook." Her voice cracked, wrought with emotion. "Are you okay? What happened?" She was shaking from head to toe and so was her daughter.

"Rudolph . . ." Brook choked out. "I couldn't find him."

Ricki let out a breath of relief. "He's probably hiding. Animals are smart that way." She prayed she was telling the truth. As she spoke, she edged her daughter away from the heat and smoke of the fire.

A man ran up to them, his hand on Ricki's shoulder. "Anyone else inside?" he asked.

Ricki recognized Hunter Kincaid, though the rest of the fire squad was still on the way, sirens wailing in the distance.

"No one else—"

"But my kitten!" Brook interrupted.

"Stay back," Hunter ordered, adding, "I'll look for it."

Immediately, he got back to work with Colton and Tyler, hacking burning embers from the porch and spraying the fire with the garden hose, which someone had apparently found in the garage.

Ricki turned away from the wall of heat and hugged her daughter again. "I'm so glad you're safe. What happened?" she asked again.

"I was Skyping and the power went out. So Sophie called me back on my cell, and we were just talking awhile." Brook's rapid-fire speech reflected Ricki's racing pulse. "And then I smelled something funny, then smoke. At first I thought it was the toaster, but when I went to check the front door was on fire. The kitchen door, too! I'm sorry about the broken window, but it was stuck and I dropped my phone and it was the only way I could get out!"

"Forget the window. The important thing is that you're okay. I'm proud of you, honey."

Brook coughed, swiped at a soot-smudged cheek. "I don't know how it happened. I didn't do anything."

"I'm just so glad you're okay," Ricki said again, her mind shying away from the terrible thought that Brook could have been seriously hurt.

I love you, she thought. Tears burned behind her eyes, threatening to spill out.

Brook pulled back, her gaze on the orange waves of fire in front of her eyes. There was something in her expression—a glimmer of fear or guilt—that sent Ricki's mind spiraling off in a different direction as aunts and cousins surrounded them, hugging and patting Brook on the back.

The image of that lighter in Brook's backpack.

She wanted to dismiss it, but there was no denying the trouble at school . . . Brook's history. The fire that had been started in New York . . .

No.

Ricki wanted to deny the thought as soon as it crowded into her mind, but it persistently remained. And she didn't need an arson specialist to know this fire was deliberate: the entire porch structure had burned quickly, as if it was doused in gasoline or kerosene. Was someone trying to hurt Brook? Send a message to Ricki by hurting her daughter? Scary as those notions were, they were better than the idea of Brook starting the fire herself to get attention. *Oh, please, God, no. Anything but that.* Ricki couldn't bear the thought that her daughter might be as deluded as the father she had escaped.

He watched through the descending night from the crest of a hill as the Dillingers ran around like chickens with their heads cut off. He could just make them out: as small and insubstantial as toy figures riding a model train, their coats and knit caps dark against the snow.

From his pocket he removed the teeth and popped them into his mouth. They still tasted of salt and blood, but he didn't mind. He was tasting the essence of his victims, woman and beast, sucking the life from them, mastering them. As he rolled them around with his tongue, he considered the chaos below him. Those Dillingers, pounding through the snow on their horses, tearing over the prairie in their vehicles. He let his tongue linger in the crevice of a molar, feeling his juices flowing once again.

He would have another Dillinger, soon.

They were concerned about the fire . . . about things that did not matter.

They should be worried about dying, because the end is near.

He rolled the loose teeth around in his mouth, his body pulsing, rock hard, as he thought of the power that would be his. He would have everything he rightly deserved. Finally.

Chapter Twenty-One

Hunter stood at the front of the cathedral-ceilinged dining room, where all the Dillingers were assembled along with Sam and Davis Featherstone and several other members of the sheriff's department and fire squad. Luckily Whit Crowley was off-duty today, so there was one less jackass to contend with. Hunter had been elected to speak to the family, though there was nothing to tell until they had time to assess what had caused the fire. It was just that someone needed to reassure them. The fire was out and the investigation had begun. The foreman's cottage had been saved, but the damage at the points of ignition was extensive.

He looked over the somber Dillingers, noting Colton and Sam's smoke-stained faces, undoubtedly a reflection of his own soot-covered skin and clothes. His gaze inadvertently landed on Delilah. That red-gold hair. That touch-me-not demeanor. Her years in Hollywood had turned her from a rawhide-tough, skinny kid to a slim woman with curves in the right places and a haughty attitude he could read from across the room. All Dillinger.

"Is it arson?" Ira demanded before Hunter could speak.

"Yes," Hunter said. "The electricity was cut from the feed

outside. And there were multiple points of origin for the fire—the front door and the kitchen door, which is around the side of the house, a good twenty feet away."

"You're saying someone deliberately started it?" Ricki's daughter asked.

Brooklyn, he remembered. Everyone had tried to get her to go to bed, but she wanted to hear what he had to say. He got it. She needed to know. She was tightly holding the white kitten Hunter had found yowling in the woodpile. The little feline had clamped on with tiny, fierce claws that had made it damn near impossible for him to extract it. Besides the smoke, he had a few bloody scratches for his effort.

"They used gasoline and an accelerant, lighter fluid like you spray on charcoal in a grill. You'd need some kind of squirt can to soak the eaves of the porch roof. That's what made it catch fire and burn at that intensity and speed. We'll know more tomorrow."

"Was someone trying to kill me?" Brook asked in a quavering voice.

"No," Ira and Ricki declared at the same moment, with Ricki adding, "That doesn't make any sense."

Hunter said, "Someone was trying to block the exits. We can't be sure they knew you were in the house, especially with most of the family gone on that sleigh ride." *But we need to pursue the motive,* he thought.

Apparently Sam agreed with him, because he turned to Ricki. "Could be a grudge against you or your family," the sheriff told her.

"Besides the Kincaids?" Ricki responded with a snort.

"Last I checked, our two families were on speaking terms," Hunter reminded. "My mother and Ira have been meeting about oil rights."

"Georgina and I are talking with Century Petroleum," Ira clarified. "There's no deal yet. No one's signed anything."

Hunter kept his expression neutral. Ira, the old dog, would hardly admit that there were ongoing negotiations. Couldn't bear for anyone to think he might have softened about the feud, though Hunter knew his mother sure hadn't. Whatever Georgina was doing with Ira Dillinger was a mystery to Hunter.

"I know some people have a bone to pick with me." Ricki spoke up. "Especially now that I'm law enforcement. First one that comes to mind is Dodge Miller. He was spitting mad when he recognized me last night."

"Yeah, there's that." Sam rubbed the back of his neck. "I'm gonna track him down. See if he left his trailer today. In the meantime, we need to be thinking about who else might have a motive."

Hunter opened his arms to include all the Dillingers at the table. "And if any of you remember anyone on Dillinger property that shouldn't have been here or seemed out of place, report it."

Tears streaked through the ash on Brooklyn's face. "I want to go home. Just take me home." She leaned into Ricki, who was sitting beside her.

"Honey, the house is filled with smoke," Ricki said. "No one can sleep there to—"

"Not there. Back to New York. I'm done with this place. I want out of this cow-shit town, out of this insane family!"

"I know." Ricki patted her daughter's back. "This is really hard, and you were very brave today. But we're going to pull through it. Your family is behind you."

"My family might get me killed," Brook declared. "What if this is because somebody's got it in for Dillingers, Mom? What if I get killed because of it?"

"You're fine now, and we're going to do everything we can to make sure you and the rest of our family are protected." Ricki's voice was loving but firm.

"What do you want to do?" Colton asked Hunter.

"For now, clean up," he admitted. "When I have more information, I'll be in touch."

Everyone rose from the table, meeting adjourned. But when Hunter looked for Delilah, she was nowhere to be seen.

"Go on up and take a shower," Ricki told Brook. The girl was pallid with exhaustion, but she did as she was told, dragging herself out of the room toward the stairs.

The main floor was empty but for family and a few stragglers from the fire squad. Ricki found Sam taking notes at the desk in the great room. She bypassed Colt and Rourke and approached Sam. "I need to talk to you," she said in a voice so quiet, it was nearly lost in the cavernous room.

Sam stopped writing. "Okay."

She drew a deep breath, exhaled, then dropped to her knees so that her eyes were level with his. "Back in New York, there was an issue with Brook and her friends, and a fire."

"What do you mean?" Concern burned Sam's smoky eyes.

Glancing toward the door, she was grateful to see that Colton was ushering Rourke out of the room. When they were completely alone, she said, "Brooklyn had a friend who was a kid on the edge. Shoplifting, smoking, drinking. She was smart and clever, but from one of those families where the kids were overlooked. She set several small fires, one of them on school grounds."

"Uh-oh."

"I know. A fire in a trash can. April said she had been trying to put out a cigarette. Maybe that was true. But the administration pulled in all of April's friends, and Brook was one of them. Though Brook says she warned April to be careful with the cigarette, who knows . . . ?" Ricki trailed off.

"I tried to forbid Brook from seeing her. They weren't close friends, but she resented my interference anyway."

"Kids do stupid things. You know that," Sam said gently. "Doesn't mean they're headed for a life of crime."

"Yeah, but the other day I found a lighter in Brook's backpack." Ricki pressed her hands together tensely. "And she hates it here. She tells me that all the time. I just . . . don't want to think that she set this fire to take away our home and pave the way back to New York."

"She's not capable of that," Sam told her.

His dark eyes held her gaze, and she envied the assurance she saw there. "How can you be sure?"

"Doesn't match up with the kid I've observed these last few days. And Ricki, look at the details of this fire. The electricity cut from the outside? A kid her age probably doesn't even know where the line comes in. And both exits burning? Seems to me she would have left herself a way out. This fire was beyond Brook's current skill set."

"My God, I hope you're right."

"I am." He rose from the desk and reached for her.

Energized by his touch, Ricki straightened and took a deep breath.

"Should I send Katrina on that interview this afternoon? You can stay with Brook and—"

"No." Ricki smoothed down her sweater, as if taking a mental inventory. "I'll go check on Brook, but then I'm going to try to reach Doc's girlfriend, keep pushing the investigation. I need to keep busy, and there's no use sitting around and waiting for Hunter Kincaid and the fire department to do their part."

"You sure you want to keep going tonight?"

"Yep."

She walked with him across the room as Delilah slipped inside, glancing behind her toward the foyer as if she didn't want to be seen by anyone. "I was outside the door and heard what you said about Brook," Delilah admitted. "I wasn't trying to eavesdrop, but—"

"It's all right." Ricki finalized her good-byes to Sam, then closed the front door behind him and leaned back against the panels, staring at her sister. "I never thought she was really involved with April, but when I found that lighter, and now the fire . . ."

"Sam's right. Brook couldn't have done this. Maybe she had the lighter because she was experimenting with cigarettes herself. Or burning incense, or something," Delilah suggested.

Ricki nodded, feeling hopeful. "Scented candles. That was the excuse she gave me."

"See? That could be it. Stranger things have happened."

"You heard Sam. You sound just like him."

"Great minds think alike."

Ricki smiled faintly. "It was nice to hear him defending my daughter. Sam's so level-headed, so sane, y'know?"

"He is," Delilah agreed.

"It's good to be home. Even with everything that's going on, I think this is the right place for us."

"Because of Sam?"

"Partly," Ricki admitted.

"Ricki, are you falling for him?" Delilah asked, a smile creeping across her face.

"Oh, no."

"You sure?"

She shook her head. "I have to work with him. I don't have time to fall in love with anyone. Besides, Sam's more like a brother to me."

Delilah's guffaw could be heard all the way to the second floor.

* * *

It was nearly seven when Ricki headed out to her truck in search of Doc's "mysterious" friend, Allison Waller, who assured her that she would be at her home in Lander tonight when Ricki stopped by. When Ricki had called her, she was just getting off work at the car dealership where she was employed, but she'd been more than accommodating.

As she climbed into her truck, she heard a distant bark and a yelp. Coyote? The plaintive tone struck a sad chord inside her, somehow reminding her of the two women who had died alone at the hand of a predator. She paused, scanning the horizon as her breath produced a white puff in the air. She could feel him, his heinous touch nearby. He was close . . . maybe even watching the lodge at this very moment.

And he was coming after her . . . or was it Brooklyn he wanted? This didn't seem like the same m.o. as the church fire. So, what did that mean? Two arsonists? Was he after her, now that she had joined the sheriff's department? Was he after Brook? Was he making a statement to the Dillingers as a whole? Or was it someone else entirely?

The coyote howled again and she touched the bulge at her hip, reassured by the pistol at her belt. It was a fact of nature—predator and prey—but not something to be tolerated in human society.

As she got into the truck, worry weighed her down. First Amber, then Mia, then . . . then a fire in her home. Oh, God, was her small family next on his list?

Putting her fears aside with an effort, she drove over to Lander and located the small subdivision Allison Waller called home. The split-level homes with picture windows had probably been all the rage when they were built in the fifties, but now they suffered from a plague of leaky windows and abandoned cars.

From the outside, Allison's home seemed well kept. The older woman who answered the door introduced herself as Allison's mother, Esther.

"You want coffee?" Esther offered, her mouth set in a tight line. Was that because her daughter was being interviewed by a cop, or did tension always permeate this home?

"No, thanks." Ricki waited just inside the door, taking in the contemporary sofa, easy chair, flat screen TV. A moment later a stunning woman came into the room. From her bleached blond hair to the spiked heels of her boots, Allison Waller was everything Ricki had expected, with one exception. She was actually beautiful.

"Hey, there. You must be Ricki Dillinger." Allison tilted her head so that her blond hair fell over one side of her face, grazing the gloss on her lips.

"Thanks for seeing me. I just have a few questions for you about the night you and Doc were at Big Bart's."

"Come in." Allison motioned Ricki to a sofa, and they both sat, staring toward the picture window.

"I guess Doc told you we have to keep this quiet." When the woman's blue eyes connected, there was a surprising alertness. "We don't mean to cause anyone heartache."

"Right." Ricki wasn't here to judge her. "It was Thanksgiving weekend."

"The night that woman went missing. The one found in the church, all . . . cut up."

"She was on her way back to California and stopped in for a bite to eat, apparently."

"I was hanging out in the Buffalo Lounge. With Stu. You know that already, don't you?"

Ricki nodded. "Do you remember Amber Barstow at all?"

"Not really," she admitted.

"Okay. Do you happen to remember what time you were there?"

"Around eight, I'd say. Doc has a reputation to protect, and he's trying to protect me, too. God knows what the folks around here would call me if they knew. We had dinner at the bar and we were just into each other, y'know. We left when the Buffalo Lounge closed, around two."

On the table behind Allison was a photo of a baby holding a ball. It reminded Ricki that Doc had delivered her, and she was barely older than Allison. Talk about robbing the cradle.

"That's good to know. It covers Doc's whereabouts."

Allison uncrossed her legs and leaned toward Ricki. "I'm not just saying that to save his sorry ass. I want you to catch that killer as much as any single woman in this town. But that Saturday, Doc was with me," she said meaningfully.

"How did you hook up with him?" Ricki asked, curious.

She smiled in remembrance. "He came into the dealership for a sports car. I sold him the Corvette, gave him a few upgrades. He got quite a ride out of it," she added impishly.

"You two go to Big Bart's often?"

"Every week or so. It doesn't draw too many folks from Prairie Creek, and usually, since we're sitting at the bar, any flirting looks like good clean fun."

"Do you remember anyone else who was at the bar that night?"

Allison reeled off a few names, all of whom had already been questioned. Sam had compiled a list of patrons from the receipts and the bartender's recollection of that night.

"Anyone there that you didn't recognize? Strangers?"

"Mmm . . . yeah. There was a dude at the bar. Kind of a cowboy." The description of the tall man in black was familiar.

"You talk to him?" This could be the guy Grady Chisum mentioned.

"Well, yeah . . . when Doc went outside to take a call," she admitted.

"Find out where he was from?"

"It was just a little flirtation," she said, as if Ricki had made a judgment call. "I asked him, 'cause I knew he wasn't from around here, but he didn't tell me." Allison's smile fell away from her face. "You think that was him, don't you? The killer?" The lines between her brows creased her pretty face. "God, I hope I wasn't coming on to a killer."

Ricki inclined her head noncommittally. "Thank you for being forthcoming."

Allison shrugged. "Stu was the one who was worried about me talking to you. He's protective that way."

Protective of his reputation, Ricki thought. "Doc's a good man. Known him all my life."

Both women stood up. Allison headed toward the door, but paused in the vestibule. "It could have been me."

"What?"

"If I hadn't been with Stu that night, I would have given that guy some play. He could have killed me instead of that Barstow woman." She squeezed her eyes shut and shuddered. "I'm telling you, Deputy, life is short, and it's scary to brush that close to death in a cowboy hat."

The phrase rolled through Ricki's mind over and over again as she drove back into town.

Death in a cowboy hat.

After today's fire, she felt like it was time for some more soul searching about her decision to move out here, to the land of cowboy hats and gun racks. Maybe Brook was right; maybe they'd be better off packing up and heading back to New York, where neighborhoods and streets were crowded with people who acted as a natural crime deterrent, and where the cops were just minutes away.

She called Sam on her cell phone. "I'm heading back home. I met with Allison Waller and she flirted with the guy in the black Stetson at the Buffalo Lounge. She said if it weren't for Doc, she mighta gone for him."

"You're thinking this stranger's the killer?" Sam asked.

"I don't know. How'd it go with Dodge Miller?"

"Fine. Better than you'd expect," Sam said with a note of surprise. He explained that the cranky butcher had actually invited Sam into his trailer, apologized for the night before and allowed Sam to search the place.

"I was hoping he could give us something," Ricki said, somewhat disappointed.

"It would have been hard for him to get to Big Bart's by midnight that Saturday night," Sam said. Miller claimed to have been visiting his kids in Cheyenne until late Saturday, and his son and daughter had confirmed his story. "It's possible if he drove the interstate at ninety, maybe a hundred miles per hour."

"In snow conditions?" She let out a breath. "Nah."

"Crazier things have been done out here."

"Now you're humoring me."

"Maybe, but I can see you're discouraged." His voice was soft, surprisingly patient. "I'm just trying to hook you back into the case, make you hungry for justice."

"Oh, I'm hungry for it," she said vehemently. "I'm starving." She thought of her daughter's tearstained face, gray with soot. "After what happened to Brook today, I'd do anything to get this killer."

"So, it's back to the stranger in the black Stetson."

"Yeah . . ." Her voice trailed off as she reached Prairie Creek's main street. "Where are you?"

"I dropped back into the station, but I'm leaving."

"Going home?"

"Heading that way."

"Okay," she sighed.

"You're playing the 'what if' game, aren't you?"

"What do you mean?"

"You can't get your mind off Brooklyn's close call today. What if the fire had spread faster? What if she hadn't made it out alive?"

Ricki felt her eyes burn with tears. "She's okay. She's with Delilah tonight." She drove by the station. "I see your Jeep."

"I see you," he said, stepping outside, the phone to his ear. He signaled her over, and Ricki wheeled into the lot.

She stopped beside him and rolled down the window. Suddenly, she was bone-weary. "All I want to do is go to bed, but my bed is not inhabitable tonight."

With the smoke damage and broken window at the foreman's cottage, it would take a few days to get the place back to normal. Even then, Ricki wasn't sure she had any desire to go back.

"Come home with me," Sam said. "I'll take the couch."

She tilted her head. "They'll find room for me at the lodge."

"Do you really want to go there?"

"No," she admitted.

"I can offer professional protection, twenty-four-seven. You know you'll sleep better with a big, strong man around to keep you safe."

He scared a smile out of her.

"And I'll be the perfect gentleman."

Well, that was disappointing. Still . . . she would feel safe with Sam near, and the truth was she didn't want to leave him. "I have to be at the house early tomorrow. Even though Delilah's taking care of Brook, I—"

"You need to make sure she's okay," he interjected.

"Yeah," she said.

"Leave your truck here and get in the Jeep," he said, and Ricki swept her jacket from the seat and did just that.

Sam's house was off a busy state road, but it was far enough back in the trees to feel secluded.

"Should I be worried about making a path through your bachelor pad?" Ricki teased as she waited for Sam to unlock the front door. "I'm envisioning a trail of socks and underwear and stacks of cardboard pizza boxes."

"I have my vices, but living with raccoons is not one of them."

He opened the door and revealed a tidy living room. Golden light washed over a rust-colored sofa, white shag rug and brown leather chair.

"Nice," she said as she followed him in.

"Here's my downfall." He turned to what should have been the dining room. Covered in newspaper, the room was a graveyard of shiny metal parts.

"What is this?"

"It's my workshop. These are parts for two snowmobiles that I'm reconditioning. I like to tinker."

"And you don't use the garage because . . . ?"

"It's cold out there. Besides, I've never used this room. You want a drink? Wine or beer?"

"Beer sounds good." She needed something to take the edge off.

He opened two bottles and started a fire in the potbelly stove. As heat began to suffuse the room, they talked about the old days in Prairie Creek, when Sam and Colton were high school students and were paid a good wage to help out with the cattle.

"Those weekends when we branded the calves . . ." Sam shook his head, looking off into the distance. "That was good money for a kid in school."

"That was one time I was glad to be a girl." Ricki would never forget those roundups. The noise and smell of bawling, mud-caked animals. The stink of manure and burning hair. "I worked one of them, and that was my last. I don't think girls are meant to witness a castration."

Sam grinned. "Maybe. But it's no picnic for a guy, either."

Somewhere near midnight, Ricki yawned and Sam said they might as well get some sleep. She rose and stretched, thinking how Sam had been true to his word—the perfect gentleman. As he grabbed a blanket from the closet and showed her into the bedroom, she realized it would be up to her to take things to the next level.

"Can I get you anything else?" he asked as they stood beside the double bed, neatly made with its puffy red plaid quilt.

"Just one more thing." She rested her hands on his upper arms, tentative. When he didn't blink, she allowed herself to move closer, her body leaning against the rock-hard wall of his chest, hips, pelvis and legs. "How about a kiss good night?"

His eyelids were nearly closed as he brushed her lips gently, then latched on, fiercely, hungrily.

His hands pressed into the small of her back, then slid down to cup her butt. When he pulled her against him and showed her how much he wanted her, she groaned in pleasure.

Before she knew it, they were rolling on the bed, stripping off their clothes, talking about a condom in a haze of woozy desire. Naked with Sam, flesh against flesh, she felt her body reel with yearning, and she couldn't get enough of the taste, smell and feel of him.

At last, he was poised over her, her bare limbs pressed to his, her hands discovering the sinewy muscles of his back and the swell of his tight butt.

"Are you sure?" he asked, his eyes afire, his voice a rough whisper.

That was the thing; in this random world, at this moment, the only thing she knew for sure was that she wanted him.

"Yes, Sam," she said, her voice clear and decisive. "Yes."

PART THREE

by
Nancy Bush

Chapter Twenty-Two

Delilah tiptoed out of the bedroom, taking a last look at Brook's sleeping form. She was curled up on her side with the little white kitten tucked around her neck. It had been a long night where Brook, in her twin bed, had actually reached across to Delilah and clasped her hand until she'd fallen asleep. The girl had been deep down scared, and who could blame her. Delilah had asked if she wanted her mother, but Brook had just squeezed her hand harder, and Delilah had been happy to be a maternal surrogate.

Now she made her way to the stables, walking through the brisk morning air, her cheeks numb from the frigid air. In the midst of the craziness the night before, she'd heard rumblings that Babylon had foaled, and she planned to see the newborn colt before anyone else was about, wanting this moment to herself.

What she didn't want was to admit to the rest of her family that she was a failure. A failure in life, a failure in love and a definite failure in her career. When Daniel Selkins had brought her in for an audition and then bent her roughly over his desk, holding her down with one hand and ripping at his belt buckle with the other, she'd been so stunned it had taken her a full ten seconds to react, and by that time he'd ripped her panties down to her ankles and was trying to drive himself between her legs.

She'd grabbed the phone charger and twisted around. It wasn't much of a weapon, but she'd yanked it from its tether and slammed it into his eye. Hard.

With a yowl of pain he released her, but needless to say, she didn't get that part or any others in the future. Her reaction had pretty much ended her career as an actress. From that point forward she'd worked behind the camera instead of in front of it, and though she liked production work all right, it wasn't the career she'd planned when she left Prairie Creek behind.

She had never told a living soul what happened. As far as her acting career went, it had died a quick death from the moment she resisted Selkins's amorous attack. She'd never been offered another seriously good role since. Still, she'd stayed on and found some happiness in production. She'd even told herself she might find a soul mate in one of the actors or directors or even production guys, but that was a dream. There had been a lot of dates, some romantic entanglements and one relationship that had lasted nearly ten months, but there'd never been any real chemistry. Not since Hunter Kincaid.

Grimacing, she stepped carefully down the path to the stables, her cowboy boots slipping a bit on an icy patch. She was a cowgirl at heart. Always had been, always would be, though she'd denied it in herself so long that she'd almost begun to believe it. Now, long years since she'd kicked the dust of Prairie Creek from her heels, she was back again. She'd pretended to Ricki that she was just here for the wedding. That there was no chance she would stay. Was that the truth? She didn't know. But even with all the fear, drama and danger going on in her Wyoming hometown now, she was kinda glad to be back.

If it weren't for Hunter, she might stay for good.

She made a growling sound beneath her breath, then sighed. How tragic. Letting one man influence her so much. One teenaged love affair. It was ridiculous, but no matter how hard she tried to dislodge the memories from her brain, it was damn near impossible.

Thinking about Hunter brought back the scene from that night: his long legs and lean body at the front of the great room, his dark hair, slightly long, his face smeared with soot, his blue eyes narrowed in that suspicious way all Kincaids seemed to view Dillingers and vice versa. She'd tried to regard him objectively. Good-looking. Lean, in that cowboy way she loved. Nice enough, probably, at least to anyone other than a Dillinger. Great smile, when he scared one up.

She'd half convinced herself that she was over him completely. Why shouldn't she be? It had been years and years since their ill-fated, secret affair. She'd started to believe that he had no real effect on her anymore, that she just didn't care. Then he'd shown kindness to Brook, and all Delilah's rationale and defenses failed her after that. She'd looked at Hunter and remembered how it had felt making love to him, had sensed the same melting feeling in the pit of her stomach, the same treacherous heat between her legs. Good. God. Those feelings had been the bane of her existence when she was a teen. She cringed inside, remembering the way she'd followed him around like the proverbial lovesick puppy. She'd been so pathetic back then, so lovestruck, so willing to lie down in the hay and beg him to take her.

Even now, with his face swimming behind her eyes, she could feel something weaken and grow molten inside her, and her cheeks heated despite the cold.

What a pisser.

Throwing open the door to the stables, she was greeted by warmer air, and she quickly rattled the sliding door back into place to keep out the cold. Kit Dillinger, her red-brown hair tied back in a braid, her attention on the newborn colt, looked up from the box and shot her a sideways glance.

"Hi," Delilah said as she approached the stall. Inside was a ruddy-coated colt with a bright white blaze, all knees and ears and eyes and skinny ribs. Delilah sucked in a breath as his mother nuzzled him, damn near knocking him over with her long nose. Her heart swelled into her throat, and for a moment she was afraid she was going to embarrass herself and actually *cry.*

Pulling herself back from that precipice, she cleared her throat and said, "What a sweetheart." Kit glanced from Delilah back to the colt and nodded. "Davis around?" Delilah asked her.

"Out with the herd."

It wasn't like Delilah had anything particular to say to the ranch foreman. She just wanted to be out of the house and near the new little guy. Give herself time to think about something other than the wedding, the terrible things going on in Prairie Creek and last, but certainly not least, Hunter Kincaid.

And she also needed to think about herself, what she planned to do next. She didn't think Southern California was the answer anymore. She wanted her life to start. Family life. With or without a man.

At thirty-three, she wanted to have a baby and she didn't want to wait.

The little colt looked at her from behind his mother's flank. Delilah could feel herself respond and she had to turn away from Kit's probing gaze as she glanced her way again. "Does he have a name yet?" she asked.

"Firestarter," Kit said. "It's what I call him. He was born last night during the fire."

"It's a good name," Delilah told her. At first she'd been taken aback, what with the fires and murders going on, but on second thought she decided the name fit the little horse with the reddish coat.

She left the stables a few moments later, tucking her chin inside her scarf, though she was almost glad of the biting wind; it helped cool the rise of emotion inside her. The last thing she needed was to break down and make a complete fool out of herself just because her maternal hormones were on overload. Good Lord, she was a mess. And everyone thought she was so capable. So in charge. So able to magically transform her father and Pilar's wedding into something extra special. Bullshit. All she really wanted to do was bury her head under her pillow and wait for everything to pass.

Which was a chicken's way out. Here Ricki was off searching for a murderer and Hunter was examining the fires for clues to the arsonist, while she spent time just thinking about herself and the dissatisfying life choices she'd made up till now.

She glanced toward the mountains, blue-gray in the distance, and her mind touched on the kidnapped girl from Big Bart's. Skinned and frozen and left at the Pioneer Church. And then Mia. And even a coyote . . . defiled out on Dillinger land . . .

And the fires.

Wiping off her boots on the front doormat, Delilah then headed inside and up the stairs to her bedroom. Just before she reached her door she saw Ricki step quietly from the room and softly close the door behind her.

"There you are," Ricki said softly, pulling Delilah down the hall away from the door. "How'd last night go? Was Brook okay?"

"She was fine. She's tough."

"I felt bad running out on her, but she wanted to stay with you."

"I was glad to be there for her," Delilah assured her.

"How are you doing? You're in yesterday's clothes. I can smell the smoke."

"Can you?" She sniffed and made a face. "Oh, yeah. I just came back to change but the cottage is a mess. I didn't even go inside. The rest of my clothes probably smell even worse."

"Where have you been?" Delilah asked.

"Well . . ."

"With Sam?"

"Shhh." She glanced back at Brook's door, grabbed Delilah's arm again and pulled her even farther away. "Okay, you caught me."

"Oh, great. Colton and Sabrina, and now you and Sam. Do you know what hell it is being around you all?"

"It just happened."

"Bullshit. Nothing just happens. We talked about this. What about working with him?" Delilah reminded her, arching an eyebrow.

Ricki lifted her hands in surrender. "I mighta overthought that. Maybe we can work together."

"It's a damn lovefest around here," Delilah said sourly.

Ricki smiled at Delilah, which did not improve her mood. "What about that guy from Century Petroleum? Tom. He was looking at you pretty hard the other day."

If I wanted blue eyes, I'd go after Hunter Kincaid . . . Nope. That wasn't true. She didn't want Hunter, either.

"I can complain about you guys all I want, but I'm not looking to date anybody. This romance stuff . . . Dad and Pilar . . ." Delilah gave a mock shudder. "So where were you heading off to?"

"Back to work."

"To meet Sam again."

Ricki glanced down at her clothes and made a face. "I hope I don't smell too bad."

"You found a way to get through last night. Oh, wait. Guess you didn't have clothes on."

Ricki ignored her. "Why are you up so early?"

"I went to the stables to see Firestarter."

"Who?"

"Kit's name for the new colt."

"Firestarter," Ricki repeated dubiously.

"He's an adorable little guy. The new male in my life, I guess."

"How was Kit? I've been worrying about her. I've tried to get her to stay with us, but she won't."

"She seemed just fine."

"Davis has been looking after her."

"Then I think you can stop worrying."

"Do you?" Ricki questioned.

"He's a stand-up guy. Why?" Delilah asked, when Ricki thought that over. "Is there something I don't know?"

"No . . . I just wish Kit would let me help her. Maybe Davis can get through to her." She shook her head, then said, "Damn, I'm going to have to buy all new clothes."

"How about I go to the foreman's cottage, pick up your clothes and Brook's and bring 'em here to wash."

"Would you?"

"Ricki, you practically made me sign in blood that I would organize this wedding and everything that goes with it. That's what I'm doing. So, yes, I'll get your clothes. Mrs. Mac'll probably help out."

"You're a godsend."

"Yep."

Ricki smiled at her, but it was clear her thoughts were somewhere else. With Sam, most likely. "Hopefully the fire department's finished with their investigation and will let you in. Maybe you can ask Hunter," Ricki suggested.

"There's an idea," Delilah said carefully, as Ricki gave

her a big hug before heading back down the stairs to leave.

"Thanks a whole lot," Delilah called after her. "Now I probably smell like smoke, too."

Ricki made a very rude gesture with her finger, which she delivered with a grin, and Delilah gave it right back. Smiling at herself, she headed back to her bedroom, tiptoeing carefully as she gathered up new clothes and her toiletries. She then headed down the hall to the bathroom, stripped naked and stepped into the shower. Turning on the spray, she let the hot water pound her skin and steam the room around her.

Ask Hunter. Oh, sure. Like that's what she was going to do.

Fifteen minutes later she was dressed in jeans, her boots, a black turtleneck sweater and was reaching for her jacket, ready to head out, when she saw Mrs. Mac arriving early.

"Gotta make breakfast for this crowd," the housekeeper-cum-cook said.

"You need some help?"

"Heavens, girl. You got enough on your plate with the wedding."

"I'm going down to the foreman's house and try to get some clothes for Ricki and Brook, bring them back here to clean," Delilah said.

"Good idea. I'll help you, but I'd wait a bit. I think the fire department's coming back this morning."

The thought of running into Hunter changed Delilah's mind about the timing of her trip to the cottage. She could go later. Instead, she turned back to the great room as Mrs. Mac headed into the kitchen. Delilah purposely pushed thoughts of the fire and Hunter from her mind as she stared up at the rough-hewn boards of the soaring ceiling.

Pilar had hired Carolina Solsby of Carolina's Table, a local caterer, the only one in town actually, but now that the wedding was going to be at the house, there were new considerations. Sometime today Delilah planned to hit a rental store—again, the only one in town—and order enough folding chairs to accommodate all the guests attending the ceremony. Pilar had blown in late the night before—Delilah had heard her as she'd lain awake in the twin bed beside Brook's—and Delilah planned to go down the checklist with her on what was yet to be done to get ready for the new venue.

She was pacing off the room, wondering how many chairs would fit and still leave space for an aisle up the center, when a shadow fell across her. She looked up. A man in a black Stetson filled the doorway. Startled, she sucked in a sharp breath before recognizing her brother, Tyler.

"Jesus, Tyler. What are you trying to do? Scare me to death?"

"Scare you?"

"Yeah, scare me." She looked past him. "Where's Jen?"

"Still in bed. What are you doing up so early?"

"Seems to be the question of the day. I have a job," Delilah reminded him shortly. "This wedding is supposedly coming off in a few days and it's not going to do it by itself."

When he didn't respond, she shot him a look, seeing tension on his face. "Okay, what's wrong?"

He swept off his hat and ran a hand through his auburn hair. He looked a lot like Colt, with maybe a little more Dillinger added in. He and Jen lived in Colorado, where he ran his own smaller ranch while Jen raised their children.

"Does something have to be wrong?" he parried.

"Word games. Great. Just what I'm looking for."

Tyler walked up to the fireplace and gazed down at the ashes left over from the blaze Ira had built the night before. "Well, there is something."

"Mmm."

"Jen and I aren't . . . getting along too well."

Delilah thought about her earlier remarks about love

with Ricki. She hadn't considered Jen and Tyler, maybe because it seemed like they'd been married forever, since right out of high school. "Oh. Just going through a bit of a rough patch . . . ?"

"Rough," he said, grimacing.

"That doesn't sound good."

"Jen wanted to come to Dad's wedding and I didn't. She loves this kind of stuff and I can't stand it, and let's face it, she always wants to remind Dad that she's a Dillinger, too, now. Doesn't want to be forgotten."

Delilah looked at Tyler closely. Even though Tyler was only two years younger than she was, he'd always seemed to be in his own world when they were kids. Delilah didn't know him as well as she did Colton and Ricki, but on the other hand, she probably knew him better than they did. Their youngest sister, Nell, was the "oops" baby who'd shown up seven years after Tyler, so none of them had ever been as close to her in the same way. Now Delilah realized, with something of a surprise, that she was probably Tyler's go-to ear in the family.

"What are you saying?" she asked him.

"This is going to sound bad, but I don't want to be married anymore."

"You're right. That does sound bad. Does Jen know how you feel?" Delilah asked carefully.

"Not yet."

"She really doesn't know?"

"Well . . . she's gotta suspect," he said slowly. "I haven't been coming home much lately."

"Dammit, Tyler." Delilah gave him a hard look. "Is there someone else?"

"No."

He said it too fast and Delilah glanced away. She'd been through this too many times not to know where it was going. Her life in Southern California had been a string of cheating males. And here in Prairie Creek wasn't any better. Her father had cheated on her mother. No one talked about it, but it was one of those rumors that moved in and out, a whispered word here, a sideways look there. Her uncle had died during a tryst with Mia Collins when the homestead fire broke out. Even Colton had left Sabrina back in the day and had a brief fling with Pilar that had produced Rourke. And then, of course, there was the real reason Delilah had wanted to run far and fast away from Wyoming: Hunter. Who'd cheated on her with his ex-girlfriend, Abby Flanders. Okay, Delilah had just been a kid then, and Abby was a few years older, but she and Hunter had been so close. She'd believed he loved her, and she'd certainly thought she loved him.

Tyler's casual words reminded her of how she'd learned he was a cheat, how much it had hurt.

Everything had all fallen apart the night of the homestead fire, when Hunter had been with Abby while Delilah was waiting for him on the tire swing beneath the lone pine tree that stood like a sentinel between the main house and the old homestead. It was their special "trysting tree," as it had been named by Delilah's mother when Ira had wooed her. Delilah had been lost in anticipation of making love to Hunter, her face turned up to the pinprick stars that pierced the dark heavens above, when she'd seen the orange glow of the fire. She'd jumped to her feet just as the old homestead windows popped and shattered. Flames shot out in a loud roar, smoke boiling out in black-gray clouds. Delilah had first run toward the fire. She'd seen a dark figure running away from it, but hadn't been able to see who it was. Heat and sparks had thrust her back and she'd turned away, choking, in the direction of the new house, meeting her father and Colton as they rushed headlong toward the blaze, both of them barking at her to get to safety. Somehow Hunter made it to the fire, too, and tried to help Colton and Ira save Judd and Mia, but it was only Mia who'd survived.

Later, there were questions about why Hunter was there, questions he wouldn't answer, so rumors abounded that Hunter had set the fire for unnamed reasons. Some even thought he might be the drifter/arsonist who had plagued the area that summer, even though the authorities later caught the man who was responsible. Didn't matter. People wanted to blame somebody and a Kincaid was at the top of the Dillinger list.

Only when Abby stepped forward and said that Hunter had been with her, that she and he had seen the fire from her nearby parked car, just over the line into Kincaid land, had the rumors died down. Questioned about that night, Abby had said she'd quickly started her engine and driven Hunter there at his insistence. Delilah had wanted Hunter to deny it, for him to say something else: that he'd been near the old homestead because he'd been secretly there to meet her. But he didn't. He let Abby's story stand, and over time Delilah had come to realize that the reason he did was because it was the truth.

Now, she looked at Tyler and said with feeling, "You need to tell Jen right away that you've been cheating. She deserves that much and more."

"Hey, I'm not the bad guy here," he protested.

Aren't you? she thought.

Before she got into a bigger argument with him, she headed toward the stairs, grabbed two black Hefty bags and slammed out the front door to the foreman's cottage.

When Ricki got to the station she was the only one there except for Chet Norcross, and even he was yawning.

"Sam's not here yet?" she asked him.

"He shows up about eight."

Ricki looked through the front window. As if to prove Chet wrong, Sam's Jeep wheeled into the parking lot at that moment. Breaking into a smile, she headed outside to meet him.

"You beat me," he said, his dark eyes warm, as he climbed out of the car.

"I'm fast that way."

"Ahh . . ." He sent her a faint smile. "How's Brook?"

"Sleeping. Delilah's taking charge and Brook idolizes her, so I left. I want to get on this arson case."

"I already put a call into Raintree. He'll get back to me as soon as he's got the report from Kincaid."

Jack Raintree was the fire chief. "And I also want to go over who was at Big Bart's again the night Amber Barstow disappeared. If we zero in on Black Hat as our guy, maybe somebody will remember something more. I know we already went over the people who were there, but there's got to be something."

"Come into my office."

"Sorry about the clothes. Mine all smell this way."

"I didn't mind last night," he pointed out, sliding her a look packed with meaning.

"But you did notice."

"Hard not to. I just didn't care."

They smiled at each other and Ricki's mind took a quick trip down memory lane that was X-rated. She hoped to high heaven she wasn't blushing.

Once inside his office, Sam closed the door but didn't turn on the lights. He pulled her into his arms in the darkness and said softly, "I'm only going to do this once at work." Then he kissed her hard until she felt her knees weaken and her body start to slip down.

Before anything else could happen, he drew back and exhaled heavily. Then he flipped on the lights and they squinted at each other in the sudden brightness.

Man, I love you, she thought happily as Sam opened the blinds and she sat down opposite his desk.

"I've got the list right here," he said, tapping onto his computer and sending a page to the printer.

"Let's start with the women," Ricki suggested. "Allison talked to Black Hat for a while, flirted a bit, but she was waiting for Doc. Maybe he tried somebody else before he chose Amber. Somebody who hasn't admitted it yet, for whatever reason."

"All right," Sam said, settling behind his desk, his gaze on Ricki.

"Don't look at me like that," she said.

"Like what?"

"Like I'm probably looking at you."

They both broke into grins. "If we take it from the top, time-wise, we start with Mariah Kincaid," Sam said, dragging his eyes away. "She was about an hour too early for Barstow, but we don't know what time Black Hat arrived."

Ricki nodded. "She was home for Thanksgiving and she stopped at the Buffalo Lounge with her brother, Blair. Katrina talked to Mariah. Couldn't get hold of Blair." Because the Kincaids had been at the bar too early, Ricki had let Katrina talk to them. But now, she wanted to dig a little deeper. "I'll call Mariah. Although we both knew her and what a liar she was."

"It's been a lot of years since high school," Sam pointed out.

"You're right." She wouldn't want anyone holding Brook's reputation against her from their old school. "Katrina never could get hold of Blair. Called his cell multiple times but he never returned her call. He lives in . . . ?"

"Cody. Foreman at a ranch out there. Lives on the property."

"That's right. And Mariah's in Jackson. Runs an interior design shop that caters to the rich and famous around there." Ricki had read the report the department had compiled, but she also was constantly fed information from the townspeople. Kincaid and Dillinger doings were always at the top of the gossip list.

"Grady said both Kincaids were there when they said they were," Sam said.

"Only because that's what it says on the receipts. I don't think he would notice the exact time," Ricki said. "He was tending bar and it was a busy night."

Sam wrote both Mariah and Blair's phone numbers on a notepad, ripped off the sheet and handed it across the desk to her.

"Who's next on the list?" Ricki asked.

"Miriam Trothbury."

The septuagenarian who lived at bars. "She's yours," Ricki said, and Sam laughed.

Chapter Twenty-Three

"So, you caught last night's fire at the Dillinger ranch," Whit Crowley drawled as Hunter stepped inside Prairie Creek Fire and Rescue's front door.

The lieutenant was leaning against the counter that ran along the back wall of the room, next to his good buddy, Bill Graves, each of them holding a cup of coffee. They were blocking the short hall that led to the fire chief's office; whether by accident or design, Hunter couldn't tell.

"That's right," Hunter said.

"Just happened to be on the scene," Crowley said. "Lucky you."

"Heard you gave a speech to the Dillingers," Graves said in his gravelly voice.

"You going back there today?" Crowley asked.

Hunter had asked Casey Rawlings to keep an eye on the burned property until he got there, which would be a bit later because first he wanted to talk to Jack Raintree, the fire chief, about a number of things. He'd called the chief and made this early-morning appointment with him. He wasn't sure if Raintree knew anything about Crowley's money-making scam to squeeze extra cash from fire victims, but he was going to find out. One way or another, Hunter was going to bring Crowley's misdeeds into the light of day, no matter what blowback came with it.

"Where's that pup of yours, Rawlings?" Crowley asked, sliding Graves a look.

"I'm not his keeper," Hunter said.

"Maybe you should be. Seems he's got kind of a big, yapping mouth. Yap, yap, yap."

Hunter didn't visibly react, but inside he felt his pulse speed up. Who had Casey talked to?

"Don't think we'll be seein' him around much more. Right, Bill?"

Graves nodded slowly, never taking his eyes off Hunter.

"He's a volunteer," Hunter reminded them shortly.

Whit Crowley's lips pulled back into the semblance of a smile as he set his coffee down on the counter behind him. "I told the chief the boy just couldn't keep his goddamn mouth shut. They're plenty of other guys who wanna play fireman. Might be a good idea to get rid of the yapper."

Hunter tried to hold down his simmering fury with Crowley. "We've got some real crime happening around here, Whit. Homicides and set fires. Not any of your manufactured stuff."

Crowley pushed himself forward. "What's that, Kincaid?"

Hunter tried to brush past him, but the older man grabbed him by the shoulder.

They glared at each other and Crowley snarled, "You got somethin' to say, firebug?"

"I'll say it to Raintree."

"Rawlings was just repeatin' what you've been sayin' about me all along, wasn't he?" Crowley's face was a mask of rage.

"Get your hands off me, Whit."

"Who's gonna make me?" He grinned like a demon and

Hunter felt Graves stiffen in readiness. Saw him also put his coffee cup down on the counter.

Hunter said tautly, "You want to fight. Good. I feel like a goddamn fight."

"You'll be out of a job, too, you little shit."

"Might be worth it, though," Hunter challenged, staring at his superior, ready for the battle.

He really did feel like punching Whit out. Slamming the bastard against the wall. Frustration was eating him alive. Someone was out there, killing women and animals, skinning them, setting fire to the Pioneer Church and the Dillinger foreman's cottage. And this weasel was using his *job,* his authority with fire and rescue, to cheat innocent victims, the people who lived in his own hometown.

Something in Hunter's expression apparently got through to Whit, who suddenly took a step back, then brushed past him, slamming out the front door, muttering obscenities. Hunter turned expectantly to Whit's crony, but though Graves regarded him with hot, angry eyes, in the end he followed Whit.

Adrenaline still pumping, Hunter stalked down the hall to Raintree's office and pounded on the door panels. When the fire chief called him in, he didn't waste time. He burst inside and said, "Crowley's cheating fire victims. He blames every blaze he can on their propane tanks and then sells them new tanks, jacking up the price. And they don't even need 'em."

Raintree, a granite-faced man with a solemn manner, pointed to a chair. Hunter shook his head. He had no intention of sitting down and being treated like a schoolboy.

Raintree said, "Sit down. Calm yourself."

"I'm tired of Crowley's intimidation. If you won't do something about it, I will."

"I thought you came in to talk about the Dillinger fire," the chief said.

"I did. But I'm not putting up with Whit and his—"

"Have you got any evidence against him?"

"No. Not yet. Nothing tangible. But I'm telling you—"

"I know about Lieutenant Crowley, Kincaid. You don't have to tell me anything. His days are numbered here, but it's gotta be done right."

Hunter had to clamp his teeth together to keep from continuing the argument. Crowley had gotten so far under his skin that it was all he could do not to rant on about him.

Raintree saw his struggle but chose to ignore it. "Last night's fire was started with gasoline."

Hunter nodded. With a supreme effort, he got down to the Dillinger fire. "Looks like lighter fluid as well."

"Same as the Pioneer Church."

"Not exactly," Hunter said.

"You don't think it's the same doer?"

"The Pioneer Church fire had multiple points of origin. Looks like he wanted to burn the whole thing down. But only the Dillinger foreman's house's exits were set to burn. Like whoever did it wanted to trap someone inside, or keep them from going in."

"So, what are you thinking?"

"I don't know. The foreman's cottage feels more like it was spur of the moment. Maybe someone who's got something against one or all of the Dillingers. The electricity was cut and then it was torched. But the Pioneer Church was planned in advance. Somebody wanted to make a big fire, send us all there, probably because they needed time to go after Mia Collins."

"You think we've got two doers?" the chief asked skeptically.

"I'm leaning that way. The first fire, the church, was set to make a statement. A big show. But the second's smaller . . . not the same purpose. Most of the Dillingers were on a sleigh ride when it went up. There were some other people at the lodge. Ricki Dillinger's daughter, Brook, who was supposed to be on the sleigh ride, was the only one in the cottage."

"Think our firebug thought the place was empty?"

"Maybe . . . but those exits were torched for a reason. Feels like a trap for someone. Maybe he got the wrong person . . . ? Brook had to escape through a window."

"Lucky she did get out," Raintree observed soberly.

"Very lucky."

"Got any theories on who?"

He shook his head. "Someone staying with the Dillingers? The foreman's cottage is easy to access from the main lodge. Or, maybe it's someone who's got a grudge against them. They could have gotten the idea from the church fire."

"A copycat?"

"It just doesn't feel like the same doer," Hunter said.

"So, what's your next move?"

"I'm going to go out there. Interview the Dillingers some more."

The chief almost smiled. "Want me to give that duty to someone else?"

"I handled it last night," Hunter said. Sure, Ira would take offense at having Hunter asking more questions. Helping to douse the fire last night was one thing, but a Kincaid interviewing and re-interviewing the Dillingers, possibly digging into their backgrounds, would be quite another.

Tough, he thought, heading out to his Chevy truck.

He wondered if he should start with Delilah.

The foreman's cottage stank of damp, burned timbers and it was guarded by a young man Delilah didn't know who looked at her uneasily when she approached the building, carrying her black plastic bags.

"You're not trying to go inside?" he said doubtfully.

"I want to rescue some clothes and get them washed."

"There's a lot of damage around the doors. It may not be safe."

"The back door doesn't look as bad as the front," Delilah said, moving forward and increasing his discomfort.

"Mr. Kincaid will be here soon. Can you wait?"

Hell, no. "I won't be long." Delilah carefully passed through the gaping black hole of the back door and stepped into the kitchen area. It didn't look quite so horrible, once she was through the burned area, but the whole place had a sorry, dispirited air from the smoke that had swept inside and stained the walls, ceiling and furniture.

Delilah moved to the back bedrooms and yanked out drawers in both Brook's room and Ricki's, piling clothes into the bags, one for each of them. By the time she was finished, she was eager to be gone. The cabin would be uninhabitable until it was thoroughly cleaned and patched up.

When she was back outside, she hefted the bags over her shoulders and ran straight into Hunter, just managing to keep from bowling over him, though her boots slid on the ice-crusted path when she tried to stop.

He caught her shoulders lightly. "Hey, Delilah. Saw you last night up at the lodge."

"Uh-huh." She hoped to God he couldn't hear her heart, which felt like it was leaping in and out of her chest as if held by a rubber band.

He glanced at the bags on her shoulders. "What have you got there?"

"Clothes," the young man burst in before Delilah could answer. "She said she had to rescue them."

"I'm taking them to the lodge to wash them," Delilah said.

"Let me help you," Hunter said, grabbing both bags over Delilah's protests.

"I can do it," she said, but he was already striding away. Quickly, she hurried after him. "You don't have to go to the house."

"You mean you don't want me to go to the house."

"No . . . that's . . . no . . ." She'd always been a terrible liar.

He shot her a sideways look and she was thrown back in time, when those blue eyes used to smolder with desire. Feeling breathless, Delilah tore her eyes away. It was so long ago that it really pissed her off that she noticed every little detail about him.

"You haven't changed a whole helluva lot," he said. "I kinda thought you would've."

"Oh, I have. I grow glitter under my armpits. We all do in Tinseltown."

He threw her a smile.

Devastating. That's what it was. Delilah kept her gaze on the ground and followed him up the steps and through the front door, where from the kitchen the smell of frying bacon greeted them along with the loud voices of Rourke and Justin, and Haley's softer tones.

"I can take the bags," Delilah said, holding out her arms. "Just point me in the direction of the laundry."

She didn't want him near the kitchen, or anywhere else, for that matter, so she led him back outside. Then they trudged through the six-car garage attached to the house and into the large laundry room that fed through a mudroom to the west end of the back porch.

Hunter set the bags down on the floor and then looked at Delilah. "You really don't want to be seen with a Kincaid, do you?"

"You were great last night," she said. "Especially with

Brook. Everyone appreciates what you've done, what you're doing."

"But . . ." he said.

"No buts. I'm just saying thank you." She crossed her arms over her chest and met his gaze directly.

"Why are you so nervous?"

"I'm not nervous. I'm just—busy."

"With the wedding."

"That's right."

"It's going to be here now?" He inclined his head to encompass the house.

"Are you coming?" Delilah asked with sudden dread.

He gave her a long look. "Maybe. I was kinda surprised to get an invitation."

No shit, Delilah thought. "How about the rest of your family? I'm going over the responses with Pilar today. Gotta know if we can fit everybody in."

"I can't speak for them, but the Major won't make it. He's not doing well."

"I'm sorry to hear that."

Hunter nodded, taking her at her word, and why not. The Major had always been a decent man, no matter what Ira said. It was Georgina who'd been the problem, and maybe Mariah and Blair and Hunter. Hunter's sisters, Emma and Alexandra, were the only Kincaids who were outside the feud, at least in Ira's opinion.

"I think you're pretty safe to knock us all off the guest list," he said.

There was a moment of awkward silence and Delilah cleared her throat. "It would be okay if your family came. Ira and Pilar have invited half the town, maybe more, although our relatives haven't been, apparently. Guess Dad just wants it to be local."

"Do you mind if I ask you some questions?"

"About what?"

"The fire."

"Last night's fire?" Delilah repeated.

He nodded. "Just want to know if you saw anything, or remember anything. Maybe something small that didn't seem important at the time. I want to ask the same thing of your whole family. Maybe someone saw something they haven't put together yet about who could have set the fire."

"Well, it's the same person who burned down the Pioneer Church, right?" Delilah asked, watching him. "That's almost a given. Two fires in Prairie Creek, just days from each other?" When Hunter didn't immediately respond, she asked, "What? You don't think it's the same person?"

"The sheriff's department will figure that out."

"You think this fire was different," she insisted.

"Possibly."

"Damn it, Hunter. Just say what you're thinking."

"Whoever killed Amber Barstow set the fire at the church. That seems pretty obvious. But whoever set the fire here . . . it feels like a separate motivation."

"Meaning?"

"More personal maybe. Possibly to trap someone inside. Ricki . . . or her daughter?"

"No." She shook her head.

"You asked me what I thought," he reminded her.

"Well, that doesn't make any sense."

"What's your theory, then?"

He stared at her and Delilah had trouble staying on point. Her mind wandered to dangerous memories. Hunter taking his shirt off and diving cleanly into the river . . . Hunter dragging himself from the water and lying atop her . . . her fingers anxiously digging at his wet jeans, pulling them off him . . . Hunter sliding his shaft inside her while they stared into each other's eyes and began a rhythm of love and desire . . .

"I don't have any theories. That's your job," Delilah muttered. "I've got to get this wash done." She practically shouldered him out of the way as she opened the bag with Ricki's clothes and began dumping them into the washer all together. *Separate, separate, separate.* She could hear her mother's voice in her ear and she paid no attention to it at all.

After several long moments of silence, Hunter headed back toward the garage.

"I thought you wanted to interview all of us," she called after him.

"I'll be back," he said.

"You might even catch Ira with your mom here, later," Delilah tossed out. "Now that they're in business together, there's bound to be another meeting."

Hunter retraced his footsteps and leveled a look at her. "What business?"

"You don't know about their oil deal? Something to do with Kincaid land?" She almost smiled, enjoying the feeling of knowing something he didn't. "I don't know what it's all about, but it involves Century Petroleum."

"Hell," he muttered, clearly unhappy. He hesitated, then said, "I'll give you my cell number," which he then rattled off to her and which Delilah immediately committed to memory, then he said, "I've gotta go," and stalked out.

Delilah pictured the conversation he was going to have with his mother and wished she could be a fly on the wall.

Davis entered the stables and moved the muscles on his face, which felt frozen from the brittle wind that had slapped at him all the while he was checking on the cattle, herding them toward the barns. He'd been anxious to get back to see the new colt and to check on Kit. She'd stayed with him reluctantly, refusing a bed, grabbing a sleeping bag and stretching out on the floor.

When he saw her by Babylon's stall, he relaxed. "Sabrina wanted to come see Babylon's foal," he said to Kit. "I'll give her a call."

As he pulled out his cell phone, Kit said, "I need a driver's license."

Davis's brows shot up. "Yeah . . . you could use one." He felt almost elated by her admission. He'd wondered if she would ever even think in those terms. So far, her main form of transportation had been on horseback.

"Mia has a car," Kit said.

"A Subaru wagon. It's probably yours now."

"That's why I need a license."

"You want some driving lessons?"

She slid him a sideways look. "Do I need them?"

"Pretty sure. And there's a written test." Carefully, because he didn't want her to turn away from him by saying the wrong thing, he asked, "You might even want a GED?"

"A GED?"

"High school equivalency exam. You haven't . . . attended class, as far as I can see."

"Are there books for that?"

"I'd bet on it."

She nodded. "I'll need them, too."

"Okay."

She turned back to Babylon, then grabbed a brush and headed down the length of stalls, clearly intending to do some grooming. Kit had never shown the least bit of interest in conventions, and the fact that she'd said she needed a driver's license and that she might even try to pass a GED was a huge step in the right direction. Her mother's death had forced a change in her.

She stuck her head out of a stall at the end of the line and said to him, "I won't be staying with you anymore. I've got my mom's house."

"I'd feel better if you stayed with someone until they catch whoever killed her."

"I'll be fine," she said in a voice that brooked no argument, and Davis could only nod in agreement, though he planned to keep an eye on her as best he could.

Pilar pinched the bridge of her nose and sighed dramatically. "I should have stayed in Jackson."

"We'll get this thing put together," Delilah assured her. "I'm taking the Jeep into town and renting some chairs. You've already got flowers. And you've picked out a dress, right?"

"Yes," Pilar said shortly. "The last one I tried on. But it's not right for the stairs."

"It'll be fine. Perfect. And Carolina was always bringing the food here, so we're good to go there, too."

"What about the guests? They don't know about the change of venue."

"You sure about that?" Delilah asked dryly. "Prairie Creek isn't that big. We'll just call them up and let them know that the wedding's here. I'll bet you there aren't two that don't know already."

"Ricki was right about you, Delilah," Pilar said reluctantly, as if it was hard to admit. "You're good at this."

Delilah smiled. What she was good at was managing expectations. Making sure excitable personalities kept their eye on reality. That's what years in Hollywood had taught her. "Have you got the guest list? Let's go over it and see."

"It's on Ira's computer."

She left to retrieve the list and Delilah stretched her arms over her head. She was already tired and it wasn't even ten o'clock. Colton had come in from the bunkhouse and rounded up the kids, and they'd all headed over to the stables to meet the new colt. Sabrina was driving over as well, and Nell had joined up with the group. Delilah didn't know what was going on with Jen and Tyler and thought maybe she was lucky not to.

Ira had gone down to his den early and when Pilar came back with the list, he came with her. "You're not gonna add anybody," he warned Delilah. "I got enough relatives around here, and if they don't live in Prairie Creek, they're not gonna make it in time."

"Fine," Delilah said. She and her father had already gone over this enough. She didn't agree with him, but it was his wedding. Glancing down the list, her eye caught on two names: Gil Flanders and Abby Flanders Bywater. *Abby* . . . "You invited the Flanderses? Gil Flanders doesn't live around here anymore."

"Gil and I have done business for years," Ira said stubbornly. "And he's in Jackson. He can get here."

Gil sold farm and ranching equipment. "Why did you invite Abby?"

"I don't have to defend every name on the list," Ira snapped. But Pilar cut in. "I invited Abby and her husband, Brent. You remember him?"

"Yeah . . ." Vaguely. What Delilah recalled was that Sabrina had dated Brent Bywater for a time.

"We've all been friends for years," Pilar said. "I thought we were going over the list to see who needs to be told we've moved the ceremony, not make judgment calls on our friends."

Ira waved a hand at them. "I'll be in the den."

"Okay," Delilah said. It wasn't for her to say. This was her father and Pilar's wedding and that was all she wrote.

Half an hour later she was driving into town, familiarizing herself with the Cherokee. In L.A. she'd driven a Ford

Edge to haul various equipment from job to job, so this wasn't that much different. The lease on her car was about up, she realized. One more thing almost over in her previous life.

The rental shop had a buzzer at the door that announced her entry into a world of everything from tablecloths and vases to gardening equipment and jackhammers. The owner was a thin woman with a dry, prairie wind–scoured face and a sharp eye. "You the Dillinger that called about chairs?"

"That would be me," Delilah said. "I think we need a hundred." She'd told the woman seventy-five, thinking extra guests could stand in the back, but she'd upped the amount, thinking they could maybe . . . *maybe* . . . squeeze them in.

"Don't know that I have that many. When do you need 'em?"

"Saturday."

"We got other events, lady. You're not the only ones havin' a wedding over the holidays."

"I'll take as many as I can get," Delilah said. She sensed a certain resentment, which she'd run across more than once, being a Dillinger. Ira had made loads of friends and loads of enemies in his quest to increase the family fortunes.

In the end she got the full hundred, putting down the deposit and signing the paperwork, working out a delivery time of noon as the wedding was at five.

She stepped back onto the street into a bright, cold day. Shading her eyes, she looked up and down the street, wondering if she should stop in at Carolina's Table and make sure everything was copacetic there, too.

A woman holding a baby in a front pack was walking her way. She was heavyset in that way new mothers sometimes looked before they'd taken off the baby weight. Delilah's eyes were on the baby, who was swaddled in a pink jacket and blanket, its head covered by a pink hood. Then her gaze traveled upward to meet the mother's eyes and she got a succinct shock. Abby Flanders . . . Bywater.

"Oh, hey," Delilah said, trying to hide her surprise. "Abby."

"Delilah Dillinger! Don't you look fabulous," she said enviously. "Skinny. I swear. I'm going to have to take up running or something as soon as Marjory's done nursing. I'm just a blubber-butt."

Her openness disarmed Delilah. "You are not. You've just had a baby."

"Yeah, and I can only use that excuse so long."

"Her name's Marjory?" Delilah asked.

"Yes, it is." Abby turned the baby so that Delilah could get a look at her face. "She's sleeping."

The baby's lashes lay against plump cheeks and her lips moved in and out in a sucking motion. Delilah was swept by emotion so intense it felt physical. My God. Twice in one day. First the colt, now the baby . . . She was going to have to get a grip on herself and fast. "She's beautiful," she said softly.

"Thanks. She's the best," Abby said. "I heard about the fire at your dad's place last night. That's terrible. What happened?"

Delilah shrugged.

"Was it arson? That's what I heard."

"Could be."

"Hunter was there, right?"

Delilah felt a jab of discomfort. "Well . . . yes."

"Strange how things circle around, isn't it?" she mused. "Hunter working for the fire department, after what everybody said about him."

"About the homestead fire? Luckily you set the record straight," Delilah said, wondering how to get out of this conversation.

She gave Delilah a searching look. "You mean, because I said he was with me at the time?" To her nod, she said, "I thought you of all people would know that was a lie just to stop the rumors. You really didn't know?"

Delilah slowly shook her head.

"They were all looking for a scapegoat and Hunter wouldn't defend himself, so I gave him the alibi. He was there to meet you, right? He just wouldn't tell anybody. But anybody with half a brain coulda figured it out, if they'd known."

"You lied for him?"

"He sure wasn't about to protect his own ass. I thought he was an idiot and I told him so."

"He should've spoken up," Delilah said. "People still believed he had something to do with the fire, even with your alibi."

"Some did," Abby allowed. "People love to believe the worst, don't they? And it wasn't even the right rumor about him."

"About Hunter?"

Abby opened her mouth to answer, thought a moment, then glanced away from Delilah and then down at her little girl. "What am I doing? I really should be going. Marjory's like a time bomb ready to go off if I get her off schedule. Don't let anyone ever tell you nursing's easy. It's its own little hell."

"What did you mean about Hunter?" Delilah pressed.

"I was just blabbing away. People talk, that's all." She hesitated, then looked at Delilah directly. "I just thought that's why you broke up. Because of the rumor."

"What rumor? About the fire?" Delilah asked, baffled.

"Look, I really need to get going. Say hi to Ira for me. Dad's sorry he can't make the wedding. It's so crazy. Those two are like twins; neither one of 'em wants to slow down."

She left in a hurry, as if she didn't want Delilah asking any further questions. It was a revelation learning that Hunter hadn't been with Abby the night of the homestead fire, and it was gratifying that it was as she'd originally thought: he'd been there to meet her. But why had he never told anyone the truth and let himself be crucified by public opinion? To protect her reputation because she was a Dillinger and he was a Kincaid? To the extent that he would let people keep thinking he set the fire?

And what rumor had Abby meant about Hunter? Something that she felt was the real reason they'd broken up?

"What the hell?" Delilah muttered, lost in thought as she headed back to the Jeep. Maybe she should just ask Hunter what Abby meant.

Chapter Twenty-Four

It was afternoon before Mariah Kincaid deigned to call Ricki back. When her cell rang, Ricki was seriously thinking about heading home for an hour or two and catching some sleep. Though she wouldn't give back a moment of her night with Sam, she was fast losing energy. A nap, if she could scare up a bed at the lodge, and a check on Brook, and maybe something to eat, she was thinking. She almost didn't pick up the call she was so weary, but she'd been placing calls all morning, waiting for responses, so she swept up the phone and answered, "Deputy Ricki Dillinger," with as much power as she could muster.

"*Deputy* Ricki Dillinger," a cool female voice responded. "*Ms.* Mariah Kincaid-Drammeur returning your call."

"Hello, Mariah," Ricki said, coming awake as if she'd been shot with adrenaline. "Thanks for returning my call."

"I told that girl who called me from the sheriff's department earlier everything I knew. She had the receipts. She knew I was there long before that poor girl who was killed."

"I know. But we really need to find this guy, so we're calling everyone again."

"I see," she said in a voice that said Ricki was wasting her time. "I thought you got married, Ricki. Still going by Dillinger?"

"Divorced."

"Ah, yes, I did that, too," Mariah said. "Kept the name, though. Couldn't get it wiped off the business, otherwise I might have done the same."

"There was a man in a black Stetson sitting at the bar the night Amber was kidnapped, who struck up a conversation with her. I know you left before Amber arrived, but maybe he was there earlier?"

"If he was, I didn't notice. Like I told the girl who called, I was with Blair and we were having our own discussion about our family. I don't know if you've seen the Major lately. Mom takes him out now and again, but he's on borrowed time. At Thanksgiving, we learned that he probably wouldn't make it to Christmas. So, no, I wasn't looking at anyone but Blair. We were having a drink in the Major's name before we split and headed home."

"Did you and Blair leave at the same time? We haven't been able to get hold of him."

"Yeah, I know. I've got a better number for him. The phone he actually answers. Blair doesn't want to talk to the family, so he gave Mom, Hunter, Emma and Alexandra a different one that he rarely checks. He'll be pissed I gave it to you."

She told Ricki the number, then said, "Mom called and said there was a fire at your place. The foreman's cottage. You think it's this same guy? The one who left the girl in the church and burned it down?"

"Looks like they're both arson," Ricki said carefully. She didn't want to give too much away.

"So, it is the same guy?"

"Don't have the answer to that. If you think of anything

else, just happen to recall something from that night, please call back."

"I told you, I won't remember anything because there's nothing to remember. I paid the bill on my credit card, said good-bye to my brother and left. There were people there, but I didn't look at them."

Ricki thanked her, ended the call and stretched in her chair. Sam had gone over to fire and rescue to talk to Chief Raintree directly, hoping to catch up with Hunter, too. She'd gone down the list of names, hit and miss in reconnecting with the patrons, and had learned precious little so far. Getting up from her chair, she cruised toward the vending machines in the break room and bought herself a Diet Coke. Maybe a hit of caffeine would keep her going.

Back at her desk she punched in the number Mariah had given her for Blair. To her immense surprise he answered on the second ring, saying, "Hello?" in a suspicious voice. Probably didn't recognize the number on caller ID.

"Blair, it's Ricki Dillinger. I got your number from Mariah."

"Well, that was ballsy of her. She knows better."

The youngest Kincaid son was nothing like his older brother, Ricki thought. Whereas Hunter had always been decent, if somewhat hard to read, Blair was as wild as a roaming mustang, and he always seemed ready for battle of some kind. The youngest sister, Alexandra, had been party to some of Blair's wilder schemes when she was a kid, but then had apparently grown out of them. It was like a division could be made between Hunter and Emma, and Mariah, Alexandra and Blair. The first two favored the Major in temperament, the last three Georgina.

Though it had been years since Ricki had lived in Prairie Creek, from talking to both Mariah and Blair, it didn't appear much had changed.

Before Blair could come up with a reason to hang up

on her, Ricki told him why she was calling, finishing with, ". . . think this guy at the bar is the killer and we really need to find him, so that's why we're checking with everyone who was at the Buffalo Lounge that night."

"Can't help you," Blair said. "I don't remember anything. We were talkin' about the Major and glad we could get the hell out of Prairie Creek. Holidays are always fuckin' disasters."

"Doesn't sound like you plan to come home for Christmas."

"Hell, no. Is Mariah? She said she wasn't."

"I didn't ask her. On that Saturday night, Mariah said she paid the bill and left. Did you leave at the same time?"

"Yeah . . . well . . . there was a guy there with a couple of his friends. Used to bronc ride and knew Colton. I remember bein' in the stands the time he got his teeth knocked out. Got tossed into the fence by one nasty piece of horsemeat. So at Big Bart's I went over to the guy, told him I was there that day. He's got some fake teeth he can push in and out with his tongue, so he did that and bought me a couple of beers. Then I left."

"What's your friend's name?"

"Not really a friend. McKewan. Ed McKewan. But he can't be your guy. He's like five foot six and kind of a dumbass. Never was much of a rider." Blair huffed out a laugh. "Was an idiot to even think he could be."

"His name's on our list. I called him earlier today," Ricki said. "He said he doesn't recall anyone at Bart's, either. He didn't mention you."

"He was shit-faced. Barely could remember his own name. But he remembered that ride."

"You didn't see a taller man in a black Stetson, maybe hanging by the bar?"

"There are always guys around in black Stetsons. You live here. You know."

"Yeah. Anything else you can recall?"

"Wish I could help you. I really do. I heard what that bastard did with a knife to that girl and then Mia Collins . . ."

"Do you remember what time you left?" Ricki asked.

"About half an hour after Mariah. Maybe a bit longer. I went out the back and had a smoke, clearin' my head a little before I got in the truck and headed back here."

"That's about the time Amber drove in," Ricki said.

"Didn't see her."

"Okay. She drove a blue Honda Civic that we think he disabled. He flattened one of her tires."

"A blue Civic?"

"That's right."

"I think I saw that car," he said suddenly, sounding surprised himself.

"At Bart's?" Ricki asked quickly.

"Yeah, in the lot. There was a guy there. I thought the car was his, cuz he was hangin' by it. But maybe it was hers, and shit, yeah, he was wearin' a Stetson. Black one."

"Can you describe him?" Ricki asked eagerly.

"Mmmm . . . tall. Face shadowed. It was dark."

Ricki waited. She could tell he was thinking hard. *Come on, come on . . .*

"Clean shaven. Black gloves. It was cold. A blizzard was comin' in." Another hesitation, and then he said, "That's about all I got."

"You didn't see him inside the place?"

"Just on my way out. But if he was at the bar, I wouldn't have seen him. Mariah and I were over by the fireplace."

"He was sitting at the opposite end of the bar from Barstow," Ricki said. Grady Chisum, the bartender, had established that. She needed to talk to him again, too, face-to-face, now that they'd zeroed in on Black Hat.

"Like I said, we were drinkin' to the Major. That's about all I was thinkin' about."

"All right. Thanks, Blair."

"No problem."

Hanging up, she stared into space for a moment, then she grabbed her coat and headed out to her truck.

It was afternoon by the time Hunter could get over to the Kincaid ranch and have a powwow with his mother. He'd met with Sam Featherstone and Raintree about the fires and they'd all pretty much concluded the same thing: there were two arsonists. They'd gone over all the evidence from both fires and had distilled their conclusions into two theories: one, the Pioneer Church fire was done as a distraction for the killer to get to Mia, and two, the Dillinger fire was an attack on the Dillinger family. With Mia being connected to the Dillinger family through Kit, there was concern for Kit's safety as well as every other Dillinger. They'd all come home for Ira's wedding and that meant they were all in Prairie Creek. Maybe that's why the fires had started happening now.

Or maybe it meant nothing at all. But there was a reason, a motivation in there somewhere, and Hunter was betting it had something to do with the Dillingers.

Georgina was sitting at the kitchen table, going over accounts, when Hunter entered. Seeing him, she swept the books to one side, trying to appear casual as she said, "You could let me know before you just waltz in."

"Want me to call ahead?" Hunter asked evenly. He'd always had a tough relationship with his mother, but this was the first time she'd made a fuss about him coming unannounced.

"The Major's napping," she said. "He could use some quiet."

As if he'd heard her, Hunter's father called out from the TV room, "Who is it?"

"Napping?" Hunter repeated.

Georgina's lips tightened. "I thought he was asleep."

She was lying. He knew her well enough to recognize the signs. Georgina was a tough nut to crack and she'd seesawed from being overprotective to damn near bordering on neglect when it came to raising her children. Hunter said, "I just learned you're going into the oil business with Century Petroleum and Ira Dillinger."

She stilled, as if she felt movement might give her away. "Who told you that?"

"Is it true?"

"It's none of your damn business, Hunter."

"You've been looking for a moneymaker for a while. That's what those cabins were supposed to be about, but that didn't work out."

His mother flushed red with fury. "Last I checked, this is *my* ranch, not yours."

"Maybe you should tell the Major that, because he wants me involved more. Not that I want to be. But if you're planning something with Ira Dillinger, I'm pretty sure he's going to want to know why. Unless you've told him . . ." He inclined his head in the direction of the TV room.

"It's all just in the talking phase. But Ira knows oil," she snapped back.

"And ranching, and how to make a deal in his favor." Hunter wondered what the hell was really going on in his mother's manipulative head. "You don't like any of the Dillingers, especially Ira."

"I have respect for Ira's business sense."

"Since when?"

"Go see your father." She gathered up the account books, slid away from the table, then stalked out of the room and down the back hallway, slamming the door behind her.

Hunter went in search of the Major, who was leaning

back in a recliner all the way, a blanket over his legs. His pallor was gray and he looked like he'd aged a year since the last time Hunter had seen him in town with Georgina. Hunter hadn't really believed that he might be gone by Christmas, but now the doctor's warning seemed prophetic. The cancer that had dogged him for years had finally gotten the upper hand.

"Hunter," the Major said, dredging up a smile with an effort.

"Hey, Dad." He tried to keep the worry out of his voice.

"I told Georgina to call you. Glad she finally did."

Hunter started to disabuse his father. His mother hadn't called him, but the Major was already on another track. "Remember what we talked about before? Your mother can't handle a thousand acres and God knows how many sheep by herself. She's gonna need your help."

"I'll do what I can, but Mom's pretty tough."

His voice lowered to a whisper and Hunter had to lean in to catch what he was saying. "I want you to take over. Georgina won't . . . be fair. I've got a will made out. You need to check with Berkley Price. You know him?"

Berkley Price was an attorney in town, but he wasn't the family lawyer. Or, at least Hunter hadn't thought he was. "I know who he is."

"You go talk to him, okay?"

"Dad—"

"Your mother has her own ideas, but they're not mine, you understand? You have to watch out for her."

Hunter's gaze shot toward the door. He felt uneasy. Did the Major know about Georgina's business dealings with Ira? Feeling a bit like a Judas, he asked, "You know Mom's been meeting with Century Petroleum?"

His eyes pinned Hunter's. "What's she plotting now?"

Plotting . . . Was that what she was doing? "Some oil deal that also involves Ira Dillinger."

"No . . ." He sank back into his chair, spent. "She won't have anything to do with him anymore."

Hunter could practically feel his father's energy slipping away, so he didn't press the issue. He was between a rock and a hard place, between his mother and father, and it was nowhere he wanted to be. His mind went back to the meeting with Sam and Chief Raintree. Featherstone had thanked Raintree and Hunter for their work, but had let it be known that the sheriff's department would be handling the arson investigations from here on out. Though Hunter understood, he wasn't ready to walk away from the Dillinger fire just yet.

Is that because of Delilah?

Maybe, he thought.

Grady Chisum rubbed his chin, his gold tooth glinting in the dim light thrown from the BUDWEISER beer sign over his head. "I didn't see him much. I wasn't looking. I talked to Amber, but the guy at the end of the bar didn't say anything. Had a couple Buds, I think. Paid cash. I've been trying to remember everybody that night, but it was pretty damn busy. He had a black hat on. So, this is the guy?"

Ricki wasn't ready to give out that much. "We think she got picked up by someone at the bar," was all she would allow. "Can you remember anything else about him?"

Grady screwed up his face in the struggle to recall. After a few minutes, he said, "Didn't have a beard. Strong jaw, I guess. Couldn't see his eyes. The hat was always dipped."

"Could you see any hair?"

"Just the hat."

Disappointed, Ricki thanked him, then interviewed the waitresses who'd been at the bar that night as both Carol and Jane came in for their shifts while she was there. She called Shelly, Bart's wife, on the phone, as she wasn't working tonight, but she couldn't offer up much more either.

It was frustrating, but they were going to have to find the guy some other way, Ricki realized. With a sigh, she called it a day and headed back to the lodge to clean up and collapse for a while.

"You want to go to the Prairie Dog Saloon with me?" Nell asked Delilah as they watched Brook play Twister with Justin, Rourke and Haley.

About the last thing Delilah wanted to do was go out to a bar, but then she didn't want to hang around the house much longer either.

She'd gone over the list of guests with Pilar and helped place phone calls. After that, she'd spent some time with Brook, glad that Ricki's daughter had seemed to bounce back fairly quickly and was now even playing with the younger kids, keeping them entertained.

But all the while her mind had been circling back to the fire and then to Hunter and what Abby had said about him and then back to the fire, and so on. It had been hard to concentrate on anything else. Then, when she'd gone up to her room for a few minutes, she'd heard raised voices from down the hall and realized Jen and Tyler were in a huge fight.

As if reading her thoughts, Nell said, "I asked Jen and Tyler to join me, but neither of them is in the mood, apparently."

"Did they say why?" Delilah asked casually.

"I just don't think they want to go."

She looked so disappointed that Delilah shook off her own doubts and said, "Sure, I'll join you."

"Good." Nell brightened immediately.

"I'll even be the designated driver. I've got the keys to the Jeep."

They left half an hour later. Delilah had changed into a pair of skinny jeans and tucked them into her boots, had pulled on a long, burgundy sweater with a cowl neck, which came down to her thighs, and had topped it off with her suede jacket. She looked half cowgirl and half Hollywood, and when Nell, who was in jeans and a red blouse and a sheepskin jacket, saw her, she said, "You do clothes well."

"Thanks."

Nell chattered away as Delilah drove them down the snow-crusted roads and along Prairie Creek's main street to the Prairie Dog. The place wasn't as large as Big Bart's, but it was closer and more intimate. When Nell and Delilah entered, an overhead silver bell jingled to announce their arrival. The floor was wood and the bar was scarred oak. Red, green and silver tinsel festooned the overhead lights, hanging in deep loops. There was a Christmas tree in one corner with a picture of Zipper, the prairie dog mascot, hanging from its front bough.

Nell and Delilah squeezed into a small table in the corner, which the other patrons had stolen the chairs from. They were finally able to barter back a couple of chairs from the group of loud guys who were in a game of darts and only using about half the seats around their own table. Shrugging out of her jacket, Delilah looked around and realized there was a man staring at her from across the room. Her pulse jumped for a moment at the intensity of his gaze.

She was taken aback when he came over to her table. "You're a Dillinger, aren't ya?" he said.

"Who's asking?" she responded.

"Whit Crowley." He extended a hand. "I'm with Prairie Creek Fire and Rescue. Shame about the fire out at your place last night."

"Yeah." Delilah shook his hand. *He must work with Hunter.*

"You're in town for the big wedding." His gaze slid over Nell.

"The wedding and the holidays," Delilah said, glancing

around the room. She hoped he would just go away, but no such luck.

"You should have your tank checked. It's propane, right?" He reached in his pocket and pulled out a card. "I got a company does this work all the time."

"It's actually my father's property," Delilah said, reluctantly accepting the card.

"Well, I won't interrupt you any longer." He gave them a smile and headed toward the door.

"Thank God," Nell said, watching him leave.

"I know, right. Where're our drinks?" Delilah scooted from her chair. "Stay here. I'll go get 'em."

He stood outside the saloon, in the shadows. He'd watched them enter the bar, feeling the hunger gnaw at him like a living thing. He'd planned on the youngest one. She was there. Nell. It was always easier to cut the weakest one from the herd, the youngest one as a rule. But the other one . . . *Delilah* . . . He could imagine her naked. Her white, smooth skin. Her long legs. The thatch of hair at the juncture of her thighs . . . would it be red or blond?

His mind imagined rubbing his hands down her breasts and along the curve of her hips and he groaned with desire. He wanted to slide himself over her and jam inside her, screw her till she screamed.

Then he would slip the edge of his knife under her skin and carve a sweet section off.

Man, he was going to have to jack off right here. Right outside the Prairie Dog. Working his hand inside his jeans he grabbed himself, but then he heard an approaching engine, so he dipped his Stetson to hide his face and turned around to the back of the building to hide and wait.

* * *

Because it was almost Christmas, Nell had a green vodka martini and Delilah had a red one. Then Nell had a red one and Delilah decided to skip a round since she had the keys. Maybe she should have another and just call up Ricki or Colt to pick them up. But no . . . with everything she needed to do, the last thing she could afford was a hangover.

But she was having a much better time than she'd thought she would. It was almost Christmas and it was time to try and be jolly, regardless of all the troubles affecting them.

"As soon as this wedding's over, we need to decorate for Christmas," Nell said.

"You got that right."

The jukebox was blasting country western music and the guys around the dart game were getting louder and louder. Delilah cupped her ear to hear Nell, and after about another hour had passed, she glanced at the clock and decided it was time to give it up. They rose from their chairs and then Delilah decided to take a trip to the bathroom.

Nell said, "Hand me the keys."

"Are you kidding?"

"I just want to get in the car. I'm not driving," Nell said, shrugging into her coat with some difficulty.

Delilah reluctantly handed her the keys. "I'll only be a minute."

Nell lifted one arm to say she'd heard as she headed for the front door.

Delilah was in and out of the bathroom in record time, feeling anxious. Not that she didn't believe Nell, she just didn't want anything unexpected to happen.

She stepped outside into a cold, clear night where bright pinpoint stars looked down from coal-black heavens. She saw Nell in the car, buckling her seat belt, but that didn't dispel the feeling of discomfort that enveloped her. For a moment she stood frozen, thinking of the killer/firebug loose around Prairie Creek. Even in Hollywood she'd never felt this freezing fear that seemed to fill her insides. In fact—

A shadow materialized from the gloom around the building. A man's shadow. He came toward her fast and she backed up and screamed for all she was worth.

"Delilah!" It was Hunter's voice, reaching out to her as he quickly grabbed her arm, shooting hard looks in all directions. Nell was scrabbling with the door handle and Delilah's heart was thundering in her ears.

"Oh . . . God . . . damn . . ." She could scarcely breathe. "What the hell are you doing? You scared me!"

"Jesus," Hunter said, drawing her close, his own heart pounding inside his chest.

Nell finally got outside, half stumbling toward them as the door to the Prairie Dog burst open, the men who'd been around the dartboard boiling out like angry bees. One of them charged up to Hunter, but Delilah shook her head.

"No, no, no. It's okay," she declared, holding up a hand.

"What the hell's going on?" one of the men demanded.

"I scared her," Hunter said.

"Yeah?" another growled, moving closer to Hunter as if readying for an attack.

"It's nothing. It's nothing." Delilah's pulse was jumping with fear. "I made a mistake. All these terrible things have been happening and I just thought . . . I didn't mean to . . ."

"That's all right, honey," the one glaring at Hunter said as he relaxed. "It's been pretty damn scary all right."

"That you, Kincaid?" The first man took a step nearer and squinted at Hunter.

"'Fraid so," Hunter said.

"Well, sheettt," he muttered, waving a dismissive hand at them.

A few moments later the men were all heading back inside and Delilah was left alone with Hunter and Nell.

"I'm sorry," he apologized.

Nell said, "You about made me pee my pants!"

Delilah gave out a laugh as Nell reopened the car door and dropped inside, slamming it shut behind her. "You scared the liver out of me," Delilah said to Hunter. "What are you doing here?"

"I was looking for somebody."

"Who?"

"Heard one of the guys from fire and rescue was here talking to Dillingers, probably trying to scam 'em."

"Whit Crowley?"

"That's the one." Hunter was tense. "What did he want?"

"He asked me if we had a propane tank."

Hunter swore so pungently beneath his breath that it took Delilah by surprise. "Why?"

"What did you tell him?" Hunter asked grimly.

"That the property's Dad's. What do you think? I don't own the Rocking D. He wants to talk about it, he should take it up with Ira."

That seemed to appease him. "Okay."

"What the hell, Hunter." She was growing annoyed with him. "What is this?"

"Just a little war I've got going," he muttered, turning toward the door. "Crowley still inside?"

"No, he left."

That stopped him. He'd been moving toward the door, but now he turned back to Delilah, looking across the dimly lit parking lot at her. The music had been turned up again and throbbed outside, feeling like a second heartbeat that resonated throughout her body.

"Sorry to scare you," he said, then headed back toward his gray truck.

Delilah watched his lanky body and long, cowboy stride

for a moment, the image imprinted on her brain as she circled to the driver's side of the Jeep.

"God. Damn. It."

The killer ground his teeth inside the cab of his pickup, seething with fury. What the fuck was going on between Kincaid and Delilah Dillinger? His hands curled into fists, then he opened them wide. He wanted to slide them around Hunter Kincaid's neck. Everything had been in place. The youngest Dillinger had got herself shitfaced, so she would be no problem, and that left slim and hot Delilah within his sights. For a brief moment he'd thought he could have them both. It was within his grasp. When Delilah had stepped outside, sniffing the air like a cautious deer, he nearly lost sight of the need for discretion and was poised to tackle her right there. Knock her out. Throw her in his truck and drive to the new secluded place he'd taken as his own. He'd damn near done it, though it was crazy and dangerous. Anyone could have come out of the Dog. But he was that ready for her. He could see himself cutting off her clothes and skimming her skin with his knife, then sliding inside her, rhythmically thrusting, watching the terror on her face slowly change to ecstasy. Her eyes would close and she would start to moan and thrash, feeling him pumping into her. Her fingernails would rake down his back and her hands would desperately clasp him to her while she begged him, cried for him, wanted him. He could feel her legs wrapping around him as he buried his shaft deep into her core.

And then he would use the knife . . .

He'd been hard as granite, his mind full of images. "C'mon, baby, c'mon, baby," he'd whispered, stroking himself even as his rage smoldered inside.

And then goddamn Hunter Kincaid. What the *fuck* did he think he was doing?

His erection dwindled and he slammed his palm against the steering wheel. Maybe he was going to have to kill him, too. Wouldn't be the same as the Dillinger females, but there might be some pleasure to it.

Hunter Kincaid . . . well, fuck yeah.

Practice makes perfect.

Chapter Twenty-Five

Delilah awoke on the couch in the family room in the middle of the night. She'd given up her bed to Ricki, who had argued with her, but Delilah wasn't listening. Ricki might want to go to Sam's, and that was fine with Delilah, but she found herself too keyed up and tense and full of thoughts of Hunter to toss and turn in the bed next to Brook's. Ricki didn't realize that it was as much an excuse for Delilah to be with her own thoughts as it was a graciousness on her part.

She was annoyed at herself at waking up, especially since she'd just fallen asleep. Too many thoughts were rattling around in her head. Nameless fears that were rooted in the fires and terrible deaths and maybe even an uncertainty about her future and definitely about Hunter.

What rumor had Abby meant? she asked herself for the millionth time. What rumor? And who had set the fire at the foreman's cottage? Someone intent on hurting the Dillingers? Some firebug drifter, like the one who'd cruised through Prairie Creek that summer long ago, the one convicted of burning up the old homestead though he'd never admitted to the crime? Were they really dealing with two different arsonists? Hunter seemed to think so, but what did that mean?

Was one of them the man Ricki had said she and Sam were zeroing in on, the man who'd been at the Buffalo Lounge the same time as Amber Barstow was kidnapped?

Then, who was the other one?

What rumor had Abby meant?

She woke up again suddenly, her eyes flying open, unaware she'd even fallen asleep. Gray fingers of light were sneaking in around the lowered blinds. She'd slept in her clothes and now she climbed a bit stiffly off the couch. She'd brought her bag downstairs last night and now she grabbed up some clean clothes and tiptoed back upstairs to the bathroom.

She was just letting herself inside when she heard the key turn in the front door. Someone was letting themselves in.

Carefully, she tiptoed to the top of the stairs, her skin rising with gooseflesh. Her sister's red hair glowed in the flash of sunlight that followed her in as Ricki stealthily tiptoed inside and placed her hand on the newel post, turning for the stairs.

"Sam, huh," Delilah whispered down to her, causing a gasp from her sister, who glared up at her.

"You scared me," Ricki accused.

"A lot of that going around."

Hunter watched the sun rise from the front window of his rented ranch-style house at the far end of town—about as far a distance from the Kincaid ranch as was possible while still maintaining a Prairie Creek address. He hadn't planned the divide, but he wasn't sorry, either. He didn't want to be embroiled in all the Kincaid messiness, no matter how determined the Major was at keeping him involved.

He hadn't slept much. He'd gone looking for Crowley when Hal, a bartender at the Prairie Dog and a friend for some time, had called and told him Whit Crowley was sniffing around some of the Dillinger women. Though Hunter had not confided in Hal about Crowley's money game, Hal just didn't think much of Whit, either. The bartender had overheard Whit throwing out negative comments about Hunter from time to time and had taken a dislike to the lieutenant. He'd told Hunter he didn't know how he worked with such a piece of scum even though Hunter had kept his mouth shut on his own feelings about the man. Tonight, though, because of the Dillinger fire, he'd called Hunter and told him what was going down.

Hunter had barreled down to the Prairie Dog, ready to take on Crowley bare-fisted if he had to. As he'd told Whit earlier, he was ready for a fight. Almost looked forward to it.

Which was kind of crazy as Hunter rarely felt this way. But when he thought of Crowley trying to weasel his way close to Delilah, it made him see red. He didn't know exactly what that meant, was pretty sure he didn't want to know, but there it was.

Now, he ran through a quick shower then dressed in his usual jeans, boots and a gray corduroy shirt, smashing his Stetson on his head before striding out to the truck. He'd told Sam Featherstone he'd stay out of the police investigation, but that apparently was a lie, because he planned on talking to as many of the Dillingers as he could find.

Somebody knew something . . . something that they might not realize they knew.

Climbing into the cab of the gray Chevy, he backed out of his drive and onto the main street that ran through Prairie Creek, cruising the gut before heading down the access road that would take him by the Kincaid ranch and onto the Rocking D. He had a few misgivings showing up so early and unexpectedly. He didn't know what he was going to ask and who to talk to first. It was a half-assed idea all around, but he was determined to keep at it.

He passed the long drive that led to his parents' house and

kept on going. The winding, rutted lane to the old Dillinger homestead passed by next and he had a moment of remembrance about those long-ago summer days with Delilah, the notes she'd left him in the pine tree.

With an effort, he pushed them aside. Past history. Long over.

As he neared the Dillinger ranch, his gaze caught on the stables. With a sense of relief, he drove there first. It was too early to start with the main lodge, but Davis might be around. Sam's brother was a man of few words but keen insight. He would start with him.

Parking outside, a sharp wind blew his hair back from his face. It was getting too long and he needed to cut it, but he'd been damn preoccupied with all the fires and Whit Crowley and the killings. He strode quickly up the ramp and inside, smelling the scents of horseflesh and hay. The Kincaid ranch had once had twenty horses, but now they were down to a couple of aging geldings. They'd had more sheep than he wanted to count once, too. Now, there were a few hundred, he would guess. The whole place had been falling into disrepair at about the same rate as his father's decline, though now the Major was ahead in that grim race. Maybe Georgina was right in working with Ira Dillinger and Century Petroleum. Something needed to be done.

The first person he ran into was Kit Dillinger. She glanced up at him and he saw a lot of Dillinger in her: the red hair, the lean, whip-tough build, the suspicious gaze. "Hi, Kit. Davis around?" he asked.

"We're going to check the herd."

He saw that she was saddling up. At that moment Davis appeared and said, "Something I can do for you?"

"I wanted to talk about the fire here," Hunter said.

"Can't help you. Kit and I weren't here. We were over at Mia's place to get a few things."

Hunter glanced at Kit who was tightening the girth on

the saddle. "You're spending a lot of time together?" Hunter asked.

"Yes," Davis answered cautiously, his eyes narrowing as he assessed Hunter's meaning.

"Good. Until we catch whoever's doing this, better to be around other people."

Davis nodded and relaxed a bit.

Hunter was glad Davis was looking out for her. He imagined it was difficult for Kit to go back to the house where her mother had been killed. By all accounts she and Mia hadn't had the best relationship, but when you lost a parent . . . your only parent . . .

"Day of the fire the Dillingers were all on a sleigh ride, except for Brook and Ira," Davis said.

Hunter nodded. "Pilar hadn't returned from Jackson yet." He thought about what folly he might be embarking on in interviewing the Dillingers. He wasn't the sheriff's office, and he was a Kincaid.

Davis said, "Ira was meeting your mother and those two Century Petroleum men. Maybe they know something."

"I'll check with them."

Hunter waited while Davis and Kit led the horses down the ramp, climbed onto their saddles and headed out slowly, swaying side by side. He had a sudden vision of doing something similar with Delilah once upon a time. They'd just been kids and he'd tried to discourage her, in the beginning. She was several years younger and he'd tried to ignore the way she tagged after him. But she'd been persistent. He'd told himself he hated all Dillingers. Really tried to adopt his mother's attitude, but Delilah had wormed her way into his thoughts, and before he knew it she was circling inside his head like a melody that he couldn't forget and writing him breathless notes of love, and they were meeting secretly every chance they could.

The first time they'd made love had been in the spring with rain hammering on the roof of the old homestead, mere months before Judd and Mia were caught there in the fire. But the homestead was just one of the places they met. They were too eager for each other, and reckless. Once he remembered they'd squeezed into the backseat of his sister Mariah's compact car and had just finished making love when she came barreling out to the garage and glared at him as if she knew. Naked, Delilah had just managed to wedge herself into a storage closet that was stuffed to the gills with leftover equipment rusting from disuse. When he pulled her out, she was covered in cobwebs, but it hadn't stopped them from making love again right then.

And there had been other times, other places. Out in the open field mostly as the summer waxed on. He could still see the shine of her eyes under moonlight, the warm glow of her tanned skin in daylight.

Damn.

He was standing outside the stables, wondering if it was still too early to approach the house, when his breath caught. Delilah was heading his way, her blond-red hair tucked into the collar of her coat, her head bent to a brisk breeze. She didn't see him until she was almost at the stables, and when she did, she stopped short and narrowed her eyes at him. Dillinger, through and through.

"You following me?" she demanded.

"I could ask you the same thing."

"You're on Dillinger land," she reminded him.

"Still looking to talk to Ira."

"Ah." She moved forward again and went around him and inside. "I came to see Firestarter."

"Who?"

"The new colt."

Hunter followed her back up the ramp, sliding the door

shut behind them. It was surprisingly warm inside, or was that just him? His thoughts had been traveling down a path that had started out as merely nostalgic but had quickly become damn near X-rated. And now, as he saw her unbutton her jacket, revealing her flat stomach and soft breasts, he felt a response that was way out of line to the moment.

"Thought you were going to the house," she said, not looking at him, sensing, apparently, that he was uncomfortable.

He dragged his thoughts back with an effort. "Still a little early."

"Ira's up," she said shortly. "Probably having breakfast."

"I'll wait a bit." He followed her down the line of stalls. "Ira was meeting with my mother and the Century Petroleum men."

"That's why he wasn't on the sleigh ride." She glanced back at him. "You ask her about the oil deal?"

"More like I accused her of going behind my father's back."

"How'd that go?"

"About like you'd expect."

"Are you working with the sheriff's department?"

"In a manner of speaking," he said diffidently.

"What's that mean?"

"I want to know who set fire to the foreman's cottage and I don't want to wait."

"Ahh . . ."

Delilah turned a corner and then stopped at a large box on the second aisle. Leaning over the rail, she waved him closer and he moved next to her. Inside the stall was a bright-eyed colt swishing his tail, looking at them from under his mother's belly.

"I come out here every day," she said.

"I see why." There was something so wonderful about new birth on the ranch. A sense of positive changes. The little colt was a heartbreaker already.

His thoughts turned to his own family's financial failings when Delilah turned and bumped into him, losing her footing briefly. Automatically, he reached out his arms to steady her and for a flashing instant he thought about kissing her.

As if she felt the same, she froze, staring at him through startled eyes. Then she blinked, breaking the spell. "Sorry. I just always want a better look."

"It's all right."

"I'd better . . ."

"Yeah."

They both moved the same way, trying to avoid each other, but the opposite happened and this time, when they inadvertently pressed against each other, neither of them moved. Or breathed. Hunter could hear his own heartbeats. Or were they hers?

His gaze dropped to her lips. Plump. Light pink. Half parted, as if she were about to whisper. Ignoring every sane thought, he leaned forward and pressed his mouth to hers, his arms sliding inside her coat and around her slim back to rest in the hollow at the base of her spine.

He didn't know what he was doing. He didn't know what to expect. He'd reacted on instinct, going for something he wanted. When she didn't rear away from him, he deepened the kiss, a bit desperately, aware that at any millisecond she might shove him away, or slap him, or scream bloody murder like she had outside the Prairie Dog.

She did none of those things. For a moment or two, a lifetime, she didn't react at all. Then her lips quivered a bit beneath his and her hands slid up his arms.

"Delilah? You here?" Colton's voice called from the other side of the stables.

Hunter and Delilah broke from each other as if cleaved apart. Without a word to him, Delilah stumbled away, toward Colton. "Right here," she called back.

"Ricki said to come and get you. We're making breakfast

for the kids. You don't have to come if you don't want to, but she—"

"No, no. I'm ready," she said hurriedly, and then their voices faded away.

Oh. My. *God.*

It was hours later but Delilah couldn't get the thought of that kiss out of her head. Her mind kept reviewing it and reviewing it and reviewing it. His urgent mouth. Strong hands. Wide, muscular chest. The sense that if they kept going she would lie down on the hay and drag him with her.

She'd wanted to unbuckle and snap open his jeans and strip him naked. She'd wanted to feel him inside her and—

Holy—shit—damn—hell.

Pilar was staring at her and Delilah realized she'd posed a question. "What?" Delilah asked.

"I said, Emma wouldn't even bring my dress over. She sent Georgina with it."

"But you've got it now, right?" Delilah asked, trying to keep to the salient point. Who cared who brought it? "It's upstairs. In your bedroom."

"Yes, but that's not the point."

"What is the point?" Delilah asked.

Pilar must have sensed that Delilah was no ally because she just shook her head, glared at Ira's den door and said, "Tell your father I'll be upstairs when he's finished."

She stalked toward the stairs and Delilah glanced toward the den door. Her father was closeted with someone, maybe Colton this time, who'd had a whole lot more questions about the fire, ones no one was able to answer. He and Sabrina were taking all the kids out riding this afternoon, which Pilar had bemoaned all morning. Ricki was into her investigation and therefore not around, though Delilah suspected a certain part of her enthusiasm was because she was working with Sam. Nell and Jen had gone into town and Tyler hadn't left his room, as far as Delilah knew. It had left her all morning with Pilar.

"You know . . ." Pilar's voice reached her from the stairs and Delilah turned. She'd stopped at the landing, one hand on the rail, but she was looking down pensively. "I kinda thought I'd be pregnant by now. I wanted the wedding to be perfect, of course, but I gave up birth control two months ago, thinking that timing-wise, I could still fit into the dress and we'd already be starting that family."

Delilah worked hard to keep the horror off her face. Yes, her father was marrying Pilar, and yes, they were bound to have a sexual relationship, but good God . . . "It's early yet," she heard herself say. "You've got time."

Pilar made a sound of disgust as she headed up the second flight. "None of us are getting any younger."

Delilah heard the den door open behind her but didn't turn around. She was too locked into her own personal hell. Of course Pilar didn't know that she wanted a baby as well, but it still felt like a knife in the back. If Pilar should turn up pregnant . . . and Delilah was still looking for a man . . . a sperm or two or billion . . .

Afraid of what might be seen on her face, she headed out the front door and headed blindly toward the foreman's cottage. The cold wind slapped at her face and she was glad for it. She hoped it slapped her silly. She needed to be pulled out of this funk.

She was standing in the frigid air, watching her breath plume, when Ricki's truck pulled up. "Hey," her sister said, alighting from the cab.

"Hey," Delilah said shortly.

"What's wrong?"

"Nothing."

"What's wrong?" she asked again with more force.

"Pilar's planning to have a baby."

"Oh . . . no . . ."

The horror in her voice made Delilah laugh. "My reaction as well. And the worst of it, it's all I'm thinking about, too. That damn biological clock has gotten really, really loud." She mentally shook herself. "Sorry. I know you're deep into figuring out what's going on around here." She managed a smile. "Anything new?"

"Nah . . . we think we know who, just don't have a name. Until we can figure out the motivation, it's hard to know where to look." She stood beside Delilah and they both stared at the burned cottage. "You can have a baby without a guy," she pointed out.

"Might be easier," Delilah said. "Might be harder, too."

"Nearest sperm bank's probably in Jackson," Ricki observed.

Delilah thought about that for a moment, then said, "You know what I want? A hot, quick affair with a sexy man. No strings attached. Someone who'd be on board with a pregnancy, should it happen, but could just walk away afterward. Go right on down the road."

Ricki laughed.

"I'm serious."

"You are not. You want the whole enchilada. The baby and the guy."

"Sure, it'd be nice, but really, it would be okay to just get the baby part."

"Okay, fine. You got someone in mind for the job?"

Hunter flashed across the screen of her mind. The kiss filled her thoughts and she felt a thrill slide through her, right down to her feminine core. "No," she lied.

Ricki's gaze had returned to the burned wreck of the cottage. "I was gonna brave going inside, but maybe I'll wait. I'm meeting with Sam again soon. He talked to Hunter about the fires and I talked to Mariah and Blair about being at Big

Bart's just before Amber Barstow disappeared. Kincaids are all over this thing, aren't they?"

She said it lightly as she headed back to her truck, but Delilah felt a flutter of alarm. "You think they're involved?" she asked.

"Nah. Only peripherally." Ricki glanced at Delilah and said, "What?"

"I don't think they are, either."

She seemed to see something on Delilah's face, so she hesitated, one hand on the driver's door. "Do you know something?"

"No, no. Not about anything going on now."

"What is it?"

"I ran into Abby Flanders, er, Bywater. We were talking about the wedding and whether she and her father would be going . . ."

"And?" Ricki persisted when Delilah trailed off.

"She wasn't with Hunter the night of the homestead fire. She lied about that because everyone wanted to believe he was the firebug who was setting fires that summer. He wouldn't say the truth, so she gave him an alibi."

"What truth?"

"That he was there, but he was there to meet me."

Ricki narrowed her eyes at Delilah. "To meet you . . . You were seeing Hunter back then?"

"Oh, yeah. I was crazy. Teenaged love, you know. I couldn't tell anybody. Dillinger/Kincaid relations weren't all that great. Then when Abby lied for him, I thought he was still seeing her and I cut it off. Left him a note and ended it."

"Huh." She thought about that for a moment. "So, now what?"

"I don't know. I . . . saw him this morning."

Ricki seemed to pull her thoughts back from wherever they'd gone with an effort. "Saw . . . Hunter?"

"In the stables. But then Colt came in and I left."

Ricki gave Delilah a long look. "You're thinking about asking him to be your baby-daddy."

"Hell, no!"

"Yes, you are," she insisted, grinning. Then her smile faded and she asked, "You sure he was there to meet you at the homestead that night?"

"What does that mean?"

"Well, if Abby hadn't lied for him . . . I don't know."

"He was protecting me."

"Protecting a secret love affair, when he was practically accused of arson?"

"Hunter didn't have anything to do with the fire! Then, or now."

"I know. I know . . ."

"Don't placate me."

"You're talking about babies, Delilah. I just thought that maybe, before you go any further, you might want to clear the air about what really happened that night. Especially in light of the recent fires, and murders."

"God, I'm sorry I said anything."

"I'm just saying . . . before you go to the next step . . ."

"I'm not going to the next step," she snapped out.

Ricki lifted her hands in surrender and climbed into the truck. "Deny it all you want, but you're thinking about making a baby with him. It's in your head. But once you have a father in the picture, they're connected to your kid for better or worse. This I know."

As she drove off, Delilah muttered, "Well, hell." Though she wanted to refute everything Ricki had said, there was an element of truth in there she couldn't ignore because yes, she was thinking about Hunter. She couldn't damn well stop thinking about him.

Pulling out her cell phone, she began to punch in Hunter's number, her heartbeat escalating. She would ask him to meet her at the stables again. If Davis and Kit were around, fine.

There was a tack room with a couple of chairs and a bunk where they could have some privacy. Was she thinking about asking him the impossible? No. Of course not. How could she? What she really wanted was to just clear the air, like Ricki had said, and then maybe . . . maybe . . .

Maybe he'll throw you down on the bunk and make love to you like it's the last day on Earth.

"Jesus," she said, cutting off the call before it could go through.

What the hell is wrong with you, Delilah?

Lost in thought, Hunter heard his cell give one aborted ring. He pulled it from his pocket, throwing a cursory glance toward Whit Crowley and his buddy Graves, who were loitering in the parking lot as he crossed to the front steps of the firehouse. But suddenly Crowley's paw spun him around, his back toward the firehouse wall. Graves was in his face, too. His big mug only inches away. Hunter stiff-armed Crowley, thrusting him back.

"You think you can get me shitcanned, Kincaid?" Crowley growled. "Your troubles have just begun."

"So, Raintree fired you," Hunter shot back through his teeth. "'Bout time."

Crowley grabbed at him but Hunter lithely moved out of range. He was balanced on the balls of his feet, ready. Two against one wasn't exactly a fair fight, and Graves was a big man, but the moment was now.

"What'd you say to the Dillinger girl?" Crowley demanded.

So, this wasn't just about Crowley's ass getting fired. "You mean besides telling her what a scumbag scammer you are? That you're no kind of fireman? That you prey on people and bilk them and their insurance companies? I was real nice about you, Whit. Said you keep your car clean. Maybe you oughta ask her on a date."

"Shut your smart mouth, asshole."

"That all you got, Whit?"

A moment later Graves delivered a punch to Hunter's gut that crumpled his knees and took his breath away. And a moment after that Raintree and several of the volunteers rushed outside.

"Get away from him, Crowley, Graves, before I have you arrested," Raintree bit out. "Get the hell away."

"He threatened us," Crowley said, his face red as a beet as he reluctantly stepped back.

"With a cell phone?" Raintree glowered fiercely.

Muttering under their breaths, Crowley and Graves threw Hunter and Raintree both hateful looks as they strode away.

Hunter had gotten his feet under him again, but his stomach hurt like a son of a bitch.

"You okay?" Raintree quickly came over, concerned.

"Yeah . . ."

"Go see Doc," he said.

"No." Hunter inhaled a deep breath. "Still in one piece."

Raintree growled, "Crowley isn't the only one losing a job. Graves is out, too."

Hunter actually laughed. He was already feeling better. Graves's punch had been hard, but Hunter had managed to move away just at the moment of impact, lessening the damage.

Looking down at the cell phone, his pulse jumped as he recognized the area code on the aborted call as being Santa Monica, California. He knew it because he'd made a point of knowing it. Because Delilah had moved there.

"Sure you're okay?" Raintree asked.

"Yup. I got somewhere to go. I'll be back later . . ."

Chapter Twenty-Six

From the stables Delilah watched Colton, Sabrina, Brook, Rourke, Haley and Justin ride away, Colt's dog, Montana, following after them. Davis and Kit had returned and there was talk of meeting with the Dillinger family lawyer to help put Mia's affairs in order. Kit had looked determined if somewhat frightened, and Delilah totally understood. The girl knew more than most of them about animals, but the world of personal finances and paperwork was completely foreign to her.

Delilah had gone back to the house just as the kids had piled down the stairs, totally excited about the upcoming trail ride. Herding them together, Colton told her Sabrina was on her way and at that moment the veterinarian had pulled up, causing them all to race outside. Delilah had been glad to see that Brook seemed to have shaken off her fears enough to join in. After they left, Delilah had hung around just long enough to get into another wrangle with Ira about the wedding.

"You know who just called me?" he asked her, exasperated. "Lila!"

"Lila called?" Delilah repeated.

"Because *you called her*." He spoke each word with emphasis. "Told her about the wedding even though—"

"I didn't. I didn't call her. I don't even have her number."

"—I told you I wasn't going to invite them!"

"I didn't," Delilah insisted, feeling herself grow hot with annoyance. "How many times do I have to say it? Yes, I thought it might be nice to invite our relatives since you asked every person in twenty-five square miles, but I did not call Lila."

"Well, then, who did?" he demanded suspiciously, not giving an inch.

"I have no idea." They glared at each other for several long moments. "Well, what did she say?" Delilah finally asked. "She knew about the wedding?"

"She offered me congratulations," he muttered. "Said she and that husband of hers couldn't make it down, as if they'd been asked. Wanted to know if Tara and Garth were invited. They're both living in Wyoming again. Asked if I'd seen 'em." He snorted. "Fool woman."

"What did you tell her?" Delilah asked. She kinda thought the old man was getting a bit of what he deserved.

"That it was a *small* wedding."

"Well, I didn't call her, and I didn't call Cousin Royal in Bad Luck, either. Again, didn't have the number. So if you get any other relative checking in, you gotta look elsewhere for your leak."

"I just wanted to keep it simple," he growled, then strode outside and to his truck before she could offer a rejoinder.

Delilah had then wandered around the lodge for a few minutes, trying to drag her thoughts back to the pending nuptials when all she wanted to think about was Hunter. Finally, she'd headed back to the stables where she'd run into Kit and Davis, and now she was alone.

She heard the shifting and snorting of the horses, and when she approached Babylon's box, Babylon came toward her and snuffled her shirt. "I shoulda brought an apple," Delilah murmured, stroking the mare's long nose as she spied Firestarter butting his own nose under his mother's flank, searching for milk.

She thought of Kit, alone now that Mia was gone. She thought of losing her own mother.

The quiet of the stables started to play on her nerves. She hadn't forgotten there was a killer out there. And an arsonist. Maybe one and the same. She needed to be on alert and she suddenly wished she'd gone out with the group. Being by herself wasn't necessarily a safe choice these days.

A blast of music played and Delilah jumped as if goosed. Her heart leapt before she recognized the sound of her own cell phone's default ring. Snatching the phone from her pocket, she stared down at the number, furious with herself for being so jumpy.

Hunter's cell.

Punching the CONNECT button, she said, "Hello?"

"Delilah?"

His voice was like honey. No, it wasn't at all. It was deep and careful and she was just *reacting all over the place.* "Hunter," she responded just as carefully.

"Did you try to call me?"

She wanted to lie. Tell him she'd pocket-dialed him, but what the hell was the point of that? *You do want to see him.* "Yeah, I—did."

"Did you think of something?"

I thought about making love to you. "What do you mean?"

"About the fire?"

"Oh, no." Of course. That's why he'd given her his cell number in the first place. "I just . . . I was talking to Ricki. I—I ran into Abby Flanders in town. Or Bywater. Whatever her name is now. Guess I'll never get that right. She told me she lied about being with you the night of the homestead fire."

There was a long moment of silence, which suddenly made Delilah's nerves scream. What was he thinking? What did that mean?

"Where are you?" he asked.

For a millisecond she thought about not telling him. What if . . . what if he was involved somehow? But she knew better. *She knew better.* Just because the Kincaids seemed to be all over the terrible events of the past few weeks didn't mean they had anything to do with them. "I'm at the stables. I told you I come here a lot."

"I want to talk to you," he said. "I'll be there in ten."

"Ten?"

"I'm close by."

She hung up, her skin tingling. Was it anticipation or worry that caused the goose bumps to rise on her flesh?

Pressing her palms to her cheeks, she walked away from Babylon's box. She needed to think. To get over this absorption with Hunter. It had been years since they were together. She'd heard about people who couldn't get over high school romances; she'd just never thought she'd be one of them.

Actually, he was there in nine minutes. Delilah had watched the clock on her cell phone, calling herself all kinds of names while she waited in breathless anticipation. It made no sense. She'd grown a thick armor around herself all those years in Hollywood that she'd believed nothing could penetrate. How wrong she'd been.

She heard him park his truck, slam the door and then the brittle *thunk* of his boot steps as he crossed the icy ground that a weak sun was beginning to glaze with water. He pounded up the ramp that led to the stables, entering with a swirl of cold that reached Delilah as she stood at Babylon's box, one gloved hand clamped on the top bar as if for dear life. She heard him slide the door closed and then stride directly to her.

"What did you want to talk about?" she asked, turning

her head just enough to catch him in her sights. He looked good, she thought sinkingly. Sober and intense and his blue eyes simmered with heat and emotion. Or was that just *her* desire she saw reflected. God. Damn. *It.*

"You called me because of what Abby said? If you think I had anything to do with *any* fire, you'd better say so right now." He gazed at her hard. "Is that why you called? To ask me if I'm the firebug who burned down your old homestead? And maybe I torched the Pioneer Church and your foreman's cottage. Maybe that's why I work for fire and rescue, because I can't control the need to just burn things. Burn them down to the ground."

"I called *you,* Hunter."

"I know you called me. I saw your area code on caller ID," he retorted, too lost in his own fury to listen to what she meant.

"*You,*" she repeated.

He stared at her, a frown slowly deepening his brow. "Yeah, and I'm trying to figure out why."

Delilah left the box and walked into the tack room. Her eye fell on the bunk with its taut blanket, and with sudden thoughts of lying down with him circling her mind, she would have turned around and left, but Hunter was right behind her, his broad shoulders blocking the door. With no exit, she backtracked a few steps, the crown of her head brushing up against one of the bridles hooked on a wall peg, setting them swinging with a soft jingle.

Remembering Ricki's admonition, she said, "You weren't waiting for me the night of the homestead fire. I was at the tire swing and you never showed. You were at the fire."

She saw his surprise before he shut it down, his mouth turning into a flat line. He thought she was accusing him of something, maybe even of setting the fire, she realized, and she opened her mouth to assure him that wasn't so, but he spoke before she could utter a word. "I was there. I got to the pine tree before you, but then I saw someone—a shadow—coming out of the house. They ran across the field to Kincaid property. I chased after them. I thought it was someone spying on us and I was gonna run them down. Then I heard voices behind me—Judd and Mia—though I didn't know it at the time. I was chasing after the shadow and then the whole damn place went up. By the time I got turned around and back there, Colton was pulling Mia out and your dad saw me and just went ballistic. Wanted to know what I was doing on Dillinger land. I told him I'd seen someone there before the fire. He thought I was lying, and he let me know what he thought of all Kincaids. Again, I wasn't going to tell him I'd been there to meet you."

"But afterward . . ."

"After what?" he said through his teeth.

"After it was all over. You never said anything to defend yourself."

"Neither did you," he pointed out.

Delilah stared at him through drifting dust motes, her mind racing. He'd been waiting *for her* to tell about their secret affair? "You should have told everyone you were chasing someone."

"You think I didn't? No one listened. They all believed Ira. It was only after Abby gave me an alibi that people started thinking it was the drifter who'd set fires around the area all that summer."

Delilah felt like a traitor for even asking. "I never thought it was you. I just wanted to hear you say it, I guess."

Hunter exhaled. "I thought it was Blair," he admitted heavily.

"You thought it was your brother?"

"He'd been up to all kinds of trouble, and it sounded like the sort of thing he mighta done. Mighta set it by mistake, just screwing around. But he wasn't anywhere near the area that night. He wasn't even in the state because he was joyriding in Colorado and got himself arrested."

Delilah vaguely remembered some trouble with Blair around the same time as the homestead fire. She'd just been too miserable over Hunter's involvement with the fire and Abby's revelations to think straight. She was embarrassed now at how juvenile she'd been, how unfair. She half wanted to defend herself, to remind him that she'd been so young, but it was a weak argument. She'd loved him, and she'd believed Abby Flanders when she'd *known* that he'd been there to meet her.

"I left you a note in the hollow in the tree," she said.

"I got it."

It had been a terse breakup note that now seemed so silly and mean that she cringed inside. "I was so young . . ." she murmured, then hated the way that sounded like an excuse.

He waved an arm to dismiss it all, then gazed past her, through the high and narrow dust-smeared window on the side of the stables that looked toward the house. "Is Ira there? I still haven't talked to him."

"He left. I don't think he's back yet."

"I'm not involved with these new fires, either," he added tautly.

"I know. I'm sorry. I do know. Ricki said I should clear the air with you, and she was right."

"Ricki." He was terse. "That's what started this. She believes the rumor?"

Rumor.

"She just knew I was . . ." *Thinking about having a baby.* Drawing a breath, Delilah shook that off and said, "When I ran into Abby, she also said something about a rumor about you."

"The fires," he said on a long-suffering sigh.

"No, it was something else."

"What?"

"I don't know."

"There have always been rumors about the Kincaids . . .

and the Dillingers." He shrugged that off and straightened. "I just want to find out who's behind these current fires."

Delilah nodded, relieved that that conversation was over. "Okay. I do, too." She walked toward the dusty window above the bunk and gazed toward the lodge. "It feels personal."

She heard him walk up behind her. Along with the aromas of leather and straw was his own particular male scent. She froze where she stood, so aware of him behind her that there was damn near a roaring in her ears. She suddenly wanted him so much that her senses swam a bit.

"Y'know," she said slowly, her pulse starting a slow, insistent beat. "I've been thinking about earlier today . . ."

He was utterly still. She could just hear his breathing.

"The kiss," she admitted.

"I've been thinking about it, too."

As if pulled by a magnet, her eyes dropped to the bunk. If he followed her gaze she couldn't tell, but suddenly his hands were stealing around her waist, pulling her back against him. They stood that way for long seconds . . . an eternity, before she turned in his arms. "Is this crazy?" she whispered.

"Yes." He was unequivocal, but his mouth came down on hers, pressing hard. She molded her lips to his and slid her arms around his waist as well. She could feel his hardness against her abdomen and she reveled in it. This was right. This was what she wanted.

He picked her up and settled her on the bunk. They stared at each other, then she threw off her jacket and lay down, her hands clutching anxiously for him until his body was lying on hers. His belt buckle dug into her skin and she reached down and grabbed it, loosening it and quickly pulling it free before unzipping his pants.

His own hands were working on the snaps of her jeans and as they popped loose he yanked her waistband down until she was lying in her pink panties, the tiniest ones she owned, that she'd put on in her haste to get ready this morning. When his mouth descended against the scrap of fabric, she inhaled in anticipation and surprise. Then he was heating her in a way that made her writhe in surprise and sudden, blinding desire. Her back arched and she grabbed his dark hair.

When he lifted his head and pulled her jeans completely off, she moved her hips and wriggled out of her panties. The air was cold but she was hot as they both hurriedly undid the buttons on each other's shirts.

When they were both naked Hunter's gaze traveled hungrily over her. Delilah hadn't made love to another man in so long she trembled in embarrassment. Her hands stole up to cover her breasts, but Hunter swept them away and held them away from her so she was pinned down. He lay down upon her and they just looked at each other.

"I think I might be out of my mind," she said on a swallow.

His mouth quirked. "No."

"No?"

"No . . ."

His hips moved atop hers and her legs eased apart, making room for him. His blue eyes were too penetrating as he settled himself between her thighs, so she reached up and dragged his face down to hers, kissing him for all she was worth as the tip of his manhood probed her wetness. She wanted all of him and she eagerly wrapped her legs around him. It had been *years* since they'd been together. Years and years, but the time fell away in the familiar, rhythmic thrusts, and it could have been yesterday.

"Delilah . . ." He whispered her name in her ear as he moved with ever-increasing tempo. She dug her fingernails into his back and held on. She wanted him. She'd always wanted him . . .

And a baby.

There was no talk of birth control. Maybe he thought she

just took care of those things. Maybe he was as swept away as she was. Maybe he just didn't care.

His tongue probed her mouth and hers answered back. *I love you,* she thought. Just like she had years before. *I love you. I've always loved you.*

The words were in her head, and when he pulled back to bend down and suckle her breast they were in her mouth. But there they stayed. She was too afraid to say them. Too afraid they would break the gossamer threads of this moment and leave reality crashing down on them.

She could feel the heat building inside her. She strained against him, holding him tight, her breath caught as desire rippled inside her. *Hunter . . . Hunter . . . Hunter . . .*

Wild thoughts filled her head. She was going to tell him. *She was.* What could it matter if he knew she loved him . . . ?

She opened her mouth, but the sound that came out was a cry of ecstasy as the explosion rocked her, shattering, sending shudders through her. He groaned and stiffened and followed after her. Her pounding heart was deafening her. Her head swam.

And then she smelled the smoke.

Fire.

Before the impact fully penetrated her brain, Hunter had already rolled away from her and was grabbing for his jeans.

"Smoke," he said, his taut gaze lasered on something through the tack room window.

Delilah scrambled up and followed his sight line. The eastern-side upper floor of the lodge was smoking, gray tendrils curling out from the windows. Inside, flames climbed the curtains of Ira and Pilar's suite.

"Oh, God . . ." she murmured.

Hunter had yanked on his jeans and was dragging on his boots. Delilah swarmed into her own clothes, her teeth chattering with sudden fear. Leaving buttons undone, she snatched up her own boots, hopping into them.

Hunter ran out of the tack room and toward the stable door. Delilah was half a dozen yards behind him as they raced to the lodge. He flung open the front door and found Mrs. Mac coming from the kitchen, looking confused. "Something burning," she said, as Hunter flung himself up the stairs and around the landing.

Delilah followed after him as Mrs. Mac held a hand to her chest and the downstairs fire alarm began bleating loudly. Hunter was at the bedroom double doors, which were stuck. He slammed his shoulder against them several times as Delilah noticed the shims that had been wedged beneath them to keep them from opening. Before she could do anything, wood splintered and the left door gave. Hunter ran in and Delilah was right behind him. She could smell gasoline or something like it. Lighter fluid? The curtains were ablaze. So were the bedclothes.

And Pilar, eyes closed, lay silent as death on the bed in her chiffon wedding gown. The fabric and lace trimmings curling into ash, the whole garment burning beneath a layer of racing, hot flames.

Chapter Twenty-Seven

"Call 9-1-1. Get a fire extinguisher. A hose!" Hunter yelled as he grabbed the blankets and dragged them around Pilar's body, smothering the flames.

Choking, Delilah stumbled from the room and yelled down to Mrs. Mac, who had already scurried back toward the kitchen and garage.

Delilah didn't want to leave Hunter, didn't want to risk losing him, but she raced down the stairs, half falling, scrabbling for the rail. Then she ran across the room and damn near into Mrs. Mac, who was on the phone. Delilah knew where the fire extinguisher was in the laundry room and she ran for it, yanking it from the wall. Then she was racing back the way she'd come, hurrying up the stairs as Hunter carried Pilar's limp, blanket-wrapped body from the bedroom and set her on the landing. The alarm was ear-splitting, but she ran past him with the fire extinguisher toward the bedroom.

"Help her!" Hunter demanded and Delilah paused.

The singed blankets were smoking as Hunter rapidly unwrapped them. Pilar was gray as he instantly began pushing on her chest. "Trade places."

She did as she was told, handing him the fire extinguisher and crossing her hands over Pilar's chest and pumping. Her head was splitting with fear and the shrill blast of the alarm as Hunter ran into the bedroom and sprayed foam onto the flames.

Delilah's world narrowed to the pumping of Pilar's chest. *One, two, three, four.* . . . She counted to ten over and over again in her head. She couldn't have said how long it was before she heard the fire truck's siren and the pounding of feet up the stairs, and then there were people all around her and someone was saying, "She's gone. You can stop. She's gone."

She realized dully that the someone was Hunter. She looked into his smoke-smudged face and wanted to stumble into his arms. But there were too many people and too much confusion and then Ricki was pulling her away.

"Delilah," her sister said, in a sharp, worried tone. "You okay? What happened?"

"I'm fine . . ."

"How did this start?"

"I don't know. Pilar's . . ."

"Dead." Ricki was grim as she half supported Delilah down the stairs. "What was Hunter doing here?"

"He was . . . at the stables . . ."

"Was he here when the fire started?" she clipped out.

"What?"

"Was he in the house when the fire started?"

"No!" Delilah came back to the moment as if she'd been slapped.

"Could he have done this? You just told me Abby lied for him," Ricki said urgently. "Maybe we've all lied for him without knowing it."

"He was with me," Delilah choked out, furious. "In the stables. He was the first one here to help. You've got him all wrong!"

"I told Sam what you said and he's talking to Hunter now."

"Ricki! Oh, my God! I never thought he was responsible

for the homestead fire. You know that." Delilah, who'd been planning to strip off her smoke-filled clothes and take a shower, wrenched away from her sister's grasp.

"Someone killed Pilar," Ricki said.

"Hunter tried to save her!" Delilah heard shouting coming from the great room and turned toward it. Her father's voice. Booming with fury and grief.

"If that's true, you need to defend him fast," Ricki said.

Hunter stared silently at Ira Dillinger, who was pale and in shock but screaming like mad at him. He'd come in just after the firemen and had zeroed in on Hunter when he'd learned of Pilar's death, raging loud enough to shake the snow from the mountains.

Then Delilah and Ricki entered and Delilah said flatly, "He didn't do it. I was with him. We were in the stables together."

"I don't believe it," Ira said, ripping his hands through his hair. He was half-wild.

"It's true," Delilah said.

Sam Featherstone said, "Let's all just take a moment."

For an answer Ira staggered out of the room and toward the front hallway and looked out to where the EMTs were loading Pilar's body into the county coroner's van, slamming the doors shut.

The wail of grief that filled the rafters was from Ira's own lips. Footsteps could be heard above their heads: the forensic team and last of the firemen.

Hunter was tired enough to want to lay his head back against the cushions and fall asleep. He sensed the suspicion and blame even though Delilah had vouched for him. To hell with them all. He didn't care. He hadn't done any of this. It pissed him off but good, that he had to put up with this shit, but when he thought about Pilar's body lying on the bed, it didn't seem to matter much.

Raintree had actually come out with the fire team. "Whoever did this used the same accelerant as your fire two nights ago," he said, shooting a look at Hunter, who'd been the one to give him that information. Better to come from the chief, though.

Ira wandered back in, his jaw set but quivering all the same. Delilah was sitting quietly now, in shock, he guessed. He wanted to talk to her, hold her, be with her, but that wasn't going to be for a while yet. Her father wanted to lay Pilar's death at his feet. He wouldn't be ready to see that Hunter and Delilah had met more than casually in the stables.

"This one is different than the Pioneer Church fire?" Sam asked.

"We're working on the theory that the church fire was a different doer than the two fires on Dillinger property," Raintree agreed.

"Someone killed Pilar," Ira rasped. He didn't look at Hunter, but Hunter could feel the old man's enmity reach him in waves.

Had they meant to kill Pilar? he asked himself now. Was she the target? He searched inside his own head, examining what he knew about arsonists and fire and the emotions tied to them.

Sam said, "ME's put a rush on to learn the cause of death."

"Cause of death?" Ira's glazed eyes raked over Sam. "She was burned, you fool. By Kincaid."

"Hunter wasn't in the house when it went up," Sam said.

"I don't give a good goddamn. He did it somehow."

"It appears Pilar was drugged first," Sam said. "The champagne glass beside the bed is being tested."

At that moment Colton rushed in. "The kids are with

Sabrina at the bunkhouse. Rourke's upset, but I wouldn't let him come up here. I saw the coroner's van . . ."

"Pilar's dead," Ricki said, coming up to Colton and grabbing his arm, pulling him to the side of the room.

"Oh . . . God . . ." Colton looked out the window toward the direction of the bunkhouse. "I gotta tell Rourke," he said bleakly.

"I'll come with you," Ricki said. "Brook's there, too?"

Colton nodded as they headed for the front door.

Hunter watched Colton leave with a heavy heart. He had the unenviable task of alerting his son to his new reality, one without his mother.

"Well, who was it then?" Ira demanded, sinking into a chair. But the fight wasn't out of him yet. "You were here," he said to Hunter. "You were on Dillinger land."

"I was here, too," Delilah reminded. "Hunter and I were in the stables. We ran to the house when we saw the smoke."

"What were you doing in my stables?" Ira asked Hunter.

"Ira." Sam tried to intervene.

"Talking to Delilah," Hunter replied.

"You just happened to be at the stables?" Ira demanded.

"He met me," Delilah said.

"After he set the fire."

"I didn't set this fire or any other," Hunter said, getting to his feet. He was sick to the back teeth of all of them, save Delilah. His head was full of images, not the least being Delilah's soft skin dappled by light through the small stable window, her soft moans that sounded like a plea, the wet heat of her. But superimposed on that glory was Pilar's still body and the smell of burning hair and flesh. Luckily, the fire had been easily put out. Whoever had set it had drugged Pilar before setting the bedclothes and curtains on fire.

Who?

"Where are you going?" Ira demanded as Hunter headed for the door.

Ignoring Ira, he strode outside and gulped lung-freezing air that helped clear his head. Someone had killed Pilar on purpose. All Ira could see was that a Kincaid was to blame, but there was a reason she'd been chosen, a method to the doer's madness.

But who? Why? What?

He wished he could just forget it all and grab Delilah and make love to her forever. That's what he wanted. Delilah. With him. In Prairie Creek or some other stretch of Wyoming. It's what he'd wanted since those early days.

She wanted to leave with Hunter. What would they do if she just got up and walked out with him? Delilah wondered. Ira would have a fit, of course, but she didn't give a rat's ass. And she was furious with Ricki for saying all those things about Hunter to Sam. Sure, sure, Ricki was just trying to figure out what had happened, but *it wasn't Hunter.* Ricki knew that! Didn't she? *Didn't she?* Delilah wanted to cut out her own tongue for talking to her sister about what had happened at the homestead. Damn it. It was so long ago, and Ricki didn't have all the facts anyway. In fact, *she'd* been the one to tell Delilah to talk to Hunter.

And who had killed Pilar? Someone had deliberately taken her life; that was clear. Delilah wondered if she should go to the bunkhouse and help with Rourke, or if maybe it would be better to wait until Colton asked for her help.

She felt ill and unhappy, when mere hours before she'd been in ecstasy with Hunter. Awed and amazed that after all this time it was still there. Desire. Craving. Attraction. Love . . .

"Who's doing this?" she asked aloud into a lull in the conversation and accusations that had still rung through the air after Hunter's departure.

Everyone looked at her, but no one had an answer.

Deciding she'd had enough, she left the great room in a rush and ran outside. Her gaze swept the area for Hunter, but all she saw was the back of his gray pickup as it burned away from Dillinger land.

Three hours later Ricki pressed the cell phone to her ear and asked, "Does the lab know anything yet?" as she walked outside and away from the oppressive mood inside the lodge.

It was a long shot, but Sam had said there was a rush job on the cause of Pilar's death.

"Preliminarily looks like she died of a drug overdose. The fire was secondary."

"What drug?"

"Looks like oxycodone." Sam gave her a quick rundown of what was in the hurried lab report: not much at this juncture. Part of Ricki had wanted to leave with him, but there was emotional chaos at the Rocking D and Brook needed her close, whether she knew it or not. Now she stared off toward the Tetons, her gaze on their snow-capped peaks as she heard the front door open and close behind her. She turned to see her daughter, pulling a heavy sweater more closely to her chest, come down the steps toward her.

"Someone killed Pilar," Brook said unsteadily. "Like they tried to kill me?"

Ricki wanted to deny it. She always wanted to minimize Brook's tendency toward "drama." But she shut her mouth before she said anything. Maybe she hadn't listened to Brook enough, had ignored or dismissed Brook's complaints. Now, she cast her mind back to several conversations between Brook and herself that had washed over her head at the time . . . and maybe shouldn't have.

Sam was saying, ". . . will know more later, but it looks like Pilar was the target in this case."

Was the same true of Brook and the foreman's cottage fire?

Something in Ricki's face must have revealed her thoughts because Brook frowned at her. "Thanks, Sam. I've gotta go," Ricki said into the phone. "I'll check back with you."

She clicked off and remained silent, thinking.

"What?" Brook asked.

"Pilar was drugged and it's likely she died of an overdose. Looks like traces of oxycodone were found in her champagne glass."

Brook blinked at her mother. "Drugs? Oh, my God."

"You bumped into Georgina and knocked her purse over and she was furious with you. And I remember you said there were drugs in her purse."

"And a gun. You said the pills were for her husband and to stop making too much of it."

"I know."

They stared at each other and Brook drew a sharp breath. "What are you saying, Mom?"

"I'm not sure. But the Major has cancer and must use some form of painkiller."

"You think *Mrs. Kincaid* killed Pilar?"

"Or someone with access to the drugs," Ricki said, lowering her voice and pulling Brook away from the house. "Don't repeat what I'm saying. I don't have all the answers. I was just remembering what you'd told me."

"You're not scaring me. If that old bitch did something—"

"Brook," Ricki broke in, exasperated. "Don't make me regret treating you like an adult."

"Geez, Mom. Come on . . . Do you think she set fire to our house, too . . . because I saw the drugs? You think she *meant to kill me!*"

"Shhh. I mean it. Don't jump to conclusions. This is

dangerous. Let me talk to Sam." She was sorry already she'd said anything to her daughter and was worried that she'd set Brook on a path of conclusions from which she wouldn't stray, when there were still too many questions left to be answered. "Come on. Get in the truck. I'm taking you with me."

"Where?"

"Wherever I'm going to be," she muttered, punching in another call to her cell phone as she grabbed Brook's arm and hurried her toward her truck. "Colton, hey . . . I'm sorry to bother you. Just wanted you and Delilah to know that Brook's going to be with me for the rest of the day . . ."

Who was at the Dillinger house at the time of both fires?

The question haunted Hunter as he took a shower at the station and changed into the spare set of clothes he kept in a locker. He was just leaving the locker room when he ran straight into Whit Crowley.

"What are you doing here?" Hunter asked, looking past the man for his buddy Graves, but it looked like Whit was alone. Maybe Graves, at least, was taking his dismissal seriously.

"Gotta clear out the old locker now that I've been . . . terminated."

Hunter was sick of tangling with Crowley and his juvenile tactics of intimidation and he brushed past the man, hoping it was the last time.

"Can't stop burning down the Dillingers, can ya?" Crowley called after him. "First that guest house and now the main house . . . didn't expect the lady of the house to be there . . . or was that planned, too?"

Hunter ground his teeth.

"Your days are numbered, y'know. Now you've killed someone. And I'm gonna make sure everyone knows it."

Hunter stopped short at the door. "Do your worst," he ground out.

"They're all gonna know what you did . . ." he went on, but Hunter was already out the door.

Hearing a text come in, he pulled out his cell and examined it as he headed for his truck. It was from Delilah, asking where he was and if she could meet with him.

His first instinct was to say yes, but he stopped himself. He thought about the stables and then the fire . . . and the way she'd been . . . the way they'd all been . . . in the aftershock of Pilar's death. He needed time to think. About Delilah. About what he wanted. About what was possible.

Climbing into the cab, he texted back: Will call you later.

Then he drove off toward the mountains, putting some time and space between himself and Prairie Creek, needing a few hours to himself, needing to shut down his mind for a while.

Even as he told himself as much, the question he'd been asking himself all day returned: *Who was at the Dillinger house at the time of both fires?*

Delilah jostled along in Ira's Jeep Cherokee. She'd stayed at the house about as long as she could stand it. Jen and Nell had returned and Jen had herded up her two children from Colton and Sabrina's care, put them in the car and taken them to the Tumbleweed Inn, the only overnight lodging in Prairie Creek worth knowing about. Tyler had been at the impromptu meeting after Pilar's death but hadn't said anything. While Jen was packing up the kids, Delilah had asked him if he was going with them, and his answer had been, "I guess not."

She'd left Nell trying to comfort Ira, who was shell-shocked, gray-skinned and spent. Delilah hadn't been able to say anything to him. She was too angry with the way he'd treated Hunter. When she'd headed for the Jeep she'd found Tyler along the fence line, looking off in the distance as if following the invisible trail that had been left in his family's departure.

"Where are you going?" he'd yelled at her as she drove off.

Somewhere else. Her answer was a lifted hand in goodbye. She just couldn't be in the house anymore, and not only because of the wet, smoky smell that permeated the place or the sense of gloom, disbelief and fear. She needed to clear her head and think things through. Too much was happening in too short a time, a free fall from her old life.

All she knew for certain was that she wanted Hunter in her new life.

She headed into Prairie Creek proper, determined to drive around in circles if need be to pass the time until Hunter got back to her. She realized with a sense of shock that tears were pooling in her eyes and she brushed them angrily away. It was terrible. Everything was terrible. She sure as hell wanted Ricki and Sam to find out who was doing this and put an end to it, but damn it all, she wanted to be with Hunter, too. Wanted to throw herself into his arms. Wanted to cry her eyes out until there was nothing left.

An hour went by . . . then two . . . Delilah had parked in the Menlo's Market lot and she woke up to find herself staring blankly through the windshield in a kind of self-induced trance. Hunter wasn't going to text her back. Had he forgotten, or . . . did he not want to see her?

Well, tough. She was going to see him. She wasn't about to let another eighteen years slip by. If she needed to prostrate herself at his feet and swear her undying love, it would be better than being separated again. When she thought about the possibility of having to leave him and go back to her old life, she wanted to rip her hair from her head and scream at the Fates.

This time she was going to have her say, and not with a note left in the hollow of a tree. This time she was going to have a face-to-face, and damn the consequences.

She knew where Hunter lived and she drove past his house, but the place looked deserted in the dull afternoon light diffused by the overhead cloud cover. Next, she went by Prairie Creek Fire and Rescue, but Hunter's Chevy truck wasn't anywhere to be seen.

Would he go to his parents' place?

Not likely. Hunter and Georgina's relationship made Kit and Mia's seem like it was out of a 1950s sitcom. But then Georgina's relationship with everyone had always been difficult. Delilah didn't really know Hunter's mother, but she remembered her from her youth: grim, suspicious and laser-focused. As a teen, as much as Delilah had worried about Ira learning about Hunter's and her love affair, she had woken up from more than one nightmare where Georgina learned of it.

"She's just an older woman now," Delilah murmured to herself as she made her way to the Kincaid property.

Swallowing her misgivings, she turned into the long drive that wound to the front of the two-story Kincaid house with its wings that flared out on both ends. Snow had been shoveled away from the track leading to the front porch and hard, dusty ground showed through. The snow that remained was in dirty piles on either side that were slowly shrinking into hard mounds.

The place was rustic. Too rustic. A shutter listed on one of the upstairs windows; another was gone altogether. Delilah felt uncomfortable as she thought of how her father gleefully had admitted that he wasn't planning to drill for oil on Dillinger land, intimating that his deal with Georgina somehow favored him and maybe shafted the Kincaids.

Hunter's truck wasn't anywhere to be seen here, either.

Maybe he'd driven around the house to the back to park, or more likely he wasn't here at all. She had no wish to meet with Georgina on her own, although the Major had always been a decent man and apparently still was, the way people talked about him.

But now Ira's Jeep was in full view. If she turned around and left, would Georgina take it as a slight? Good God, she was annoyed at herself for her indecision.

Maybe she should just leave well enough alone . . .

Instead, she found herself heading up those cracked wooden steps and crossing the porch to the front door. Several hounds began baying at the sound of her knock and when the door opened suddenly, Delilah wondered if Georgina had been on the other side, just waiting for her.

"Hello, Georgina. I was wondering if, um, Hunter was here."

Georgina looked her up and down, then said, "Come in," waving her inside.

Delilah crossed the threshold and Georgina shut the door behind her. A frisson of fear began to slide down Delilah's back. Feeling how tense she was inside, she tried hard to relax.

"Sad business up at your place. Come sit in the kitchen," Georgina said, stalking toward the back of the house.

Delilah followed her reluctantly. She sensed Hunter wasn't around and she did not want to be around his mother any longer than she needed to be. "Doesn't look like Hunter's here," she said, entering the kitchen where Georgina was standing in front of the back door, looking through the door's window onto the fields beyond.

"Nope. He was yesterday. Talked to the Major." Her face was grim and Delilah got the impression that she was having some inner dialogue with herself.

Delilah fingered her cell, which she'd stuffed in her pocket. She wanted to text Hunter but had to wait till she got through talking to Georgina.

"So, Pilar's dead, huh."

"Yes . . ." Delilah didn't want to talk about it, least of all to Georgina, but she managed. "Hunter and I tried to save her."

"Fire got her? The smoke?"

"Seemed more like she was unconscious from something else."

Georgina lifted a brow. "What?"

"You'd have to ask the sheriff's department. I don't know."

"Why are you looking for Hunter?"

"I just wanted to see how he was doing, I guess."

"Care about him, do ya?"

Delilah hardly knew how to respond. "He really tried to save Pilar. It was just too late."

"I know you're sleeping with him," she stated flatly, surprising Delilah so much she almost choked.

There was no way Hunter would have told her about the stables. No way. Not with everything that had gone on today, and not anyway. There wasn't time and he just wouldn't do it.

"I'd better get going," Delilah said.

"You Dillinger girls. Think you can have anything you want."

Delilah stared at her. This woman was the mother of the man she loved. She didn't want to completely ruin any hope of renewed Dillinger/Kincaid relationships, but it was amazing how rude Georgina was. She fought out, "Say hello to the Major for me," and turned for the front door.

"You can't have my son," she said. "I told him the same thing before he left."

"I don't think that's your decision," she said, hesitating.

"Didn't know I'd have a chance to be telling both of you the same thing. You can't be together."

"I'll let Hunter tell me that," Delilah answered coolly.

"Sometimes a rumor's true, you know?"

Delilah felt the hair on her arms rise and she slowly turned around to look into Georgina Kincaid's avid eyes. *She's enjoying herself.* "What rumor?"

"Ask your father."

Georgina looked like she could hardly contain herself. She wanted Delilah to keep asking her questions, but it was clear she would keep up this strange cat and mouse game. Delilah turned her back on her, then headed for the front door and Ira's Jeep. Climbing inside, she tore away from the Kincaid house and out onto the main road, aiming for the Rocking D, driving faster than she should. But she didn't care. There was something going on . . . something uneven beneath her feet that threatened to trip her. Did Hunter know what Georgina meant? She'd said she'd warned him off Delilah as well.

About three miles separated the Kincaid ranch house from the Dillingers' new one. The lane to the old homestead was in between. As she passed the turnoff to the homestead a truck lumbered out from the lane and followed after her in the direction of the Rocking D. She wondered what someone was doing up there; there wasn't much other than the ruined house and more Dillinger property. Maybe it was one of Ira's workers?

Glancing in her rearview mirror, she realized the truck was suddenly gaining on her. Here she'd thought it was slow moving, but it suddenly seemed to be pursuing her as if it were jet-propelled.

"Hey!" Delilah stomped on the accelerator. She didn't know what the hell he was up to, but by God she wasn't waiting around to find out.

The road was patchy with ice and snow. Her tires slipped, caught, slipped again. Her hands were sweaty on the wheel. "Shit," she murmured, beginning to feel real fear.

Bam! The front end of the gray truck smacked into her.

Delilah hung on to the steering wheel, madly fighting for control. *BAM!* He hit her again and now her wheels locked and she screamed as the Jeep tore off the road and over a ditch and through a fence. She threw one arm up to protect herself, her head slamming into her side window. Dazed, she smashed the heel of her hand down on the horn, blasting it. *WWWAAAAHHHHHHHHHH!*

The truck kept on going, zipping past her and fishtailing as the driver stomped on the brake. Then it suddenly whipped fully around, facing back at her. Delilah saw it all through a haze. If he came at her again. If he hit her broadside . . .

She saw the truck's front tires spin and catch. The grill was coming toward her.

She unbelted herself with stiff, unresponsive fingers. Tried to scrabble across to the passenger seat. *Hurry . . . oh, God . . . hurry!*

Whoosh!

The truck zoomed right past her, racing back the way she'd come. She looked up and tried to see the license plate but it was crusted over with dirt.

Her heart was thundering. Her breath coming in gasps. Minutes passed.

Then she heard another horn and turned her head slowly toward the Rocking D. A vehicle was fast approaching.

One hand strayed to her forehead and came away bloody. When she'd banged her head into the side window, she'd split the skin next to her hairline above her left eyebrow.

She saw that it was Colton's truck. She wanted to tell him to speed after the truck, which had disappeared around a bend in the road, but was struggling to find the energy. He sprang from the vehicle and ran to hers, yanking open the driver's door. "Delilah. You all right? What happened?"

"I was . . . run off the road . . ."

"*What?*" He whipped out his cell phone. "I'm calling an ambulance."

"No." Delilah made a concentrated effort to get out of the car and show him she was all right.

"Then I'm calling Sam. Did you see who did this?"

"No . . ." All she'd seen was a gray truck, like Hunter's.

Chapter Twenty-Eight

Delilah lay on the den couch as Nell fussed over her. "I'm okay. I'm really okay," she said for about the hundredth time.

"Someone's trying to hurt our family." Nell's face was drained of color as she leaned forward and tried to put another wet compress on Delilah's forehead.

Delilah blocked her with one arm and sat up.

"You've got a cut right at your hairline," Nell said.

"It's a scratch," Delilah muttered.

"It's a cut. You should probably have it stitched up."

"A Band-Aid will do. Head wounds bleed a lot. Doesn't mean they're serious."

Colton had tried again to call 9-1-1, but Delilah had managed to talk him out of it. Just. Now he was back at the bunkhouse with the kids and Sabrina. He'd been walking to his truck, planning to head into Prairie Creek for some pizza to feed the troops, when he'd heard the Jeep's horn. Immediately, he'd jumped into the truck and driven as fast as he could to find her. He hadn't known what to expect, but with all the danger and tragedy surrounding them, he'd acted first, figuring he could ask questions later.

"I'm okay. Better than okay," Delilah insisted as she got to her feet. "I've got some things I need to do."

"Colton's coming right back."

"Good. I need his truck."

Nell shook her head. "You're as stubborn as Dad. Worse."

"Where is Dad?"

"In town."

Delilah didn't really want to see Colt. She wanted to see Hunter. But as she took three steps toward the kitchen her head felt woozy, and though she managed to hide it from Nell, she sank into a kitchen chair as soon as she was out of her sister's sight and sighed. She needed to find her cell phone and call Hunter but didn't have the energy to find her purse yet. She'd told Colt to grab it from Ira's Jeep, but she wasn't sure that had happened.

She was getting to her feet again, definitely feeling better, when she heard her father's truck rumble into the yard. A few moments later Ira slammed inside the house. Something about the sound of that didn't bode well for her father's frame of mind.

But Delilah was pissed, too. At the way her father had treated Hunter, and at the wild driver who'd run her down. It gave her a cold feeling when she thought about how deliberate that attack had been. Was this the arsonist . . . the killer? The one who seemed to have something against the Dillingers?

Ira stuck his head in the kitchen and said, "What the hell happened to the Cherokee?"

"I put it in the ditch." She found she couldn't explain, but as it turned out she didn't have to because Nell was right there. Before he could ask anything further she started regaling her father with the events that had led to the crash, and then Colton returned and joined in, and Delilah felt the first twinges of a headache coming on and just tuned them all out.

It would be too embarrassing to admit, but she just wanted to push everything aside for a few minutes and talk to Hunter. They'd made love and it had been wonderful and they hadn't had a moment together since. Where was he? She had an uneasy feeling inside that he'd run away from her, like she'd run away from him so long ago. But no. That wasn't how Hunter was made.

Thoughts of Georgina and her insinuations intruded on her thoughts and she tried to push them away. She didn't want to let Hunter's obsessive mother inside her head. She really didn't give a damn what either she or Abby had meant.

The din around her had turned into a shouting match with Ira blaming Hunter Kincaid for damn near everything, and Nell and Colton trying to get him to listen to reason. Delilah wanted to clap her hands over her ears.

And none of them knew yet that it had been a similar truck to Hunter's that had run her off the road. Gray . . . well, maybe dirty white, but she didn't think so. Just wait till that shit hit the fan.

"I've gotta lie down," Delilah said.

"Told you," Nell said.

Actually, it was more an excuse to get away from them than anything else, but they didn't have to know that. As Delilah moved past Ira, she said, "I may need to use your truck tomorrow. I've got some things to do."

"So you can put it in a ditch?"

"She was run off the road," Colton reminded him tersely.

"By a Kincaid. They're all rattlers lying under rocks. That's what I've been saying!"

"The truck," Delilah said again, and her father pursed his lips and nodded. With that she headed back to the den.

After a full day tagging after her mother, Brook's enthusiasm for any kind of police work, not that she'd had much to begin with, had taken a serious hit. It was so boring. Sitting around, discussing who was where at what time, and there were lists of names and phone calls to be made . . . Initially she'd been eager to be a part of things, to tell her tale about the Kincaid lady, glad that her mother was finally listening to her. But then hours had passed and nothing had really happened, and she was flat-out tired of hanging around the station.

Sam had wanted to hear her story and so she'd told it, expecting action. But there were "considerations" and all kinds of reasons why they didn't seem to want to piss the old lady off.

"She came out of that dress shop and ran right into me," Brook had told him when he'd asked. "Her purse went flying and she dropped an 'f' bomb, I'm pretty sure. Then she acted like it was all my fault and practically knocked me over grabbing up her purse."

"What exactly did you see in her purse?" Sam asked.

"Bottles of pills. You know, like drugs. And a gun."

Apparently Mrs. Kincaid was known for having lots of guns, because nobody even batted an eye on that one.

"How do you know that they were drugs?" her mom had asked, looking really intense.

"I'm not a baby."

"What happened after she ran into you?" Sam asked.

Brook was gratified that he at least recognized Mrs. Kincaid ran into her, not the other way around. "She snatched up her purse and tucked it under her arm, like she thought I was going to steal it, or something. And then she said, 'You're Ricki Dillinger's girl,' real mean-like. Or something like that, and I told her I was a *Vakalian* from New York. I told her she could just bite me."

"You didn't," her mother warned.

Okay, maybe she hadn't said exactly that. "Well, I told her my last name. She's like . . . psycho."

"Brook . . ." Her mom had sounded annoyed, and after that she and Sam had pretty much forgotten about her, which really pissed her off.

Now, she got up stiffly from the chair she'd been sitting on in Sam's office and headed out the door to find out where they'd all gone to. As if she'd known she was looking for her, her mother was coming down the hall. "Brook, come on. We gotta go," she urged, doing an about-face and heading for the front of the station.

"It's about time. Where are we going?" Brook demanded, hurrying to keep up with her.

"To the lodge. Delilah was in a car accident."

"Oh, no. She's okay, though, right?"

"Yes. She just has a cut on her forehead."

"What happened?"

"The Jeep's in a ditch. Colt said someone ran her off the road."

"Who ran her off the road?" Brook demanded, scared. When her mother didn't answer, she declared fiercely, "I bet it's something to do with *her*." She was walking fast to keep up with her mom's fast footsteps. "She's *awful*. A total bitch. I bet she drugged Pilar with those pills and killed her. And she probably set the fire at the cottage, too. She wanted to kill me!"

"That just doesn't make sense," her mother muttered through her teeth as she stiff-armed the door and headed outside. Brook caught up to her and they both slammed into the truck. "Why would she do that?" her mother added. "Because you saw the drugs?"

Brook stared at her, slack-jawed. She'd been just bitching, really. It freaked her out a little that her mom was taking her so seriously. "Are you going to arrest her?"

"No. Good grief. We don't know anything. We can't just throw around accusations." She yanked the seat belt over her shoulder. "But if I find out Georgina Kincaid, or anyone else, is responsible for setting our house on fire while you were in it . . ." She left the threat unfinished, but Brook felt a little better.

Her mom's cell phone rang and she snatched it up, glancing at the screen. "Don't know it," she said, then answered anyway, "Deputy Dillinger." As soon as she heard the voice on the other end of the line, her attention was grabbed hard.

"Who is it?" Brook asked, but her mother paid her no attention.

"That's a real help, Mr. Griffin," she said. "I'll tell Sam. Thanks."

She hung up and switched on the engine. Brook asked again, "Who was that?"

"Just part of the investigation." They headed out of town. Her mom was lost in thought and didn't say much for a long, long time. The light was fading as they rattled down the road that ran in front of the Kincaid and Dillinger properties. Just past the road to the old homestead they came across a Thomas Towing truck winching up the rear end of Ira's Jeep Cherokee.

"Oh, my God . . ." Brook said in a hushed voice. "Mrs. Kincaid ran Aunt Delilah off the road. Her house is just back there!"

"What did I say about jumping to conclusions?"

"She tried to kill *me,* in case you've forgotten."

"Brook . . . stay out of this. If anyone's going to jump to conclusions, it's going to be me. And I'm not there yet," she said grimly.

Hunter watched his sister stow the dress she'd been fixing onto a hanger, tugging on the hem and examining it critically. "Mom's crazy," Emma said to him, never taking her eyes off the dress. "She's crazy, and Dad's sick. The ranch is going to shit. But you know all this."

He'd shown up at her dress shop after he'd gone back to the station and checked with Raintree who'd seen his preoccupation and asked him what he was thinking about the fires. Hunter had tried to go over everything he knew again, and he'd come to the same conclusion as before: two doers. He'd left the station, stopped in at Molly's for a quick sandwich, had dodged questions about the fire and Pilar's death, then had plucked out his cell to call Delilah.

She hadn't picked up, so he'd left a fairly terse message, saying he'd call her the next day. He was annoyed with her family. Half of them blamed *him* for the fires. Ira, Ricki . . . maybe not Delilah, but it sure as hell was goddamned convenient for them to point fingers at the Kincaids.

He'd stopped by Emma's dress shop in a dark mood, and she'd taken one look at his face and ushered him into the back room, hurriedly shooing the other employees out. "The Major?" she'd asked anxiously as soon as they were alone.

No, not really. That hadn't been what was driving him, but their father's health was definitely something they needed to discuss, so he'd nodded and they'd talked about his rapidly failing health for a while.

Hunter finished with, "He asked me to call Berkley Price." He'd already told her how their father didn't feel Georgina was capable of keeping the ranch going, which wasn't a surprise based on the dilapidated state it was in. What he didn't tell her was the Major's belief that Georgina wouldn't be fair to her own children when she was in total control.

"Why Price?" Emma asked. "He's not the family lawyer."

"I don't know, and I don't want to know."

His sister gave him a long look and said, "Something else is bothering you. What is it?"

He didn't talk to Emma often. He certainly didn't come

to her place of work, so he got why she thought there was something else. And, well, there was something else.

"When I was at the ranch Mom guessed that I was seeing someone."

"You are? Who?" Emma asked, a smile forming on her face.

"Delilah Dillinger."

Emma didn't hide her surprise. "How did that happen?"

Like everyone else, Emma had been kept in the dark about his teen love affair with Delilah. And, well, he didn't feel like going into it now. "It just did. Mom knows and she told me I couldn't see Delilah anymore."

Emma half laughed. "I'm sure you listened to her."

He snorted. "Like always."

"Why does she care, because Delilah's a Dillinger? I thought we were past that."

"I thought so, too, but maybe not for her. Although she is in that oil deal with Ira."

"What oil deal?" Hunter quickly brought her up to date with what he knew, and Emma made a clucking sound in her throat. "She doesn't hate Ira Dillinger as much as she puts on. And the way she hated Pilar, you'd think she was a jilted lover. Wonder if she feels bad that Pilar's dead."

Her words twigged something in his mind. He had to search around for what it was and finally remembered. "When I saw Dad yesterday, I told him about Mom and Ira meeting about oil rights with Century Petroleum. He didn't believe me. He said that Mom didn't have anything to do with Ira *anymore.* She's never had anything to do with Ira, as far as I know."

Emma made a face. "Well, there are those rumors."

"The only rumors I know are the ones about me being a firebug, and those are alive and well."

"There've always been whispers about Ira and other women, Mom included. You musta heard them."

"They're not true. Not about Mom."

"Well, how would you know?" Emma posed. "It was before she got with Dad, supposedly. They haven't always been at war."

He tried to imagine his mother with Ira Dillinger, but the picture failed to materialize. Ira had married Rachel about the same time Georgina had hooked up with the Major, and before that he was pretty sure his mother had been involved with some guy from Cheyenne.

"It just doesn't sound right," Hunter said.

Emma shrugged her slim shoulders. "She doesn't want you with Delilah. Maybe it's because she's jealous of your relationship with a Dillinger."

"That's not even worth answering," he said.

"I'm just telling you," she said, unconcerned, never realizing she'd left Hunter with a bad feeling that followed him all the way back to his house. As he climbed out of his truck, he yanked out his cell phone. Delilah hadn't called him back. Maybe she was upset with how long it had taken him to call her.

Grimacing, he headed into the house. Tomorrow, he thought. Tomorrow he would straighten that out with Georgina and put the whole damn thing to rest. If her aversion to Delilah had something to do with Ira, he wanted to hear it.

He drove to the end of the rutted lane and then along the fence line, miles back from the Dillingers and Kincaids, toward the foothills of the mountains. He'd cut through a section of fence to make way for his vehicle and had found many other places to hide ever since the sheriff's department had found his shed on Horseshoe Ridge where he'd kept

Amber, and the cave he'd used for skinning. It hadn't been easy, keeping ahead of them. There had been a lot of riders swarming over Dillinger and Kincaid property and beyond. He'd had to throw everything into the back of the truck and hide it beneath a blue tarp, but then, he didn't actually stay at his chosen lairs; they were just used for his work.

The sheriff's department's scouting had eased up since the two fires at the Dillinger spread. The last few days they'd stayed closer to home, assuming, he suspected, that they felt he was closer in as well. All of it made it possible for him to concentrate on his next conquest.

"Delilah," he said, savoring the syllables as he fingered the teeth in his pocket.

His cock was a flagpole as he pulled the truck into the heavy brush that he used as a blind. In the dark he removed the license plates, which were purposely covered with mud, and buried them about a quarter of a mile away. He had more in his lair, along with his tools. It was a long trek from where he felt comfortable to park to his new hideout, but he looked forward to slinging Delilah's body over his shoulder and carrying her there. His mind swam with the thought.

But he had to be careful. He had to keep moving. If they found his lair again, he could take to other caves in the mountains, find a way back to his truck. He could live a good while without them finding him.

Delilah . . .

He'd wanted so badly to take her. Had slammed into her truck in a frenzy of desire. Had wanted to rip her away from that fucker, Kincaid. When he thought about her with him he felt downright sick, his stomach clenching when he pictured Kincaid's hands sliding over her flesh. That flesh was *his* property. *His.* He could scarcely wait to slip his knife into that sweet place just below the epidermal layer, separating it from the muscle, slicing it free.

But it had been too bold a move. Before he could collect her she'd slammed on the horn. She would pay for that mistake with her lovely flesh.

Thinking about her was exquisite torture, but he indulged himself. First he would mount her like a stallion and they would make love to exhaustion. How long would that last before he took her skin? A week had seemed like an awfully long time with Amber. Too long. He'd wanted the lovemaking to last. He really had. A couple of weeks, more, but he hadn't been able to. With Delilah it wouldn't even be a week. Three days, he told himself. Maybe two . . .

God, it had to happen soon. This waiting was excruciating.

He needed a plan. A way to make her his, before he went after the rest of them. They all deserved to die, but some deaths would be more pleasurable than others.

He smiled in the darkness. They didn't even know he existed. He was invisible to them. They ran around like ants in all directions. Couldn't imagine who was after them. He wanted to crow to someone . . . *Delilah.* Wanted to tell her everything.

He pictured her tied up in his lair. Her hands behind her back, her legs pulled up to meet her hands so she was in a bow, arched. Her breasts and thighs straining. He would run his knife along her flesh, and then he would slide his cock into her wetness and ride her like the little whore she was. Daddy's girl. All of them Daddy's girls. They would do anything for Daddy's money. But then they all had, hadn't they?

But he would show 'em. One by one. And after she'd satisfied him he would pluck out a tooth. Just one . . . well, maybe two. Trophies. Only then would he begin skinning. His mind burned with the thought. Maybe he would pour water on her and freeze her like he had Amber, leave her in some public place. God. He could see the terror on their faces when they found her and wondered who would be next.

But how to get her?

Kincaid.

He ground his teeth, just thinking about the man. She was a bitch in heat around him. He'd seen them outside the Prairie Dog. If they'd been alone they would have thrown themselves into the dirt and rutted away. He'd smelled the desire on them.

If he wanted her, he just needed to get Kincaid first. He knew that. All he had to do was lure him into a trap and let Delilah know where he was.

She would come running.

Chapter Twenty-Nine

Davis watched Kit saddle up, her rolled-up pack tucked behind the saddle. He didn't like what he was seeing one bit. "It's not safe for you to be by yourself."

She didn't answer, just tightened the girth and threw him a look that said she'd heard it all before and hadn't believed it then, either.

"The animals will be fine," he said. "We'll sort it out later."

"I'll find 'em," she said, which exasperated Davis.

They'd located several places along the fence line that divided Dillinger land from Kincaid land that had been broken out. Kincaid sheep had wandered onto Dillinger land and Dillinger cattle had taken a trip over to Kincaid property. Kit had galloped onto the Kincaid land without a qualm, but Davis had great respect for Georgina Kincaid and her "shoot first and ask questions later" attitude.

"You don't want to go on Kincaid land uninvited," he warned.

"I can handle them."

"Ira won't like it."

She refused to answer.

"Kit, it's too dangerous."

She glared at him and he knew the more he said, the less she was going to listen. He'd really thought they'd reached a new understanding, but Kit lived by her own rules. He had to keep reminding himself of that fact. No, he didn't like it one bit.

"Just wait until I can talk to Ira," Davis said urgently, as Kit mounted Sirocco, the white and gold Arabian she preferred. When she acted like she hadn't heard him, he said, "I'll come with you."

"I'll be fine."

"When will you be back?"

"When I'm done."

He almost jumped on his own horse and tagged after her, but he knew enough about her to know the more he tried to control her, the further and further she would push him away.

"Damn it all," he muttered fiercely as she rode off. He would have to talk to Ira and maybe he should warn Georgina Kincaid, just to make sure she didn't do something stupid. But that woman was as cold as a mountain lake in winter.

After some hard thought he put in a call to Hunter.

Ricki was pacing in front of Sam's desk. "I think I should be the one to follow up on this," she said for the third time, and for the third time Sam said right back, "Let Katrina go through the list again."

She growled in frustration and threw herself into the chair opposite his desk. "I don't know what it means anyway," she muttered.

She'd gotten a call from Catfish Griffin, who'd been at the Buffalo Lounge the night Amber Barstow had been kidnapped. He'd been on Katrina's call list, but then Ricki had been the one to call him the second time and ask him about the cowboy at the bar in the black hat. He hadn't offered anything new when they'd talked, but apparently he'd thought it over some, and when he phoned Ricki back he said, "I remember his boots. The guy at the bar that night. Had him some black alligator ones. If he's really the sick bastard yer after, he don't deserve those boots."

Ricki had thanked him for the information, but with Brook in the car and in a race to find out if Delilah was all right, she'd shoved the information aside for the moment, then had had all night to ruminate on it. Now, she was convinced it might lead her to their killer, but Sam was infuriatingly calm and deliberate.

"I want to get this guy before something else happens to my family," she said determinedly.

"Thought you were zeroing in on one of the Kincaids."

"Only because of Georgina. This guy could be a Kincaid."

"Hunter . . . or Blair . . . ?" Sam looked at her dubiously.

"There's some kind of connection with the Kincaids. I don't know what it is," she growled. "We just need to find those boots. Black Hat killed Mia and Amber and burned the Pioneer Church down. Maybe he didn't do the other fires. I don't know."

"He could have left Prairie Creek."

"No." Ricki was positive. "He's around. And he's got something against us Dillingers." She looked at him. "You think I'm grasping at straws."

"The boots are somewhere to start. If he's like most of us around here, he's probably wearing 'em every day. We don't change 'em much."

"Then I should go through the list again."

"Maybe you should take a day off."

"What does that mean?" she demanded.

He held up his hands. "A helluva lot's happened, Ricki. To your family. Besides the fires and Amber Barstow and Mia Collins, we're looking for whoever killed Pilar, and the truck with a bashed-up front end that ran your sister off the road. Just thought you might want to go home and circle the wagons."

"This your way of trying to get rid of me?"

"You really think I'm trying to get rid of you?" he tossed right back at her.

Ricki felt a small smile steal across her lips. There was a reason she'd fallen in love with Sam Featherstone. "Then let me keep going on this. I'll split the list with Katrina. I don't care if they all think I'm bugging them."

"Maybe you should try it from the other end. See if you can find out who wears boots like that."

"Could be a lot of people."

"Could be just one," Sam rejoined.

She exhaled heavily, thinking hard. "What does this guy do when he's not setting fires and killing people . . . skinning them?"

"He goes to bars. He was at the Buffalo Lounge."

"You're right," Ricki said with renewed energy. "So, maybe he's been to the Prairie Dog, too. And maybe someone there saw him in a pair of black alligator boots."

Hunter's cell phone rang and he ignored it as he turned up the drive to his parents' ranch for the second time in two days—a new record since he'd moved out when he was a teen.

He circled the house and parked in the back, climbing out of the cab into a crisp morning that was growing colder as gray clouds moved in. As he walked to the kitchen door, he glanced at caller ID and saw that it was Davis who'd called. That was odd enough to get his pulse thumping. Maybe the man had remembered something.

Punching the number into his cell, he said, "Davis, it's Hunter. You called me?" when the Dillinger foreman answered. Hunter held his breath, waiting for some big reveal, but Featherstone just asked him to tell his mother that Kit Dillinger was finding errant Dillinger cattle and Kincaid sheep and moving them back to their respective properties. He wanted to make sure no one mistook her for a trespasser.

"I'll tell her," Hunter assured him. He hung up, disappointed. He'd wanted somcthing to break.

Someone was after the Dillingers, but it wasn't him. And it wasn't the psychotic monster who'd filleted Amber Barstow and Mia Collins, either. There were two distinct crime patterns. Were they working together? Setting fires and killing people?

"Mom?" he called as he stepped inside the unlocked door. Normally he would have walked right in, but Georgina had been so testy the last time he'd shown up, he waited for a few moments before he stepped farther inside. His family had never felt the need to lock their doors, but in the quiet kitchen he felt a whisper of fear. So silent. He strode urgently through the kitchen and down the hall to the TV room.

The Major was in his chair, his eyes closed. Hunter walked in front of him, noting the white, wisping hair, the sunken cheeks. "Dad?" he asked, his pulse accelerating again. He reached forward to touch his father, make sure he was alive, when the Major pulled in a slow, labored breath.

Hunter relaxed slightly. His father wasn't gone yet, though it didn't look like death's door was far away. He glanced at the table beside his father, noting the bottle of oxycodone.

Georgina came from somewhere down the hall and followed his gaze to the bottle of pills, her mouth tightening. "What are you doing here?" she asked, her voice slightly hushed.

"My father's sick."

She ignored his tone and brushed past him, heading toward the kitchen.

The Major's eyes fluttered open and his breath caught. "Hunter?"

"Right here." He clasped the older man's hand.

His tongue slowly swept his dry lips, then he asked, "Did you talk to Price?"

"You said to call him if something happened to you."

"Call him . . ." With a sigh, he sank back into the chair.

Hunter stared at him for a few moments, watching the shallow, irregular rise and fall of his chest. Then he left the room in search of his mother.

Georgina was in the kitchen, gazing out the back windows toward the fields that stretched toward the horizon and the distant mountains beyond. He'd seen her stand in just that position a lot of times, he realized. "Kit Dillinger is looking for Dillinger cattle on our land. Davis Featherstone wanted you to know in case you thought she was a trespasser."

"That's what you came for? To tell me that?"

"How many pills is Dad taking?"

She turned on him. "You're going to criticize how I'm taking care of your father!"

"He's dying," Hunter said bluntly. "I was going to say it doesn't matter. Just give him enough so he's not in pain."

"Don't think you can tell me what to do."

Hunter felt his temper rise. "Is the rumor true about you and Ira Dillinger?"

"What?" He'd shocked her.

"Did you have an affair with him? Is that why you're doing this oil deal with him?"

"Your father's dying and you think you suddenly have the right to say *that* to me?"

"You're the one who hinted about some other rumor," he reminded her.

"You've been talking to the Dillingers."

Not really, but if that would get him answers, so be it. "Yes."

"Delilah." Georgina said her name as if it tasted bad. "She came by yesterday."

"Here?"

"Yes, here. She didn't find you? I thought she'd run right to you. She was looking for you and I told her that she couldn't have you."

Hunter stared at his mother in disbelief. He'd never been close to her, but more and more she was a stranger. "Didn't you just tell me I had no right to tell you what to do?"

"This is different."

"Oh, yeah?"

Georgina lifted her chin. "You want to know about me and Ira? Yeah. We loved each other once."

Hunter stayed silent. Whatever had been between his mother and Ira, he doubted it was love.

"Judd wasn't the only Dillinger catting around. Ira was worse. I was beautiful in those days and he had to have me."

"Musta been a while ago."

"A long while." There was the faintest quirk of her lips. "About thirty-seven years ago."

Hunter stared at her hard, wondering if she really believed what she was saying or if this was some sick Georgina trick. "Ira Dillinger's not my father," he said.

"Yes, he is. And Delilah Dillinger's your half sister," she reminded him with a bit of triumph in her voice.

It wasn't true. He was too much like the Major. There was no way *Ira Dillinger* could be his father. He couldn't believe the lengths she would go to. "Delilah is not my half sister," he said through his teeth.

"What do you think started the feud? The Major and I didn't have any problem with Ira and Rachel before Ira seduced me. And when your father found out, all hell broke loose."

"I thought you were in love."

"You just don't want to believe it because you want to fuck your precious Delilah!"

"You're lying. The feud was over land rights, and it started before you married the Major."

"Who are you to tell me?" Twin spots of color rose in her cheeks.

"I don't know why you're doing this," he grated out. "But it's a lie."

"Better keep your dick in your pants when you're around your sister," she snarled.

"I'm going to call her right now. Tell her what you've been saying. Get a DNA test. Prove you wrong." He yanked his phone from his pocket and placed the call.

A flicker of fear crossed Georgina's face, replacing her rage. "Leave her alone," she muttered.

Hunter had called her bluff and now she was backpedaling. He could have throttled her!

Delilah answered on the third ring. "I'm sorry. I was separated from my cell phone and just got it back. It was . . . in the Jeep . . ."

"Can I see you?" he asked urgently, ignoring Georgina's growl of frustration behind him.

"Sure. When?"

"Right now. Are you at the lodge?"

"Let's meet somewhere else," she said. "Your house?"

"Okay. I—"

A loud, rasping gasp came from down the hall, a death rattle. Georgina's head snapped around as did Hunter's. His father. His body went cold. He knew, without being told, that the Major had just taken his last breath.

"I'll have to call you back," he told Delilah tersely.

"Should I go to your house?" Delilah asked.

"Let me call you back."

He hung up and strode after his mother, who'd scurried around the corner and into the TV room.

The Major looked much as Hunter had left him except his eyes were half-closed and his mouth hung open further. His mother was leaning over him, grabbing his arm, checking his pulse.

"He's gone," she said.

In disbelief, Hunter looked from his father back down at the cell phone still in his hand. He touched the button for Delilah's number again and when she answered, said, "The Major's gone. We'll have to meet later. I'll call you when I can . . ."

Delilah hung up in shock. She'd been striding toward the garage, ready to head out and meet Hunter at his house, but now she retraced her steps to the kitchen. She'd spent the night in the room Jen had vacated and had gotten up early, prowling around, anxious to get her cell phone back. When Tyler came down she asked him to take her to the auto body shop and sure enough, there was her phone, but it was dead.

She'd just gotten home, plugged the cell into its charger on the kitchen counter, and had just seen Hunter's message when he'd called. She was so glad to hear the phone ring, she'd damn near dropped the thing while sweeping it into her hand.

It had been a hellish twenty-four hours, starting with the lodge fire and Pilar's death, then being run off the road by persons unknown, and now the Major was gone . . . *Gone.* She hardly knew how to feel.

Delilah walked into the foyer and glanced toward the den door. After Colton had gone back to the bunkhouse to be with Sabrina and Rourke, Ira had barricaded himself in his den. Nell had finally given up playing nursemaid and had left Delilah alone. All yesterday she'd had to push thoughts of Hunter's and her lovemaking aside. Too many terrible events had gotten in the way. But finally she'd been able to sit down in the great room by herself. She'd settled into Ira's deep chair, and then she'd run Hunter's and her lovemaking over in her mind again and again and again. It was the one good thing that had happened.

But then Ricki and Brook had burst in, riling everyone up again. Ricki was wound up and pacing, but it was Brook who got Delilah's attention when she declared, "Mom, tell her about Mrs. Kincaid."

Ricki seemed at a loss of what to say, so Delilah prompted, "What about her?"

"Nothing." Ricki shot Brook a speaking look, then said to Delilah, "I just want to know who ran you down. *Purposely* ran you down."

"I don't know."

"Well, what kind of vehicle was it?" Ricki asked.

"A truck."

"What make and model? What color?"

"I didn't get that good a look at it." Delilah turned away, afraid her sister would see something in her face.

Brook wasn't about to be put off. "I ran into Mrs. Kincaid outside of the dress shop. She dropped her purse and she looked at me like she *hated* me and then she grabbed up her purse but it was full of pill bottles and a gun. Mom told me it was for her husband, but she doesn't think so anymore."

"That's not quite what I said," Ricki disagreed.

Nell, who'd been watching the back-and-forth exchange, asked, "What kind of pills?"

"Like what killed Pilar, probably," Brook said.

"Brook," Ricki said, long-suffering.

"So, it was an overdose that killed her," Delilah said.

"Looks that way, but I don't want to sit here and theorize. I want to know what happened to you, Delilah. Did you see anything? Was it a man at the wheel? How many were in the truck?"

"Just one . . . man."

"Mom . . ." Brook had been annoyed with what she apparently saw as Ricki putting her off. "That old lady is out to get us. She set our house on fire because she wanted to kill me because I saw the drugs and the gun."

"You can't just turn supposition into fact," Ricki told her tautly.

"You think she did it, too!" her daughter charged.

Delilah hadn't wanted to think about any of it and had pretty much shoved it to the back of her mind. Georgina? That was preposterous, wasn't it?

Ricki clearly had wanted to derail Brook and had again tried to change the subject back to the truck that had run Delilah off the road, but Delilah hadn't wanted to go into that, either. In the end she'd admitted that she thought it was dirty white or gray, and luckily no one had jumped on the fact that Hunter's truck was gray, too.

Finally satisfied, Ricki had called it a night. Just before she headed upstairs, she'd added that the department's suspect, the man at the bar the night Amber Barstow was kidnapped, had worn black alligator boots and that if Delilah or Nell knew any man who wore that type of boots to tell Ricki immediately and steer clear of said boot-wearer.

Delilah's mind's eye had instantly recalled the brown supple leather of Hunter's boots as he'd yanked them off in the tack room, the hard *plop, plop* they'd made as they'd hit the floor. Once more she'd run through their lovemaking and after a late meal of leftover pizza, she'd taken herself to bed.

Then this morning, after Hunter's first call, Delilah had felt huge relief. She couldn't wait to see him. Her mind had been bubbling with all the things she wanted to talk with him about.

Then he'd called back to say the Major was dead.

Now, Mrs. Mac looked up from where she'd been putting sandwiches together for lunch as Delilah came into the kitchen. "You all right?"

"That was Hunter Kincaid. The Major's dead."

"Oh, no . . ."

"I think . . . I don't know." She sank into a chair, stunned. Then a moment later she got back to her feet. "I'm going to leave for a while. Dad said I could take his truck."

"Honey, your father already took it. Said he was meeting with someone whose company will repair the fire damage."

"Oh. Thanks." He must've left when she and Tyler were picking up her phone.

She walked outside into a biting wind and stared across the windswept plains in the direction of the Kincaid house. She wanted to be with Hunter, even if Georgina would have a fit if she showed up. The closest way to the Kincaid house was straight across the fields as the lodge, the old homestead and the Kincaid ranch house were set back from the road that wound around the edge of the properties. Still, it was a ways and the Major had just died.

Chafing, she went back inside. She would think about it before making the trek and just barging in. She wished Hunter would call her again.

* * *

The trickle of arriving vehicles grew to a steady stream as Hunter stayed to help his mother deal with the aftereffects of death. When Emma arrived he let her take over, not that there was that much to do besides collect the food and cards and condolences from sympathizers who apparently went into high gear as soon as the word got out. Luckily, most of them had come after the Major's body was taken away to the morgue.

The day wore on slowly, but throughout it, his mother acted pretty much like nothing had happened. Her attitude was so cavalier, in fact, that it pierced the daze of grief surrounding him and made him wonder what the hell was going on with her.

Emma noticed, too, and pulled him aside. "What's with Mom?"

"I'd say she's glad he's gone," Hunter said.

"You mean the burden of taking care of him?" His sister gazed at their mother with concern.

"That's one way to look at it."

Actually, he was thinking about her remarks about Ira Dillinger, and though he was certain she'd been lying about his paternity, he believed her feelings for Ira were intense, something she'd actually played down in their conversation. She'd said she loved him, but it seemed more like she was obsessed with him . . . then and now . . .

After the last well-wisher departed and Georgina, Emma and Hunter were alone again, Hunter half expected to talk to his mother about what she wanted to do next. But almost immediately Georgina went down the hall to her bedroom, leaving him and Emma in the kitchen. Then she came out a few moments later dressed in a black dress and boots. Her hair was pulled into a dark chignon and she had on more makeup than she'd worn in years. "I'm not sitting here and crying," she said to their surprised faces. "I'm going into town and raise a glass to the Major."

Hunter forced himself not to look at Emma, knowing he would give himself away.

A cell phone began singing in Georgina's purse and she pulled it out, eyeing it suspiciously. "Century Petroleum," she muttered, walking away from them.

"Good God," Emma said. "Who is that woman?"

Hunter was beginning to think she was someone neither of them had ever known.

"You think she'll go through with the oil drilling?" Emma asked.

"With Dad gone, she can do what she likes."

"This place needs money. She doesn't have anyone working here anymore. She'd rather be helping at the dress shop than at the ranch, and she doesn't like that much, either."

Suddenly Georgina's voice rose. "If Ira Dillinger's pulling out, so am I!" She listened a moment longer, then added furiously, "You're not drilling on Kincaid land if you're not drilling on Dillinger property. That wasn't the deal. Ira's a part of this. I don't care what his reasons are. *Ira's a part of this!*"

She clicked off and let out a roar of fury. When she stomped back through the kitchen, her eyes glittered with rage. "What are you both still doing here?"

"Mom," Emma said, aghast.

"The oil deal's off?" Hunter asked.

"Ira pulled out!" Georgina sputtered.

"He just lost Pilar," Hunter pointed out. "He's got to be reeling. Maybe his priorities changed."

She was so enraged she struggled for words. "He never loved that money-grubbing whore. He should be thanking whoever killed her that she's gone! My God. How can he do this to me? After all I've done for him. Well, he's not getting away with it!"

"Where are you going?" Hunter asked.

"I'm going to drink on it. And I'll take care of things like I always do." She waved her hands furiously, motioning them out of the house, and Hunter and Emma had little choice but to leave. Hunter held the door for Emma and they walked down the back steps together and toward their respective vehicles.

Emma stopped at her car and stared back at the house. "What the hell's wrong with her? Has she always been this way?"

"Maybe."

"Why does it feel like she was married to Ira more than our father? She absolutely hated Pilar, and I thought she hated Ira, too, but . . ."

Hunter didn't respond, and after a few moments and a shake of her head, Emma climbed in her vehicle and drove away. Hunter followed after her a few moments later, his thoughts churning. His mother was acting like Ira had jilted her again. She'd been involved with him romantically once, and she'd gotten involved with him again recently, at least in a business sense. Maybe she'd just never gotten over him.

She absolutely hated Pilar.

Emma's words haunted him. He ground his teeth together, thinking about the bottle of oxycodone sitting beside the Major's tray. He felt like a traitor even letting his mind touch on the thoughts that plagued him. But the thoughts wouldn't go away. He worried them like a tongue against the hole left by a missing tooth.

Was his mother a killer?

Pilar was overdosed and the killer had set the place on fire. Like an afterthought. An emotional choice, like the foreman's cottage. Not like the Pioneer Church.

Two different arsonists.

No!

But she had the means, and she'd been at the Dillinger

house, over and over again, meeting with Ira and the oilmen. Her SUV had been there a lot. It was an expected car. No one would consider it suspicious.

She'd been there the day of the sleigh ride . . . the day the foreman's cottage was torched. She and the oilmen were the reason Ira hadn't gone with the others.

Was she there *yesterday?* When Pilar was drugged and killed?

He shook his head, clearing it. No . . . no . . . it didn't make sense.

And Delilah Dillinger's your half sister.

He didn't believe that for a second. He didn't. He was too much like the Major.

But why did she say it? There had to be a reason.

Or was she the monster he was starting to believe she might be . . . ?

He needed to talk to Delilah.

He needed to talk to Ira.

With a last look in his rearview mirror at his parents' ranch, he drove away, turning west toward the Rocking D.

Chapter Thirty

Delilah saw Hunter's truck coming through the front window and hurried outside to greet him. She wanted to throw herself in his arms and let out all her fears from the accident, fears she'd hidden from everyone else. Instead she stopped about ten feet away and waited until he'd climbed from the cab.

"Hey," she greeted him.

"Hey," he responded, walking toward her in that slow, cowboy way that she loved. How had she ever thought she could find a man for herself in Tinseltown?

"I'm so sorry about the Major," she said, heartfelt.

"We knew he didn't have long. Doesn't mean it wasn't a shock." He'd been looking past her at the house, his thoughts elsewhere, but now his attention zeroed in on her. "What happened?" He gestured to the bandage at her hairline.

She reached up and touched it. "I was going to call you, but there just hasn't been the time. I was run off the road last night by a man in a gray pickup."

"Run off the road." His laser gaze cut into her.

Drawing a breath, she told him about the events when she'd come back from talking to his mother, finishing with, ". . . the license plate was mudded over."

"The sheriff's department is looking for this gray truck. Where did it come from? Was it behind you when you left my mother?"

Something in the cold way he said "my mother" caught at her attention, but she had to confess, "It might have been dirty white. I don't know. It was growing dark."

"But it's somewhere around that color."

She lifted a hand and then dropped it to her side. "I didn't want to say gray. After what had happened the night before with Ira blaming you, I just didn't want a witch hunt."

"You thought they'd think it was me." He drew a long breath. "God. How do you know it wasn't? Everybody else thinks I'm an arsonist hiding out as a fireman. What's wrong with you?"

"Nobody thinks that."

"Yes, they do."

"They're just scared," Delilah defended. "So am I. So sue me. I didn't tell them right away because I didn't want Ricki and Sam and everybody else coming down on you. I *know* it wasn't you, and they do, too, but everybody's on edge. And . . . no, he didn't follow me from your mother's. He came out of the road from the old homestead."

"There's nothing down there but the house," Hunter said, caught by her words.

Delilah looked at him. "Maybe he was just . . . lying in wait."

"You think he followed you?"

A cold feeling filled the pit of her stomach. "Is he one of us?"

When Hunter headed back for his truck, Delilah was at his heels. "Where are you going?"

"To the old homestead."

She wrenched open the passenger door. "You're not leaving without me."

"I don't want you—"

"Shut up. I mean it. You're not leaving without me."

She surprised him. She could tell. Then a faint smile slid across his lips as he sent her a sideways look that warmed her heart.

Fifteen minutes later Hunter's truck was shimmying along the rutted lane that led to the old homestead house. Delilah clung to the hand grip above the door to keep from being thrown around. As they approached the burned wreckage, she recognized a vehicle already parked in front: her father's Dodge Ram truck.

"What's Dad doing here?" she asked.

"Good question." Hunter's gaze traveled past Ira's truck and the house, and he was looking at the fence line that divided Kincaid and Dillinger property.

"Is he inside?" she asked as Hunter pulled the truck to a stop beside Ira's.

She reached for the door handle, but he put his hand on her arm, stopping her. "I gotta tell you something," he said. "The reason I want to talk to Ira. I didn't think we were going to run into him so soon."

She gazed at him expectantly, waiting.

"My mother said the Major wasn't my father. She said Ira was my father."

Delilah half laughed. "You're kidding."

"No."

Delilah remembered how Georgina had been with her, too. "No . . . no . . ."

"I don't believe it, but she told me to talk to Ira about it."

"Why would she say something like that?" Delilah sputtered.

"She and Ira had an affair. I think maybe she wanted it to be true."

"But they hate each other."

"I think we might've been sold a bill of goods. I just wanted you to know, in case it comes up."

She shook her head in disbelief then looked toward Ira's truck. Her father was nowhere to be seen. "What's he doing here?" she asked again.

At that moment the boards creaked and Ira stepped outside from beneath the aged and blackened timbers above what had been the front door. He stared across the frozen ground to where they were parked as Delilah climbed out of the passenger side and Hunter got out of the driver's.

"What are you doing in there?" Delilah demanded.

"Just looking around." To put action to words, he glanced from left to right, along the rotting, burned porch.

"It's dangerous, Dad. Condemned. You're the one who's always told us not to go inside."

"What are you doing here . . . both of you?" he asked, stepping off the porch and crossing the weed-choked ground toward them. It was as if he'd aged twenty years since Pilar's death.

"The Major died this morning," Hunter said.

Ira's head jerked up and he gazed at Hunter in surprise. He ran a hand over his mouth. "He's battled it a long time. I thought he'd beat it."

"Not this time," Hunter said.

"I'm sorry." He looked like he wanted to say something else, but he just shook his head and sighed. Then, as if recalling himself, "How's your mother?"

"Drinking to my father somewhere."

Ira frowned. "That doesn't sound like Georgina."

Hunter's gaze traveled back to the fence line. "Did you make those tire tracks along the fence?"

"Onto Kincaid land?" Ira grunted. "More likely it's one of your people."

Delilah didn't think Georgina had any "people." "The truck that ran into me pulled out of here," she said.

"Well, there's nobody here. I've been through the place,

as much as you can walk through it, and it's empty," Ira said. "And I sure as hell didn't run you down."

"Somebody's been here," Hunter said.

"The oilmen have been all over Dillinger and Kincaid property, but the place is vacant most of the time."

Hunter said, "My mother got a call from one of those Century Petroleum men today, who told her you'd backed out of the oil deal."

Ira demanded, "Who called her?"

"I don't know. One of them. I thought she might have come after you. She was upset and furious."

Ira started to defend himself then clamped his mouth shut. Delilah had known that he never intended to drill on Dillinger land; he'd said as much. Georgina and Ira had played cat and mouse with each other for years. Maybe that's what had prompted her to say what she had about Hunter.

She suddenly wanted to clear the air on that issue once and for all. Address it and put it to rest. "Georgina also told Hunter that . . ." She stumbled a bit, finding the words harder to say than she'd expected. Gathering her courage, she finished in a rush, "That she and you had an affair and that Hunter could be your son."

Ira reacted as if he'd been slapped. "What the hell? Hell, no. She knows that's not true! What the God . . . damn . . ."

"Why would she say something like that?" Delilah demanded. "Abby Flanders mentioned a rumor about Hunter. She knew it, too, and it wasn't about the fires."

"Well, it's not true. If you were my son . . ." Ira gazed at Hunter, wrestling with himself. "I was wrong about you and what happened," he said. His way of apologizing.

Hunter nodded, silently accepting.

"Why did Georgina say it?" Delilah demanded again. "How did Abby know?"

He shrugged. "Georgina's always had a crazy streak. She liked saying stuff . . ."

"The rumor came from her?" Delilah wasn't giving up. "Were you lovers? Was that part true at least?" she demanded.

"I loved your mother," her father sidestepped.

"Nobody's saying you didn't," Delilah said.

"When Rachel was gone, I was lonely. Georgina came by right after she died . . . and I told her to get the hell out."

"But before," Delilah pressed. "Years ago . . ."

Ira rubbed a hand tiredly over his chin. "What we had . . . was small. Nothing, really. Years after you were born," he added quickly to Hunter. "A mistake from the beginning, so I ended it. Ended everything with her, and she was just as happy to be rid of me. Wouldn't have even started the oil deal with her if she hadn't been so pesky about it. Bothering me, all the time, so I thought I'd just go along and pretend I was in, but I never intended to drill on Dillinger land. They can drill on Kincaid land all they want. That's what I told 'em, and I guess that's what they just told Georgina."

Delilah was silent, absorbing. She'd always heard about her father's infidelity, but it disappointed her all the same.

Ira looked back at the house. "Georgina and I used to meet here," he admitted. "That's what gave Judd the idea to bring Mia. He was in love with Mia. He kept going on about leaving Lila, and I tried to talk him out of it." He lifted a hand to encompass the crumbling, ruined house. "Then it all ended with the fire." Ira shot a look Hunter's way. "I thought it was you. I thought you knew about me and your mom and burned the place down. I just didn't ever believe it could be plain bad luck. Some drifter cruising through and setting fires. Couldn't be just some firebug chose my house and I lost my brother because of it."

"Hunter was meeting me," Delilah put in. "That's why he was here. We were seeing each other."

Ira looked from her to Hunter. "S'that right?"

"Yes," Hunter said.

"It sounds like my mother's had ideas about you and her all along," Hunter added to Ira.

"No. It was years ago," Ira protested.

Hunter said, "I don't know. Sounds like this lie about you being my father, she started years ago. Maybe she wanted it to be true."

Ira shook his head. "You were a kid running around when Georgina and I . . . started seeing each other."

They were all quiet for a few moments, thinking things over, then Hunter said, "She hated Pilar. Maybe she thought that after Rachel was gone . . ."

Delilah stared at him in horror. Her mind traveled over what Brook and Ricki had said about Georgina. "What are you saying?"

"She's been in and out of your house for weeks with this oil deal. She hated Pilar and maybe never got over whatever she had with Ira. I think I need to find her and ask her some questions."

"I'm going with you," Ira said, heading to his truck.

Delilah quickly let herself back into the passenger's side of Hunter's Chevy. "I'm going with you, too."

Ricki looked around the Prairie Dog Saloon. It was afternoon by the time she'd left Sam and the station, and the bright sun outside reached into the darkened interior of the rough-and-tumble bar, throwing the scuffed chairs and worn floorboards into sharp relief. The Prairie Dog was popular but not as well kept up as Big Bart's Buffalo Lounge, and right now there were only a few people seated at the tables, two couples, three guys watching a fishing program on the soundless television and a bald guy in the corner with a large belly and nursing a beer.

"Can I help you?" a woman bartender asked. She wore a

red checkered shirt, a matching neckerchief and a white cowboy hat as she gazed at Ricki expectantly.

"I hope so. I'm working for the sheriff's department and we're looking into the deaths of two women. Maybe you've seen it on the news."

"Sure have. The one at the church fire and Mia Collins. I knew Mia a little. She's got the animal whisperer daughter. Kit." She leaned forward eagerly. "You're a Dillinger, right? Your sisters were in here the other night."

"That's right." Ricki was surprised by how much she knew.

"I wasn't working when they were here, but I heard about them. We've got a group of regulars who play darts and they were distracted by your sisters." She snorted. "Men, huh. The brains go right down to their crotches when they see a pretty girl."

The bartender wasn't half-bad-looking herself. Ricki could imagine she'd had her share of unwanted male attention and had grown somewhat cynical. "I'm looking for a guy who was at Big Bart's the night Amber Barstow disappeared. I don't have much of a description. He's a big man and that night he wore a black Stetson and black alligator boots."

"You think he's the guy that killed her and Mia?"

"He's a person of interest."

"We get a lot of guys that kinda fit that description." She exhaled and thought hard, frowning. Ricki could practically see the wheels turning. "Alligator boots, huh?"

"Black ones."

"You know, my relief, Hal, comes on in half an hour. You should talk to him 'cuz he remembers everything. You want something to drink while you wait?"

"Uh . . . water?" Ricki asked, seating herself at the bar. She grabbed her phone and texted Sam. He knew she'd planned to stop by the Prairie Dog on the way home, but she wanted him to know she might be hanging around a bit longer. They'd put off talking to Georgina about the Major's pain medication when they'd learned about his death. Instead, they'd checked with the local pharmacies to see about other prescriptions for oxycodone, and Ricki, after talking to Colton, as her father wasn't around, had learned the Dillinger clan planned on sending flowers to Georgina and maybe calling on her the next day or the day after, when some of the shock had worn off. Maybe by then the sheriff's department would have some more definitive evidence about the cause of Pilar's death.

The front door opened and a shaft of sunlight burst in. Ricki glanced over and was surprised, stunned really, when Georgina herself sailed through the front door in a long black coat that was nearly off one shoulder, revealing a rather tight black dress underneath, and a pair of black boots. She'd pulled her dark hair into a bun that was now losing strands that fell into her eyes. The effect was oddly sensual, and the bald guy with the big belly straightened up as if he'd had a rod put up his ass.

Georgina didn't immediately see Ricki, but when she did, a furtive look came over her face and a flush of emotion stained her cheeks.

"Where's Ira?" she demanded. "I've been toasting the Major into the next world. Thought he might like to join me."

Georgina's voice could cut glass. "I'm sorry for your loss," Ricki said. "Everyone liked the Major."

"He was a likeable guy. Not true of your father." She smiled coldly. "Ira's a two-timing bastard. Always has been." She pressed a finger to her lips. "I shouldn't say that to you, should I?"

"Did you come from the Buffalo Lounge?" Ricki asked.

"Aren't you nosy, nosy." She ignored Ricki and said to the bartender, "Give me a glass of Jack."

Big belly had relaxed back in his chair, but his attention

was focused on Georgina. It was a revelation to Ricki, who'd never seen her in a dress before. She'd seemed to pride herself on being hard as prairie dirt. Good with a gun. Implacable as stone.

"Is your dad coming here?" Georgina asked, not even looking at Ricki, but something in her tone suggested she really wanted to know.

"I don't know where he is."

"Probably between some other woman's legs." Her glass of Jack Daniel's came and she took a big swallow, shuddering as it went down. "You Dillingers," she said, throwing Ricki a dark look. "Think you own this town and everybody in it. Well, Ira can't play with me anymore. You can tell him that for me."

"Maybe you oughta slow down," Ricki said as Georgina reached for her glass again.

"Maybe you oughta keep your fucking advice to yourself."

Ricki tried to hold herself back. She really did. Georgina's husband had just died and it seemed wrong to go after her so soon, but everything just seemed to coalesce in her head: the fire at the foreman's cottage with Brook inside . . . the drugs and the gun Brook had seen in Georgina's purse . . . the way Georgina had focused on Pilar's champagne glass that day in Emma's dress shop . . . the traces of oxycodone found in the glass beside Pilar's bed . . . the hatred Georgina felt for Pilar . . . anger toward Ira, maybe even mixed with a little jealousy . . .

"You were at the lodge with Ira just before the foreman's cottage went up. And you were around the house the day Pilar was killed. Ira told me you were there. And you have access to the drug that killed her, because of the Major."

Georgina's glass stopped halfway to her lips. She was staring straight ahead, refusing or afraid to meet Ricki's eyes.

"My daughter, Brook, thinks you torched the foreman's cottage because she was inside and she saw the pills in your purse. Maybe you were planning Pilar's death all along and you saw an opportunity to get rid of someone who could point the finger at you—my daughter."

Georgina was shaking her head. "You're crazy." But her voice trembled with emotion.

Ricki had been probing and she'd struck a nerve. *Oh, my God,* she thought. Everything felt like it slowed down. "You killed Pilar because she was marrying my father," Ricki realized.

"I'm through talking to you." Georgina slid away from the bar and stumbled toward the door.

Ricki immediately punched in Sam's number on her cell. The bartender, who'd heard most of what they'd said, was staring after Georgina openmouthed. Throwing some bills on the counter, Ricki raced after Georgina, pushing through the door with a straight arm, ready to give chase if necessary.

But Georgina was standing stock-still in the parking lot, staring into the blockade of Delilah, Hunter and Ira, all of them gazing at Georgina as if she were the devil incarnate.

"What did you do to Pilar?" Ira demanded.

With the screech of a banshee, Georgina dug in her purse, yanked out a handgun and aimed it straight at Ira.

He'd damn near run straight into them. There they were, standing outside the Prairie Dog Saloon. Ira Dillinger, Hunter Kincaid and Delilah.

He'd managed to turn the truck onto a side street rather than go right past them. Even with the changed-out license plates, there was still some damage to his front end, which he'd worked on, but anyone with half an eye would be able to tell he'd run into something.

Goddammit, what had he been thinking?

He had to be careful. So . . . careful.

Parking three streets away from the Prairie Dog, he stepped out into a cold afternoon. He crossed the street, away from them, where he could hide and watch behind a half-fallen fence around the old gas station.

He'd barely gotten in place when Georgina Kincaid suddenly burst from the Prairie Dog with Ricki Dillinger right behind her.

"What did you do to Pilar?" Ira demanded.

And then Georgina let out a shriek and yanked something from her purse. A gun. Which she aimed at Ira. He damn near gasped himself, but Hunter jumped forward, grabbed his mother and knocked her sideways. The gun she'd reached for spun through the air to slam against a black Ford sedan then clatter to the ground.

And then Sam Featherstone's Jeep was screeching into the lot and he was out of the vehicle, snapping handcuffs on her, marching Georgina back to the Jeep and placing his hand on her head to duck her inside.

Well, what do you know. He wanted to laugh. Georgina Kincaid. He would bet she was the one who'd set the fires at the Dillingers', too. He'd kind of suspected that was her work, though he'd kept his thoughts to himself. For an old woman she sure seemed to run hot. The way she'd been looking at Ira when she thought no one noticed could damn near melt steel.

He knew the feeling.

His eyes searched out Delilah, but the group was starting to break up and leave. He waited till they were gone, then he quickly hurried back to his truck. He'd determined that tonight would be the night he would have her.

He figured they might all be going to the sheriff's department and in that he was right. From a far distance he watched their vehicles park outside the station, making sure to avoid detection. But he wanted to know how this played out. Weak sunlight glinted off the back of Hunter Kincaid's gray Chevy truck.

His fingers automatically reached into his pocket to rattle the teeth within. A smile spread beneath the brim of his hat.

Thank you, Georgina, you crazy old hag.

She'd shifted the focus and it might be all he needed to cut Delilah from the herd.

Chapter Thirty-One

His mother had pulled out a gun and charged at Ira Dillinger. *Pulled out a gun, intending to kill him.* God. It was unbelievable. No . . . that was wrong. It was entirely believable. Georgina played for keeps.

Hunter looked around the reception room of the sheriff's department. Sam had hauled Georgina into a back room and was questioning her, and Ricki was with him. He, Delilah and Ira were waiting outside, and Ira had called Colton, who was on his way. Probably Nell would come, too. And Tyler.

He hadn't phoned any of his family yet.

Delilah was right beside him and he felt her hand steal over and clasp his. He wanted to take her in his arms and crush her to him, but this wasn't the place and there was so much he had to do.

Squeezing her fingers, he reluctantly released her hand. "She set the homestead fire," he said aloud. Ira looked over at him but didn't say anything. "It wasn't any drifter passing through. She set it, and then let the blame fall on me."

Delilah stirred. "She's your mother," she said.

"She's obsessive." Hunter hadn't really thought about his mother's psyche other than to know she was hard and stubborn. But the events of the last few weeks had revealed a disturbed personality lurking inside her that was darker than anyone had known. "She tried to kill you when she thought it was you with Mia that night," he told Ira. "She got Judd instead. But she's wanted you all along. She waited for you and thought she had her opportunity when Rachel died."

"But then there was Pilar," Ira said.

Delilah asked, "What's going to happen to her?"

"Depends on how much they can prove, I guess." Hunter inhaled and exhaled heavily. "She pulled a gun on Ira."

"Aimed for the heart," Ira said.

"You think she set the fires?" Delilah asked Hunter.

"The ones at your place. Yes."

"The church fire?" she asked.

"I think that one just gave her the idea again. She wanted Pilar out of the picture."

Delilah said dully, "So, she tried to kill Brook? Because she'd seen the pills in her purse."

Delilah had given him a quick rundown about what Ricki's daughter had said, and Hunter thought it could very likely be the motivation.

As if he'd read his mind, Ira spoke up. "She wouldn't kill my granddaughter."

Wouldn't she? Hunter didn't know what all Georgina's reasons were, but he believed her capable of anything.

Outside they heard car doors slamming, and Hunter looked through the front window to see Colton, Tyler and Nell heading for the station's front door. He felt bone-tired and said to Delilah, "I gotta talk to Emma."

"Want me to come?" she asked.

"Think I need to do this alone. I'll call you later."

"Don't disappear on me again," she said in a low voice. "I mean it."

He would have kissed her to reassure her if the door

wasn't already opening, allowing in a cold breath of air and the rest of the Dillingers.

Once outside Hunter inhaled a deep lungful of air. Yanking out his cell phone, he walked through the deepening twilight to his truck. But he didn't place the call to his sister. Tired as he was, his mind was moving on a line of its own. The old homestead house. There were tire tracks through the shrinking snow, which led away and onto Kincaid land. They could be from Sam and his deputies, but they could be from whoever had chased down Delilah.

He and Delilah had gone to the old homestead to try to learn something about the truck that had slammed into her, but had encountered Ira instead and the mission had gone sideways. But the tracks had maybe been left by the man lying in wait, and Ira had said the tracks weren't his.

Putting back the cell phone, he grabbed up his keys. He'd go to the old homestead and check out—

SLAM!

Pain exploded in his skull as something hard smacked into his head, throwing him against the side of his truck. He tried to grab for the sides of the truck bed, but he slipped down, the world blackening, turning into a long, dark tunnel.

At the end of the tunnel stood a pair of black alligator boots.

SLAM!

Hunter lost consciousness.

As soon as Hunter left, Delilah wanted to, too. She was going to have to cadge a ride with Ira, but realized he was looking pretty worn down as well. "Let me take you home, Dad."

"Ricki might need my statement," he muttered.

"She can get it later. And if she needs support, everyone's here."

"Georgina tried to kill me." He sounded more in wonder of that fact than fearful.

"I was there."

"You really think she tried to kill Brook?"

"I don't know, Dad."

"But Pilar . . ."

"Yeah."

She talked him into letting her drive, and after saying their good-byes to everyone—with Colton giving her a surreptitious nod of approval in getting Ira out of there—they headed home.

Her father went straight to his den and his bottle of Jack Daniel's. Some of Mrs. Mac's sandwiches were still in the refrigerator, and as she pulled out the platter, Sabrina came in from the great room where Rourke and Brook were still watching television. "Georgina pulled a gun on Ira?" Sabrina asked quietly.

"She sure did." Delilah gave her a quick rundown as she readied a plate for Ira.

"Is Hunter going to be all right?" she asked.

She sure as hell hoped so. "He's probably with Emma."

She took her father the plate with a ham sandwich, which Ira glanced at but ignored. "Eat something," she told him, and he seemed to surface enough to pick up half a sandwich and take a bite.

Sabrina was clearly babysitting, and as Delilah passed by the great room she heard Brook asking dozens of questions.

Delilah was heading in to help Sabrina out when her cell phone buzzed with a text. Hunter! She read the message eagerly: Meet me at the old homestead. I found something.

The old homestead. Their meeting place.

"Sabrina, I'm going out," she called.

"Where're you going?" she yelled back.

"To meet Hunter."

She still had the keys to her father's Dodge truck and she hurried to the garage. Night had fallen and she stopped as she backed out, checking in the glove box for a flashlight. It was there. Her father always had one. Hunter probably had one, too, but it could be blasted dark on the prairie at night.

It wasn't all that far to the homestead road and she drove as fast as she dared. Had Hunter learned something about the truck that rammed into her?

His truck was parked in front of the old homestead and the open front door gaped like a black tooth. Glancing toward the pine tree, she hoped to see a light there. Hoped he hadn't gone inside the house.

What the hell was this about?

Grabbing the flashlight, she stepped from the cab. "Hunter?" she called, her finger searching for the switch.

She heard movement beside his truck and turned her head.

SLAM!

She was suddenly on the ground, her head aching. He'd hit her. Someone had hit her! Before she could collect her wits about her, he'd jerked back both her arms and was whipping them together behind her back with twine. She struggled with all her might, but he was fast. He threw her face down into the dirt, hitting her jaw against the ground so hard that she saw stars.

She slowly surfaced to realize her hands were behind her back and he'd bound them to her feet, bowing her backward in a painful arc.

Then he squatted down and shined the flashlight in her face. All she could see was bright light crowned by a black Stetson.

"Who are you?" she asked in an unsteady voice.

"You know me," he said. The voice was familiar. He

turned the flashlight on himself and she blinked until she recognized him.

"Tom . . . Unger?" The oilman from Century Petroleum?

"The name's Garth Dillinger, cousin."

"Garth . . . Lila's son? I—what are you doing?"

"Getting payback," he said, smiling. Then he hauled her up as if she weighed nothing and tossed her into the back of Hunter's truck. Hunter was already there, unconscious, lying beside her, a mat of blood on the side of his head. "Oh, he's not dead. Yet," Garth said at her gasp. "Had to hit him a little harder than you to convince him to stay down."

With that he scrabbled around and found an old blanket, threw it over them, slammed into the truck and suddenly they were bumping alongside the homestead down a track that led past fence posts, then through a gap that led onto Kincaid land.

Ricki glanced at the clock on her cell phone and said, "I gotta get back to the Prairie Dog. The bartender I want to talk to came on at six."

It had been hours with Georgina, and though the Kincaid matriarch had lost it out in the Prairie Dog parking lot, she'd lapsed into sullen silence now, angry and cold. And she'd asked for a lawyer.

Georgina was in the end cell, and there was no one else in the jail. Sam motioned for them both to head to his office and when they were inside, he closed the door behind them.

Ricki said, "I want to ask about the boots."

"I'll come with you," Sam said.

"We caught one of our firebugs. Maybe we'll catch the other."

* * *

The ride was interminable. Delilah had no idea where they were. She tried to talk to Hunter, but he was out cold.

She was freezing herself. And terrified. And worried sick about Hunter. Garth Dillinger . . . how . . . why?

Suddenly the truck jerked to a stop. Delilah braced herself, but her limbs were strained to breaking and she had no strength. He threw back the blanket and pulled her out as easily as he'd put her in. Dropped her onto the cold ground for a moment, then hauled Hunter out of the vehicle. He slung Hunter over his shoulder, but it took a hell of a lot more effort as he strode toward one of a series of cabins.

The Kincaid cabins. Delilah had never seen them, but there were only two finished, with several others in varying stages of completion. *Georgina's folly,* her father had called it. But now Garth Dillinger was using them.

She heard his stomping steps as he came for her and she braced herself.

"Won't be long now," Garth said, hauling her up. The twine cut into her wrists, but she was so cold she hardly felt it.

Then they were in the end cabin and she was glad to see there was a fire in the fireplace. Skinny limbs from a pine tree were stacked and burning, their needles crackling. "We're gonna fuck like animals," he whispered to her. "In front of your boyfriend."

Delilah's teeth were chattering. Her eyes were on Hunter. He was lying on his side, his hands tied in front of him, his legs tied as well, but he wasn't in the joint-wrenching bow she was.

And then Garth pulled a knife out of a backpack, its blade glowing yellow and red in the firelight.

Hal Bremmerton was hard at work mixing drinks and taking more orders when Sam and Ricki walked into the Prairie Dog. As soon as he saw them, he nodded once, as if he'd been expecting them. They had to wait a few minutes until he was free, but then he came down the bar to where they were standing.

"Black alligator boots?" he asked. "Carrie told me. I know two guys who wear them."

"Really," Ricki said. "Who?"

"Well, there's Ronnie over there at the dartboard. See?"

Ricki and Sam looked at the men playing darts. One of them was indeed wearing black alligator boots, but he was a slight man and nowhere near six foot two or three, which was what they'd determined Black Hat must be.

"Who else?" Sam asked.

"One of the Century Petroleum guys. The younger one."

"Tom Unger?" Ricki said.

"That's the one. He's only been in once, maybe twice. If you'd asked Carrie about his 'amazing blue eyes' rather than his boots, she woulda known who you wanted."

"Thanks," Ricki said.

She and Sam moved outside and Sam said, "They're staying at the Tumbleweed."

They slammed the doors to the Jeep and ran the five blocks to the motel. The girl at the desk looked up at them in alarm, but when Sam showed her his badge she quickly relinquished the number for Unger's room on the second floor. They were quickly heading for the stairs when they ran into the older Century Petroleum man. Len Mercer, Ricki remembered.

Mercer looked from one to the other of them. "What's up?"

"Is Tom Unger here?" Sam asked tautly.

"Don't think so." He looked through the windows to the parking lot. "His truck's not here."

"What kind of truck does he have?" Ricki asked quickly.

"Chevy. White. What's going on?"

Sam didn't bother to answer. "We'll check his room," he told Ricki grimly, and left Len Mercer staring after them.

* * *

To both Delilah's relief and dread, Garth untied her from her torturous position, but it was only to strip her of her clothes. When he began to retie her, she tried to talk to him, keep him busy.

"You killed Amber Barstow," she said, struggling to keep her chattering teeth under control.

"You wanna know all about me, right? So did she." He smiled.

"Why did you kill her?"

"Because she was there. A stranger. With no ties to me. It was easy. Much easier than getting a Dillinger." He drew the flat side of the blade along Delilah's thigh.

"But I'm your cousin. I'm not a stranger."

"All the Dillingers forgot my mother. Fuckin' forgot her. Don't worry, you're not the only one. You're just the first. They'll all die, too."

"No one forgot Lila."

The knife was suddenly under her throat. "Don't lie."

"I—wasn't."

"You've all been taking care of poor Mia and her fucking backward daughter."

Your half sister, Delilah thought, but didn't say it. Garth was too volatile, too ready to slice into her skin.

"Century Petroleum is mostly a cover," he said. "Had to go into the oil business like my stepfather, John Unger. Turned out it was useful, when I finally decided to take care of things for Mama. The girl in the bar was just practice, like the coyotes and deer and cats and dogs and rats . . ."

Fear slid an icy finger down her back. "Please . . . don't . . ." she pleaded when he began to tie her again.

"Please, don't," he repeated. "You need to save your begging for later, Delilah. De-li-lah." His tongue moved around the syllables.

Delilah swallowed, searching her brain for something more to say. Her gaze darted to Hunter, but Garth caught her at it. "Look at him again and I'll cut him," Garth snarled. Immediately she shot her gaze back to Garth. "That's better. You know Mia had to go. The whore. Sucking up all that Dillinger money that should have been my mother's . . . should have been mine."

"There's a lot of money. Ira will give you whatever you want."

"That's another lie, Delilah. You're trying my patience." Quickly he dropped the knife to retie her hands and feet. She didn't think she could bear being pulled back again.

"I'm not lying. Ira talked to Lila the other day. He likes her. Someone told her about the wedding . . ."

"I did. And she was pretty upset that she'd been left out." He pulled on the twine and wrenched her into a bow again. Delilah groaned. "Dessert first," he whispered, sticking his tongue in her ear.

"Aaayyyyyyyyeeeee!"

From out on the prairie came an ungodly scream. A shriek to the heavens. Garth froze, then swept up his knife, crouched by the door.

"Aaaayyyyeeeeee!"

"Fuckin . . . what?" He opened the door, stepped outside, his hand still on the door for a moment. Then he was gone.

Delilah struggled hard. This was her chance. Her only chance. But she couldn't do it. The bonds were too tight.

"Hey."

Her gaze shot around the room in fear, settled on Hunter. His eyes were open. And he was working to untie his legs.

Thank God he was all right! She wanted to yell at him to be careful, to hurry, that she loved him, but she stayed quiet as a church mouse, her gaze darting from Hunter, to the door, to Hunter and back again. His legs were free! She sucked in a breath and then inclined her head to the backpack. Where there was one knife, there could be more. Hunter was ahead of her, already searching for a weapon. Sure enough, he withdrew a wicked-looking blade and he moved to Delilah and sawed her free. As soon as her hands were untied she tried to take the blade to cut him loose, but it slipped from her cold, frozen fingers. She picked it up, tried again.

The door flung open and Garth stumbled in with a roar of fury. He charged at Hunter, who drove his knee into Garth's gut. Garth fell forward and Hunter's knee came back covered in blood.

"She stabbed me . . . she stabbed me . . ." Garth garbled.

Delilah looked at Hunter, who'd staggered back away from Garth and was again trying to cut his hands free. She looked at Garth, who was curled over himself on the floor. And then she looked to the open door where Kit stood, holding a blood-stained knife in front of her.

"He killed my mother," she said.

PART FOUR

Epilogue

Christmas morning the scents of cinnamon and frying bacon filled the kitchen as Ricki pulled the rolls from the oven and Nell lifted the sizzling pan off the stove. Delilah was peeling kiwis and adding them to the glass bowl already layered with oranges, blueberries and red grapes.

Looking up from her task, Delilah watched Jen serve coffee to the adults and hot chocolate to the kids. Jen had decided to stay on in Prairie Creek after all, now that both Georgina and Tom Unger were in jail. She'd returned to the lodge with her kids and apparently with Tyler, who seemed to be making a greater effort than before. Maybe it would work out, maybe it wouldn't. Since Mrs. Mac was spending the holiday with her family, they were all pitching in to make a Christmas brunch to remember.

Ira was seated in his chair in the great room and Jen strolled over to give him a refill. She began laughing and talking to him in her suck-up way, which made Delilah smile. Colton noticed and smiled as well, and both of them ignored their father when Ira lifted his eyes and sent them a "please save me" look. Tyler, who'd been making Irish coffees and was following after his wife, gave Colton and Delilah long-suffering looks, which changed their smiles into out-and-out laughter.

They'd forgotten to get a Christmas tree in the midst of the wedding plans, and with everything that had occurred, it was Christmas Eve before Colton, Sabrina, Rourke, Brook, Tyler, Justin and Haley set off to find one. Gifts that had been purchased prior to Pilar's death were suddenly remembered, dragged out from their hiding places and quickly wrapped and put under the tree. There was a mad dash into town to buy new gifts, which had resulted in some completely useless items that nobody needed or wanted and yet everyone loved. The leftover wrapping littered the floor, and Brook's white kitten was jumping in and out of the rustling paper.

Delilah accepted one of the Irish coffees, bringing it to her lips. Ira had gotten a team of construction workers to repair the damage in his bedroom, and though there was still painting to be done, the charred scent that had permeated the air was gone, and all the damaged walls and flooring had been removed. All in all, there was a sense of new beginnings.

The doorbell rang, and Sam and Sabrina arrived at the same time. Delilah watched as they were greeted warmly by Ricki and Colton. She'd invited Hunter to join their brunch, and he'd said he might swing by later, but with all the revelations about Georgina she knew that was a long shot. It might be too early for him to drop in on the Dillingers, though Delilah wasn't going to wait much longer before she revealed that she and Hunter were definitely a couple.

Rourke ran to meet Sabrina, binding himself to both Colt and Sabrina as the three of them had a group hug. Colton ruffled his son's hair and Sabrina slid her arm affectionately around Rourke's back. Delilah felt those same treacherous tears burn her eyes at the sight of their newly formed family. Colt had told her he was planning to stay in Prairie Creek and was going to ask Sabrina to marry him.

Ricki asked Sam, "Where's Davis? You did ask him to come, right?"

"He's trying to talk Kit into joining us, so who knows," Sam said.

Though she'd saved the day, Kit had shied away from joining the Dillingers in their Christmas celebration. She'd been bringing back stray sheep from Dillinger property to the Kincaids when she'd stumbled across Garth's newest lair. She'd been in the process of returning back to tell Davis, when she'd seen the lights of Garth's truck. Apparently, he'd never driven all the way to the cabins before, but with both Hunter and Delilah in the back, he'd pulled right up. She hadn't seen him haul Hunter and Delilah inside at first, but when she'd gotten a peek through the window, she'd stepped away and let out her war cry. When Garth came into the dark, she waited for him to get near and then attacked him.

"What's the story with Kit and Davis?" Ira asked, climbing out of his chair and walking toward them, away from Jen. "Should I be talking to your brother about a few things?"

"Go right ahead," Sam said with a smile. "Don't think their relationship's like that, but it wouldn't hurt to put him on notice."

"Family," Ira said.

Family . . . The room went quiet for a moment and Delilah suspected that, like her, all of them were thinking about Garth Thomas Dillinger. He was family, too. Ira had placed a call to Lila to tell her about her son's arrest, and had gleaned through Lila's tears more about Garth's troubled past. He'd tortured and killed animals from a young age, and when they'd caught him skinning a rabbit before it was dead, Lila's husband had put his foot down, seeking psychological help for the young boy. The therapy appeared to work in the beginning; at least they never caught him again. Garth went through school and was well-liked and popular, but he never had a girlfriend. He followed his stepfather into the oil business and everything seemed fine. The only blip on the radar was that he'd listened to his mother's accounts of his real father's infidelity, and by the time he was in his teens had developed a deep, abiding hatred for both Mia Collins and all of the Dillingers, especially the women. But that was high school, and when he was older, there'd been no further mention of the Dillingers at all. Lila had believed it was just a phase of teen angst that he'd gotten over. She hadn't even recalled his threats by the time he moved to Wyoming, and when he'd called and told her Ira was marrying Pilar, all she'd thought was how upset she was that she and her family weren't invited.

Brook sidled up to Delilah. "Are you going back to Hollywood when Aunt Jen and Uncle Tyler leave tomorrow?" she asked anxiously.

"No, actually, I'm planning to stick around. I like it here."

The look of horror on Brook's face made Delilah laugh. But then Brook broke into a smile herself and said, "If you stay, then I'll stay."

"Glad to hear it," Ricki said dryly.

"But I'm moving to New York as soon as I turn eighteen," she added quickly, looking around as if she'd been caught in some nefarious act.

They sat down to breakfast around the huge dining room table just as an enormous dark cloud darkened the sky and then snow started to fall. Delilah watched the drifting flakes and listened to the hum of chatter around her. She looked down the table at her father, who was once again getting his ear bent by Jen, seated on his right. Ira wasn't the kind of man to be without a woman for long, so even though he'd been sad and bereaved at the small memorial service for Pilar overseen by Reverend Landon, she believed he would be back on the dating scene very soon. He'd been slightly flattered by Georgina's obsession and attention, no matter what he said to the contrary.

The doorbell rang again.

Hunter!

"I'll get it." Delilah jumped up and hurried to the front door. Sure enough, Hunter stood outside wearing his jeans, boots, a fleece-lined jacket and a brown Stetson. He was holding a large manila envelope, but he pulled Delilah into his arms and dragged her outside, kicking the door shut behind her.

"Don't you want to see my family?"

"Not yet," he said.

"Chicken."

He grinned, his blue eyes filled with warmth. She kissed him hard on the mouth, then pulled back to look at him. "What have you got there?" she asked, nodding to the envelope.

"DNA."

"What?" She stared at the envelope with growing dread. What did this mean?

"Before he died, my father told me to go see a specific lawyer, Berkley Price. When I did, Price gave me this. He'd held the results at his office per the Major's wish." Opening the envelope, he slid out the contents. "Turns out my father had DNA tests done on all his children. He always suspected Georgina had an affair with your father, so when it became just a matter of swabbing a cheek to get DNA and sending it in, he started collecting samples."

"But you're not—"

"Nope. Ira was telling the truth about me."

Now she gazed curiously at the printouts. "Georgina didn't know?"

"None of us knew. He actually got a sample of my blood from when I cut my arm once when I was screwing around with Blair in the backyard. I don't even remember it, but he got me tested."

"And you're not a Dillinger."

"I'm a Kincaid."

"But . . ."

"Alexandra isn't the Major's daughter."

Delilah gasped. "Is she Ira's?"

"Well, she's the only one of us with red in her hair. I'm going to give her a call and suggest she check. Or maybe I should drop this bomb on her in person."

"I need to tell Dad that he might need to give a DNA sample, too. Wow. That's going to be . . . a little bit of hell. He reacted so warmly to the idea that you might be his."

Hunter choked out a laugh. "I should also tell you that I'm taking over the ranch. My mother's practically let it go to ruin, and it's what my father wanted, so I'm going to try to bring it back, without the half-assed cabins in the back. I'm trying to get through to Blair. I'd like him to come back and help. Mom doesn't want to give up control to any of us, but she doesn't really have a say anymore."

"So, she just said what she said because she knew or guessed about Alexandra and just wanted to torture us."

"My mother's a master at stealing ideas. The old homestead was because of the drifter. The two fires on Dillinger property were because of Garth burning the church. The lie about me . . . the rumor . . . was because of Alexandra."

"Prairie Creek is a dangerous place to live," Delilah said. "If I were smart, I'd hightail it back to Santa Monica as fast as I could." She smiled. "Good thing I'm not that smart."

He laughed. "You're planning on sticking around then."

"That's the idea."

"So, what are you doing with the rest of your life?" he asked casually.

"Well, I don't know. I'd like to find some kind of job. Not a wedding planner. Something else. Oh, and I want to have a child. Soon. Very soon. As soon as I can. In fact, I'm already hoping I'm pregnant, although I really haven't had a chance to talk to the potential father about any of this."

"A child . . . huh." He rubbed his chin pensively.

"That's right."

"A Dillinger/Kincaid child."

"Yes."

"Would you . . . also say yes to marriage?"

She searched his face to see if he was serious. "Is this a proposal?"

"Kinda sounds like one."

"Then, yes. Yes, I would say yes." Feeling bold, she added, "And I kinda think there may be a few weddings coming up. Ricki and Sam . . . Colton and Sabrina . . . any chance we could be first?"

"A Kincaid, beating out Dillingers . . ." he mused. "How about New Year's Eve?"

"Yes," she said again, wrapping her arms around him tightly and sealing the deal with a kiss.

Dear Reader:

I hope you had a good time reading *Sinister* and hanging out in Prairie Creek, Wyoming, with the Dillingers and Kincaids! I can't tell you how much fun Nancy, Rosalind and I had working on the story together. (We're even thinking of heading back to Wyoming again. If we do, I hope you'll join us.)

However, there are quite a few other books on the horizon before I can even think of returning to Wyoming. I've got the paperback edition of *Tell Me* coming to stores in March of 2014. This is the story I truly love. Remember reporter Nikki Gillette and Detective Pierce Reed from *The Night Before* and *The Morning After*? Well, they're back. In *Tell Me*. Set in Savannah, *Tell Me* is the story of the release from prison of Blondell O'Henry, one of the most reviled and beautiful women in Savannah's dark criminal history. Her son has recanted the testimony that put her behind bars. Was she guilty of the heinous act of killing her own child and maiming the others, or is she the innocent victim of bad press and an incompetent lawyer? Nikki intends to find out as Blondell's dead daughter was a close friend of Nikki's, closer than anyone suspects. Things, of course, are never what they seem and as Nikki uncovers the truth, she discovers well-kept secrets that bring her into the killer's sights.

In June 2014, look for *Summer Days*, a collection of novellas in which my contribution is entitled *His Bride to Be*.

In August, the next installment of the "TO DIE" series, *Deserves to Die*, featuring the female detectives Selena Alvarez and Regan Pescoli, whose lives have become complicated in Grizzly Falls, Montana, is available. This book takes up where *Ready to Die* leaves off, so if you're a fan of the series, be sure to look for it!

By the time September rolls around, I'll have a new stand-alone thriller on the stands, *Close to Home*, which is a bit of a departure for me. When Sarah McAdams returns to the run-down mansion where she grew up, she expects to find a haven for her and her children. Instead, she discovers evidence of a heinous hundred-year-old murder within the dilapidated walls. Worse yet, her younger daughter claims to talk to ghosts, while her older girl is crossing boundaries that she shouldn't, evidenced by the recent rash of teenagers disappearing in Stewart's Crossing, Oregon.

To cap off the year, *Under the Mistletoe* is my contribution to a collection called *Our First Christmas*, being published in October 2014, and Nancy Bush and I have teamed up again in *Wicked Ways*, the fourth installment of the "COLONY" series, which will be available in December 2014.

Phew! It's going to be a busy year, and to help you keep track of my releases, just log on to www.lisajackson.com, where there are excerpts and more information about the books. Also catch up with me on Facebook, Twitter and Pinterest! We have tons of fun, so join in!

Here's to a wonderful New Year; 2014 looks fantastic!

Keep Reading,
Lisa Jackson

Dear Reader:

I hope you enjoyed *Sinister*, a book born of Hot Tamale candies, walks on the beach, and a glass or two of wine. I had a blast working with Lisa and Nancy, and I would love to return to Prairie Creek, Wyoming, to kick up some dust and stir up some more stories.

Hold on to your hat, because my next book, *And Then She Was Gone*, is coming out next month from Kensington Publishing. As with most of my novels, this was inspired by true events: the kidnappings of girls who were released many years later. What happens to these young women and their families after they're recovered? What is the "new normal" when years of your life have been stolen away?

And Then She Was Gone is the story of eleven-year-old Lauren O'Neill, who vanished one sunny afternoon as she walked home from school. Her parents, Rachel and Dan, spent six years scouring their Oregon hometown and beyond. When Lauren is finally rescued, Rachel's relief turns to heartbreak when she sees that the bright-eyed, assertive daughter she knew has been transformed into a wary, polite stranger.

Lauren's first instinct is to flee. For years she's been told that her parents forgot her; now she doubts the pieces of her life can ever fit together again. But Rachel refuses to lose her a second time. Little by little, they must relearn what it means to be a family, trusting that their bond is strong enough to guide them back to each other. Like most of my novels, this story dovetails into a suspense plot, but I don't want to give too much away! I hope you enjoy *And Then She Was Gone*, available January 2014.

All Best,
Rosalind Noonan

Dear Reader:

I had a blast writing *Sinister* with my sister, Lisa, and my good friend Rosalind Noonan; so much so, in fact, that we're all thinking of writing another story together, set in Prairie Creek again. There's just something about cowboys and wide-open spaces and, well, a killer or two on the loose.

Hard to believe it's the end of another year, but I've got several new projects developing for 2014. In July, it's the debut of my newest thriller, the story of Callie Cantrell, who's lost her husband and young son in a tragic car accident. Callie works to overcome her grief and guilt on the Caribbean island of Martinique and befriends Tucker, a "street urchin" who is at the center of a dark mystery. Callie's relationship with the boy puts her in the crosshairs of West Laughlin, an implacable and determined man who's on a mission to find his brother's missing son. As the mystery surrounding Tucker unfolds, Callie begins to realize that her own family's deaths may not be quite what they seemed, and that both she and West are unwittingly embroiled in someone else's dangerous game.

In the fall, look for the return of Jane Kelly! Yes, it's really happening. For those of you who've asked me about whatever happened to Jane, Dwayne, The Binkster and all the other characters from the Jane Kelly Mystery Series, they're BAAACCKKK! Look for Jane to be reintroduced next holiday season in a Christmas anthology, headlined by *New York Times* bestselling author Fern Michaels, available in October 2014.

To end the year, there's the fourth installment in the Colony Series: *Wicked Ways*. If you haven't caught up with the Colony Series yet, look for *Wicked Game*, *Wicked Lies* and *Something Wicked*, the first three books in the series, and meet the strange and gifted women who live together at an isolated lodge along the Oregon coast, named Siren Song.

For everything you've missed, or I've forgotten to tell you, check in on my Web site, www.nanbush.net, or catch up with me on Facebook or Twitter. You can also join my blog at www.nancybush.blogspot.com.

Happy Reading,
Nancy Bush